NOREELIUS COMMUNITY LIBRARY
1403 1st Avenue South
DENISON, IOWA 51442

54766

Hylton, Sara

Summer of the flamingoes.

DATE DUE

Oc 29 '91	Jl 3 '92	AUG 06 2015	
No 23 '91	Se 3 '92		
De 9 '91	Ap 29 '93		
De 26 '91			
Fe 6 '92	JUN 05	2003	
Fe 12 '92			
Fe 25 '92	SEP 28	2004	
Ma 5 '92	NOV 11	2010	
Ma 12 '92	NOV 26	2012	
Ma 17 '92	DEC 13	2012	
Ma 25 '92	DEC 13	2012	
Ap 9 '92	JUN 17	2014	

WITHDRAWN

10-2-91

Norelius Community Library

1403 1st Avenue South

Denison, Iowa 51442

Phone: (712) 263-9355

DEMCO

P9-CRE-126

Summer of the Flamingoes

By the same author

Fragile Heritage
My Sister Clare
Tomorrow's Rainbow
The Hills Are Eternal
The Whispering Glade
The Talisman of Set
The Crimson Falcon
Jacintha
Caprice

SUMMER OF THE FLAMINGOES

Sara Hylton

St. Martin's Press
New York

Library of Congress Cataloging-in-Publication Data

Hylton, Sara.
    Summer of the flamingoes / Sara Hylton.
      p.   cm.
    ISBN 0-312-05970-1
    I. Title.
  PR6058.Y63S8   1991
  823'.914—dc20   90-27703
                                                          CIP

First published in Great Britain by Random Century Group.

First U.S. Edition: May 1991
10 9 8 7 6 5 4 3 2 1

PART I

CHAPTER 1

I had slept badly, and I awoke with a strong sense of foreboding. It was a typical November day with leaden skies and a glassy grey sea and I looked down dismally at the few withering asters in their urns along the terrace. I decided that as the day progressed it would probably rain; even the dogs hated the rain that drove inland from the sea.

I bathed and dressed unhurriedly and when I reached the kitchen was surprised to see that it was still only a little after eight. In my sleepy state I had misread the time on my bedside clock, and there was over an hour to go before Mrs Pearson made her genial appearance in the kitchen.

The two spaniels barely raised their heads, merely flicking their stumpy tails in acknowledgement of my appearance.

I made a cup of coffee and took it into the morning room, where I could look down the long curving drive towards the tall wrought-iron gates, and my spirits lifted slightly when I saw the paper boy. At least there would be something to read before the arrival of Mrs Pearson.

As I went into the hall I heard the telephone ringing in the study and I hurried to answer it with a resurgence of the night's foreboding. I recognized the voice immediately; in good days and bad Aunt Edwina's voice had a plaintive air.

'Is that you, Lisa? I was hoping you would be up,' she announced.

'Yes, Aunt Edwina, how are you?'

'I'm well enough, it's your grandmother. She died at four o'clock this morning, I thought I should let you know by telephone and I hope you will be able to come here. Can you come today?'

'I'm sorry about Grandmother, Aunt Edwina, but I'm

not sure about today. Andrea and her father are returning from the Far East tomorrow and they'll expect me to be here. I'll come the day after, we'll probably all come then.'

'Most of the family are arriving today, Lisa. There are a great many things to discuss and I don't think you should make an excuse on this occasion.'

It was unlike Aunt Edwina to be so forthright and I felt faintly irritated by it even when I admitted to myself that her tone was more than justified. And still I prevaricated.

'What are the roads like round Carnforth? The sky here looks heavy with snow.'

'It snowed in the night but it's quite bright now. Don't think of coming by car, take the train to Lancaster and Uncle Raymond will meet it. We've looked it up, there's one arriving at seven this evening.'

'I'll do what I can. If it isn't possible I'll be sure to let you know.'

'We'll expect you, Lisa. Goodbye.'

I was trembling as I put down the receiver. I had not seen my grandmother for six years and felt no real sorrow at her death. She was ninety-six years of age and had been enjoying imaginary ailments ever since I could remember. It was the meeting with the rest of them that I was not looking forward to. It had been too long, too many harsh words had been said, even in all the long years of separation I had felt their acrimony, their disturbing disapproval. Now I would be expected to face them at a time of family bereavement and it could all start over again, particularly if Jessica was there.

Disconsolately I wandered back to the morning room. The coffee was cold and there was rain on the windows. Mr Longton, our gardener, was walking up the drive, his head bent against the wind, and making up my mind suddenly I ran to open the front door.

He came when I called to him, touching his cap respectfully although his long lugubrious face remained unwelcoming.

'Mr Longton,' I began, 'I have just heard that my grandmother has died and they are expecting me to go up

8

there today. I may have gone by the time Mrs Pearson arrives, so will you tell her what has happened?'

'Ay, ma'am, I will. I thought the master was arrivin' back tomorrow.'

'Yes he is, I shall have to leave notes.'

He looked up at the sky, frowning. 'If ye takes my advice, ma'am, ye'll leave the car in the garage. It'll snow afore mornin'.'

'Do you really think so?'

'Ay. Them clouds are full o' the stuff and it'll not get any better the further North ye go.'

'You're probably right. I'll order a taxi. You'll be sure to give Mrs Pearson the message?'

He nodded, and touching his cap once more, lumbered off along the drive.

It didn't take long to throw a few things into a suitcase and I changed into a warm angora dress, hesitating between high-heeled court shoes and soft beige suede boots. The sound of hail on the window decided me to wear the boots and after snatching my fur coat from the wardrobe I hurried down.

Mrs Pearson was already in the hall. 'I've spoken to Longton, Mrs Hamilton, he's told me about your grandmother. My but I thought the old lady was goin' on for ever.'

'Will you ring for a taxi, Mrs Pearson? Ask them to come up right away.'

I went into the study to write a note saying I would be away until after the funeral and there was no need for them to attend, it was too far and they had already done enough travelling.

It was all so false. It had been false of me to tell Aunt Edwina that we would all attend Grandmother's funeral. I didn't want my family to meet the rest of them, I didn't want my husband to meet Jessica and I preferred to face their disapproval on my own two feet, the sly innuendos and open criticism, even Jessica's martyrdom.

I told them what sort of food they would find in the freezer and asked Andrea to see to the dogs, then quickly I penned off a short note to Jeremy at the university and

9

Linda at her digs in Cheltenham. I was just sealing the envelopes when Mrs Pearson came to say the taxi had arrived.

'I've written messages, Mrs Pearson, and could you possibly post these two letters for me on your way home?'

'Of course, Mrs Hamilton. You'll be back as soon as the funeral's over, I expect?'

'I hope so.'

'Maybe the snow'll lay off, I hates funerals in the snow.'

I smiled at her, and hurried out. The driver had taken my case and I sat shivering at the back of his taxi, huddled in my fur.

I had only minutes to spare before the London train left the tiny country station. I had been lucky, and would make a good connection in London for the northbound journey.

I passed the time on the train in contemplating who of the family had already gathered at Grandmother's house. If Uncle Raymond was to meet me then Aunt Georgina would be there and probably their sons and their wives whom I had never met. It would be a large funeral. Grandmother Marston had lived in the village all her married life and had been prominent in every village activity, there would probably be a great many people at the funeral I wouldn't even know. They would know about me though, a younger edition of my mother who had not been ashamed to steal my cousin Jessica's fiancé and was therefore responsible for the shocks and disasters which had coloured her life.

The bustle of London was a relief from my thoughts. I arrived at Euston with over half an hour to wait for the train so I went into the tearoom. My heart sank, for sitting at one of the tables was Margery Harris.

Margery had been a close neighbour of Grandmother's and when we were children we always called her Aunt Margery. I had no doubt she was going up for the funeral and there was no way I could avoid her. Catching sight of me, she waved her hand in welcoming delight.

'How nice to see you, Lisa, I hate travelling alone. I expect we're both heading for the same destination.'

10

'Do you mind if I get myself a cup of tea?'

'Of course not. The tea's not bad and the toasted teacakes are bearable.'

When I came back with the tea she was smoking a cigarette out of a long ebony holder and I noticed the ashtray was filled with stubs. Seeing me look at it she trilled, 'I've tried to give them up, Lisa, but I can't. It's my only vice so why should I worry? After all I've no trouble with my health. How is your handsome husband? And the children?'

'They're all very well, but they're hardly children any more. Andrea is twenty-two, Jeremy is twenty and Linda is almost nineteen.'

'Heavens, how time flies. What are they doing with themselves?'

'Andrea is good with languages. She's been working in Hong Kong for the last six months, in fact she should be travelling home today with her father who's been there on business.'

'Don't tell me she speaks Chinese.'

'And French, German and Spanish.'

'Gracious, what a clever girl. I was always hopeless at languages. Is she also a pretty girl?'

'Yes, I think so.'

'Is she like you, Lisa?'

'No. She's a true Marston, not like me at all.'

I saw her eyes narrow with speculation. 'I call that very strange. Your mother was always different from the others and so are you; still, I suppose the family strain is bound to come out at some time or another. What are the other children like?'

'Jeremy is a younger edition of his father and Linda is like me; she's a lot like me in disposition, also.'

'And I take it Andrea is not?'

'No.'

She stubbed out her cigarette and lit another, and I could feel my eyes beginning to sting and the tiresome tickle at the back of my throat.

'Is your son going to be a civil engineer like his father?'

11

'He's at university at the moment making up his mind, right now he leans towards archaeology.'

'Digging up old bones, that is, isn't it?'

'It can be a good number of things.'

'And your other daughter?'

'She's an art student in Cheltenham.'

'Everybody seems to be painting pictures these days, either that or writing a book. If I'd had children I'd have hoped they'd go into something permanent like the law or banking.'

Regretfully I started to cough and she looked at me in some alarm. 'I say, Lisa, I hope it's not my smoking that's causing you to cough. It's a filthy habit but I must have a smoking compartment for that long journey.'

'Then I shan't be able to join you, I'm afraid,' I said between choking, 'I'm sorry.'

I felt impatient with my streaming eyes and throaty voice but at the same time I blessed them for enabling me to travel without the companionship of Aunt Margery.

As we made our way to the platform I felt very much better, my eyes stopped their streaming and my voice lost its croak so that Aunt Margery said, 'You really are allergic to cigarette smoke, Lisa. Some people only say they are, and they're killjoys. We'll meet up at the other end, then. Are you getting off the train at Lancaster or going through to Kendal?'

'I'm being met at Lancaster.'

'I wish I'd known, I'm being met at Kendal. But no doubt we'll meet on the day of the funeral. Who's meeting you off the train?'

'Uncle Raymond.'

'Oh well, I'm glad he and Georgina are going to be there, Raymond was always a pet even if your grandmother disapproved of him most of the time. I suppose your Uncle Henry will be officiating at the funeral service?'

'I don't know. I last saw my grandmother just before her ninetieth birthday but it's many years since I saw any of the others.'

'It's not going to be easy for you, Lisa, it's a pity your

husband couldn't have been with you. But don't worry, you'll soon adjust. There's nothing like time for healing old wounds. See you at the funeral, darling. I'm staying with the Walfords.'

I smiled politely and then she was climbing into a first-class smoking compartment and I was walking along the train to find a non-smoker.

There were not many people travelling north on that cold autumn afternoon and apart from an elderly man and woman I had the compartment to myself.

Seeing Aunt Margery again after all these years had brought my grandmother and my childhood rushing back to me. Much of my early life had been spent in her lofty Pennine stone house and I was remembering it vividly.

From my window at the front of the house I had been able to see the silver line of the sea and the curve of Morecambe Bay. Across the bay I had learned to read the message of the lakeland hills and to understand that if they stood out sharply against the sky we were in for harsh weather but if they were bathed in gentle mist the weather would be fine.

In those days there were often children staying at Grandmother's house, the offspring of her four married daughters, and I looked forward avidly to the visits of my cousins – all except Jessica, that is.

Grandmother had desperately wanted a son but to her disappointment she was blessed with five girls. She was so sure that one day one of them would be the longed-for boy that she chose only boys' names, so when another girl arrived the name had to be adapted to suit the new infant. Aunt Claudia was the eldest, and the next one was called Georgina. Then came Aunt Cecily and my mother, Stephanie. Aunt Edwina was the final attempt.

My grandfather has remained a vague shadowy figure who shut himself away in his study or spent his time on plants and butterflies. After the birth of Aunt Edwina, Grandmother became a woman obsessed with the search for health cures at various spa towns both at home and abroad, while Grandfther went his gentle way and died

13

quietly alone and without the ministrations of his wife or any of his daughters.

On the day of his funeral, while Grandmother wept copious tears, we were all lined up in a respectful file before his coffin. The fact that I shut my eyes and refused to look earned her utmost displeasure and Cousin Jessica's derision.

I have often been told over the years that Grandmother's attempts to find suitable husbands for her daughters provided the county with the utmost amusement. 'Suitable' meant that only the sons of local landowners, wealthy businessmen and even the nobility were ever allowed to escort the Marston girls. Fortunately the Marston girls were all pretty, intelligent and lively company.

Aunt Claudia was the first to marry, a vicar from the West Riding. Uncle Henry was tall, pale and thin, surely the most scholarly cleric ever to mount a pulpit. They had one daughter, Cousin Angela, a pale fair little girl who grew up to be a replica of her father and who distinguished herself by taking a first-class honours degree in History at Oxford.

Aunt Georgina was the next one to marry, Uncle Raymond, a young veterinary surgeon on leave from Kenya and staying with his aunt and uncle Sir John and Lady Chandler at Reverston Hall. To have captured the nephew of a baronet against all opposition never failed to delight my grandmother yet ironically Uncle Raymond was not a favourite with her. He was too fond of race meetings and gambling and possessed a wicked sense of humour which she never understood. The fact that he always seemed to view her with cynical detachment did not weigh heavily in his favour; at the same time he and Aunt Georgina had a reasonably happy-go-lucky marriage which produced three sons, Roger, Rodney and Robin, all of whom I adored.

Grandmother had decided that her daughters should be married off in order of their seniority and now it was Aunt Cecily's turn. A newcomer to the area was a Mr Neville Mapleton, a chartered accountant with a thriving practice in Preston. Mr Mapleton was however a bachelor in his

14

mid forties who let it be known he intended his condition to be permanent. He had reckoned without Grandmother, who set about inviting him to weekend tea parties and in no time at all he was escorting Aunt Cecily to country shows and hunt balls and within ten months they were married and living in a large ostentatious house she had persuaded him to build on the outskirts of Whalley. The year after, their one daughter Jessica was born.

Now there only remained my mother Stephanie and Aunt Edwina. With three daughters off her hands Grandmother concentrated her considerable energies on cultivating Brigadier Ralston and his wife who had recently moved into the area, particularly when she learned they had two sons of marriageable age.

It transpired that Philip, their elder son, was already engaged to his cousin, and their younger son Malcolm was gamekeeping in Kenya. Undeterred by such trivialities, however, and encouraged into thinking it would be very nice to have two daughters living in close proximity, even if it was in Africa, immediately Malcolm arrived home on three months' leave she set about cultivating him as a suitor for my mother, tragically as it turned out since by this time Mother was in love with Philip and he with her.

This was an age when children obeyed their parents, even when the future loomed desolate and empty. Philip Ralston married his cousin Constance and after a brief courtship my mother married Malcolm and went to live with him at the house in the big game reserve in Kenya where he was employed as a gamekeeper. I was born a year later, and I was five years old before I saw England for the first time and Grandmother's house north of the city of Lancaster.

With only Aunt Edwina left, Grandmother's searching for husbands dramatically ceased. With four daughters married and scattered it became increasingly essential that Edwina should be there to care for her in her declining years. Suitors were discourged, and Aunt Edwina fetched and carried and danced attention on a mother who became heavily involved in searching out one health cure after another. It became worse after Grandfather died, and for

Aunt Edwina there was no escape. She very quickly became the uncomplaining dowdy spinster Grandmother wished her to be.

The cynicism with which I could view my mother's family had long since ceased to surprise me but my first glimpse of the snow-covered Pennines from the train filled my heart with a strange nostalgia.

By the time we left Preston, powdery snow had begun to fall. It was dark now, but I knew the countryside: miles of flat farmland through which the Ribble wound its way to the sea. Long furrowed fields and hedgerows of hawthorn with here and there stunted trees which leaned away from the sea, scattered farmhouses and winding roads over narrow bridges with here and there rows of whitewashed cottages.

Soon, after we had left the Fylde countryside, it would change to low rolling hills and we would soon be approaching fell country, rumbling moorland streams of clear water that wound their tortuous way through the Forest of Bowland and beyond, what I considered the most enchanting vista of all, the lakes and mountains of Cumbria.

It still felt strange to me that all that beauty should now be called Cumbria. When I was a girl growing up in the shadow of those mountains, Windermere and all Coniston were in North Lancashire and there had been a Westmorland then as well as a Cumberland. Why had they needed to change it all? Sombre industrial Lancashire had been so proud of those lakes and the other two counties had vied with each other in their separate beauty.

For years I had closed my senses and cheated my memory of their beauty, knowing full well that we could not return to them without spending time at my grandmother's. What an abject coward I had been, now I felt ashamed that I had allowed the past to separate me from places and people I had loved.

We were approaching Lancaster now, where the domed Ashton Memorial stood high over the city, its illuminated whiteness vying with the softly falling snow, turning the grey stone city into a medieval wonderland.

I looked round quickly as I handed in my ticket and

saw Uncle Raymond bearing down on me, his raincoat flapping in the wind, his tweed hat set at a rakish angle. He was smiling broadly, and I could smell the whisky on his breath as he kissed me.

'Here you are at last, Lisa,' he said.

The wind hit us like a knife as we emerged from the station and Uncle Raymond said, 'Blasted wind. Your grandmother could have lived anywhere, but no, she had to stay halfway up the north Lancashire fells. This part of England's always one of the first to feel the winter biting. But don't mind me, Lisa, I'm just being a bit peevish.'

'Because you had to turn out to meet me?' I asked as we got into his car.

'Gracious no, that was a bonus. I needed to get out of the house.'

'It's as bad as that, is it?'

'Well I don't honestly know how your Aunt Edwina's going to cope, the old lady'd taken her over completely. And the week won't pass without a few home truths being spoken, you can be sure.

When I remained silent he said, 'I'm not thinking about you, love, there's other matters to consider, and in the trauma of those I expect they've not even been thinking of you.'

'Aunt Edwina was insistent that I come to the funeral, so insistent it seemed out of character.'

'She probably thought it would take the heat out of the rest of the proceedings. Why are you here on your own? Edwina said something about your husband and a daughter being in the Far East but couldn't your son have come with you?'

'I preferred to come alone,' I answered shortly. 'What do you think Aunt Edwina will do about the house? Surely she won't live in it alone.'

'If there's any justice in heaven she should be a wealthy woman now. But the old girl was unpredictable and one never knows how many others have been dipping into her nest egg,' he said darkly.

'Who would have the nerve, Uncle Raymond?' I asked but he simply grinned at me.

'We'll be left in no doubt, my girl, when the will's read after her funeral. There's all the aunts, my wife among them, and the nieces and nephews. The old lady was always very fond of Robin but didn't think much of Marcia, his wife. She would have preferred him to marry a North Country girl, but he's married a girl he met up at Oxford, pretty as a picture and clever, though she's no good in the kitchen.'

'Will all your family be at the funeral, Uncle Raymond?'

'All except Roger, who's out in Australia. He married an Australian girl and they live just outside Perth.'

'It's going to seem awfully strange meeting them all again. There'll be many changes, I expect.'

'Not as many as you'd think. Claudia's plumper but as sharp-tongued as ever, Cecily's forever complaining about her health, and Jessica's still very beautiful, beautiful and as hard as nails – though everybody else would no doubt disagree with me.'

'She's not married again?'

'I've rather lost count and I never ask. Usually I'm told that poor Jessica's once again been cheated by some man or other so whether it's a third marriage or a twenty-third love affair she's embroiled in I can't honestly say.'

I didn't answer him, I was looking through the window at the familiar city. Traffic had churned the falling snow into a grey melting mass but the solid grey stone buildings were as I remembered them. I realized that Uncle Raymond was detouring through the city as if to make this journey a nostalgic one.

'Lancaster doesn't change much, Lisa,' he said softly. 'There's the old castle and the prison, same as always, and we'll be driving over the Lune presently across the same old bridge. Is it all coming back to you?'

I nodded wordlessly. It was coming back to me with a vengeance and I couldn't prevent a shudder of fear when I remembered a Halloween night many years before at my grandmother's house. I was seven years old, and apart

18

from Jessica and me the rest of the family were over at the Daltons attending a Halloween ball.

Meg was looking after us. She had been a servant in Grandmother's house since her early teens and she was now well past middle age. She delighted in telling us stories of old Lancashire, and on that night what could be more appropriate than a tale about the Pendle witches?

By the time I went to bed my head was spinning with the story of the grisly goings on up at Newchurch and how the women were at last brought down to Lancaster to stand trial for witchcraft. They were all found guilty and executed, the last people to be executed for indulging in the black arts in England.

I remember lying shivering in my bed. Every creak on the stairs, every patter of rain on the windows and the sighing of the night wind through the beeches filled me with terror. The full moon sailed fitfully through clouds and the room seemed to fill with misty shapes. Then suddenly there was a bloodcurdling cry and a black figure in a tall pointed hat was leaping howling about the room, finally coming to rest on my bed with her fingers around my throat. When I felt I must surely die, the figure collapsed into helpless laughter. Then Meg was there, snatching off the cloak and tall hat to reveal Jessica clad in her nightgown and well pleased with her antics.

She had cared nothing for my fright or Meg's scoldings, or even threats to tell her mother and grandmother. She had demanded hot milk and biscuits before she promised to go to bed.

'Here's the old bridge now,' Uncle Raymond was saying. The lights along the river reflected in the water and I knew that if we turned left we would be heading for Morecambe, but if we turned right, we were entering the wild Pennine fells and the lakes and mountains I loved, and Grandmother's house, which lay halfway between Lancaster and Kendal.

I hoped Uncle Raymond would remain silent, for I wanted to relive the days when Grandfather's ancient Morris travelled this road, bringing me home from school. Familiar inn signs leapt at me through the gloom, and rows of whitewashed cottages, and I was glad that the darkness hid my tears.

It was along this road that I had been taken for Sunday tea with Grandpa and Grandma Ralston. Sitting on a velvet stool in my best silk dress, my fair hair tied back by ribbons, my shoes neatly polished, I was mostly silent, since I had been lectured while we were still on the front doorstep to speak only when spoken to.

We always drove over in the trap with Mother handling the reins, and the ritual was always the same. Grandpa would present me with a new shilling on leaving, and Grandma a white lace handkerchief. Uncle Philip would wait until the grown-ups were not looking before he pushed a bar of chocolate into my pocket, and Aunt Constance would look down her haughty nose at me, while I was glad that it was a whole week before next Sunday.

I had been so engrossed with my thoughts that I was surprised to find we had reached the house. My heart raced as we drove through the ornamental iron gates and along the virgin snow of the drive. Lights burned in the downstairs rooms and a lamp over the front door had been thoughtfully left on for us.

'Shall I drop you here, Lisa? I'll have to put the car away,' he said, stopping at the door.

'I'd prefer to come to the garage with you,' I replied, 'that way we can go in together.'

He nodded, and drove on to the back of the house.

The snow had drifted almost halfway up the garage doors, and while Uncle Raymond shovelled it away from the doors I looked across to the snow-covered firs and Scotch pines, and the sloping lawns looking like the white icing on a Christmas cake.

Oblivious to the beauty of the scene, Uncle Raymond said, 'Come on, Lisa, hot toddies for both of us.'

'I just want to get into a room with a fire,' I replied.

'When did you last eat?' he demanded.

'In London, at the station buffet. I'm not very hungry.'

'In weather like this you need some food inside you. The rest of 'em dined ages ago and I had something in Lancaster. It was a relief not having to look round the table at their doleful faces. After all, Grandmother Marston had a mighty good innings, better than most of us'll get.'

Suddenly he said, 'Here, let me take a good look at you under the lamp. While I waited at the station all I could remember was a little girl with flaxen pigtails and braces on her teeth, then I remembered the night you went to the ball at the Bartons'. You were so very beautiful that night, let me see what you look like now.'

He took hold of my elbows and spun me round to face him. His red face burst into a smile and he hugged me enthusiastically. 'I knew it,' he said jubilantly. 'It's still there, Lisa, all the beauty you had on that night.'

'I never thought of myself as beautiful.'

'Well of course not, you were always pushed into the background in those early days, but there's no need for you to take a back seat now. You are beautiful and elegant, the sort of woman a man looks at and admires. I'm a good judge of beauty, Lisa, as good a judge of a pretty woman as I am of a flighty filly. Now you're going in there with your head held high and you're not going to let any one of them get to you, am I right?'

I nodded tremulously.

'That's my girl. Nobody ever talks about your mother and father, that's a scandal they prefer to forget and one they can't blame you for. As for the rest, you've been married nearly twenty-four years, it's time they forgot about it.'

'But they won't.'

'Your grandmother's gone, Lisa, she's not here to dictate policy any more and she was responsible for a lot of what happened.'

He kept a firm grip on my arm as we walked up the front steps but I was still trembling as he lifted his hand to the bell pull.

CHAPTER 2

A girl in a white apron opened the door and smiled as Uncle Raymond said, 'Here we are then, Jenny. Will you tell Cook that Mrs Hamilton hasn't eaten since London and she's starving.'

The girl hurried away, and the door to the drawing room opened and Aunt Edwina came into the hall. For the first time in many years we looked each other in the face before she came forward and kissed me.

'I'm glad you could come, Lisa, I'll take you up to your room. I've given you the corner turret room, you always wanted to sleep there when you were a little girl.'

'How nice of you to remember, Aunt Edwina.'

'A fire's been lit so the room should be quite warm. What sort of a journey did you have?'

'Very comfortable. If the snow continues it could be thick by morning.'

'I'd like it to be gone for the funeral but it doesn't seem very likely. Your grandmother wanted to be taken to the church so we've complied with her wishes. If you want to see her there in the morning one of us will go with you.'

'I'd prefer to remember her as she was the last time I saw her.'

'How are the rest of the family?'

'Very well, thank you, but I doubt if they'll be able to get up for the funeral.'

'We are not expecting them, Lisa. I've only seen Andrea twice, and the other two not at all. I don't blame you, Lisa, it was hard to return to a family who had showed you so much antagonism, but perhaps death should erase all the hurt and anger we have all experienced.'

I said nothing and by this time we had reached the turret room. My eyes lit up at the firelight which played on the velvet drapes, soft chintz bedspread and cushioned chairs.

'It's every bit as charming as I remember it,' I told her, smiling.

'We had a bathroom built across the corner,' she said. 'We've done a lot to modernize the house over the years. Now would you like to eat in the dining room, or would you prefer a tray in here?'

'I would prefer a tray in here, if it isn't too much trouble. I'd like to freshen up and I do have the beginning of a headache. I expect it's the cold.'

'Here, give me your coat. Is it very wet?'

'I don't think so, the snow is fine and dry as yet.'

I shrugged out of my coat and she took it from me. I watched as her hands lingered lovingly on the thick dark fur and a vague pity took possession of me when I looked at her old-fashioned grey dress which was too long, ill fitting, and unflattering to her brown hair peppered with grey.

'What a beautiful coat, Lisa. I love fur.'

'Yes, it's ranch mink.' Then I said impulsively, 'If there's any justice in heaven, Aunt Edwina, you should be able to afford a dozen of them now that Grandmother's gone. If anybody did their duty it was you.'

Her face seemed suddenly to close as she turned away to put the coat in the wardrobe. She said briskly, 'I was always very happy to care for Mother, I never longed for the fleshpots, and I am certainly not expecting to be the recipient of more than my share. There are other claims on whatever money she had, far greater than mine.'

'Who could possibly deserve more than you, Aunt Edwina?'

'That was for your grandmother to decide. She made her last will three years ago and she kept all her faculties to the end of her life. She never altered it.'

'She never told you how she made it?'

'No, and I never asked. Now, can we expect you downstairs this evening, Lisa, or would you rather meet up with everybody at breakfast?'

'Has everybody arrived?'

'Most of the family have arrived, the rest will be here in time for the funeral. I'll make your excuses tonight, Lisa, you'r probably very tired.' She smiled absently and left me to my own devices.

After unpacking, I went to the window. The snow was still falling and already our footsteps from the garage had been obliterated. The room was deliciously warm and I was pleasurably aware of being back in a room that I had once loved, although in those days I had never been allowed a fire. Grandmother had said it would make a softy of me.

Jenny arrived, carrying a large brass coal hod. She gave the fire a good poke, then started to place the coals while I stood watching. She was a pretty, round-faced country girl.

After a few minutes she sat back on her heels, well pleased with her handiwork.

'There we are, that ought to do it. Mrs Harris's preparing a tray for you, ma'am, as soon as it's ready and I've washed mi hands I'll bring it up.'

'Thank you, Jenny. Who is Mrs Harris?'

She stared at me wide eyed. 'Why she's the cook, ma'am, didn't you know?'

I shook my head. 'Is Meg still here?'

If anything her eyes opened wider. 'Why, ma'am, she's bin retired over five years now. She lives in the village in one o' them cottages just by the church. If she's well enough she'll be at the funeral, I'm sure.'

'Thank you, Jenny. It all goes to show how I've lost touch.'

I felt sure our conversation would be repeated in the kitchen. No doubt I was the curio, the granddaughter who never visited, and in talking about me they would remember my mother and all that came after. In a village like Branley when old folk gathered, old scandals would be milled over, long-gone romances would be revived. I had little doubt that my mother would be cast as the scarlet woman who had cheated her husband, destroyed another marriage and brought death and tragedy to them all; and I would be cast in the same mould.

24

I should go downstairs with my head held high and face the rest of them but I had neither the will nor the courage. Besides I was painfully aware of the insistent throbbing that heralded a migraine, an affliction I had not suffered for some considerable time.

Jenny brought the tray containing a piece of deliciously cooked halibut and vegetables, fresh fruit and cheese. I made myself eat in spite of the increasing pain in my head and the sickly feeling that accompanied it, then sat back and closed my eyes.

When Jenny came back for the tray she looked at me curiously. 'Ye don't look well, ma'am, would ye like me to tell the mistress?'

'It's just a headache, Jenny, I'll be perfectly all right when I've had a night's sleep.'

''Ave ye taken aspirin or somethin'?'

'No, aspirin won't help, I just need to be quiet and get some sleep. It's been a very long day. Goodnight, Jenny.'

She left me shaking her head doubtfully and I went to the door to turn the key. I sat on the bed to take off my jewellery, opening the drawer in the bedside cabinet. I had expected to find it empty but found it contained a sachet of handkerchieves smelling faintly of lavender, and a photograph album.

The album became a voyage of nostalgia, every page brought the past back to me so vividly that scalding tears rolled down my cheeks. Why had Aunt Edwina left it for me to find? Was it cruelty that had prompted her or a plea for me to remember the past kindly and forget the anguish that had destroyed it?

My mother's face looked back at me from the album, so very beautiful it brought an ache into my heart; and there was me as a child in gingham frock and white socks, my fair hair tied back in ribbons, running with the dogs across the fell.

There was a photograph of Grandmother sitting like a queen surrounded by her family, her silver hair piled high on her head, the lace collar of her gown worn high above row upon row of jet beads. Uncle Raymond was there, young and debonair, with an arm around Roger and

Rodney, while Robin sat with me at the front. There was Aunt Claudia, and Uncle Henry looking every inch the perfect cleric in his severe garb, and Angela gazing up at him adoringly.

Jessica's parents, Aunt Cecily and Uncle Neville, were a handsome couple, looking straight in front of them while I sat at their feet, exactly as Uncle Raymond had remembered me, my hair in thick plaits over my shoulders, my mouth set in determined lines to hide the hideous disfiguring braces on my teeth. And there was Jessica, tall and dark, lithe as a young gazelle and incredibly beautiful – the beauty I had envied and admired all through my schooldays and beyond.

Irritably I snapped the album closed, the tears stinging my eyes and my head a mounting torture. I knew that sleep would not come immediately. I had not thought to bring the tablets the doctor in Dorset had prescribed for migraine, so miserably I crept between the sheets and closed my eyes.

For years I had thrust the past behind me, shutting it out. I had been clever at thinking of something else quickly whenever it had intruded into my thoughts. But now I was being made to face it, the trauma of its sorrow, as well as the joys of one golden summer, which in my heart I treasured as the summer of the flamingoes.

PART II

CHAPTER 3

We left Mombasa in the early morning before the town was yet awake and I remember standing looking through the ship's rail at a quayside strangely deserted except for the horde of negro porters who grinned up at us expectantly and were rewarded by a shower of silver coins from the passengers. I was five years old and miserably unhappy.

I had said a tearful farewell to Rinta, my baby impala, only hours before, and Father had impatiently hurried me away with the tears still wet on my cheeks. Mother was already sitting in the truck and we drove in silence through mile after mile of tea plantations until we reached the smoother roads leading into the city.

We had brought flasks and sandwiches, and on any other day it would have been a picnic, but not today, not with Father's stony silence and Mother's sulky indifference. I stood beside her on the quay while father said coldly, 'I don't suppose you can say when you expect to return?'

'I'll write to you as soon as we arrive, Malcolm, and I'll let you know how we're getting on. Please, Malcolm, this isn't a holiday, it's a necessity. I can't stand these sulks and long silences, can't you see how unhappy it's making all of us?'

'I can't pretend I'm happy to see you leaving the reserve just now, Stephanie. I just don't see the necessity for it.'

'You could have come with us.'

'Don't be ridiculous, this is our busiest time, and you know very well I can't be spared. The truth is you've never tried to like it here, but you can't say I didn't warn you what it would be like. If you wanted balls and garden parties you shouldn't have married me, Stephanie.'

'Now who's being ridiculous? Never once in all the years we're been married have I ever even hinted that I

29

was missing the old life. I'm not going home because I miss that, I'm going because I'm not getting better. I've had six years of Africa, the heat, the dust and the fever, now I need to see a decent doctor and build up some sort of resistance to the climate before I can face it again. Besides, there's Lisa.'

'There's nothing wrong with Lisa.'

'She needs to see a dentist, her teeth are overcrowded. And the only children she knows are the natives in the village. I don't want my child to grow up lonely and inhibited.'

For a long moment they stared at each other stolidly, then Mother held out her hand to me. 'Come along, Lisa, time to go aboard.'

I walked between them to where the great ship towered above us, dismally aware of Father's stern expression and mother's pale face.

We paused at the gangway and Mother said softly, 'You needn't come aboard, Malcolm, I hate goodbyes. And I'll be back before you know I've gone.'

He said nothing and anxiously she went on, 'I'll see Lisa settled in at a decent school and I'll try to see a lot of your parents so that I can bring all their news when I come back in the spring.'

'You *are* coming back in the spring, then?'

'Or before. Please, Malcolm, trust me.'

Their embrace was swift and then suddenly his face relaxed as he looked at me, so that I too smiled and welcomed the roughness of his face against mine. Then I was walking with my mother up the steep gangway and he was standing back to watch. At the top we turned and waved to him. He lifted his hand in acknowledgement, then strode away.

'I'm going to find the purser, darling,' Mother whispered. 'Stand here at the rail and I'll come back for you shortly.'

'Will you be back before the ship sails?' I asked plaintively.

'Yes, I'm sure I shall.'

The truck had gone and now several other small groups

30

were arriving. I watched as they performed tearful embraces and several people boarded the ship while others stayed below.

Father hadn't waited because he was angry with us, and I hadn't missed the relief in my mother's face as she stepped along the deck almost blithely. Were all marriages like my parents'? I had no yardstick by which to measure it. Our nearest neighbours were miles away and they were elderly; Father's partner Johnny Harris was a bachelor, and when he came to the house all they ever talked about was ivory poaching and the hiring and firing of negro hands.

Mother had not been well for over a year now and the doctor said she was anaemic, lethargic and needed a change of scenery. Father suggested a holiday in the hill country so that he could be quickly recalled should he be needed, but tearfully Mother said she needed to go home, she wanted to see her mother and sisters, she was tired of Africa and the climate.

I had met none of our relatives and Mother pointed out that Aunt Georgina and Uncle Raymond went home every two years and their sons were already at school in England, even the youngest one. Six years was too long to expect her to stay in Africa without sight of home.

'If your father had his way you'd grow up a complete ignoramus,' Mother said angrily. 'You have to receive an education, Lisa, you have to learn how to dance and mix with other young people and he's not going to spoil it for you – or me either.'

Every day of the voyage she seemed to recover some of her high spirits and she became once again my beautiful mother. Her hair was glossy once more, and her eyes sparkled as she talked animatedly to our fellow passengers.

I sat at our table watching happily while she was invited to dance at the tea dances. One afternoon I overheard a conversation which I kept to myself but remembered for a very long time.

It took place between two middle-aged ladies, Mrs Gill and Mrs Brady, who were travelling home from Singapore. They had made a fuss of me because there were very few children on board, and Mrs Brady knew my grandmother.

Watching Mother dance by with one of the ship's officers, Mrs Gill said, 'How much better Mrs Ralston is looking now. She's hardly the same woman who boarded the ship in Mombasa.'

'I've noticed, dear, and she's having such a lovely time, I don't suppose she's seen much of civilization since she was married. They've never been back to England, you know.'

'Really, not even on leave?'

'Not even then. Malcolm probably has his reasons, there was some talk before their marriage but you know how wrong gossip can sometimes be.'

'What sort of talk?'

'Well, Stephanie was around and about quite often with Philip Ralston but he was engaged to Constance Ralston, his cousin. Indeed they've since married, so whatever there was between Philip and Stephanie is all in the past.'

'The past can have a nasty habit of catching up on one.'

'Yes, that's true. However Philip and Constance are abroad. He's in the diplomatic service, you know.'

'I hope he's abroad for a while yet, just in case gossip rears its ugly head. I expect you'll hear all about it if there's anything to hear.'

'Well yes, gossip in the country never loses anything and I know both Stephanie's family and Malcolm's equally well.'

Just then Mother returned to the table to be greeted by smiles and compliments and I sat back in my chair marvelling at the sudden change in their conversation.

CHAPTER 4

I always thought about the Maples as being Grandmother's house even though Grandfather was there. It was
a large Pennine stone house set in green lawns and ordered
flowerbeds, and the fact that there wasn't a maple in sight
hadn't deterred Grandmother from calling it the Maples
when she moved into it as a bride.

There were pines and firs and beech trees in plenty, so
she set about having maples planted. The soil however
was not conducive to their growth and in time they all
perished and were never replaced. She never renamed the
house, but then she was not a person who ever went back
on anything she had set her heart on. The maples were a
disaster she chose to forget, particularly in the days when
more potent and far-reaching disasters took precedence.

It was almost dark when we arrived at the Maples
and I looked round the panelled hall with interest, and
particularly at the blaze in a fireplace that coverd most of
one wall. I was immediately overawed by my grandmother, a tall statuesque lady in a black dress, her ample
bosom adorned with row upon row of jet beads.

Grandfather was less alarming: a tall slender man with
a shock of silver hair, and blue eyes that twinkled at me
from behind his rimless spectacles. Aunt Edwina too was
nice, putting her arms around me and holding me close,
and I could smell her light floral perfume. Then Grandmother led the way up the wide curving staircase and
Grandfather and Aunt Edwina were left to cope with our
luggage.

'I've given you your old room, Stephanie, but I didn't
know what to do about Lisa. She's old enough to have a
bedroom to herself, I think, even though the house is
bound to be strange to her.'

'Oh, Lisa won't be any trouble, Mother. What about
the old nursery?'

'Well yes, there's that of course. I'll get one of the girls to put a match to the fire, I expect you'll both feel the cold after Africa, although I've never been one to encourage young people to want fires in their bedrooms. Just for tonight perhaps.'

I was left in the old nursery after warm embraces and kisses from mother and Aunt Edwina, and I was not afraid. I was accustomed to being much on my own. In Kenya the nearest village was miles away and there was only our house in the middle of the reserve and the house where father's partner lived. Surrounding us were miles and miles of scrubland, tall leathery grasses and delicately fashioned spires and pinnacles which had been created by the most skilled and industrious architects of all, the ants.

I was a tidy child and found a cupboard where I could place my outdoor clothing, then I looked around with interest.

There were bookshelves ranged all along one wall and my eyes lit up at the sight of thick picture books with large print. I could read quite well for my age, indeed Father had once remarked that I would probably grow up into something of a bookworm.

On another wall sat shelf after shelf of dolls, their lovely porcelain faces and wide blue eyes staring back at me – dark-haired dolls and fair-haired beauties, dressed in silks and satins, some of them with velvet cloaks, and baby dolls in exquisite lace. I had never been one for dolls. My favourite toy had been a battered teddy bear and I preferred paints and colouring books as well as the miniature tinkling grand piano that Aunt Georgina and Uncle Raymond had given me for Christmas. Then Father took it away, saying it got on his nerves when he was trying to do his accounts.

I had wept long and bitterly and there had been a stormy scene between my parents until he promised I should have it back if I would not play it when he was trying to work. After that I hardly played it at all because somehow much of the joy had gone out of it.

I pulled back the curtains to gaze out into the night, then my eyes lit up with pleasure. The house was built against a hillside and I could see the lights of Lancaster shining in the distance and the scattered lights of villages and homesteads. Back home in Kenya the dark came suddenly and it closed in sharply and threateningly after the fierce glow of the sun. Occasionally the sparks flew upwards from native camp fires and we could hear their music or the insistent beat of their tomtoms and I could visualize them dancing. Occasionally too there came the night calls of animals and there were even times when they ventured into our compound. Fires kept them at bay, and in the hours of darkness they were always lit.

The door opened and Mother came in accompanied by a young servant girl carrying a tray.

'Here's your dinner, darling,' Mother said, drawing up a small table.

She looked round the room with interest while I tucked into my dinner. I was hungry. The girl smiled at me and I smiled back, liking what I saw: a pretty brown-haired girl with warm brown eyes.

'There's apples and custard to follow,' she said softly.

Mother said, 'This is Mary Stevens, Lisa, she is going to look after you while we're here. Mary will know the things you ought to see and where to take you.'

'Won't you be there, Mother?'

'Yes darling, of course I will, but I know an awful lot of people round here and I'll be paying them visits. I can't think you'd enjoy it, their conversation would bore you, about people and places you don't know anything about. Mary's family have a farm on one of the fells, you'll like it much better going there and meeting all the animals and Mary's younger brothers and sisters.'

'We'll go tomorrow, luv,' Mary said happily. 'Mi mother'll be right glad to 'ave a visitor.'

I went with Mary willingly the next day and as she tucked my woollen scarf firmly round my neck she said, 'It's allus windy up there on the fell, luv. Are ye sure ye can walk across the moor?'

'Of course, I walk a long way back home in Kenya.'

'Is that right, then? Well come along, and ye can stay wi' me at the farm all afternoon.'

She was right about the wind. It swept through the harsh moorland grass like a knife, taking my breath and bringing the tears to my eyes, but it was exhilarating too, and Mary took hold of my hand and we ran laughing towards the farm.

It was a rambling affair, the farmhouse surrounded by outbuildings. As we crossed the cobbled yard we were surrounded by excited barking dogs, and several cats who eyed us cautiously before leaping on to the walls.

'Down Ross, ye'll ave all mi dress muddied fer sure. I 'ope yer not scared o' dogs, luv, we 'ave to 'ave them on the farm."

'I'm not scared, I like dogs.'

'That's a good job, then. Mind 'ow ye goes, down Towser, down Jed.'

We went into a huge kitchen where a stout lady was vigorously mixing batter. 'So this is the young lassy then,' she said. 'Welcome to Lower Crag Farm, luv. Will you be wantin' to watch me mixin' cakes or take a look round the farm with our Mary?'

'We'll watch ye mix the cakes, Mam. Maybe Lisa'd like to scrape the bowl.'

I sat on a high stool entranced as Mary's mother ladled great spoonfuls of the mixture into at least a dozen tins, which she thrust one after the other into a vast stove on one hand and an oven next to the roaring fire on the other. Then she pushed two mixing bowls over to us and I watched for a few seconds while Mary scooped up the leavings in her bowl, then I followed suit. The mixture was delicious, rich and sweet with a hint of spice and ginger.

They both laughed when I got much of it over my face and Mrs Stevens brought a warm wet cloth to clean my face.

'We can't 'ave yer grandmother seein' ye like that, can we? She'd not be lettin' ye come again. Now, our Mary, come along and give mi a lift wi' the dinner, the lads'll be in an' wantin' their food.'

The dining table was a huge white wood affair in the middle of the kitchen and there were no formalities.

36

Knives, forks and spoons were laid out, then Mrs Stevens fetched a pile of hot plates straight from the top of the stove. I watched in amazement as she placed them round the table and when she caught sight of my round eyes she laughed merrily. 'Nay lass, they're not all mi family, and the children are away at the school, it's mi 'usband and the farm lads that'll be comin' in for their meal.'

They came one after the other, big red-faced men with strong gnarled hands, good-humoured and smiling, and after washing their hands at the big stone sink in the corner they came to the table. Mr Stevens sat at the head, watching his wife pile roast beef and potatoes on to their plates, then with twinkling eyes he looked at me. 'And who 'ave we 'ere, then? What's yer name, luv?'

For a moment I sat tonguetied, overwhelmed by the sheer force of so much male activity, then Mrs Stevens said, "Er name's Lisa, and she's Mrs Marston's grand-daughter, so I'll be askin' all of ye to watch yer manners.'

'So we're in the presence of the gentry, are we? Well, they need to eat like the rest of us.'

There was no way I could have eaten all the food piled on my plate, but I did my best with it. The food was good and wholesome and the apple pie that followed was so scrumptious I had two helpings.

As soon as the men had eaten they trooped back to work and I set about helping Mary and her mother to clear the table.

'Do your brothers and sisters come home now?' I asked Mary.

'Not until 'alf past four they don't, they go to the school over at Carnforth so they gets their lunch down there.'

'How many are they?'

'There's Joe, 'e's the one next te me so 'e's the eldest o' the boys. He's goin' to be a farmer one day, just like mi Dad. Then there's our Danny, 'e's good at school 'is teacher sez, 'e'll never want to come into farmin'. There's two sisters, Emmie and Pauline. There's only a year between 'em but yer'd think there was all the time in the world. Emmie's feckless and Pauline's a dreamer but clever when she sets 'er mind to it.'

37

'Then there are five of you,' I said brightly.

'That there are. Would you like brothers and sisters?'

'I don't know, I haven't thought about it. I have cousins, three boys who live in Kenya.'

'And ye 'ave cousins 'ere too, luv, I've seem 'em when they visits yer grandmother.'

'What are they like?'

'Well there's Miss Angela, the Reverend's daughter, she's a quiet little girl, only speaks when she's spoken to and minds 'er manners, not like the other one.'

'The other one?'

'Miss Jessica. She's a haughty little minx, gives ye two words for one she does, and a right little bossy-boots. Don't let 'er take it out on you, luv.'

I forgot about Miss Jessica in the excitement of the afternoon. I fed the chickens and the geese with Mary, and I watched the milking when the dogs brought the cows up.

'What time are ye to 'ave the lassie back for?' Mrs Stevens asked.

'I thought mi dad might take us back in the truck, I'd like 'er to meet the rest of us afore we go.'

At that moment there was a sound of running in the farmyard and laughter and children's voices, then the door was flung open and a young girl with bright red hair and freckles almost fell into the room, followed by a tall gangling boy who could never have been anything but her brother.

'Wipe yer feet afore yer comes into my kitchen,' their mother admonished, 'and put them muddy shoes at the side door. Yer slippers are on the hearth.'

More subdued, they obeyed her, then the door opened again and another girl and a boy came into the room. The girl had a fresh bright face and her hair was brown, shining and bobbed, while the boy was very thin, with a sharp intelligent face and the most startling blue eyes I had ever seen. They swept over me curiously as Mary performed the introductions. He was the only one who held out his hand to take mine, while the older boy shuffled his feet and the two girls eyed me curiously.

The red-haired one was Emmie, the dark one Pauline, and after a few minutes it was Pauline who came to sit with me to show me the drawings she had done that afternoon. She was so warm and friendly I hoped fervently that she would be my friend, but even as we looked at her pictures Emmie came and snatched them away. 'Stop showin' off, our Pauline, yer not the only one that can draw pictures.'

'Show us yours then,' the younger boy commanded, but she only tossed her red head and ran through the door shrieking with laughter and taking Pauline's colouring book with her.

Pauline's eyes met mine with resigned patience. 'She's only showin' off,' she said gently.

'Will she give it back?'

'Oh yes, when she's 'ad 'er fun with it.'

We sat down at the table to a feast of home-made bread and strawberry jam, scones fresh from the oven and large slabs of fruitcake.

Emmie cheekily remarked, 'What's it like livin' in that big 'ouse o' Mrs Marston's then?'

'I don't know, I only arrived last night.'

'Don't you be askin' so many questions our Emmie,' Mary said. 'Lisa's come 'ere all the way from Africa and that's where she's going back to.'

"Ave ye seen lions and tigers?' Emmie asked, her eyes popping wide.

'I've seen lions, there aren't any tigers in Africa.'

She tossed her red head defiantly. 'Just because you've not seen any doesn't mean they're not there,' she said adamantly.

'Tigers don't live in Africa,' Danny retorted, 'everybody knows that.'

'You think you know everythin', old clever-boots,' Emmie said sharply.

Her mother said, 'Stop showing off, Emmie, and look at all them crumbs yer makin'. See there's not a crumb in sight where Lisa's sittin'.'

Whereupon she pulled a face at me which her mother'd

39

didn't see and Pauline asked, 'Are ye coming to see us again, Lisa?'

'Oh I do hope so, perhaps tomorrow if my mother is visiting again.'

'If you come on Saturday we'll be on holiday from school, we could go up on to the fell.'

'I'd like that.'

'There's an old castle up there. Nobody lives there now but the grass inside is so short and green, we often play there.'

'I don't like you going up to the castle,' her mother said sharply. 'The walls are crumbling, one of these days they could fall down and you could all be 'urt.'

'They won't fall down, Mother,' Danny said firmly. 'Walls were made to last i' them days.'

'Then why is it in ruins?' Emmie demanded.

For the first time the older boy spoke. 'Why don't we go down to the river, there's swans and we could go fishin'.'

'Wait and see what sort o' day it's goin' to be,' Mrs Stevens said firmly, now if yer've finished yer tea ye can clear away and wash up the plates.'

I was helped on with my coat and the woollen muffler, then Mrs Stevens said to her daughter, 'Get off with ye now, luv, and p'raps I'll expect ye on Saturday. Yer father's not back yet.'

Mother and daughter kissed each other warmly then we were once more out in the farmyard and it was almost dark.

So we ran down the fell until we reached the stile and Grandmother's house with the lights shining across the gardens.

CHAPTER 5

For the first time in my young life I was truly happy. Every day I went with Mary to the farm and spent long happy hours watching Mrs Stevens baking enormous jam tarts, apple pies, loaves of bread and steak puddings. Mary helped her mother at the farm and I soon learned how to feed the chickens and collect their eggs.

After the children came home from school I played with them around the farm or in the old barn which had become their playroom and was heated by an ancient oil stove.

The days shortened, and in the morning frost covered the hedgerows and adorned the trees so that I delighted in their beauty. I had never seen frost before. In the middle of December it began to snow and the two boys made ramshackle toboggans which we carried to the summit of the fell. Then, howling with glee, we tobogganed down, quite often coming to grief in a snowdrift.

I knew that one day we must go home to Kenya, but it would not be until I had had something done to my teeth. The dentist had not been able to take me for several weeks after we arrived because both his children were ill with scarlet fever and he was not making any appointments.

Mother wrote long letters to Kenya telling Father about the dentist's report and urging him to try to join us for Christmas.

'Isn't he coming to see us at Christmas?' I asked.

'I've left that to him, darling, he may be too busy and you know how he hates leaving the reserve when he's busy. On Sunday I'm taking you to see your other grandmother, they've been on holiday in the South of France but they're home now and will want to see us both.'

Immediately after lunch on Sunday I was dressed in my best silk and my hair was brushed and plaited, then taken back and caught in a blue ribbon to match my dress. My shoes were polished and I wore short white socks and my best tweed coat. Last of all Mother set a blue tam-o'-shanter on my head and took me in to Grandmother for a final inspection.

'You look very nice, Lisa,' she said. 'Now be on your best behaviour, don't make crumbs on the carpet, speak only when you're spoken to and let Grandmother Ralston see that you are a young lady.'

'Yes, Grandmother.'

'And if your Aunt Constance is there be sure to say please and thank you when she speaks to you.'

'Why should you think Constance will be there?' Mother asked sharply.

'She may or may not be. I have heard they are coming home for Christmas.'

I looked up curiously at Mother. Her face was quite pink, and catching hold of my hand firmly she hurried me towards the door. Outside the room she stood for a long moment with her back to the door, and I felt anxious, she looked so strange.

We drove in Grandmother's trap, pulled by Sally who was invariably frisky and with a mind of her own, and the fact that we drove in silence I attributed to Mother's anxiety to keep a firm hold on the reins.

I loved riding behind Sally's round chestnut rump and swishing blond tail. The country roads were a joy and for the main part they had been cleared of snow although it lingered on the fields and trees. My hands in woollen gloves were warm under the rug which Mother had spread across our knees, our breath froze in the sharp wind and I felt strangely exhilarated.

'Do I call the lady we are going to see Grandmother?' I inquired after a while.

'No, darling, that would confuse you. Why not call her Grandma? I think she might like that.'

'Is she a nice lady?'

'Yes indeed, very nice, and Brigadier Ralston you can call Grandpa. He's sure to be there.'

'Grandfather Marston is hardly ever there.'

'No dear, he likes to spend most of his time in his study. Daddy's never been one for socializing.'

'He's nice though, I like him. I like him better than Grandmother.'

For the first time she laughed. 'I'd advise you not to let her hear that, Lisa. She likes to be the centre of attraction.'

'Who is Constance?'

'She's Uncle Philip's wife. Uncle Philip is your father's brother.'

'Is she nice?'

'Nice enough . . . Over there, Lisa, that's their house, Bartley Hall.'

'It looks very big, a lot bigger than Grandmother's.'

'Yes, a lot bigger, but don't let her hear you say so, she's rather touchy on such matters.'

We were approaching a big stone house with pillars at the front and a long winding drive lined by tall trees. The parkland was vast and there were deer roaming through the trees, reminding me nostalgically of my impala. For a moment I felt the sharp sting of tears.

Mother halted the pony at the front door, clambered down and lifted me after her, and immediately two men seemed to appear from nowhere.

The older man said, 'I'll take the pony, ma'am, and give her something to eat.'

'Thank you, Anderson.'

'Do you know everybody here, Mother?' I inquired curiously.

'Most of them, darling. Remember this was your father's home when we married.'

The girl who opened the door to us reminded me of Mary with her fresh pink cheeks and bright smiling eyes.

'Good afternoon, Mrs Malcolm,' she greeted my mother. 'The family are in the drawing room.'

'Thank you Lucy.'

Lucy helped me off with my coat and Mother straightened my skirt and eyed me critically.

'You look very nice, Lisa. Now don't be afraid, nobody is going to eat you.'

43

'I'm not afraid,' I protested stoutly.

She laughed. 'No, I don't suppose you are, you've always been a very self-possessed child.'

The drawing room was very large and a bright fire burned in the tall Adam fireplace. An elderly man and a woman came forward to greet us. We were both embraced, then Mother went to sit with the lady near the fire and Grandpa showed me a small velvet-covered stool for me to sit on.

Their inspection of me was brief, all the same I felt absurdly conscious of my overcrowded teeth and was careful to sit with my feet together and my skirt pulled down firmly over my knees.

'What a pity Malcolm couldn't have come with you,' Grandpa was saying, 'and he's such a bad correspondent, I can't remember when we last received a letter from him.'

'I know, I tell him he should write more often.'

'You haven't been well, Stephanie. What has been the trouble?'

'I've probably been too long in a hot climate, I wanted to come home for a spell. Six years is a long time to spend in Africa without coming home.'

'I do agree with you.'

During this conversation I was busy scanning the room. The pictures and ornaments fascinated me. Through the long windows I could see the deer wandering through the parkland, and I startled the others by clapping my hands with glee when a brightly coloured peacock strutted past.

They all laughed and Mother said, 'I see you've still got Orlando. He must be quite old by now.'

'We don't know how old, he was here when we took over the house and his temper doesn't improve with age. Don't be tempted to go too near him, Lisa, he's not the friendliest of creatures.'

A small fair-haired woman came into the room. She was elegantly dressed in pale beige, and pretty in a pale, aloof sort of way. Mother rose to greet her and they embraced briefly.

'You look well, Stephanie,' the lady said, then as though

she had seen me for the first time she turned to me, saying, 'Hello, Lisa, I'm your Aunt Constance.'

I smiled, and felt her eyes appraising me carefully before she said, 'How strange, I had always thought she would be like Jessica. We all hoped she would be like Jessica.'

'The child's like herself,' Grandma said sharply, 'and children change all the time. Have you seen your sister and her husband during your visit, Stephanie?'

'Yes, of course, I've visited them but Jessica's away at school.'

'She's the most beautiful child I've ever seen, I've often heard that children of late marriages can be beautiful.'

I felt I had been sized up and found wanting. Jessica was beautiful and I was not, Jessica had charmed these people as I was failing to do.

As if she too sensed the hurt, Mother said, 'Lisa is waiting to see Mr Cranston about her teeth. They're beautiful and strong but overcrowded. I hope he'll be able to take us this week.'

'Does that mean she will have to wear those disfiguring braces on her teeth?' Aunt Constance said, shivering delicately.

'For a time perhaps. It will be worth it in the end.'

'You'll be enchanted with Jessica, she's a quite delightful child.'

'I can't wait to meet her,' Mother said dryly.

'She's quite tall for her age, she has the loveliest blue-black hair and green eyes. Quite a beautiful combination, don't you think?'

'Oh quite, and my Lisa is going to be the perfect English rose with corn-silk hair and cornflower-blue eyes. A plain child can grow up into the most startling beauty.'

I had now been informed that I was plain, and that was probably the moment when I resented Cousin Jessica even when at the same time I wished I was like her, tall and slender and incredibly beautiful.

'Is Philip with you, Constance?' Mother was asking.

'Why no, he had things to see to in Geneva but he'll be home for Christmas. After that I hope to persuade

Philip to take a holiday in the sun, Egypt perhaps or the Canaries. I expect you've had a surfeit of sun?'

'Shall we just say I'm enjoying England in the winter, I've had six years of tropical sunshine.'

'You're here over Christmas then?'

'Yes. I have to make inquiries about Lisa's schooling and there are other things I need to see to.'

'Jessica's at a private girls' school in Lancaster,' Grandma Ralston said. 'It has a very good name but they don't take girls until they are seven. Jessica's done remarkably well there and it would be nice if you could enrol Lisa for when she's old enough.'

'Couldn't I go to the school in the village?' I couldn't resist asking. 'All Mrs Stevens' children go there and Danny and Pauline are clever.'

Mother laughed and the others smiled tolerantly. 'I can't leave you here from the age of five, darling. Seven is going to be bad enough.'

We were saved from further argument by the arrival of Lucy pushing a tea trolley and for the next half hour I was too busy trying to balance a plate on my knees to think about schools, the Stevens children or Cousin Jessica.

An hour later we left. Grandpa and Grandma came to the front door to see us climb into the trap, but Aunt Constance had settled into an armchair with a magazine after kissing us briefly on the cheek. I had formed the opinion that while I liked my grandparents I was not particularly fond of Aunt Constance and as we drove through the gates I said, 'Do we have to go there again, mother?'

'Well of course we do, darling, they're your grandparents and besides you have to meet Uncle Philip.'

'Is he like Aunt Constance? Because I don't like her very much.'

'Oh no, Lisa, he's not at all like Constance. I promise you will love Uncle Philip.'

Down the road we came across a woman climbing over a stile, and when she saw us her face broke into a smile.

'Hello, Stephanie, I heard you were back. Is Malcolm with you?' she called.

'No, Margery, not this visit I'm afraid. Do you want a lift?'

'No thank you. I'm putting in some walking, trying to lose a little weight. So this is your daughter Lisa?'

'Yes. Lisa, this is Mrs Margery Harris, your grandmother's neighbour.'

'I see Constance is visiting. Nasty one of Fate to have you both here at the same time.'

'We must go, Margery, you know what Mother's like when we're late home for tea.'

Mother urged the pony on in sharp tones and I turned to look back at Margery Harris trotting doggedly up the road.

CHAPTER 6

Although my mother promised me the Christmas of my young life I was not looking forward to it. For one thing the dentist had at last removed the offending teeth and my gums were sore so that I was only able to eat silly sloppy food, and apples and nuts and the like were denied me.

I was constantly assured that in no time at all I would look prettier and my teeth would grow straight, particularly when the brace was fitted, but in the present I hated my reflection in the mirror with the gaps where the teeth used to be.

Neither tinselled tree nor bright holly berries consoled me, and Emmie was scolded soundly for laughing at my misery.

'Ye should be ashamed of yerself,' her mother said sharply. 'Ye were a right crybaby when ye had teeth out, so ye've no call to be laughin' at Lisa.'

Most of the time I got along with Emmie very well. I had learned to give as good as I got, and though I had more in common with her sister Pauline I found Emmie's gamin face and mischievous humour infectious.

Grandmother's Christmas present to me was a corded velvet dress which I hated on sight and over which I wept rebellious tears of frustration.

'Darling, you must wear it on Christmas Day, she'll expect it,' Mother admonished me.

It was far too long and felt bulky round my waist. When Mother said she would shorten it a little, Grandmother snapped, 'The child will grow into it, by next Christmas she'll probably be too big for it anyway.'

'I can leave the hem to let down later, Mother, but it really is very long on her, she feels uncomfortable in it.'

'Oh well, you'll no doubt do as you think fit, I should have learned by this time not to expect gratitude for any-

48

thing I do,' Grandmother remarked, and swept from the room.

Mother said to her sister, 'How can you stand it day after day and year after year, Edwina? The dress is too long, and how stupid simply to buy a dress without consulting either Lisa or me.'

'She means well, Steph, the dress will be lovely when you've shortened it.'

'The dress is hideous. Does Cecily allow her to buy clothes for Jessica?'

'No, but that's different, Jessica is in school uniform most of the time and Cecily's always been fashion conscious. She buys all Jessica's clothes from Marianne in Lancaster.'

'How fortunate for Jessica. We've been hearing about Jessica's beauty from this person and that ever since we arrived. The child's going through a period of misery with her teeth, I don't want her upset by unkind comparison with Jessica.'

'Well of course not, nobody would be so cruel.'

'Constance has already said she expected Lisa to resemble Jessica, and made it quite obvious that she was disappointed. Oh, I know she's getting at me, but I won't have her getting at me through Lisa.'

'Why should she get at you, Steph? You've been married to Malcolm for six years, what happened between you and Philip is all in the past.'

'The past has a habit of catching up in a village.'

'But it's over, isn't it – at least I hope it's over. Please, Stephanie, promise me you won't start anything up with Philip. There was such a lot of talk the last time, Mother was mortified by it and so was I.'

'How did it affect you?'

'Having to listen to Mother going on about you, having all conversation suddenly ceasing whenever I walked into a room, people's smiles and smirks, and knowing even the villagers were gossiping. Having Constance cut me dead in the street and having to watch Philip's misery deepen day by day after you went away.'

'It didn't stop him marrying her.'

49

'No, and it didn't stop you marrying his brother. It's over, Steph. Please promise me you won't see Philip alone, if there's any more gossip it will kill Mother.'

'Oh I think you'll find Mother is more resilient than that. I'll have to see Philip, it would look worse if we avoided each other.'

After a long sorrowful look Aunt Edwina left us alone, and Mother hugged me unexpectedly. 'Leave it to me, darling, I'll do something about the dress and I promise you won't have to wear it when we go to see Grandma Ralston next Sunday.'

'Will Uncle Philip be there?' I asked, seeing my mother blush bright pink and dissolve into embarrassed laughter.

'I don't know, Lisa, I don't know when he's coming home.'

'Doesn't Aunt Constance like you?'

'Well, we don't like her much, do we, darling? Now come along, we're going to decorate the tree.'

I had always had a vivid imagination, making up stories about all sorts of people. Already Aunt Constance had the role of a wicked witch, whereas Uncle Philip was my handsome knight on a white charger. My mother I had cast as the beautiful princess he was to rescue from her imprisonment in the grey stone tower, and I sensed in all their talk of scandal and intrigue the beginnings of a beautiful fairy story.

In spite of my hopes that the snow would linger until Christmas it disappeared in a torrent of rain, leaving grey slush and dark sullen skies.

Pauline Stevens was in bed with bronchitis and Grandmother thought it best that I didn't go up to the farm so I mooned about the house miserably. I was considerably cheered by the mounting volume of Christmas presents wrapped in fancy paper that were beginning to pile up under the tree in the hall, and at night when the tiny lights were switched on it became a magical thing.

'Who are the parcels for?' I asked Mother.

'For the family and the servants, dear. We are sure to

50

have lots of people arriving bringing more and some of the parcels will be for you.'

'I wish there was more for me to do. I've read all the books in the nursery.'

'You'll probably find some more among your presents. If the rain clears up after lunch we'll go into one of the villages and have tea.'

I cheered up considerably after that and sat on the window seat in the nursery waiting for the clouds to lift. To my relief they did so shortly after lunch and a pale sickly sun appeared.

Wrapped up warmly in scarves and woollens we set out in the trap. Mother loved driving it, she said she could drive a car any time but only Grandmother still persisted in having the pony and trap, and I too revelled in the pony's high-stepping grace. It was Mother who said Sally was in a temper.

'You only have to look at her to realize that,' she informed me. 'I wouldn't try to get too friendly towards her today, Lisa, she's rolling her eyes and swishing her tail. All this goes against her judgement.'

Indeed before the day was out we had reason to respect the pony's weather forecasting when the wind worked itself up into a squall and the rain came down in torrents.

We were passing Grandma Ralston's house when a car came suddenly through the gates and Sally shied so hard that the trap was flung into an embankment and almost capsized. The car driver ran across the road to see if we were hurt.

He was a tall man who stared at my mother incredulously and the next moment she was in his arms and I was forgotten in the urgency of their embrace. Then, remembering that they were not alone, they looked at me sitting in a heap in the corner of the trap and the man reached out his hand and pulled me towards him.

'Philip, this is Lisa,' Mother said softly.

He smiled, and in that sweet sudden smile I recognized a resemblance to my father in one of his lighter moods. He didn't smile very often.

51

'Hello, Lisa, I'm your uncle Philip, I'm very pleased to meet you.'

I looked at him solemnly and Mother said, 'She's not smiling at the moment, Philip, she's had some teeth extracted.'

'Oh dear, did it hurt much?'

'No. They don't hurt at all now.'

'I'm very glad to hear it. Were you on the way to see us?'

'No, we've been to tea in the village, we were going home.'

'In that case we'll have to see what we can do about the trap. You shouldn't be in that contraption on such a day.'

'The sun was shining when we set out.'

'Well it isn't shining now. Sit in the car, Stephanie, while I get the trap back on the road. If you'd like to drive the car you can take Lisa home and I'll follow with the trap.'

'I'll take the trap, Philip, as soon as you've got it back on the road. I don't want to cause any more talk than there's been already. You do realize the whole area will be watching us?'

He didn't speak, but set about righting the trap. Then he lifted me up and settled me down on to the seat. When he handed Mother into the trap she allowed her hand to remain in his while they looked deep into each others' eyes and the rain beat down mercilessly on our heads.

That was the beginning of it, the day that altered the rest of my life, and the miracle is that unlike the others I was not consumed by the flames.

CHAPTER 7

My first English Christmas Eve – and the rain poured down. Sitting curled up in the nursery window seat I reflected on the Christmas card pictures I had believed in implicitly while we celebrated Christmas in the heat of Kenya.

I had yearned over those wonderful snow scenes and perky robins on trees decorated with frost. I had believed in stage coaches pounding through the winter night, but I had never visualized a parkland where the puddles stretched as far as I could see, and where everything felt damp.

Grandmother had proclaimed the uselessness of my silk and cotton dresses and had insisted that I wear serge, woollen jumpers, thick stockings and flannel nightdresses.

I stayed in the nursery largely forgotten while the household prepared for the arrival of the family on Christmas morning: Jessica would be arriving with her parents and Cousin Angela with hers. The only bright spot was that Uncle Raymond and Aunt Georgina were home on leave with their three boys.

Halfway through the morning Mary brought hot milk and biscuits to the nursery.

'If it clears up I can take you to the farm this afternoon,' she said brightly. 'Yer'll be out of the way of all the preparations and I 'ave to go home with the order for milk and eggs. Only if it clears up, mind ye.'

That meant that I spent the rest of the morning looking for a rift in the clouds and to my utmost joy it came shortly after lunch.

It was heavenly to walk into that warm kitchen with the smell of new bread and the sight of Mrs Stevens with her sleeves rolled up icing a huge cake.

I was carrying a small attaché case which mother had filled with presents for the children.

'Mother says they can be put with the rest of their presents,' I told Mrs Stevens solemnly.

'Nay luv, I'd rather ye gave them to the children yerself, they're all in the parlour.'

I had never been in the parlour before because normally it was reserved for Sunday when, Mary told me, the covers were removed from the chairs and sofa and where her mother and father sat after church in the evening when the children had gone to bed. Usually her father did his weekly accounts and her mother sat knitting. Occasionally they entertained their friends and relatives and her father would bring out his best port and her mother would produce sandwiches and rich fruitcake.

Today however the covers remained on the furniture but a roaring fire burned in the grate and Emmie lay in front of it on the bright red rug. Pauline and Danny sat at the table with a jigsaw puzzle and Joe sat in one of the large chairs with a book. They all looked up expectantly, and Mary said sharply, 'I've brought Lisa up to see ye, let 'er play with some of yer toys.'

Emmie eyed the valise with interest. 'What 'ave ye got there?' she demanded. 'Books?'

'No, Mother's sent you Christmas presents.'

She jumped up quickly and ran to the table where Pauline and Danny hastily made room for the case.

'Your mother says I can give them to you now, you can put them with the things Father Christmas will be bringing.'

Emmie hooted with laughter. 'Don't tell me ye still believe in Father Christmas?'

'Yes, of course I do, he's coming tonight.'

'Not he, it's yer parents who put out the presents. Last year I crept downstairs and watched mi mother fillin' a stockin' with oranges and apples and mi father was layin' presents out under the tree.'

I could feel my eyes growing round with outraged surprise.

Pauline said sharply, 'Shut up, Emmie, if Lisa wants to believe in Father Christmas it's not for you to tell her any different.'

'But there's no such person,' she said admantly.

'Well, I think there is,' I stormed. 'My father's in Kenya so he won't be here to lay out presents. There must be a Father Christmas.'

'Oh well, there's yer mother and yer grandmother, they'll be puttin' out yer presents.'

'Don't believe her,' Pauline said urgently. 'She's always showing off and thinking she knows everything. Can we see what you've brought?'

I watched while they tore off the wrappings impatiently. For Joe there was a warm woollen scarf in plaid and edged with fringe in beige, green and brown, and for Pauline a huge box of water-colours which she exclaimed over delightedly. For Danny there was a book of adventure stories and for Emmie a wicker workbasket containing silks and reels of cotton.

I had told Mother all I knew of the Stevens children and she had chosen her gifts with care. At the bottom of the basket Emmie found a linen traycloth ready to be embroidered and she curled up happily in an armchair, completely absorbed, while Pauline and Danny made room for me at the table.

'Are you better now?' I asked Pauline hopefully.

'Yes, thank you, Lisa, I allus has the bronchitis in the winter. The doctor sez I might grow out of it.'

'We're having the family for Christmas, they're coming in the morning.'

'That's nice. I've seen Jessica sometimes, riding' 'er pony on the fell.'

'I wish she wasn't so pretty. Everybody's always going on about how beautiful Jessica is and I'm so ugly with my teeth gone and my hair so pale. Beside her I'm going to look worse.'

'Oh Lisa, you're not ugly, you're pretty too and your teeth won't always look like that,' she replied stoutly.

'It'll take years for 'er teeth to look right,' Emmie said from her armchair, 'and 'er cousin Jessica *is* pretty. I don't like 'er, she's a stuck-up snob.'

Some degree of family loyalty made me snap back at

her, 'Everybody says Jessica's pretty and nice. I don't believe she's in the least snobbish.'

'Yer'll find out,' Emmie muttered darkly.

Pauline changed the subject. 'Will yer father be comin' all the way from Africa?'

'No. He's too busy, and we'll be going back as soon as I've got the brace fitted on my teeth.'

'What's yer father do then?'

'He's a game warden. He looks after the animals and sees that there's no poaching of ivory. Sometimes he brings baby animals home who have lost their mothers, they're beautiful and I always cry when they're old enough to leave us.'

'What sort of animals?' Danny wanted to know.

'Gazelles, elephant calves and sometimes a lion or a leopard cub.'

'Ow about a tiger cub?' Emmie asked.

Danny turned on her sharply, 'We've told you afore there's no tigers in Africa.'

At that Emmie flew at her brother with her fists flying and they set about each other with no holds barred. It took Mrs Stevens herself to separate them with the threat that they would both go to bed without supper if they didn't behave.

Danny left the room, slamming the door, and Emmie went into a far corner and sat on the floor in a deep sulk.

Pauline grinned at me. 'They're always quarrelling', Lisa, don't take any notice. Come and 'elp me finish this jigsaw puzzle.'

After a while I asked in a whisper, 'Tell me some more about Jessica.'

'She doesn't speak to the likes o' me.'

'Why not?'

'Well not with mi father bein' a farmer, we're not gentry like yer family.'

'I think that's terrible.'

'We don't mind. Our Mary's in service in yer grand-mother's 'ouse so we couldn' really expect to be friends as well. She's very good to our Mary, she let's 'er come 'ome to 'elp with the 'arvest and Miss Edwina's given 'er many a blouse and skirt. Beautiful they are, and there's never anythin' wrong with 'em.'

I didn't speak, but I was thinking of the huge box of jams and cakes I had seen Mary struggling to carry up to the house, sent by Mrs Stevens.

For the first time I was learning about the divisions in society, the haves and the have nots, the invisible bars the humble could not pass. Barriers of manners and speech, and the unchecked pride of class.

My expression must have been truly puzzled because with a little laugh Pauline gave me a little squeeze.

'Eh Lisa, there's no need for ye to be worryin' yer 'ead about it. Mi father sez it's changing since the war, but it'll be a long time afore it changes in the country.'

At that moment Mrs Stevens came in with fresh milk, shortbread and fruit loaf, which induced Emmie to come away from her corner and Danny back into the room.

Soon afterwards Mary came to say it was time we returned to Grandmother's. I went reluctantly, wishing with all my heart that I could have stayed to eat supper at the farm.

'Didn't you want to stay?' I asked Mary.

'I've work to do at yer grandmother's, luv. Cook would 'ave bin furious if I'd stayed away any longer, what with all the family comin' on Christmas Day and another lot on Boxin' Day.'

'Who's coming on Boxing Day?'

'That's when yer grandmother entertains friends and 'er daughters' in-laws. Yer other grandparents'll be coming over with Mr Philip and 'is wife. We'll not 'ave a single minute without somebody or other arrivin'.'

'I wonder why my father couldn't come. Uncle Raymond's coming from Kenya, why couldn't he?'

'I don't know, luv. Most folk make an effort to get 'ome for Christmas, but mi dad says times are changing', it's not as important as it used to be.'

I trotted by her side in silence but my thoughts were with my father spending Christmas alone in the heat of Africa with only the cries of the wild animals for company.

I wished he was jolly like Uncle Raymond. I loved our

visits to their nice house in Nairobi with the fruit trees and the swing which Robin and I fought over. I loved it even better when we went to their other house near Lake Nakuru in the Great Rift Valley. Even Father loved Nakuru although I was aware of his resentment that Uncle Raymond owned it when he would like to have it himself.

I had somehow always known that they had a lot more money than we did. I had seen Aunt Georgina give Mother dresses she no longer wanted, and Mother took them gratefully and nearly always altered them so that they looked completely different.

I once asked Robin why they could own two houses and we could only own one and he said it was because his father was a veterinary officer and my father was only a gamekeeper. Apparently vets earned a lot more.

Robin hastened to say, 'I'd rather be gamekeeper any day. Vets only look after sick animals, gamekeepers care for well ones.'

Mollified, I decided not to ask further questions on the wealth of our respective families.

CHAPTER 8

I was awake before it was properly light on Christmas morning and I longed to go downstairs to look under the tree. My ears strained to hear if anybody else was awake but the house was quiet. All I heard was the patter of hail on the window, and I ran to look out.

The trees tossed in the sharp wind that came off the fell and I gasped with delight at the snow which covered the lakeland hills. *This* was more like the Christmas cards, and as if to prove it a tiny robin came to sit on the window sill, his sharp eye watching me through the glass.

It was a cold grey morning and I ran back to my bed and snuggled beneath the clothes.

Over the back of a chair hung the corded velvet dress, and my heart sank. It had been shortened, but it still seemed bulky round my middle and too stiff round my neck. With it were beige woollen socks and black patent shoes with a single strap. I would have staked my life on it that Jessica would not be wearing corded velvet or ankle socks when she arrived.

I wished I could have gone to my mother's room but she was sharing with Aunt Edwina over Christmas since all the rooms in the house would be needed for the rest of the family.

Mother said she couldn't see why Uncle Raymond and Aunt Georgina and the boys couldn't have stayed with their other relatives nearby, but Aunt Edwina said Grandmother would be horrified at such a suggestion. I was fast becoming aware that Grandmother's word was law, even with Grandfather.

Mary came in with tea and toast, saying, 'There's no cooked breakfast this morning, luv. There's to be a buffet lunch in the dining room and Christmas Dinner tonight. Can ye get washed yerself and put on yer clothes?'

'Yes of course.'

The house was a hive of activity. Mother and Aunt Edwina were in the dining room setting the table with sparkling glasses and silver and the side table with huge platters.

Mary Stevens crossed the hall as I stood mournfully contemplating the Christmas tree and she said sharply, 'Don't you be opening any o' them parcels, Miss Lisa, they're to be opened immediately after lunch when all the family's arrived.'

'I wasn't going to touch them,' I denied stoutly.

'That's all right then,' she replied, smiling.

'Mary,' came Cook's voice from the door to the kitchens, 'I'm waiting for ye and I've only one pair of 'ands.'

Disconsolately I started up the stairs and at that moment Mother came out of the dining room. 'I'll come upstairs with you, darling, and help you to get dressed. The family will be starting to arrive any time.'

Her eyes twinkled down at me. 'You must be so bored, darling. I've finished helping Aunt Edwina now, as soon as we've changed we can go downstairs and start the day's festivities.'

'I'll bet the Stevens children opened their presents ages ago.'

'I expect they did, but we can't start before the others arrive.'

'It's not a bit like I thought it would be. I thought there'd be snow, and I haven't heard a single church bell.'

'There's snow on the hills, darling, and we don't really want it round the house. It can be an awful nuisance. I've driven through it in early May, we don't want that, do we?'

'No. I just wanted it for Christmas.'

'Wait until they all get here, you'll have such fun. You like Uncle Raymond's boys, don't you?'

'I like Robin best, the others are too old for me.'

'Oh well, you and Robin can disappear into the nursery if the others find you too juvenile. They're bringing another boy with them, a schoolfriend whose father is abroad.'

'Robin's schoolfriend?' I asked hopefully.

60

'I don't think so, darling, I rather think he's as old as Roger.'

How I hated the corded velvet dress, which even Mother looked at doubtfully.

'It's better now that it's been shortened,' she said, avoiding my anguished eyes. 'You'll look lovely, darling. See, I've found a hair ribbon just the right colour.'

We walked down the staircase with me clutching her hand, desperately conscious of the stiffness of my dress, the new shiny patent shoes with a strap that was too tight and the heavy watered silk ribbons at the end of each plait.

Below us in the hall a tall thin man was being helped from his overcoat and a fluttering plump lady turned round to stare at us. In a moment she squealed with delight and rushed to the bottom of the stairs, crying, 'Steph, how lovely to see you

From the hall a tall thin fair-haired girl looked up at us with interest. She wore large horn-rimmed glasses and she was pretty in a quiet, insipid way. She smiled as Mother and I were dragged forward to meet her, and she offered me a limp chilly hand in greeting.

The plump lady was Aunt Claudia and the tall man was Uncle Henry. I liked her, she was warm and soft and giggly, but he looked down at me solemnly and I wondered why he was wearing a funny white collar.

'Take Lisa and sit beside the fire,' Aunt Claudia said to her daughter, 'the room'll be crowded in no time. Darling, we must talk about Kenya,' she gushed to Mother. 'One of these days I shall persuade Henry to visit.'

Angela and I sat on the padded seats beside the fireplace. She said quietly, 'Are you going to school in Kenya?'

'No. I have a lady who comes to teach me, and when I'm seven I'm coming to school here in England. The same one Jessica goes to, I think.'

'Oh, that one?'

'Don't you like it then?'

'I don't know anything about it, I go to school in Yorkshire where we live.'

I got the impression that wherever Jessica went Angela's school was infinitely superior.

Just then Grandmother and Grandfather had come into the hall. I thought he looked decidedly out of place in his formal lounge suit instead of the woollen jacket he usually wore.

Grandmother was doing most of the talking and Grandfather was handing round glases of sherry when from outside came the laughter of boys and Uncle Raymond's voice telling them to shut up and help with the luggage.

I always thought Uncle Raymond's family was larger than life, three boys who laughed and teased and all seemed to talk at once. Aunt Georgina sailed through the clamour unconcerned followed by Uncle Raymond with his debonair smiling face, his trilby set at a rakish angle, his raincoat thrown theatrically round his shoulders.

Robin came over immediately, clutching a large model powerboat which he proceeded to explain to Angela and myself. He was a chubby ginger-haired boy with an infectious smile, remaining untroubled when Angela said, 'We haven't opened any of our presents, you know Grandmother likes them opened here.'

'Oh, there's plenty more,' he said airily, 'besides Alex was at our house and we couldn't expect him to wait until the middle of the afternoon before he opened his presents.'

Robin was six but his dealings with two older brothers had made him more assured and assertive. I looked across to where Roger and Rodney were circulating among the grown-ups and introducing a tall dark-haired boy. When eventually they reached us, Roger said, 'This is Lisa, I told you her father was gamekeeping in Kenya. Gracious, Lisa, what's happened to your teeth?'

'I've had some out so that the others will grow straight.'

'You look like the very devil.'

His friend Alex favoured me with a cool grave smile before they turned away and I heard Roger say, 'They live in the middle of one of the big game reserves, we might get to visit them next year if you'd like to.'

'I'd like that very much,' Alex replied.

Angela murmured, 'How can you bear to live with all those wild animals?'

I didn't answer because just then in swept a tall fashionably dressed woman in a fur coat, her dark hair shoulder length and shining. She carried several large parcels and was followed by a short portly man equally laden and a girl of about Angela's age.

My cousin Jessica was lovely indeed, and she moved about the room graciously giving and receiving embraces with the confidence of a girl who knew she was beautiful and admired. When at last Edwina brought her across to us I stared at her flawless face with undisguised amazement. Her hair was dark, with dancing blue lights in it under the tree lights. Her eyes were unlike any I had ever seen before, greener than Jade, startling in a magnolia-skinned face whose lips smiled prettily, showing small even white teeth.

She kissed my cheek, brushing it swiftly with her lips, and I could smell the perfume of her hair, feel its silkiness against my face. Then she treated Angela to an equally brief embrace.

She did not linger but moved on with Aunt Edwina. Then, with all the guests assembled, Grandmother moved towards the dining room and we formed a solemn procession behind her with Uncle Raymond and the boys bringing up the rear.

I sat between Mother and Robin who immediately disgraced himself by upsetting a glass of water on the damask cloth. Across the table Uncle Raymond winked at me quite unperturbed while Aunt Georgina's red face proclaimed her embarrassment.

'Separate the two children,' Grandmother commanded, 'or there'll be more disasters before the end of the meal,' whereupon Robin was placed between his mother and Uncle Henry and I found myself between Mother and Aunt Cecily.

As a five-year-old somewhat solitary child I adored the conversation of grown-ups, and although I sat in silence the conversation between Mother and Aunt Cecily was most entertaining.

'Why hasn't Malcolm come?' Aunt Cecily said. 'I thought he might have made the effort at Christmastime.'

'I expect he's very busy, and it's also awfully expensive.'

'I suppose it is. What a pity that illness prevented him continuing with his medical degree.'

'Malcolm wanted to be a vet, Cecily, he was never on a medical course.'

'Of course, how silly of me. Well, what a pity he had to leave the veterinary course. He must be very envious of Raymond – they've all managed to get here, the five of them.'

'He seems happy enough to be a gamekeeper. He's working with animals which is what he always wanted.'

'Well of course, darling, but he's not making nearly as much money, is he?'

'No, I suppose not.'

'It must be quite galling for him, particularly with a brother doing so well in the diplomatic service. Have you seen Philip and Constance since you've been here?'

'Yes, once or twice. They're coming here tomorrow.'

'Of course. I'd forgotten it was in-law day.'

'Is Jessica happy at her school, Cecily?'

'Oh, I think so. It's got a very good reputation but Miss Baker's a stickler for discipline, which perhaps isn't a bad thing. Jessica's not exactly clever but she's made a host of friends there, girls with the right background and hopefully with brothers in good positions when the time is ripe.'

'You can't surely be looking out for a husband for Jessica so soon? You're beginning to sound like Mother.'

'I'm a lot like Mother. It must have been hell for her with five of us to marry off, and like her I don't want my daughter to marry a boy who doesn't have a future. What are you doing about Lisa's schooling?'

'I have an appointment to see Miss Baker in the New Year.'

'Oh, good. Jessica's come on remarkably well since she

went there. She's no bluestocking, but she likes sport and she invariably gets the lead in the school plays.'

'I can imagine she might want to be an actress one day, she's very pretty.'

'She'll be an actress over my dead body. It's a precarious living and I doubt if she's that good. Neville spoils the girl terribly, everything she asks for she gets, I tell him he's ruining the child.'

'Who is the boy Raymond and Georgina brought with them?'

'Alexander Hamilton. His father's an explorer, you must have heard of him, Sir Noel Hamilton. Terribly wealthy but a bit of a recluse since his wife died. Quite a tragedy actually, killed while climbing with her husband in the Alps. The boy's at school with Georgina's boys. Handsome, don't you think?'

I permitted myself a sly look down the table to where Alexander Hamilton was chatting to my grandfather, who for once was looking pleased and animated.

My cousins were the only boys I knew apart from the native boys who moved about the compound. My cousins were happy-go-lucky boys with auburn hair and rosy faces, they had stalwart round limbs and made a lot of noise. But Alexander Hamilton was very different. He was tall and slender with hair as dark and shining as Jessica's and his profile was grave and strangely sweet. At that moment he turned his head and his eyes, a deep intense blue, met mine. He smiled, a sudden sweet smile that filled my innocent young heart with a gentle warmth.

Aunt Cecily had started to speak again and I listened with renewed interest.

'It's terribly expensive at Miss Baker's, Stephanie. It'll make a considerable hole in your money.'

'I know. Malcolm's parents are going to help. Lisa is after all their only grandchild.'

'She may not always be, but I must say Constance doesn't strike me as being particularly maternal. Do you two get on?'

'I think so, we've never actually spent much time in each other's company.'

'I wonder if she knows about you and Philip.'

'Why should she? It was before they were married.'

'Oh, word gets around, and neither of you was too discreet about it. Does Malcolm know?'

'Really, Cecily, not in front of the child, and in any case he doesn't need to know. Whatever went on between me and Philip is in the past, I'm Malcolm's wife now.'

'Constance is a dull stick. She serves on one or two committees I'm on, and the other woman all say we never get any nearer coming to know her. Do you think she's attractive?'

'In a way, yes, I do. She's remote and fairly standoffish but she does have a certain glacial appeal.'

'Mmm, perhaps. Did Mother choose that dress Lisa's wearing? It looks very much like it.'

'Yes, it *is* hideous, isn't it? I've shortened it – much to her annoyance – but it still doesn't look right.'

'There might be something of Jessica's she can have, something she's outgrown. Actually her school uniform is quite pretty, navy and pale pink, but then anything one puts on Jessica seems right, she's very fortunate.'

I was becoming impatient. The meal dragged on while in the hall that mountain of presents was waiting to be opened. At last Grandmother looked down the table to see if we were all finished before rising to her feet.

Only Uncle Raymond sat with a glass half filled with port, and drinking it quickly he indicated that we might make our way out of the room. On the way out he pulled my pigtail playfully, saying, 'Well, Lisa, enjoying your first English Christmas?'

'I wish it was snowing,' I answered.

'So do I. We could have taken our toboggans up there on the fell and had the time of our lives.'

'I doubt if you'll ever grow up,' Aunt Georgina said sharply.

'The kids would have loved it. This isn't their idea of an exciting Christmas, waiting until the middle of the afternoon to unwrap their presents.'

'It won't do them any harm, they've already opened most of their presents.'

'I haven't,' I said in my piping treble. 'I've only had this dress, the rest of my presents are in that pile over there.'

The laughter was general, except for Grandmother who glowered at me, saying, 'Patience is a virtue, Lisa, and should be endured with good grace. Now all of you, go in turn to the tree, you'll see I've placed your gifts in separate piles, we should start with Grandfather.'

So off we went, one after the other. As I followed Robin I heard Uncle Raymond remark, 'The youngsters should have gone first, it's taxing patience too far.'

In turn we retrieved our parcels. I had to go to the tree twice to fetch mine, and even then Robin had to help me. I noticed that nobody had opened their parcels but had placed them on the floor at their feet, then with a sign from Grandmother they started to remove the wrapping paper.

This was the best part of the whole day, sitting with Robin on the floor while the parcels disclosed picture books, boxes of water-colours and crayons, warm scarves and gloves and bedroom slippers, boxes of chocolates, packets of nuts and raisins and fruit. At last I was able to look around me to see what the others had received and there was Jessica whirling round the room in a pale pink party dress whose skirts billowed round her graceful legs in rich folds of shimmering silk.

The boys looked up from their parcels indulgently, and catching hold of Alexander by the arm she laughed up into his face, inviting him to dance.

Grown-ups and children alike watched as they waltzed together round the room while Aunt Edwina played for them on the piano. I saw Uncle Raymond whisper something to Roger, after which he went across to Angela who blushed furiously before she stood up and went to dance with him.

'Come on you two,' Uncle Raymond called across to Robin and me. But Robin only tossed his head impatiently, saying, 'I'm not dancing, it's soppy. Besides Lisa doesn't know how.'

'I do so,' I cried angrily, 'I can dance better than you,'

whereupon Rodney came and pulled me out on to the
floor. For a few minutes I stood confused, then falteringly
I followed his steps round the room and Robin laughed
derisively.

The dance over, Jessica was urged to change her dress,
which apparenty was required for a birthday party. The
grown-ups retired to the drawing room while we were told
to stay in the hall, amuse ourselves quietly and put our
presents away tidily.

'What happens next?' I asked Robin hopefully.

'Oh, we play around in here until it's time for Grandmother to give the servants their presents, then we have
Christmas dinner.'

I was beginning to enjoy Christmas Day until Jessica
suggested charades, though she said Robin and I were far
too young and we were duly banished to the top of the
hall to play any games we pleased as long as we didn't
interfere with the rest of them.

Robin produced board games but I must confess to
being far more interested in the goings-on at the other
end of the hall where Jessica was in her element organiz-
ing, play-acting and bossing everybody about. After a very
short time Angela decided she didn't want to play any
more so she retired into a corner with a book, and when
Robin got too excited with the game we were playing
Jessica looked round angrily, saying 'Can't you children
play quietly? We're trying to concentrate here.'

'She makes me sick,' Robin complained, 'I don't know
why they always have to do what Jessica wants. She's only
two years older than me anyway.'

'I wish I was as pretty as her,' I said wistfully.

'That's why they're all round her,' Robin snorted.
'She'll not boss me like she bosses them.'

'Was she pretty when she was my age?'

'I suppose so, I can't remember.'

'I expect she must have been.'

'What does it matter? I like you better.'

I felt faintly cheered by his stout regard, all the same I
desperately wanted to be as pretty as Jessica, it wasn't

enough to be relegated into a corner to play board games with Robin for ever.

Robin produced other games and I began to concentrate more. In no time at all we were whooping with delight and suddenly Jessica was there sweeping the counters into a heap on the floor and flinging our board into a corner. Her eyes were like sparkling flint as Robin leapt after it, while I cowered back in the face of her rage.

'If you can't play quietly,' she stormed, 'play in the nursery, you're spoiling it for us.'

With her head held high she stalked off with tears of outraged anger on her cheeks. Subdued, Robin and I bent down to collect the scattered counters and then Alex was there helping us.

Somehow the game of charades had fallen flat. Jessica stood at the end of the hall looking at us with haughty anger while Rodney and Roger shuffled their feet.

'Are you coming back, Alex?' she demanded shortly. 'If not, I'm joining Mummy and Daddy and the rest of them.'

'I'm a little tired of charades,' Alex said with a brief smile. 'Isn't there something we could all play?'

Without another word she turned on her heel and marched out of the hall and after a few minutes Roger and Rodney followed her. Alex settled down to play one of the board games and after a few minutes Angela came over to join us. I was happier than I had been all day, and in this fashion we spent some time before Aunt Edwina came to tell us we must return to the drawing room to hear the Queen's speech.

To us in Kenya the Queen had always seemed a remote person, almost like God. Somebody who was there but never seen. I was disappointed that she was not wearing her crown and jewels. She looked just like anybody else, she could have been one of the people sitting round the fireplace. Robin too was uninterested and received a hearty slap for zooming about with a small aeroplane in his hands.

After the Queen's speech we were once more assembled behind Grandmother and trooped back into the hall where the servants were assembled. There were four of them: Cook and Mary Stevens, Mr Atherton the gardener and Meg who was a sort of maid of all work. They stood in a respectful line while my grandparents spoke a few words to each of them in turn and handed over a wrapped gift.

I heard Aunt Cecily say to Aunt Edwina, 'Mother's very lucky to keep servants, she wouldn't be so lucky if she lived in the city. I've had three daily women in six months, they earn more in the factories. Nobody, just nobody goes into service these days.'

'We *are* lucky,' Aunt Edwina replied. 'If Mary leaves I doubt we'll be able to replace her.'

Cook was being congratulated on the excellence of her buffet lunch and in high good humour she said, 'I 'opes the dinner's as good. If yer'll excuse us now, Mrs Marston, we'd best be gettin' back to it.'

Dinner was eaten very early on that Christmas Day to accommodate the younger members of the family. My eyes grew round with the sight of numerous dishes and the enormous turkey which Grandfather was about to carve.

It was all coming true, the Christmas Mother had told me about, and even more so when Mary carried in the Christmas pudding which Uncle Raymond set alight after he had liberally poured brandy over it.

Afterwards we trooped back to the drawing room and Robin whispered, 'We could go up to the nursery, Lisa, and play some more games.'

Grandmother, however, had other ideas.

'Now we are all going to sit round the fire while Jessica plays for us,' she announced.

Robin groaned, Angela clutched her book a little tighter and I heard her Mother say, 'Here we are again, Jessica, always Jessica.'

Uncle Neville produced sheet music which he placed on the piano for her. Then she tested the stool for height before sitting at the piano. Normally the baby grand was locked, I knew, because I had tried it. I would dearly like to have touched the keys even though I couldn't play.

Jessica played prettily. Actually I thought she was marvellous until Uncle Raymond said, 'Come along, Alex, let's give Jessica a rest while you take over.'

Alex seemed reluctant but Uncle Raymond would have none of it. So with some condescension Jessica left the piano stool to Alex.

Child that I was I recognized that this was different, this was music as it should be played, hauntingly beautiful, filled with pathos and with an expertise that made Jessica's demonstration seem faulty and immature. After the playing of one piece of music Alex made as if to leave the piano but he was pressed to remain and for me Christmas night was filled with a rare and wonderful enchantment.

CHAPTER 9

All Boxing Day morning people were coming and going. Jessica was shown off charmingly in a pretty navy blue dress with snowy white organdy collar and cuffs.

I had been spared the wearing of the blue corded velvet and felt much happier in my familiar tartan skirt and blue woollen sweater, but I was painfully conscious of the gaps in my teeth and kept running my tongue across my teeth to assure myself that the gaps were becoming narrower.

Uncle Raymond and his family went to relatives for lunch, and the house seemed empty and silent. I had nothing in common with Angela, I was too young and she preferred her book to conversation of any kind, and Jessica preferred the adoration of the rest of the family.

Mother came to sit with me on the bottom step of the stairs.

'Are you very bored, darling?' she asked. 'If it stays fine perhaps we'll go out for a long walk this afternoon.'

'I thought Grandma Ralston was coming this afternoon,' I said in surprise.

'Yes of course, but they won't stay long.'

'Mother, will I ever be as pretty as Jessica?'

'Lisa, you'll not be in the least like Jessica. But one day my little duckling's going to be the most beautiful swan.'

'Your ugly duckling, mother?'

'No, darling, my little fluffy yellow duckling.'

I was watching Jessica displaying her pretty dimpled smiles as she moved gracefully from group to group carrying a tea tray piled high with mince tarts and tiny sandwiches. Her green eyes flashed when she was spoken to, and people were enchanted with her. I wished with all my heart that I could make my escape into the nursery to read my new books and hide away.

Lunch was another buffet meal and promptly at two o'clock Grandma and Grandpa Ralston arrived with Uncle

72

Philip. Aunt Constance was suffering from a very bad cold and had stayed at home.

I sensed the constraint on all of us, the polite conversation, the undisguised watching whenever Mother and Uncle Philip spoke together. Mother was nervous and totally unlike herself. Halfway through the afternoon she jumped to her feet, saying, 'I promised to take Lisa for a short walk if the day was fine, I do hope you will excuse us.'

Not waiting for a reply she took me by the hand and pulled me into the hall.

Her hands were trembling as she buttoned my coat around me and pulled the hood over my head.

The icy wind hit us like a knife as we emerged into the garden and there was sleet in it. I expected her to turn back, but she hurried me towards the front gate. The wind took my breath away and brought sharp tears into my eyes but we tramped on, climbing towards the fell and the lights shining in the Stevens' farmhouse.

The sleet turned to heavy wet snow and we walked in the centre of the lane, oblivious to anything until we became aware of a man's voice shouting behind us.

It was Mr Stevens, driving his milk float back to the farm, and his astonishment was comical.

'Gracious me, Miss Stephanie, what are ye doin' out on such a day? Come on, get in the float and I'll take ye back for a cup o' tea.'

The farmhouse was warm, and scented with baking bread and roasting meat. Two cats slept in front of the stove and in a corner of the kitchen a small yellow bird jumped about its cage, trilling shrilly. I ran to look at it and Mrs Stevens called out, 'That's mi Christmas present fro' mi 'usband, Lisa, 'e's a roller canary, they make the best singers. We've called 'im Peter.'

'He's beautiful, Mrs Stevens.'

Mother pulled her chair close to the stove and rubbed her hands.

'It's no day for walking the fells,' Mrs Stevens admonished her.

'I'm sorry to be such a bother, Mrs Stevens, I just wanted to get some air.'

'Not this air, ye don't. Joe'll take ye back in the truck, I can't let ye walk.'

'No, Mrs Stevens, your husband has work to do, I know how busy a farmer can be around this time. I'll be perfectly all right when I've had a cup of tea, the wind was making my eyes run.'

Mrs Stevens looked at her keenly. Her cheeks were wet and I couldn't tell if it was the effect of the sleet or if she had been crying.

Fruit loaf and scones appeared on the table, and a large brown teapot. then Emmie looked round the door, her eyes wide as saucers.

'Get back into the parlour, Emmie,' her mother said. 'Lisa's not come to play, she was walking with 'er mother.'

'Can we go out then?' Emmie demanded.

'No ye can't. It's not fit to turn a dog out, now get back to the others.'

When Mother smiled Mrs Stevens said, 'That's our Emmie, she's that frightened o' missin' somethin'. If I 'ave any trouble with any of 'em it'll be our Emmie.'

'My mother's very satisfied with Mary, Mrs Stevens, she's a good girl.'

'Ay, she is. She's allus bin considerate and 'elpful about the 'ouse. Our Pauline's got 'er 'ead in the clouds and our Emmie can be feckless, but our Mary's always bin a good lass. When are ye thinkin' on goin' back to Africa, Mrs Ralston?'

'Very soon now. I have to see about Lisa's schooling, then we must go home.'

'Well, yer've bin 'ere some time now and I allus says a family's best kept together.'

'Yes, I'm sure you're right.'

Mother rose to her feet and started to button her raincoat.

'Are ye sure ye won't 'ave another cup of tea?' Mrs Stevens said quickly. Don't be takin' any notice of anythin' I've said, I never 'ave known when to keep mi thoughts to miself.'

74

'No really, we must get back before dark.'

Mrs Stevens came to the door with us and shook her head dismally at the state of the weather.

'I wish yer'd let Joe take ye in the truck, e'll be in directly and a bit put out that I've let ye go in this.'

'We'll hurry, it isn't far.'

Mother took my hand and we started out. It was impossible to hurry. The wind tore at our clothes and the road was slippery with freezing snow. We were gasping for breath by the time we reached the gates of Grandmother's house and then we saw a man striding towards us, his head bent against the wind. He looked up and said with relief, 'Thank God, Stephanie. What possessed you to go out on such a day?'

'I'm perfectly all right, Philip, we just wanted some air.' Her voice was trembling.

He took her in his arms and for what seemed an eternity they stood together and I was forgotten, then her arms stole round his neck and they were kissing, desperate hungry kisses, and I turned away in embarrassment.

The snow was falling thickly now and at last they became aware of it. Uncle Philip picked me up and with Mother slipping and sliding beside us he strode to where the light streamed out through the open door, and there was Aunt Edwina, calling out in a fearful trembling voice, 'Were *were* you, Steph?'

'Please don't fuss, Edwina, it wasn't snowing when we left the house,' Mother answered, pushing me into the hall before her. She was very pale, and there was a haunted stricken look in her eyes.

Aunt Edwina whispered urgently, 'Please don't go into the drawing room just yet, Mother's very upset and so is Mrs Ralston. We thought you were lost.'

'Perhaps you'd better tell them we've returned, then. I'm not likely to get lost around here, I've known these lanes and hills all my life. We called at the farm and Mrs Stevens gave us tea.'

'It was inconsiderate,' Aunt Edwina insisted.

'Perhaps it was, but please don't say any more. Let me get out of this wet coat and help Lisa off with hers.'

75

All this time Uncle Philip hadn't spoken, now he strode into the drawing room where we heard him saying cheerfully, 'It's all right, they called at the farm for tea. There's nothing to be alarmed about.'

His words were greeted with silence and in the hall Mother was smoothing her hair in front of the mirror and I was looking regretfully at the pools of melted snow on the polished floorboards.

The others all came into the hall, my grandparents Ralston already wearing their coats.

'I'm sorry, Mrs Ralston,' Mother said in a low faltering voice. 'We really hadn't intended going to the farm but Mr Stevens saw us on the road and insisted. I had no idea it was so late, please forgive me.'

'But of course, my dear, we're just very glad that you are both back safe and sound.'

Mother kissed Grandpa and Grandma and shook hands formally with Uncle Philip while I was embraced by them in turn. Then we watched at the door until Uncle Philip's big car went out of the gates.

Back in the hall Grandmother turned on Mother. 'Well, I hope you're proud of yourself, Stephanie. Malcolm's parents came here specially to see you and Lisa, only to be treated by such a show of bad manners that I feel ashamed for you. Before the end of the day Mrs Ralston will be thinking how fortunate she is in her other daughter-in-law. Constance would never have done such a thing.'

'How do you know, Mother?'

'I do know. Really, Stephanie, I don't know why you do these things. You've had the best that money can buy, a good education, a happy home life, and yet you embarrass your father and me by behaving like a spoilt child. If you think that for one moment Philip Ralston approved of your bad manners you are very much mistaken. He wasn't pleased to be forced out in the snow to search for you.'

'Please, Mother, I don't want to talk about it any more. I've said I'm sorry, there's nothing else I can say.'

Grandmother swept off, displeasure evident in her

straight back and erect shoulders. As for the rest of the evening, there was an atmosphere felt by all.

In bed that night I lay thinking about Mother and Uncle Philip. I had never seen her kiss Father with that terrible yearning, or look so stricken and defeated when the kiss ended. Suddenly I became aware of voices raised in agitation – Mother and Aunt Edwina. I crept out to Aunt Edwina's door with my heart hammering against my ribs.

Aunt Edwina was saying, 'It's time you went home, Stephanie. If you don't it's all going to start up again and I can't see any future in it. Surely you must see how wrong it is.'

'Don't you think I don't know all that? I love him Edwina, I've loved him since the first moment I looked at him, and he loves me. We didn't want it to happen. I thought when I married Malcolm and he married Constance we'd forget each other, but it hasn't happened. It's a torment in my heart, being without him is like death.'

'You're just being melodramatic.'

'Oh Edwina, how could you know? You've never been in love, Mother's seen to that.'

'You should fight it, Steph, you have a daughter to consider. Go home. Philip will never divorce Constance, and in any case she'll never let him go. Think how much misery you'll bring to so many people if you don't get away.'

'How can I go back to Malcolm and pretend things are normal? I'm no good at pretending, he'll know things are different.'

'Then you'll have to lie and lie, if not for Malcolm's sake, for Lisa's.'

I heard a noise in the corridor and ran back towards my room. I had almost reached it when I saw a white figure at the top of the stairs and I gasped with fright.

I wanted to scream, but no sound would come, then the figure came towards me and I saw it was Jessica in a long white dressing gown. Her eyes were glittering strangely in her pale face and for the first time she did not seem beautiful. Perhaps it was the darkness, perhaps it was the pain in my heart, but her pale oval face seemed filled with a strange vindictiveness. Catching hold of my arm with a grip of steel, she hissed, 'You heard what Aunt Edwina said, why don't you go home? You're spoiling it for everybody.'

'How, how am I spoiling it?' I stammered.

'By just being here. Christmas hasn't been the same with you and your mother here. She's a bad woman.'

'She's not, she's not,' I stormed, aware that my voice was raised in anger, then she dragged me towards my room, pushing me inside and closing the door behind me.

CHAPTER 10

Fate took an unpredictable hand in our plans during the next week. Mother was ill and I stood miserably outside her bedroom door, listening to her struggling to breathe. The doctor came and diagnosed bronchial pneumonia.

This necessitated her removal to her own bedroom and the removal of the rest of the family to their own homes. Jessica was furious, though her parents didn't seem in the least put out. Uncle Raymond was positively glowing and even Uncle Henry, who was a dry old stick and not given to showing his feelings, declared that it was time he went home, there would be matters in his parish needing attention.

Grandmother was, predictably, very angry with Mother, saying it was all her own fault because she'd caught it by going out in the snow on Boxing Day.

I was banished from outside Mother's door by Grandmother. 'Why don't you go and play in the nursery, Lisa? You can't go in and somebody is going to fall over you if you insist on sitting there.'

'Is my mother going to die?' I asked plaintively.

'Certainly not, but she is being severely punished for being stupid. Perhaps it will teach her a lesson. Now run along.'

'May I go to the farm?'

'No. I don't want you going out at all. It's far too cold and we don't want another invalid on our hands.'

Two days later Aunt Edwina took me to the dentist to get my brace fitted.

I hated the ugly steel clamp fastened on my teeth. I hardly spoke at all because for the first few days it hurt too much and caused ulcers on my gums, so that I was constantly rinsing my mouth with salt and water.

Mother was much better and I was allowed to see her and show her my brace. She assured me that when it was

79

taken off I would have the most beautiful teeth in the world but I couldn't believe her, it was a story I had heard too often.

'Mother and Edwina will have to take you to see Miss Baker, darling. The doctor won't allow me out yet.'

'Can't it wait until you're better?'

'No, we must keep the appointment we made, she's a very busy person.'

On the table by her bed was a large vase of roses and carnations and when she saw me looking at them she smiled brightly. 'They're from Uncle Philip and Aunt Constance.'

'Does Grandmother mind?'

'Mind, Lisa?'

'Well yes, she gets so cross when you're with Uncle Philip.'

For a long moment she looked at me sorrowfully, then she pulled me close to her. 'Grandmother gets cross about a lot of things. When I'm better we shall be going home. Do you want to go, Lisa?'

'Oh yes, I want to see Daddy and my impala again. Do I have to come to school in England?'

'Yes, you do.'

'And shall I have to live here with Grandmother and Aunt Edwina?'

'I'm afraid so, darling, but you'll be able to come to Kenya for the summer holidays. Uncle Raymond's boy's have been doing it for years.'

Miss Baker's school, Ashlea, was a large stone building which had once been the property of a wealthy cotton manufacturing family from Manchester. It was surrounded by playing fields and tennis courts and in front of the long french windows were formal flowerbeds which Aunt Edwina said looked very pretty in the spring and summer.

It was on the north side of Lancaster and from the terrace we could see the curve of Morecambe Bay and the storm clouds which hung low on the lakeland hills. We saw a group of girls in navy gaberdine raincoats and pale pink felt hats and Aunt Edwina whispered, 'That is the uniform you'll be wearing, Lisa. It's quite nice, isn't it?'

I nodded wordlessly. I could hide behind such a uniform, melt into the background so that the ugly disfiguring brace wouldn't show. Then my heart lifted, for it would be two years before I could come to the school and in the meantime nobody in Kenya would care how I looked.

Miss Baker was a small neat woman who sat behind a huge walnut desk from which she rose to shake hands with us. Grandmother did most of the talking, then Miss Baker spoke to me. 'What do you like to do Lisa, are you musical at all?'

I looked up at Grandmother, expecting her to answer for me, but instead she pursed her lips in some annoyance, and shyly I said, 'I would like to play the piano, I love music.'

'Do you have a piano in Kenya?'

'Yes, but Mother doesn't often play it.'

'You must ask your mother if you can have some lessons, perhaps there is someone nearby who could teach you.'

I didn't answer, there seemed little point when I thought of those eternal acres of unpopulated country where we sometimes didn't see anyone else for weeks, even months.

'I want Lisa to receive an education which will help her to earn her own living when the time is right,' Grandmother declared stoutly. 'My daughter's husband is a gamekeeper at one of the large game reserves so obviously they do not have the capital enjoyed by Jessica's parents. Lisa's grandparents are Brigadier Ralston and his wife, perhaps you know of them.'

'Yes of course, Brigadier Ralston has been prominent on many of the committees I have sat upon. He is a very charming man.'

'Well, of course. I merely wish to point out that Lisa will not expect to enjoy the social activities of her cousin. I wish the child to have a good education, but do you really think music is necessary?'

'I think so if the child has an aptitude for it.'

'Well we will have to see, won't we? Jessica has been playing for us over Christmas, I expect Lisa merely wishes to be like her.'

In some annoyance I turned on Grandmother. 'I don't want to be like her, I want to be like myself.'

Smoothly Miss Baker intervened, saying, 'Two years is quite a long time, Lisa, and we may see many changes. Are you quite happy with the way Jessica is developing, Mrs Marston?'

'Well of course. Are you?'

'She needs to study more. It often happens that when a girl sees no need to work for her living her school work suffers. She doesn't see much point in making the effort.'

'Are you telling me that Jessica doesn't make an effort?'

'She could do better, Mrs Marston. She prefers the tennis court to the classroom, her music is indifferent and her dedication to discipline leaves much to be desired. I have spoken to her mother, because if Jessica isn't careful she will fritter away the golden opportunities she is being offered here.'

'And what did my daughter say, Miss Baker?'

'I was not at all happy with her reply. She seems to think that the social benefits Jessica obtains from the school vastly outweigh the other advantages. She left me feeling that making the right sort of marriage was infinitely more important to Jessica than receiving a good education.'

'She is very popular at the school.'

'Jessica is a beautiful girl, she moves like a gazelle and is bound to be popular with girls who do not have her physical appeal, but since you are here, Mrs Marston, I am asking you to speak to your daughter, and to Jessica also. She needs to work harder otherwise she is wasting her own time and that of my teachers.'

Grandmother's face was red and haughty. 'You can leave this in my hands, Miss Baker,' she snapped. 'I'll speak to Jessica's parents as soon as possible. In the meantime, do I take it that you are willing to take Lisa?'

Miss Baker looked at me and smiled. 'Do you promise

to work hard with your teacher in Kenya, Lisa?' she asked quietly.

'Yes, Miss Baker.'

'Very well then, when you are seven you can become a pupil here.'

The interview was at an end. We shook hands and departed but grandmother sat silent in the car all the way home. We were driving towards the house when Grandfather said drily, 'I notice both of you have little to say about your visit to the school. Do I take it Miss Baker isn't willing to take Lisa?'

'Of course she will take her,' Grandmother snapped. 'She'll take her in two years' time.'

'Then why are you both so silent? What else did she have to say?'

'She's not very happy with Jessica's schoolwork. It's all a lot of nonsense. If you ask me, there's a lot of jealousy at the school.'

'You mean our granddaughter is so brilliant all the other girls are jealous?'

'No, James, I don't mean that at all, and there's no call to be so sarcastic. I'll speak to Cecily very soon. I'm quite sure Miss Baker's completely misunderstood her.'

Mother was up and about now but she was still confined indoors because of the stormy weather. Uncle Philip drove over with his parents on several occasions and once he brought Aunt Constance. Grandmother was always present and to me the conversation was boring. When at last Mother was allowed out it was always in the car, and Sally was left in her warm stable to await the spring.

Once when I was returning with Mary from the farm we saw Mother's car parked in a lane near Grandma Ralston's house. Mary hurried me past, her face rosy with embarrassment, and I knew Mother was meeting Uncle Philip in the lane.

That evening when she came into the nursery to say goodnight I said innocently, 'We saw your car this afternoon near Green Lane, but Mary wouldn't stop.'

For several seconds she stared at me thoughtfully, then

she said, 'Uncle Philip and Aunt Constance are returning to the continent soon. Perhaps we should drive over to say goodbye.'

Grandmother thought it was a foolish thing to do but Mother was adamant. 'It will look more foolish if we don't go. After all it may be years before we meet again, if ever we meet at all.'

'You are not the slightest bit interested in seeing Constance.'

'No I'm not, but Malcolm's parents will think it strange if we don't see them before they leave. Lisa and I will go tomorrow. The day after I must make arrangements about going home. I've written Malcolm to say we'd be home before Easter, on the first available boat calling at Mombasa.'

'I see. And in two years I take it you'll return with Lisa so that she can attend school? I would like to think Malcolm will be with you.'

'That's up to him, I shall certainly encourage him to travel with us.'

'And I shall hope that if you are seen in the area with your husband all the gossip will stop.'

Nobody spoke, and after a while Aunt Edwina picked up her knitting and Mother sat staring into the fire.

I felt excitement when I thought about Kenya and the big ship that would be taking us home. I would never have to wear that stiff velvet dress again, but would roam the compound in cool cotton with the sun warming my bare arms. In Kenya there would be Benjamin's deep musical baritone echoing across the grass while he fed the animals, and his wife Beaulah for ever scolding him for his indolence. There would be hot scented nights, the glow of guardfires, and the roar of a lion which, Benjamin had told me, meant 'as far as my voice carries, this is my kingdom'.

CHAPTER 11

A week before Easter we arrived at Mombasa. Father met us when the ship docked and we travelled to Tsavo the next day.

I had forgotten its remoteness, the savage glory which seemed to belong to the darkest Africa most people only read about. Scattered nimbus clouds floated in a sky of hyacinth blue while herds of buffalo, appearing no bigger than insects in the distance, caused puffs of red dust to spiral upwards on the hot air like smoke signals. A few vultures fell quickly from the sky in an almost vertical descent, legs extended, on to a carcass.

I was a child of Africa, and the sight of vultures was normal. In some ways I had grown up with the knowledge of death and its inevitability.

I sat between my parents in the Land Rover and at times had to hold on for dear life as we encountered washboards where rain, wind and sun had moulded the sand into an iron finish of closely-spaced ripples. The noise of the wheels made conversation impossible but that hardly mattered. Conversation had been minimal since we arrived. Father's stern face had been baked nut brown by the sun while Mother seemed unnaturally fair.

I was asleep long before we reached the compound and only awoke when Father lifted me down. Then Benjamin was there with his deep booming voice and Beaulah holding me tightly against her ample bosom.

Benjamin lifted our big trunk on to his shoulders as if it had been thistledown, while all around us was the barking of dogs and from the trees the chattering of monkeys.

A tall slender woman stood at the steps. She made no effort to help with the luggage but stared at us with arrogant curiosity until Father spoke to her curtly. With a shrug she turned and walked away.

In the flickering light of the guard fire I had only been

able to see that she was a native woman. Mother stared after her, and when we were inside the house she said stonily, 'Who was that woman, Malcolm?'

'She's a servant, I took her on to help Beaulah.'

'I didn't notice her offering to help.'

'She's had no dealings with white women. She was expelled from her tribe for some misdemeanour and I found her wandering in the scrub. She wouldn't have lasted the night if I hadn't brought her here.'

'You've always been opposed to female natives about the place. What's so special about this one?'

'I've told you what happened, if you don't want her to remain here I'll listen out for something else for her . . . Let me have a look at your teeth, Lisa. How long are you expected to wear that wretched thing?'

I opened my mouth for his inspection while Mother said, 'She'll wear a brace until her teeth grow straight.'

'And when does she go home to school?'

'When she's seven.'

'You'll be going with her, of course?'

'And you too, I hope. Your mother desperately wants to see you. I promised her that the next time we would go together.'

'Two years is a long time, circumstances often alter facts,' was all Father said, and impatiently Mother turned away to sort out our luggage.

'Anything happened during these last three days?' Father asked Benjamin, and I watched the wide grin split his dark face showing two rows of perfect white teeth.

'No, Bwana, all nice, you see for yourself.'

'Good. What about the fencing the buffaloes destroyed? I don't suppose Harris has done anything about it.'

Benjamin spread his hands and if anything the smile became wider.

Father snapped, 'I thought as much.'

He went to the side table and poured himself a drink while Mother watched, frowning.

'We'll leave the cases here until the morning, Lisa, then you can help me to unpack,' she said. 'Come along, I expect you're very tired. I know I am.'

Father raised his glass to Mother with a half smile. 'Goodnight, my dear, I'll see you tomorrow.'

I saw her face grow pink in the lamplight and I could feel her hand trembling.

I was wide awake before it was properly light, and immediately became aware of the incessant barking of baboons and the vibrating rumble of elephant talk. The wild was calling to me, the compelling call of untamed Africa which for a few months I had almost forgotten but which was now a throbbing incessant song in my heart.

I ran out into the compound in dressing gown and slippers, calling to Rinta, my impala. My voice aroused a great agitation in the trees but there was no answer from her. For over an hour I searched the compound for her, going right to the southern fence, but there was no sign of her and with the utmost desolation filling my heart I retraced my steps, still calling urgently.

Benjamin came through the morning mist, his face troubled. He knelt on the grass and took me in his arms.

'Benjamin,' I wailed, 'where is Rinta? I've looked everywhere.'

He looked at me solemnly, his dark eyes filled with compassion, and said sadly, 'You have no Rinta, love, a leopard took her one morning when there was nobody to save her.'

I stared at him incredulously, then pulled away and raced to the house. Father was helping himself to breakfast from the side table but without a second's thought I ran at him and started to pound him with my fists. My voice was harsh and filled with tears as I told him how much I hated him, that it was his fault Rinta had died. Then Mother and Beaulah were in the room and Father was striding out of the door, leaving his breakfast untasted.

There was so much anger in my heart that morning. I hated Africa with a hatred so intense it felt like physical pain, and I hated my father. All morning I sat rigid and tearless, staring out into the scrub and at last mother came and sat beside me.

'You mustn't blame your father for Rinta's death, Lisa,

it is a story that will be happening today all over Africa, some animal will die to feed another. Try to think that perhaps the leopard that killed Rinta had cubs to feed. It is Nature, darling.'

'It's cruel, I hate Africa.' And I vowed that never again would I take to my heart some wild baby creature my father had rescued for a little while from the terrors of the bush.

It was a ridiculous vow. In the next two years I found many creatures to love and the pain was still the same when they left the compound because their survival was always in doubt.

Soon after, Mrs Evans arrived. She lived about ten miles away at the edge of a native compound where her husband ran a missionary school for native children with the help of three graduates from the university in Nairobi. his wife had been a teacher in England, but merely occupied herself in housekeeping since she spoke hardly any Swahili.

She had jumped at the chance of teaching me and saw little difficulty in driving her truck across the rough terrain between the mission and our house.

I liked her on sight. She was a small wiry woman with dark hair sprinkled with grey, and she had a delightful sense of humour. She and Mother became instant friends and Mrs Evans had a fund of humorous stories centred round her husband's activities as a missionary.

I looked forward to my lessons and I heard Mrs Evans tell Mother that I was coming on extremely well and would be well equipped to attend Miss Baker's school.

One other thing happened to cause me pleasure and that was my music lessons. One evening Mrs Evans brought her husband over to tune the piano. He had learned to do his own piano tuning since he arrived in Africa because there simply wasn't a professional tuner available. After that the piano was much nicer to play and I began on easy pieces of music and, after constant practice, more intricate compositions.

I didn't realize for some time that we were not seeing a great deal of Father. It was invariably late in the evening when he returned to the house and there were times when I heard my parents quarrelling. Sometimes his words were slurred and I knew that he had been drinking over at Mr Harris's place.

We saw little of Mr Harris, until the morning he called to say he'd found several dead elephants close to a water-hole, killed by poachers. While Father was making a telephone call Mr Harris came to sit next to Mother at the breakfast table. She sat stonily silent, looking down at her plate, and he smiled cynically.

'What's the matter, Stephanie?' he asked quietly. 'Aren't we having a word to say to each other this morning?'

She looked up sharply. 'It doesn't please me that you keep Malcolm drinking at your place half the night.'

'I thought you'd become accustomed to living without Malcolm.'

When she didn't reply he said quietly, 'What do you think happens to a man when his wife deserts him for three or four months? He either turns to drink or he finds another woman. Such is the nature of us brutes, Steph.'

When she still didn't answer he said shortly, 'Open your eyes, woman, drinking with me is the lesser evil in your husband's life.'

Later that morning Mother sent for Beaulah who came into the living room with a big smile.

'Beaulah,' mother began quietly, 'what exactly does that other woman do in the kitchen?'

The smile vanished, replaced by a strange wariness. 'The master brought her, she help with the cooking, the work in the house.'

'How is it we never see her, then? What is her name?'

Beaulah gave some quite incomprehensible name, and when Mother raised her eyebrows the smile came back momentarily. 'We call 'er Jubilee, ma'am, she half Masai,' and she pursed her lips comically to show her contempt for the Masai.

'Does she speak any Swahili?'

'No. Masai and some English.'

89

When Mother seemed surprised Beaulah said, 'She no good, that one. Masai threw her out, she has the evil eye.'

'Send Jubilee to me, Beaulah, I would like to speak to her.'

Beaulah seemed glad to go, and in a few minutes Jubilee sidled sinuously into the room and I saw her for the first time in the light of day. She was tall and very slender, dressed in a loose African garment almost like a jellaba. Her black hair was twisted into a mass of tiny plaits and she wore long silver earrings. She was the most strikingly unusual woman I had ever seen. I did not think she was beautiful, she was too strange for beauty to my Western eyes, but there was something in the angular mobility of her face that made me unable to take my eyes off her.

She stood in front of my mother graceful and arrogant, and it seemed to me then that it was Mother who was at a disadvantage rather than this dark contemptuous stranger.

'Beaulah tells me you speak English,' Mother said quietly.

She nodded.

'Where did you learn English, Jubilee?'

'Different places,' the woman answered her.

'Beaulah also tells me you are half Masai. Why did you leave your tribe?'

Jubilee shrugged. 'They not want me, they left me to die. Master Ralston save me and bring me here.'

'I know all that, but why didn't your people want you?'

'They call me evil, say I see things because I know things that will happen. I cannot help that, I have always seen things, always known the future.'

'The Masai have witch doctors who profess to know what the future holds, why should it be so wrong for you to know it also?'

'Because I am not a witch doctor, I just know these things.'

'You speak English remarkably well. Could it be that one half of you is English?'

'My father.'

'I see. Where is your father now?'

Again came the familiar shrug. 'He not care about me,

not since the police took him in Nairobi. I shall never see him again.'

'What do you do around the house to help Beaulah?'

'I can do anything she asks of me, anything you ask of me, lady.'

'Did the master say you could live here indefinitely?'

Jubilee raised her eyebrows and Mother said, 'Did my husband bring you here to work in the house?'

A veil seemed to fall over Jubilee's eyes, and with bent head she said, 'He said there would be work for me to do. I have tried to please, you must ask him.'

'Very well, Jubilee, you may go.'

We watched her sidle gracefully out. Mother was sitting at her sewing table, frowning, when Mrs Evans arrived.

When Mother didn't respond to Mrs Evans' bright chatter she said, 'Is something wrong, Stephanie? You're sitting there staring into space while I'm prattling on here.'

'Oh, it's nothing, Jean. I've just been talking to Jubilee, who says she can see into the future.'

'That's not unusual. A great many of the natives profess to know what the future holds. They live so close to the soil, so close to Mother Nature, perhaps it's inevitable.'

'She also tells me that her father was English.'

'That doesn't surprise me – some poacher or hunter who took his fun where he found it. Are you keeping her on?'

'If she helps Beaulah I probably shall, but Beaulah doesn't like the girl. The Masai and the Bantu have never had much time for one another.'

'The problem is, what would happen to the girl if you let her go? We've come across trouble of this kind so many times. The problem is the Masai women are very sensual. One of these days she's going to want a husband and children – if not a husband most certainly a man – and Beaulah is probably thinking about her husband.'

'I rather think Beaulah is quite capable of taking care of the man who belongs to her.'

'You're thinking about John Harris, are you? I would have thought he was more into scotch than women.'

'Perhaps you're right. Time will tell.'

'If Jubilee's as fey as she says she is she'll already be aware of what the future holds.'

Most of what I heard that morning was not properly understood, but as the months passed I knew that the normality of our life in Africa had gone for ever.

I began to sleep badly and have nightmares, and would wake wet with perspiration and with a stifled scream in my throat.

One night when I'd had a nightmare and couldn't sleep, I pulled back the curtains on a scene of indescribable beauty. A full moon sailed omnipotently in a dark blue sky, silvering the tall coarse grasses and the distant trees, while from somewhere in the scrubland came the long lonely cry of a wild creature.

The guard fires had died low, and a male lion strolled arrogantly into the compound below the verandah. He was a splendid creature with a magnificent black mane and for a minute he kept absolutely still. He looked up at the sky as if paying respect to the Creator, then lowered his head and gave a full-throated roar which swept across the compound as a thunderous rumble.

It was a magnificent sound that pulsated cold excitement up my spine and made goose flesh stand out on my arms, then without hurry he turned and padded off.

I felt no fear at the lion's intrusion into our domain, and by this time I was wide awake, the nightmare forgotten. From the compound I heard voices, then saw two figures standing motionless against the trees. Whoever they were the lion had disturbed them. One of them moved towards the dying fire, and I recognized my father. Then the other figure leapt forward and two slim arms dragged him back into her embrace.

I was unable to take my eyes away from her dark naked figure as she wound it sinously like a snake into his embrace, then he put her away from him and strode to the house. I heard the soft closing of a door and footsteps passing my room, then in all the house there was silence. I slept no more that night and the morning found me as hurt and miserable as I had felt when I saw my mother and Uncle Philip kissing.

CHAPTER 12

We had been back in Kenya almost a year, and terrible arguments occurred every day between my parents. Mother was anxious to spend Christmas with Uncle Raymond and Aunt Georgina in Nairobi, but Father didn't want to go. He presented her with all sorts of reasons why he couldn't be absent from the reserve – from poachers in the area to shortage of workers – and then John Harris had an attack of malaria and this gave him the final excuse he needed.

The week before Christmas therefore Mother and I set out alone for Nairobi. I was miserably aware of her pale angry face and that she was driving far too fast over roads made treacherous by rain.

It was a journey made largely in silence. She was busy with her own thoughts while I reflected unhappily on my parent's antipathy towards each other. There were times when I almost looked forward to going away to England.

Jubilee, that dark enigmatic shadow, added much of the acrimony to my parents' arguments. Mother wanted to send her away. Jubilee was useless in the kitchen and constantly quarreled with Beaulah.

Mrs Evans had noticed the underlying insolence in Jubilee's attitude towards Mother, and one day she said, 'Why don't you send her packing, Stephanie? She doesn't have to go back to her tribe, there must be plenty of work in the area. Surely Malcolm can see what she's like, you shouldn't have to put up with her.'

'I think he's far too busy to notice,' Mother said quickly, and changed the subject.

Under the tutelage of Mrs Evans I learned to write essays and letters, and Mother encouraged me to write to Aunt Edwina and Grandmother. Grandmother never wrote to me, but in her letters to Mother she said she was

93

pleased to see that I was coming along, as she quaintly put it.

I wrote to Pauline Stevens because I thought she was the one most likely to answer, and I was pleased when she wrote me a long letter. She had passed her scholarship for the girls' High School in Lancaster and was enjoying herself there. Danny too had done well and was attending the boys' Grammar School but Joe had left school and was working with his father. Emmie was staying on at the village school and would probably go into domestic work.

I had sent them some wooden carvings done by the native children. In the main they were crude but the wood was quite beautiful and I promised that when I returned to England I would bring some more sophisticated carvings from the shops in Nairobi.

Mother informed me that the grandparents had promised to buy my school uniform and any other things I would need – a great relief since they were expensive and Father would grumble at the cost. As it was, all he would have to find was my school fees.

It was late when we arrived at Uncle Raymond's house on the outskirts of Nairobi. Dogs were suddenly leaping all over us, and then the doors were flung open and lights streamed out into the night. The house was decorated for Christmas, including an artificial spruce in the hall decorated with tinsel and baubles.

The boys would be flying into Nairobi the following day and Uncle Raymond invited me to go with him to meet them at the airport.

'Why didn't Malcolm come?' Aunt Georgina asked. 'Surely he can bury his animosity over Christmas.'

'I don't know, sometimes I don't understand him at all, I don't even think it's envy of Raymond any more,' Mother replied.

'But you're not happy, Steph.'

'Please, Georgina, not in front of Lisa.'

They didn't need to spare my feelings, I knew all too well that my parents were unhappy. But I was determined to enjoy Christmas in Nairobi, and my spirits were high as I waited with Uncle Raymond at the airport next afternoon.

We spotted the boys immediately, waving enthusiastically as they crossed the tarmac. Then my heart sank dismally as I recognized the two people walking behind: Alexander Hamilton and Jessica.

All my joy in the holiday disappeared when I looked into Jessica's beautiful face with its stony stare. Her greeting was perfunctory, probably unobserved by the others who were all talking at once, except for Alexander. He took my hand with a brief smile and murmured, 'Hello, Lisa.'

Very soon we were all in Uncle Raymond's big brake heading for home. I sat silent while Jessica enthused about the flight, the holiday in Kenya and everything in general.

'You've been mighty lucky to get out of the usual holiday with Grandmother Marston, Jessica. How did you manage it?' Uncle Raymond asked.

'Mother said I needed some sunshine, I hadn't been too well after a bad cold in October, and Granny said she didn't mind this year because she'd had enough the year before when it was such a large party.'

I had looked forward to Christmas in Nairobi, now it was spoilt. We ate the usual turkey and plum pudding on Christmas Day and went to church, but there the similarity to an English Christmas ended. We sat in the sun and swam in the pool, and twelve months had made such a change in Robin he now felt too old and superior to spend much time with me. Instead he clung closely to his brothers and they had eyes for nobody but Jessica.

I spent much of my time with my nose buried in a book. Most of my presents had been clothing or books.

We were sitting round the pool watching the boys and Jessica playing in the water and Aunt Georgia said, 'Why do you suppose Mother agreed to Jessica coming here instead of spending Christmas at home, Stephanie?'

'Could it have something to do with Alexander?' Mother answered. 'She was always so anxious to find young men with the right connections for us, she's sure to want the same for her grandchildren.'

'That's what I think, even though they're so young.'

'Not *too* young. Alexander is at the age when he's going to meet other girls and Jessica is quite the young lady and very beautiful.'

'Perhaps a little too beautiful. She's a minx, playing one boy off against the other, even Robin who's so young, poor lamb, that he doesn't know how to cope. I'm going to have a word with him tonight, he's hardly spoken a word to Lisa all week and they used to be such friends.'

'I'd rather you didn't scold Robin about that, Georgina, it was bound to happen sooner or later and I don't want Robin to feel he has to be kind to Lisa.'

I was glad to be going home. There would only be one more Christmas in Kenya and then I would be at school in England.

'I suppose you're coming to Miss Baker's school,' said Jessica on the morning of my departure. 'I doubt if you'll like it there, the lessons are very advanced and yours is such an unusual background.'

'What do you mean, unusual?'

'Well, living in Africa, I mean. We have one girl whose parents live in Hong Kong and another whose parents live in Egypt, but their fathers are something big in the diplomatic service.'

'My father's a gamekeeper, that's better.'

'Well of course it isn't, it's not even as good as being a vet like Uncle Raymond.'

Just then Alexander and Roger joined us, and turning to them sweetly Jessica said, 'I'm just telling Lisa I hope she enjoys herself at Miss Baker's, I'll be there to look after her.'

I was beginning to get Jessica's measure. I could expect little help from her, I knew, but her duplicity astounded me. On the way back I was silent for so long that Mother asked, 'Is something wrong, darling? You've hardly said a word.'

'I just don't want to go to Miss Baker's school.'

'I suppose that's because of Jessica.'

'How did you know?'

'I know my sister Cecily, and Jessica is very like her.

96

She made life very difficult for me when we were growing up with her hoity-toity ways, and every day we spent in Nairobi I could see Cecily in Jessica. Don't let her get to you, Lisa, and remember that one of these days you'll be a match for her.'

I didn't speak. I was wishing I had more confidence in my ability to cope with a girl who quite often said one thing and meant another. I would badly need a friend in the strange and terrifying environment of school, but I would find no friend in Jessica.

I voiced my fears to Mrs Evans.

'I wish I could go to the High School in Lancaster with Pauline Stevens,' I said plaintively. 'I like Pauline, we would be friends, but there won't be anybody at Miss Baker's school. Jessica doesn't like me and I don't like her.'

'She's probably had all her own way with no female cousins close by. I'm sure she'll get over all that and you'll probably be the best of friends.'

I decided to drop the subject. Nobody would understand that Jessica could never be my friend, it was almost like asking Beaulah to be friends with Jubilee, like asking a tiger to make friends with a lamb.

I wasn't at all happy with the metaphor. Comparing Jessica to a tiger had some merit but I certainly didn't intend to be a lamb for the rest of my life.

CHAPTER 13

I shall always remember the morning when Father threw the mail across the breakfast table to Mother. Most were in the familiar handwriting of Grandmother and Aunt Edwina, but there was one which brought rich warm colour into Mother's face.

She read it through twice, then told Father, 'It's from Philip and Constance, they've been living in Egypt with her sister since their little boy was born now they want to visit us before returning to England.'

'Oh Stephanie, do we really want Constance here with her vapours and supercilious disdain of anything remotely primitive? They'll probably bring a nanny and expect the same sort of comforts they get at home.'

'Philip and Constance are accustomed to living in remote places.'

'Yes, and she's hated every one of them. She stuck them for a month or two and then she was back in England waiting for him to get home on leave. I suggest you make some excuse, say you're preparing to go home with Lisa and can't do with visitors at this time.'

'It's several months before I need to go home with Lisa, and they know it. Besides, your parents will expect you to travel with us. I don't see what possible excuse we can make, and in any case it's too late, they've left Egypt and will be already on their way.'

'How old is the boy?'

'Just a few months. Philip says Constance has been ill since he was born but she's now much better. They want to see us both, Malcolm.'

'I can't think why. Philip and I never had much in common and Constance and I quarrelled whenever we met. Are you quite sure it's not you he wants to see?'

'What do you mean by that?'

'My dear girl, you surely don't think everybody in

North Lancashire except me knew about your carryings on?'

'Oh Malcolm, please don't start that. It was all over before we married, I told you so.'

'But I never believed you, Stephanie. Philip only had to come into a room to set your heart racing. If his wife was blind to it, I certainly wasn't.'

'Well, it's over now. They have a child and we have a daughter. I hate you for talking about such things in front of Lisa.'

I sat hunched over Pauline's letter but my face was flaming scarlet and my heart was filled with resentment.

'Oh well,' Father snapped, 'if they're on their way I don't suppose there's very much we can do. You'll have to do most of the honours, I'll be busy most of the time. Harris isn't up to it since his last malaria attack, and in any case he's drinking too much.'

'And you're drinking with him.'

I heard him open the door but he paused to say, 'We must try to act the loving couple before my brother and his wife. I hope it won't be too difficult.'

When I looked up Mother sat with the tears streaming down her face. I rushed to put my arms round her and we wept together.

'Your father doesn't really mean it, Lisa, he's so terribly overworked at the moment. You'll see, darling, when Uncle Philip and Aunt Constance get here it will all change.'

In my child's heart I could only believe it would change for the worse and I became desperately afraid.

My aunt and uncle arrived in a flurry of luggage at the beginning of June, just a month prior to our departure for England. Uncle Philip looked fit and handsome, but Aunt Constance was visibly wilting in the heat. So was Miss Edwards, their English nanny.

Mark the baby was adorable. I loved him instantly and resolved to spend as much time with him as possible, but I had reckoned without Aunt Constance's determination to shield the baby both from human contact and strong sunlight.

I heard Miss Edwards remark to Mother, 'She'll spoil the child rotten, Mrs Ralston. It's foolish to smother him with attention, he'll grow up to expect it.'

Aunt Constance was obsessed with insects and snakes, wild animals and birds of prey. She looked askance at the few animals living in the compound recovering from some illness or accident before being released into the wild, and she maintained that if her son slept on the balcony one or another of them would harm him.

Father told her nothing would happen to him, and I could see that both he and Uncle Philip were exasperated by her behaviour but it made no difference. The baby spent most of the time sleeping in his cot inside the house, no trouble to anybody.

Aunt Constance spent most of her time indoors, only venturing out in the cool of the evening. She was afraid for her complexion, saying she didn't want her face to look like some dried-up old prune, and the creams and lotions she produced to protect it would have stocked a shop.

Beside Mother's sun-kissed face she appeared pallid and fragile, and she was so obsessed in her efforts to protect herself that she quickly became a bore.

There were whole days when Uncle Philip accompanied Father round the reserve and beyond, and others when he set out with Mother in the truck to visit our nearest neighbours.

Father was busier than usual because some of the native population were losing their cattle to a black leopard and Uncle Philip went with him to the clearing where they had staked out a young goat.

'Will you catch him that way?' Uncle Philip asked.

'Perhaps,' Father replied, 'but that black-hearted villain is as cunning as the devil. I don't know why it should be, but they're three times as dangerous as their spotted brothers.'

The outcome was that a young cheetah ended up in the

pit, the kid escaped but the panther lived to kill another day.

Uncle Philip was charmed by Kenya and one Sunday in particular will always stand out in my memory as the perfect day. I drove with my parents and Uncle Philip in the Land Rover through the rain forest on to a small, sunny plateau where the road ended. From here there was the most magnificent view of Africa's grandeur.

We picniced there, far above the Momella Lakes, which shimmered in shades from forget-me-not blue to emerald green. Beyond them lay deep clefts of distant volcanoes where an isolated storm was sweeping through one of the valleys and rainbow tentacles were falling from the black sky like carnival streamers.

It was quite still up on the plateau, with no sign of human habitation, and the variegated pattern of clouds moving across the rolling plains stamped the final touch of vast splendour on this wilderness.

Above us rose Mount Meru with its wicked rock face and we set off from the plateau in single file, climbing the lower slopes adorned with clusters of alpine flowers, and where the atmosphere was damp and misty and much loved by the ferns and mosses through which we passed.

Eventually we reached the trail and walked easily over gently undulating hills which were covered by thin rain forest. The forests were airy fresh, lit by filtered sunshine, and colobus monkeys frolicked and chattered among the trees.

Further on the vegetation grew sparser until finally the scene opened up to reveal a small circular lake and beyond it a lost world, an oddly colourless landscape bathed in cold sunshine and belonging to another dimension of time. Even the trees excuded an eeriness. Centuries ago they had perished in a fire, and now their lifeless frames were enveloped in lichens.

None of us spoke, it was as though words would dispel the magic, and it was only later as we made our way back down the slopes of Meru that Mother said softly, 'Our clothes are damp, I hadn't realized it was raining.'

'It wasn't raining,' Father said, 'it was the atmosphere up there.'

The sun was still shining when we reached the Land Rover but darkness fell quickly and as we drove back to the reserve the eyes of numerous animals reflected constantly in our headlights, blazing points of red, green and even yellow.

As I lay in bed I reflected on the day we had spent and I prayed silently that every day would be as good. Father and Uncle Philip had behaved like brothers, without the sarcasm which covered much of their conversation, and there had been humour too in the antics of the monkeys and the unhurried ambling of a huge bull elephant with typically delicate steps as if walking on thin ice.

Almost silently he disappeared amidst the vegetation and our last impression was of his lolloping skin which hung in deep folds like an outsized suit.

It was a long time before I went to sleep. Over and over again I thought about the events of the day, a day that had been so perfect I was never able to understand the tragedy which followed.

CHAPTER 14

The day started badly. Mrs Evans had a puncture on the way, and was late. She arrived perspiring and complaining of a headache and Mother insisted that she took aspirin and rested before lunch.

The baby was fretful and Aunt Constance berated Miss Edwards for leaving him too long on the verandah.

John Harris arrived for lunch with his voice slurred and his eyes bloodshot, and with his peculiar sense of humour insisted on addressing most of his remarks to Aunt Constance with his face close to hers so that the whisky on his breath nauseated her.

Halfway through lunch there was a weird unearthly cry from the kitchens which sent shivers up my spine. We all looked up askance, then almost fearfully at each other. Mother hurried to the kitchen but still the unearthly keening went on and in a few moments Father followed.

Beaulah came carrying plates which she placed sullenly round the table and Mrs Evans asked, 'What's wrong, Beaulah, has anybody been hurt?'

'No, Mees Evans, eet Jubilee, she been like dat all morning, moanin' and cryin', tearin' out her hair, she say eet a bad day, somepin' terrible weel 'appen.'

We heard father's angry voice, then the kitchen door slamming. I saw Jubilee run across the compound, her black hair streaming, and crouch against the perimeter wall like a wild animal, her arms above her head.

My parents returned to the table, and although we looked at them for an explanation neither spoke.

After lunch father and John Harris went out in the Land Rover and Aunt Constance returned to her room with the baby. I settled down with Mrs Evans and my books on the verandah, leaving Mother and Uncle Philip in the house. We could dimly hear the murmur of their voices, and a little later they left the house and walked into the scrub towards the river and still Jubilee crouched against the wall, and now and again we heard her haunting cries.

Mrs Evans shivered delicately. 'I wish that girl would shut up,' she complained, 'that noise goes through me. I've heard it too often not to be troubled by it.'

I stared at her. 'Why are you troubled?'

'Oh, I'm being imaginative. The girl wants to draw attention to herself, I'm sure it's nothing more than that.'

All afternoon I worked at my books while the sun shone glassily out of a colourless sky. Heat hung over the compound like a cloud and in their pens two zebras took a dust bath so that the reddish-yellow dust swirled everywhere, covering themselves with fantastic shades of yellow, orange, red, white and grey, their stripes almost obliterated.

We became aware of a loud hissing, and saw six hooded vultures circling lazily in the sky. Very soon they would be squabbling heatedly over a piece of flesh.

We saw Father and John Harris return to the compound and into John's house, where no doubt the whisky bottle would be produced. About half an hour later Mother and Uncle Philip sauntered slowly out of the shadows. She paused to speak to Jubilee but the girl only whimpered, and Mother turned away.

They walked separately now. They had been holding hands when they left the trees, and I hoped Mrs Evans hadn't seen them.

I could no longer concentrate on my studies, and she said, 'I know how you feel, Lisa, it's stifling, and I'm having the utmost difficulty keeping awake. What do you say to a cup of tea?'

Mother and Uncle Philip were standing close together, and immediately separated when we entered the living room. She seemed nervous and too eager to talk, while Uncle Philip was silent, his face strangely sombre. Then Aunt Constance came in.

'I can't possibly stand this climate for another week, Philip,' she said fretfully. 'Why can't we go home?'

104

'You've made no attempt to like Kenya. The country has great beauty if you'd only make the effort, Constance.'

'It was you who wanted to come here, I never wanted to come, and now I want to go home.'

'You hated Japan and you hated Geneva, I sometimes wonder if you can settle anywhere outside England. You knew when we married that I would have to spend most of my time abroad. It's time you tried to see that there are other lands and other peoples, Constance.'

'I'm prepared to like Brussels, but we don't have to be *here*. Kenya was never on your schedule Philip, and I really can't understand why we had to come here or remain so long.'

Her voice was querulous in its anger and in the uncomfortable silence which followed Mrs Evans said quickly, 'I'll ask Beaulah if she'll make a cup of tea. Tea's so civilized, it will calm us all down.'

Two bright spots of colour burned on Aunt Constance's pale cheeks. 'Surely you can understand how I feel, Stephanie. When you came to England you were in no great hurry to get back, what's so terrible about me wanting to go home? I want my son to be able to lie out in the garden in his pram without forever worrying that some wild animal is going to tear him to pieces, and I want to entertain our friends to civilized meals in a civilized house.'

'Are you suggesting that this isn't a civilized house, Constance?' said Uncle Philip. 'It isn't a good reflection on Stephanie or my brother, who have made us very welcome here.'

'Well of course it isn't a civilized house with that girl wailing like a banshee around the place, and your brother won't be sorry to see you go. Malcolm's always been resentful of you, even your mother acknowledges that.'

'Perhaps he was at one time, but not now. Stop raking up the past, Constance.'

'I'm not raking up the past, it's here with us now. Philip, I intend to go home. If you won't make the arrangements then I'll do it myself, and we'll go home without you.'

105

'You know I won't allow that.'

'Then you do it. If you don't I'll ask Malcolm.'

'Ask Malcolm what?'

It was my father's voice from the doorway, deep and slurred. His face was red and angry, his eyes bloodshot with the dust or the whisky, I never knew which, and he carried a gun.

'Malcolm, I want to go home, now.'

He looked across the room at his brother and I saw hatred raw and desperate in his gaze. Sarcastically he asked, 'Don't tell me Philip's refused to take you home. Is he coming out into the open at last?'

Uncle Philip had grown pale and tense. 'This is all nonsense. If Constance really wants to go home then I'll make arrangements immediately.'

'You'd like that, wouldn't you, Philip. To hide it away, to cover it up as though it didn't exist, just like you've always done. You must think I'm an imbecile not to know what's been between you all these years, not something that ended when she married me but something to be resurrected every time you met because you didn't have the guts to marry her in the first place.

'Did you really think I didn't know that every time I held her in my arms it wasn't you she saw? And you, Constance, when he made love to you, when he fathered your child, it wasn't you he was making love to, it was her. And he never had the courage to alter things and make them different.'

That scene will be emblazoned in my memory for always. Like actors in a play we stood about the stage: Mrs Evans with an arm about my shoulders; Aunt Constance, her pale face shocked out of its usual petulance, staring at him out of anxious bewildered eyes; and Mother suddenly rushing across the room to beat her hands against Father's chest while Uncle Philip stared gravely at his brother.

Mother was saying over and over, 'It isn't true, it isn't true!' Then suddenly the sound of a shot turned us to stone and she sank in a heap at his feet.

Aunt Constance screamed and from out of the kitchen

Beaulah came screaming like a mad thing, and then Uncle Philip was lifting Mother up in his arms while Father stared down at her, the smoking gun in his hand.

Tenderly Uncle Philip carried her across the room but he had only gone a few steps when my father raised his gun again, and in anger and madness he fired three times into Uncle Philip's back. He sank to the floor with Mother in his arms and I tore myself out of Mrs Evans' grasp and ran to them. There was blood everywhere, my hands were covered with it and there was no sound from either of them. Then my shoulder was taken in an iron grip and I was brought to my feet and propelled across the room and out on to the verandah.

Father dragged me screaming to the Land Rover. Jubilee came running as fast as her legs would carry her. Her eyes were wide with terror and as she clutched at Father's arm he roughly pushed her away.

He lifted me bodily into the front seat and Jubilee climbed up beside me, then we were racing across the compound and into the setting sun.

I have no memory of how far we travelled, only of the dust and the bumpy road which made every bone in my body ache. At one time we hit some particularly vicious ruts which brought deafening crashes from the back and sent us all bouncing to the roof, then we were descending a steep, soft earth ramp to cross a fast-flowing river.

At once the current twisted us sideways but father drove like the madman he surely was and then we were on the opposite bank and the rain forest closed over us. As the track snaked upwards we found our way barred by a monstrous old bull elephant, and even in his madness Father stopped the Land Rover and Jubilee and I sat huddled together in trembling anticipation.

The elephant watched us with eyes that slowly opened and closed in a methodical rhythm. Characteristically, his face appeared fixed in a permanent smile as if laughing inwardly at some obscure witticism, while the overall expression was of patience and wise understanding. Then without even twitching an ear he moved off into the scrub.

On we drove, and I became convinced that Father was

taking us to some place he knew where he would kill us. Jubilee moaned and whimpered while great tears rolled down her face.

We were climbing steeply, the engine roaring until it splurted, spluttered and was suddenly still. We were out of petrol.

He rested his head on the wheel for several minutes before he raised it to look at me, and I heard myself whispering, 'Please, Father, please don't kill me.'

Some sanity entered his expression, and in a croaking voice he said, 'Stay where you are, don't leave the truck.' He climbed down and pulled Jubilee out on to the track. They both stood staring at me for some time before they walked on up the track and as she clung to him for support I heard her sobbing.

Daylight had almost gone and all around me were the sounds of Africa: the barking of baboons, the vibrating rumble of elephant talk, the penetrating snort from a disturbed rhino and the whinny of zebras gathered at a waterhole, and I cowered back in my seat when I heard the full-throated roar of a lioness after she had made her kill.

Suddenly I heard a shot in the encroaching darkness, followed by another, and then came the chattering of animals and the fluttering of a thousand wings as the birds flew upward into the night.

CHAPTER 15

It was midday when they came for me and by that time I was terrified, painfully thirsty and hungry. From early light I had been aware of the vultures circling almost above my head and my imagination was conjuring up frightful pictures.

The Kenyan police brought Benjamin with them, and as I clung to him with sobs in my throat he soothed me gently, saying, 'You're not goin' home, missy, Benjamin will take you to Mees Evans, you'll be safe there.'

The Evanses were kindness itself to me. They fed me and nursed me, and in the night when I woke up screaming Mrs Evans took me in her arms with soothing words of comfort. It was days later when I asked about my home.

'I've spoken to your mother's sister on the telephone dear, she and your uncle are coming for you on Saturday.'

'Am I to live with them?'

'Until you go to England, yes,'

'What happened after Father took me away?'

'Are you sure you want to talk about it, Lisa?'

'Yes, I want to know what happened. My mother was dead, wasn't she, and Uncle Philip?'

'Yes, they were both dead. An inquest was held the next day, the coroner came from Nairobi and the funeral took place immediately after – because of the climate, you know.'

'What happened to Aunt Constance and the baby? And the nanny?'

'They have all flown home to England. Lisa, all this has been a terrible experience for you but you must remember that your father was not himself when he did those terrible things. Try to think that he was ill, that he didn't really mean to kill your mother. Perhaps the gun went off by accident.'

'Not when he killed Uncle Philip it didn't. He meant to shoot him.'

'Then you must put it all behind you, dear, not here perhaps where everything is so familiar, but when you go home to England.'

'Shall I still be going to Miss Baker's school?'

'Of course, after their summer holidays are over and the new term starts. You'll be very happy there, Lisa. You'll learn to dance and play tennis and Miss Baker's very anxious for her girls to take up music, which I know you love. You must try to concentrate on the good things in your life, dear. In time you will think about the bad things less and less.'

'What will happen to Beaulah and Benjamin?'

'They will stay on to serve the new gamekeeper when he comes. In the meantime Mr Harris is there with a man they've sent out from Nairobi.'

'I hate Mr Harris, if he hadn't made my father drunk it wouldn't have happened.'

'Nobody can make anybody else do what they don't want, Lisa. Mr Harris is filled with remorse for what happened, he's sworn that he will never drink again as long as he lives.'

On Saturday Aunt Georgina and Uncle Raymond came for me. As soon as she saw me my aunt burst into tears while Uncle Raymond with his usual heavy-handed kindness attempted to calm her.

I sat between them in their Land Rover and we went to their summer home in the Great Rift Valley near Lake Nakuru. At any other time I would have been thrilled because I loved Nakuru more than anywhere else, but on this morning I could only think of other times when I had sat with Mother on its banks watching the hundreds of birds that made their home there.

I showed little interest in the scenery and after a while they gave up trying to entertain me. We had almost arrived when Aunt Georgina said, 'You haven't asked about the boys, Lisa. They're all arriving on Wednesday for two months.'

Even in the midst of my misery I had to ask, 'Will Jessica be with them?'

'Why no, dear, I believe Jessica will be with her parents in the South of France. But Alexander is coming. You like him, don't you?'

'Yes, he's very nice.'

There the conversation stopped once more and we drove on in silence.

How did they put up with me those first two weeks at Nakuru, silent and sullen, miserably withdrawn?

Occasionally I saw Alexander watching me with a sympathy which made me want to cry. But I couldn't cry, my misery was like a dark stone where my heart should have been. All I could feel was deep terrible anger, and I began to hate the boys who could play and laugh because their parents were alive.

It was only just light one morning when I left the house but I had been unable to sleep. It had been dinned into me that I should never walk through the scrubland alone because the animals only respected vehicles, but today there was no fear in me, not even when I surprised a shaggy-coated wildebeest before he galloped away.

Mist hung across the lake and I went to sit on a crag looking down into its depths. The water was so clear I could see deep down to the swirling vegetation and after a while it had a hypnotic effect on me. I began to think how easy it would be to drift down into those emerald waters and simply float away. Who would care? That way I would no longer be a trouble to anybody. Grandmother didn't want me, I would be a disruption in her peaceful home, and the aunts would consider me a nuisance with my sullen disposition. It would be different if I was beautiful like Jessica.

I did not hear Alexander until he sat beside me and I looked at him with anger and resentment. He was an intruder into my misery.

He seemed cheerfully unaware of my feelings, however. 'I couldn't sleep either, Lisa, and it was so hot. I'd made

111

up my mind to come down to the lake when I saw you leaving.'

'I wanted to be by myself.'

'And I've intruded, is that what you're saying, Lisa?'

'Yes.'

'I'm sorry, but I know exactly what you are feeling. I was five years old when my mother died.'

He was looking pensively across the lake, but he was not seeing it. His thoughts were sad and on something that had happened years before.

'What happened to your mother? Your father didn't kill her!'

'No, but death is death however it happened. My father was climbing in Switzerland, it was something he wanted to do to prepare himself for the Himalayas later on. My mother went with him, she lost her life on one of those mountains.'

He was remote and tense beside me, his expression bitter even after all the years.

'I was younger than you when that happened, Lisa, but I can still feel the anger and bitterness. I hated my father. There had been no need for her to go with him, no need for her to go up on to the mountain, he was the climber, not her. Every hour of every day I told myself that she had cared more for him than for me, I hadn't mattered when it came to a choice. The hatred grew and festered until it became a living vicious thing between us and I didn't want to see him or speak to him.

'I never thought that he was suffering too. He blamed himself for the accident, he probably hated himself far more than I hated him. For years we didn't meet. He paid my school fees and gave me a good allowance and for holidays I stayed with his sister or with the parents of friends. We've both missed so much, Lisa.

'Eighteen months ago he came home. He spent six weeks at my aunt's house because he'd been ill, and we met again. He didn't seem like my father, he was more like a stranger, but as the weeks went by I realized that one can't endure a hatred like that for ever, it was destroying me. Gradually, in the little time we had, we grew

112

closer together. I discovered he was the most wonderfully exciting man I had ever met and he was my father.'

I couldn't speak, my throat was aching with unshed tears. Then slowly the floodgates opened and they rolled unchecked down my face. Alexander put his arm round my shoulders and I wept against his breast.

We were silent for so long I started nervously when he gave a little cry and the next moment he had put me away from him and was pointing to the sky.

'Look up, Lisa,' he commanded. 'You will never see anything more beautiful in your life.'

My eyes followed his pointing finger and there sweeping down the sky was a ribbon of flame as hundreds of flamingoes came down to rest on the lake. They floated like a wide pink raft, setting the water alight with fluttering wings, wings that formed curving beaches of soft pink sand, and in that moment my heart lifted and reality took the place of misery. Life *would* be beautiful again, the world and all that was in it was a wonderful place.

I was back in the land of the living, I walked and swam and played ball games with the boys, and in the evenings Robin and I were back with the old board games. I basked in Alexander's approval.

One morning when I was helping Aunt Georgina, she said, 'Your uncle and I are so glad you're more like yourself Lisa, I've always said that the young heal quickly. Next year we're going home to Grandmother's for Christmas so we shall all meet there.'

'Will Alexander be there too?'

'Yes, I'm sure he will. I expect his father will be somewhere abroad.'

'Does Alexander want to be an explorer and go mountain climbing like his father?'

'I rather think he leans towards civil or water engineering. Wouldn't it be nice if one day he and Jessica got together?'

I stared at her in astonishment. 'You mean for them to get married?'

'Why yes, dear, I know Mother has her heart set on it,

they make such a handsome couple and I think he's half in love with her already. They're terribly young, I know, but I do think it would be nice, don't you?'

I was out of the kitchen and running towards the lake. Not Alexander and Jessica, never Jessica, I thought wildly. Jessica with her dark beauty and her way of being nice when it suited her and horrid when it didn't.

Since that morning when I had sat with Alexander at the lake watching the flamingoes he had been mine, my young foolish fierce little heart had made him mine, he belonged to me. Now I was hurting again because he had never been mine, and everybody in the world was making sure he would belong to Jessica.

For the rest of the holiday I was with Robin. If I had to live without Alexander it might as well start now, I thought angrily.

There were times he looked at me puzzled and faintly hurt, and Aunt Georgina said one day, 'Have you and Alexander quarrelled? I thought you were getting along so well.'

'I'd rather be with Robin,' I said airily, 'the others are too old for me.'

'You didn't think so last week.'

'I like them all, it's just that Robin is younger. Alexander is probably very sorry that Jessica isn't here.'

'I hope you're not jealous of Jessica, Lisa. She's a lovely girl, we all adore her. When you get to school do try to be like her, dear.'

At that moment I felt very grown up and superior. 'I don't want to be like Jessica or anybody else, Aunt Georgina, I want to be myself.'

'Yes, well of course you do, I was meaning for you to be as sweet as Jessica. You don't look a bit alike.'

'You mean I'm not as pretty as she is.'

'I didn't say that, I simply said you were different. How can we tell how you're going to mature? You'll feel a lot better when you get that brace off your teeth. How long does it have to stay there?'

'I shall need two more before I'm fifteen.'

'Oh dear. Well, lots of girls will be wearing them so I

wouldn't worry too much about if it I were you. And don't be jealous of Jessica because she isn't wearing one, she's been very fortunate to have such pretty teeth.'

'Are you and Uncle Raymond coming to England with us?'

'I'm going home for a few weeks, I want to see you settled in all right. And I want to see Mother, she's not been at all well recently.'

It was on a warm golden morning that I looked through the small window of the plane at my last view of Kenya. I knew I would never come back.

I never wanted to see Kenya again, but that didn't mean I hadn't loved it. I would remember for the rest of my life its panoramic skies and equatorial sunsets, remote forest camps and snow-capped mountains. The wild untamed magnificence of Africa would always be with me.

I shuddered a little in remembering the lion's roar which said, 'As far as my voice carries, this is my kingdom.' The memory of that roar would stay in my heart for ever.

PART III

CHAPTER 16

I ran upstairs as fast as my legs would go. There was nobody about, Grandmother was visiting and Aunt Edwina was in the garden and hadn't seen me come in.

In my bedroom I flew to the mirror and stood for several minutes grinning at myself. The braces were off my teeth. Incredibly the once crowded teeth were strong and even, beautiful ivory-white teeth as glorious as Mother had predicted. At that moment it didn't matter that my pale hair was straight and bobbed, or that the heavy horn-rimmed glasses Grandmother had chosen did nothing for my eyes. Somehow the ugly duckling was halfway to becoming the swan I had always dreamed of being.

With a whoop of glee I rushed downstairs and out into the garden where I confronted Aunt Edwina with a bright smile. She stared uncertainly, then suddenly smiled. 'Why Lisa, you've had the brace off! I'd forgotten it was today, let me have a good look at you.'

Obligingly I smiled, and she laughed approvingly.

'I wish I could let my hair grow, I don't like it like this,' I cried longingly.

'But it's so trouble free, Lisa. Grandmother doesn't like long hair, she says it gets all over the place and is untidy.'

'It doesn't have to be untidy, Aunt Edwina. Jessica's hair is much longer than mine.'

'Oh well, Jessica can get away with anything, dear. Please don't antagonize Mother by talking about your hair.'

'Then there's my glasses.'

'What's wrong with them?'

'They're so heavy and ugly. I'm jolly glad I don't need to wear them for distance.'

'When you're older you can choose your own glasses, for now be guided by Mother. Are you going in to school this afternoon?'

'Yes, I have a music lesson straight after lunch. Grandfather's driving me down.'

I found him in his study poring over his butterfly collection. I hated to see them stuck through with pins but he was so enthusiastic I tried to hide my shudder. I smiled brightly and showed him my teeth.

I had been a pupil at Ashlea, Miss Baker's school, for eight years now, and my reports were very good. I was an attentive and industrious scholar but it was at the piano where I really excelled. I played solos at the school concerts and after hearing me for the first time Grandmother decided that the piano should be unlocked for me to practise on. She even went so far as to call in a tuner.

Jessica had left Ashlea at sixteen and immediately her mother packed her off to a Swiss finishing school. When Grandmother heard she said angrily, 'How ridiculous. We are not the aristocracy, we are gentry. It's going to give the girl ideas above her station.'

Aunt Cecily snapped back, 'My daughter is beautiful and I want her to marry well. Ashlea was not the beginning or the end, if she wasn't academically bright, so what! She'll learn to be a good hostess, how to behave in public and in private, and she doesn't need to find a job. Neville and I never intended her to be a secretary or a shop girl.'

Catching Aunt Edwina's pained eye, I began to realize that Aunt Cecily was the only one who ever answered Grandmother back.

I was happy at Ashlea and I had made friends. In the first few months after my arrival at the school I was a sort of curio and the trauma of my parents' deaths had been well and truly milled over. Jessica had been making the most of the tragedy as the niece of the couple concerned, and my arrival on the scene stole much of her thunder.

She made no effort to pave the way for me, indeed she resented my presence at Ashlea because I was clever and musical. She was still prominent at drama classes and always had a leading part in the school plays, but there her acumen ended and no amount of lecturing from Miss Baker produced anything better.

Christmas was still a gathering time for the family. Uncle Raymond and Aunt Georgina only came every other year because of the expense. The boys came to visit from their schools, and usually Alexander was with them.

We were polite to each other but I wasn't able to get rid of that totally illogical sense of betrayal I felt regarding him. Jessica monopolized him, and I did not miss the nods of approval from the rest of the family.

During the Christmas Alexander spent with his father in Austria Jessica went about with a long face and I hated myself for enjoying that Christmas better than any other.

My best friend was Pauline Stevens, and she had been the subject of my first quarrel with Jessica.

It was the night of the school concert for the end of term and we were both going to Grandmother's to change for the evening. Grandfather met us at the school gates and as we drove down the road we saw Pauline waiting at the bus stop. I asked Grandfather to give her a lift and he did, despite Jessica's objections. She sulked and didn't speak a single word to Pauline all the way home. At the house I turned on her furiously, saying she was a snob, and Pauline Stevens was as good as her any day.

'I'm not a snob. Her sister was a servant here, so why are you so friendly with her?'

I ran at her then, grabbing for her hair, and Grandfather had to separate us and admonish us quietly before Grandmother saw us.

Mary Stevens had left us three years before to marry a farmer in Wensleydale.

Later that evening Jessica came into my room and announced, 'Other girls have their cousins for bridesmaids, I've decided that when I marry Alexander you won't be mine, I shall ask Angela and Daphne Meachem.'

I didn't answer. If she was going to marry Alexander wild horses wouldn't make me be a bridesmaid. It was all so silly and childish but I heaved a sigh of relief when Jessica went off to Switzerland.

Sunday was my favourite day. In the morning I went to church with Grandmother and Aunt Edwina and in the

121

afternoon they went off together on one of their visits while I sat at the piano.

Invariably they were out to tea, so after grabbing a sandwich I made my way across the fell to the Stevens' farm to visit with Pauline.

Danny had left school and was articled to a firm of accountants in Kendal, Joe was still working alongside his father, and Emmie was giving her parents trouble. She was keeping company with a most unsuitable boy who had been to prison twice for petty theft, and nothing her parents could do had been able to break the alliance. Emmie was pretty, her small gamin face framed by red curls, her green eyes as clear and shining as a cat's.

I was coming to visit one Sunday when I heard raised voices. As I reached the door it was flung open and Emmie rushed out, almost knocking me over as she struggled to put her arms into her coat.

I went in to find Mrs Stevens at the kitchen table with her head in her hands, while her husband stood at the window looking out across the yard. His face was red and strained and Pauline came to me instantly and said we should go into the living room.

'It's our Emmie,' she explained when we were out of earshot. She's going to have a baby and the boy's in prison again for stealing from one of those big houses on the rise. He's got nine months.'

I stared at her in appalled silence.

'Mi mother says she's not to marry him when he comes out, but I know our Emmie, she's so determined once she's set her mind on anything.'

'What does your father say?'

'He's that upset. It's the first time I've ever known him raise his hand to any one of us, but today he hit our Emmie, knocked her right across the room he did.'

'Because of the baby.'

'Nay, we'd give the baby a home, it's her determination to have that boy.'

'Perhaps this time he'll go straight when he comes out.'

She shook her head gloomily. 'He's always been light-fingered.'

Ted Hibbert came out of prison after serving half his sentence, and tears and tantrums on Emmie's part brought about a change of heart in her parents. The wedding was at the village church with Emmie looking quite enormous in a billowing white dress and Pauline looking pretty and pensive in pale blue. The village was askance although most of them turned out to watch.

They moved into a tiny one up and one down cottage belonging to the farm and the following Sunday when Mr Stevens came to the house for his money Grandmother asked to see him.

We sat at the breakfast table, Grandfather buried behind his newspaper, Aunt Edwina pouring coffee, and myself wondering why Grandmother needed to see her milkman at all.

He hovered on the threshold with the excuse that there was dirt on his boots.

Grandmother produced her purse, and said, 'I'll pay you for a month's milk, Mr Stevens, but I don't want you to deliver any more. From now on I'll be getting my milk from Fairbrother.'

He stared at her stolidly, then he put the money in his purse and took out some change. 'You don't 'ave to pay for what ye 'ave'nt 'ad, Mrs Marston, a week's money is all I want. Might I ask why ye've stopped mi comin' 'ere after all these years?'

'Of course, Mr Stevens. It's your son-in-law I object to. He's just out of prison and he's living on your land. I don't think there's a house in the neighbourhood he hasn't tried to break into at some time or other. My grand-daughter has always been friendly with your daughter, I feel sure her sister's husband will be well aware of the valuables in this house.'

'Grandmother, that's unfair,' I stormed.

'Be quiet, Lisa. I'm sorry, Mr Stevens, but a lot of the people are anxious now that this boy is out of prison. The fact that they've set up house on your farm was bad news for us all.'

'She's mi daughter, Mrs Marston.'

123

'I'm not blaming you, indeed I'm very sorry for you all, but we have to do what's right to protect what is ours.'

'I wishes you joy in what's yours, Mrs Marston. I'll not be round 'ere again,' he said with a simple dignity that made me want to cry, and turned away.

Grandmother turned her attention on me. 'And never interrupt me again, young lady. Emmie Stevens is a slut, her father should have given them a sum of money, I'm sure he can afford it, there was no need to have them in the vicinity.'

'It sounds like something out of Dickens,' Grandfather said mildly. 'I thought we did away with homes for the fallen and workhouses years ago.'

'There's no need to be sarcastic, William, I did what I thought was right to protect your property and mine.'

'You've probably lost Lisa her friend.'

'All to the good then. I don't want Lisa to continue the friendship, now more than ever. I'm sure Pauline Stevens is a nice girl, she's studied hard and I sincerely hope she makes something of herself but she's not the sort of companion I want for my granddaughter.'

'She's nicer than Jessica, and three times as clever,' I said angrily.

'Jessica would never have become so involved with that girl.'

'Well of course not, the Stevens children think she's a rotten snob.'

'If that's what they think about your cousin you shouldn't be wanting to know them anyway.'

I never won with Grandmother but I couldn't be like Aunt Edwina or Grandfather, both negative people who allowed her all her own way even when their innermost thoughts must surely have been opposed to her.

I was not unhappy at the Maples, they fed me and clothed me and put a roof over my head. I didn't always like the way they clothed me and the school uniform was a happy relief from dark serge skirts and woollen jumpers. Grandmother's imagination didn't seem to go beyond dark grey, beige and navy.

My Ralston grandparents seemed to have aged a hundred years. Grandma was so thin, and Grandpa stooped where once he had stood erect. When I went to see them they hardly knew what to say to me. They gave me tea and cake, and we talked about my new school, the weather, Grandmother Marston's health, until I longed to say, 'Why don't you ask me about Father and Mother, why don't you talk about Uncle Philip and Kenya?' I started the ball rolling by asking about the baby and Aunt Constance.

Grandma's eyes filled with tears but she answered me bravely enough. 'They are now living in the West Riding, Lisa, where most of her family are. The baby is splendid, he's already been enrolled in his father's old school.'

Still nothing about the shooting, and in fact we never did talk of it. They clearly didn't want to see me again, I was too potent a reminder of the tragedy in Kenya, and for years I felt their rejection keenly.

Pauline too was giving me a wide berth. If we met on the fell she hurried away with her head down and one day when I could stand it no longer I chased after her and caught her at the farm gates.

'Please, Pauline,' I gasped, 'please don't go on avoiding me like this. I haven't done anything and I didn't agree with what my Grandmother did to your father.'

Staring at me solemnly, she said, 'All the same, Lisa it's best we don't meet. I'm not the friend your Grandmother wants for you, and thanks to her mi father's lost a lot of custom. The milk round's not worth keeping and even the cottage folk are having doubts about us.'

'Pauline, I can't help what my Grandmother does. I've missed you, we've been friends a long time.'

'Emmie's mi sister, Lisa. We've got to do the best we can for her. I don't bear you any grudges, I just think it's better we don't see each other. I'm sure that's how your Grandmother wants it.'

With a small bleak smile and without a backward glance she went into the house.

That was the afternoon I vowed to concentrate on my music to the exclusion of everything else. My music teacher, Miss Nelson, applauded my decision.

Miss Baker called me into her office one afternoon. 'Have you given any thought to what you want to do with your life after you leave Ashlea, Lisa?' she asked quietly. 'Most girls of your age are already beginning to think about a career. I have had good reports from all your teachers and I thought perhaps you had your heart set on going to university.'

'I'm not sure what I want, Miss Baker.'

'I thought that was probably the case. Miss Nelson is enthusiastic about your music, Lisa. Have you thought of making that your career?'

My eyes opened wide. 'Grandmother says it's an over-crowded profession unless one is particularly brilliant. And I don't think I'm that.'

'Learning music here at the school isn't enough, Lisa, you need an accomplished teacher and I am going to suggest to your Grandmother that you go to Madame Levison. Have you heard of her?'

'No.'

'She used to have a place here in Lancaster but two years ago she moved and is now living just outside Kendal. She has a studio in the town and only takes very special pupils. Do you think your Grandmother would consent to your being interviewed by Madame Levison?'

'I could ask her, Miss Baker,' I said doubtfully. I had no hope that Grandmother would agree.

'I think it might be a good thing if we spoke to her together. She is quite a formidable lady and if you were to approach her in the wrong way it might blight your future without hope of any redress. I'll ask her to visit me.'

Wednesday afternoon saw me sitting on the edge of my chair in Miss Baker's study while Grandmother and Aunt Edwina sat opposite the headmistress. She came quickly to the point, firmly telling Grandmother that I was more than an adequate musician, that I ought to go on with my music with a better teacher, and that only if I failed in this respect should I even contemplate a career in some-thing more ordinary.

Grandmother listened with an expression of comical

126

dismay. Then she asked, 'What sort of career could my granddaughter have in music? How do we know she's good enough?'

'Only time and practice will tell, Mrs Marston, but I think Lisa should be given that chance. Madame Levison has agreed to hear her play, and I should tell you that several of her pupils have gone on to play on the concert platform with world-renowned orchestras.'

Grandmother agreed grudgingly, and on the way home she said angrily, 'I knew Madame Levison when she was plain Minnie Jeffries. We were at the same village school. Her father was a violinist with the Hallé Orchestra and she could never come out to play, she had to sit at that piano and practise six hours a day. If she wants Lisa to do that we wouldn't be able to stand it.'

I sat silent beside Grandfather in his old Morris and once he winked at me in a conspiratorial way and my heart lifted somewhat.

That night Grandmother eyed me across the table, saying, 'Are you sure this is what you want, Lisa, or are you being pushed by the school?'

'It's what I want, Grandmother, if I'm good enough.'

'And how long is it going to take to make a musician of you?'

'I don't know.'

'And if you're not good enough?'

'Then I'll have to think of something else. I'll have a better idea when I've seen Madame Levison.'

Grandmother sniffed. 'I'm not going to Kendal to ask any favours of Minnie Jeffries.'

'Miss Nelson will go with me,' I said quietly.

Later, when I took Grandfather's coffee into his study, he said, 'So you're going to be a musician, Lisa, the first one we've ever had in the family to my recollection.'

'I can't believe that Grandmother's agreed.'

'Most of the time she gets her own way but this time I insisted you should be given your chance. Oh, I know you think I'm a weak and silly old buffer who lets her walk all over me, that's because I like my peace and quiet. But now and then I stand up for what I think is right.'

127

'Thanks, Grandfather.'

Impulsively I hugged him with the feeling that in my Grandmother's house I had at last found an ally.

On the following Wednesday Miss Nelson accompanied me to my interview with Madame Levison. Grandmother insisted that I wore my beige and brown check skirt and beige silk blouse although I didn't think they did anything for my colouring. I had very little jewellery: the gold chain and locket that had been Mother's, a single row of cultured pearls and, more exotic, a piece of agate called a monkey's eye, on a fine gold chain which Mother had bought me in Nairobi. This I decided to wear although Grandmother hated it, saying it was obscene and primitive, fit only for negro women and children to wear.

Madame Levison occupied a studio above an optician's shop in Kendal, with an entrance around the side of the shop. While we waited we listened to a pianist in an adjoining room.

'Do you think that is one of her pupils?' I asked Miss Nelson anxiously.

'It's more likely to be Madame Levison herself, she said she was completely free all afternoon.'

A thundering chord ended the recital, then the door was flung open and a small plump woman entered.

My illusions were shattered. I had thought she would be tall and slender, with haughty assurance and an elaborate hairstyle, instead she was homely and motherly. With a bright smile she ushered us into a sparsely furnished room with oriental rugs and two tapestry-covered chairs.

On a dais near the window stood a Steinway grand piano and for the first time I began to appreciate the momentousness of the afternoon for my future.

Madame Levison reached in the pocket of her long woollen cardigan and brought out a bag of pear drops, which she offered to us, and immediately my fright began to evaporate.

'Well, Lisa,' she began, 'so you want to become a pianist, a concert pianist perhaps?'

I didn't speak, and in a moment she went on, 'But you know it's not going to happen tomorrow or the day after,

128

perhaps not even five years after. Are you prepared to wait that long, to work that long?'

'Yes, Madame Levison, if you think in the end I'll succeed.'

'And what if I don't think you are the right sort of material, have you thought what you'll do then? There are other branches of music, Lisa, could you turn to one of these?'

'I don't know, Madame Levison.'

'Well, come along then, let me hear you play.'

I played Debussy's 'Clair de Lune' and Bach's 'Jesu Joy of Man's Desiring', then she gave me Chopin's Nocturne No. 2 in E Flat which I had never played before.

I did the best I could with it, and afterwards there was silence for so long I could almost hear my heart thumping and felt sure that we would leave the room with her rejection ringing in my ears. When I felt I couldn't bear the silence another minute she said, 'You will come twice a week, Lisa, and my fee will be a hundred guineas a term. Are you parents prepared to pay it?'

I stared at her horror struck. The subject of money had never entered my mind, and even Miss Nelson seemed a little taken aback.

'I hadn't realized it would be so much,' I said anxiously. 'I haven't any parents, I will have to ask my Grandmother.'

Your Grandmother, Annabel Marston?'

'Yes, she told me she was at school with you.'

'I remember her very well, and her daughters. Then you must be the unfortunate child whose parents died in Kenya.'

I could feel my face flaming with colour but I met her gaze bravely as I said quietly, 'Yes, Madame.'

Wisely she did not pursue the subject, saying instead, 'You have talent, one I would like to encourage. If you come to me you know what is in front of you, what I expect of you. Now I suggest you go back to your Grandmother and tell her what I have said. If she agrees I would like you to come every Tuesday and Friday at two o'clock for two hours.'

On the bus back to Lancaster I said to Miss Nelson, 'Grandmother will never agree and the money Father left is in trust until I'm twenty-one. Anyway, I don't think there's much of that.'

'Perhaps she'll surprise you,' Miss Nelson said optimistically.

There was no pleasant surprise. Grandmother said firmly, 'It can't be done. I have five other grandchildren, it wouldn't be fair to spend all this money on you.'

I knew it was hopeless. I would not be going to Madame Levison's.

Miraculously the following week something happened to change matters. On Sunday afternoon Meg came in to say we had visitors, Brigadier and Mrs Ralston. Grandmother, in spite of her arthritis, jumped up with alacrity and went out into the hall to greet them. They had come to say they were leaving the area and a cotton manufacturer from Manchester had bought their house. They were moving to a house near Ashburton in Devonshire in the next few days.

'What does a cotton manufacturer want with a house round here?' Grandmother asked.

'He's interested in fishing and hunting, and he's obviously a very rich man. He likes to entertain a great deal and is semi-retired, with two daughters, one of whom is already married to a Solicitor. I expect you'll meet the family, he means to make himself known to people in the area,' Grandma Ralston said.

They talked about property and the new buyer, and at last Grandmother spoke about me.

'I'm worried about Lisa,' she began, 'she's a very good musician and would like to take it up as a career. Unfortunately all that takes a great deal of money and I'm afraid it's quite outside our means.'

Across the room my eyes met Grandpa Ralston's and he must surely have seen the desperation in mine because almost immediately he said, 'We have come to see what we can do for Lisa. We feel we've neglected her shamefully during these last few years but it has been very painful for us. Lisa was a reminder that we had lost both

130

our boys, and we had to come to terms with it in our own good time.'

'I hope you haven't forgotten that we lost a daughter, a very dear daughter,' Grandmother Marston said.

'We appreciate that, but you have four other daughters, for us with both our children gone there are only Mark and Lisa left. We would like to pay for Lisa's schooling from now on, and if it is to be music then we will pay for that. There will also be a further sum put in trust for when she is twenty-one. The money will appreciate, she will be quite a wealthy young woman when she comes of age.'

'And what of Constance,' Grandmother Marston asked, 'will she be a constant visitor to your home in Devonshire?'

'We do hope so, as often and for as long as she wants. She said she would never come here and for that we didn't blame her, there was too much talk.'

'Well, *we* have no intention of running away from gossip. This is our home, our roots are here. In time they'll find something and somebody else to gossip about and leave us alone,' Grandmother responded stoutly.

'I hope you're right, but this was never our home, we came here when Gerald retired from the army because we liked the house,' said Grandma. 'I was born and brought up in Essex and Gerald's a Surrey man by birth.'

Grandmother Marston was silent, and after tea our visitors took their leave. They didn't ask me to visit them in Devonshire, and I was glad. All that mattered to me was that I would be going to Madame Levison's and that I had some money of my own. One day in the not too distant future I would show them all that Lisa Ralston was a force to be reckoned with.

CHAPTER 17

Madame Levison was a hard taskmistress but under her guidance my music flourished. Apart from one traumatic episode the days passed uneventfully between school and music.

One June afternoon as I returned home I was surprised to see a man running from the back of the house. He climbed swiftly over the wall and dropped into the lane at the back of the house.

Grandmother gave casual work to one or two gardeners but they always used the gates, so I ran back to the road and turned in the direction of the lane. I had only just reached it when I almost ran into Ted Hibbert who was walking swiftly and passed me sheepishly with his head averted.

The episode bothered me and I checked round the house. A kitchen window was open but nothing seemed disturbed. It was only later, when Aunt Edwina announced that she had misplaced her gold wrist watch, that I became seriously worried.

'I can't think where it can be,' she said doubtfully, 'I always leave it in my dressing table drawer but it's not there now.'

'When you're not wearing it it should be locked up. Was the clasp good?' Grandmother asked sharply.

'Yes, I'm sure it was. Oh, I do hope I haven't lost it outside.'

'You've been careless, Edwina,' Grandmother snapped. 'You'll have to advertise for its return.'

I ran up to my room and checked the drawer my jewellery case. It was empty. I sat miserably on the edge of my bed, certain that Ted Hibbert had entered the house. But how could I accuse him? He would deny it.

Nothing else was missing from the house and after a few weeks Aunt Edwina replaced her watch by a cheaper one. She had taken the trouble to advertise, but when nothing came up she said dismally, 'I can't think where I lost it. Whoever found it can't have been very honest.'

For some weeks I forgot about the incident, but on the day of the summer fair organized by the church, I was brought face to face with it.

I walked with Aunt Edwina among the stalls, chatting to people we knew. At the tombola stall I saw Pauline Stevens with Emmie and her little girl. Aunt Edwina had walked on ahead and I didn't want to speak to them, but they turned and my eyes met Pauline's.

I smiled and it was her turn to look embarrassed.

Then I saw the monkey's eye hanging on its gold chain round Emmie's neck, and suddenly burning with anger I reached out and touched the charm, saying, 'Where did you get that, Emmie?'

She coloured instantly. 'Ted bought it for mi.'

'You mean he stole it,' I said angrily. 'I would have recognized it anywhere. You can't buy such a thing in this country, it came from Nairobi and it was taken from my bedroom a few weeks ago.'

Her voice rose shrilly. 'Are you accusin' my Ted of takin' it? 'Cause if you are you'll apologize, Lisa Ralston.'

People were staring at us and already we were surrounded by a crowd. Pauline looked at me miserably. 'Please, Lisa,' she said, 'if you've anything to say we can't stand here.'

'In the marquee then,' I said, starting to push my way through the crowd.

Emmie, however, said, 'I'm not goin' into any marquee, I'm goin' 'home ter fetch mi 'usband. 'E'll soon tell you where 'e got this thing.'

She went off, and Pauline, looking at me stonily, said, 'Are you quite sure that charm was yours? I do know Ted gave it to Emmie on her birthday.'

'My aunt had a watch stolen the same afternoon my jewellery was taken. I had a string of pearls and a gold locket and chain. The pearls weren't worth much but I expect the locket was fairly expensive. The charm mattered most because mother gave it to me. It's a monkey's eye, Pauline, capped with gold. Surely you must know nothing so unusual can be bought round here.'

'Ted said it was a piece of ivory, but he didn't know much about it either. Could he have bought it from the person who stole it?'

'I saw him climbing over the wall out of the garden, Pauline. I'm sorry, but when I saw Emmie wearing it, I had to ask.'

Tears filled her eyes and rolled slowly down her cheeks and I felt terrible. 'What are you going to do,' she whispered, 'send for the police?'

'I don't want to do that. If she'll bring back the chain and my aunt's watch I won't do anything. Please talk to her, Pauline.'

She moved away then, and some days later came to meet me in the street. Her face was pale and wretched as she placed a small envelope in my hand.

'Here's your monkey's eye, Lisa, but I couldn't get the watch, he's already parted with it.'

'Parted with it!'

'Pawned it for money. He's gone away, we don't know where, he's gone but he's left our Emmie and the child. Two days he's been gone now. You can imagine what she's like, hysterical most of the time. Mi father says Emmie can come home any time but he'll not have Ted, he'll have no thief living in his house.'

'Oh Pauline, I am sorry. What's going to happen now?'

'He'll go to prison again – if not for this, for something else sooner or later. He can't help it, Lisa, he'll never go straight, it isn't in him.'

'And Emmie and her child?'

'I don't know. She's besotted with him, she says she'll stand by him, and if he goes to prison she'll be waitin' for him when he comes out. I can't understand how she can love a man like Ted Hibbert.'

'I'm sorry for the rest of you.'

'Our Danny's out of it. Gone to live in London he has, with a good job, but farmin's all our Joe knows and the farm's gone down and down these last few years. I'm sorry about your aunt's watch. Are you going to tell her?'

'I don't think so.'

She smiled swiftly and walked away. The monkey's eye was burning a hole in my hand and I was glad to put it away at the bottom of my satchel. I was blaming myself for Emmie's plight, but by the time I had reached Kendal I was beginning to realize that the misery of her life was her own fault. Emmie, who had always been self-willed and too sure of herself, had met her Waterloo.

Several days later, Grandmother said that Mr Stevens was selling the farm and had bought a smallholding somewhere. He had sold most of his dairy herd, and she'd also heard that the cottages where Emmie lived had to come down.

At the beginning of September Pauline once more waited for me near the bus stop, where she said goodbye.

'Mi mother and dad and our Joe are going to a little place in Shropshire. Mi dad's got a smallholding, and there's room for our Emmie and the child if she'll go.'

'Will she go?'

'I expect so, she doesn't know where Ted is and he's not contacted her.'

'What about you, Pauline, where will you go?'

'I've got a place at the university in Leeds. It's a three-year course and when I get my degree I hope to get a job in law. I've always wanted to be a lawyer.'

'I hope you do well, Pauline. Will you write to me?'

'I'd rather not, Lisa. It's not that I'm fallen out with you, I like you, I always have, but we're not likely to meet again because I'm never coming back here and I doubt if you will, once you make the break. I wishes you luck. I'll be listening out for you, Lisa, and one day I'll be in your audience, never fear.'

I put my arms around her and kissed her, then from the platform of the bus I looked back until I could see her no more.

Normally I loved the scenery from the bus windows on the way to Kendal, but that day I didn't see it. In my mind's eye I was remembering the farm's big kitchen, the clatter of pots and pans and Mrs Stevens standing at the table with her sleeves rolled up while she spooned great heaps of currant loaf mix into tins, with five pairs of eyes watching as we waited to scrape the bowls.

CHAPTER 18

For the first time I was being allowed to perform at the school, a special dispensation from Madame Levison because it was my last day at Ashlea.

In the afternoon I had gone up to the dais to receive my school certificate and Miss Baker had smiled at me, whispering, 'Well done, Lisa.'

I had a new dress for the evening concert but I hadn't been allowed to choose it. It was a dark and sombre green, reaching well down my calves, but it did fall gracefully and it showed off my slender waist as no other dress had ever done. Without Aunt Edwina's help, Grandmother would have had me in a particularly frumpy navy. She insisted too on low heels, but after a battle in the shoe shop I came away with medium-heeled court shoes – something of a victory.

I was indeed fortunate. Aunt Claudia and Angela had come to hear me perform and as I stood on the platform peeping through the curtains I was startled to see Aunt Cecily and Jessica sweeping down the centre aisle. There was a commotion with people moving up to make room for them near Grandmother and suddenly I felt my palms grow moist with perspiration and something intangible made me wish I hadn't been allowed to play.

I hadn't seen Jessica for ages. She was now a sophisticated and glamorous woman, tall and willowy in a long black dress. She walked down the centre aisle as confidently as a model might walk along the catwalk, carrying a silver fox cape nonchalantly in one hand. Aunt Cecily too was elegant in beige and mink.

Beside me Miss Latchford remarked, 'I hadn't realized this was to be such a formal occasion, Lisa, your family have done you proud.'

Her sarcasm was not lost on me and when my face coloured with embarrassment she laughed and putting her arm round my shoulders said lightly, 'We could always rely on Jessica to do something different, even when she was here. Tonight she's come to steal your thunder, and don't you let her. Play that piano as you've never played before.'

I was in the second half of the concert and came on right after the interval, wishing my shoes were daintier and my dress was longer, wishing I wasn't so long-sighted and didn't need the horn-rimmed glasses, and wishing Jessica and her mother were a million miles away.

Miss Baker herself introduced me as 'possibly the most gifted pupil we have had for a great many years. She has chosen to play Chopin's "Military Polonaise" and his "Fantaisie Impromptu".'

There was enthusiastic applause and then I was bowing to the audience before sitting at the piano, and with the familiar keyboard in front of me all my disquiet left me.

The audience seemed to melt away and I was alone with my piano somewhere in space, aware only of the music, the vigour and the melody. The haunting sadness of Chopin filled my entire being, shutting out every other sound, every other emotion, and then I was lifting my hands from the keyboard and the applause was in my ears, deafening and enthusiastic.

Miss Baker came and pulled me to the centre of the stage and I was bowing, most professionally, and the family were nodding their approval – all except Jessica, who sat bored and applauding in a most perfunctory manner.

My encore, the opening movement of Beethoven's 'Moonlight Sonata', brought more enthusiastic applause before I was allowed to leave the stage.

I spent the rest of the evening in a state of euphoria, and it was only when I joined the family group that I came down to earth.

Jessica, settling her furs round her shoulders, said, 'You'll forgive me if I don't like classical music, won't you, Lisa? I never have, I've always thought it a bore.'

'I'm sorry.'

'Oh, it's not your fault, darling, we can't all be geniuses.

I like musical comedy and popular stuff. I suppose you must play very well, everybody else enjoyed it.'

'Thank you, Jessica.'

'I hope you're not going to practise every hour that God sends when I'm staying at Grandmother's while Mother and Daddy are away in Australia. It'll drive me mad.'

I looked at her in dismay. 'You're staying at the Maples?'

'Well, I'm not going with them and Mother's insisting I stay at Granny's. You will do your practising when I'm out, won't you, Lisa?'

'When are you coming?'

'Oh, it's not for ages yet. Before then I could be working on some job or other, I might even be married.'

'Married!'

'Well yes, except that I've never met anybody I like more than Alex and he's elected to become a civil engineer, which will take him abroad for some time to come.'

'I see.'

'It's ages since we met, but of course we were terribly in love, it'll probably all start up again when next we meet.'

'Of course.'

'Isn't there a boyfriend in your life, Lisa?'

'No, I'm far too busy for boyfriends.'

'How dull. Well, I must go, I can see Mother's getting impatient. See you.' With that she was gone in a flurry of perfume and fur.

Grandfather squeezed my arm gently as I settled into the car beside him. 'We were proud of you, Lisa, you played beautifully. Now we'd all like to know where you go from here.'

'Back to Madame Levison's and a lot more practice, I exect.'

'While all the other girls who were at school with you find jobs, I suppose,' Grandmother said dryly.

'I'll find a job too, Grandmother. I just hope it's in music.'

'I think you'll find in music that only the cream rises

to the top. I think we should have a chat to Minnie Jeffries before long.'

I could feel myself cringing until I saw Grandfather winking at me. At that moment I realized that Grandmother resented Madame Levison because she was talented.

That night as I lay in bed I thought about my future. I visualized appearing on the concert platforms of Europe in elegant gowns. I would grow my hair into a more becoming length and I would wear contact lenses. I would earn large sums of money and I would please myself what I wore and where I went. Then suddenly I thought about Alexander and I remembered with tears in my eyes the morning when we sat at the lake watching the flamingoes descending like a ribbon of flame. Alexander who was warm and sensitive, who had made the effort to comfort a sad lost child by telling her something of his own feelings after his mother's death. How would he ever fit into Jessica's world when all she had to offer him was her beauty?

CHAPTER 19

I was eighteen when Madame Levison told me that she could teach me nothing more. I stood staring at her incredulously.

'I'm a good teacher, Lisa,' she went on, 'but you want something more than I can give you. It's time you went to a good music college, indeed I would have suggested it before but I thought you were special, I wanted to bring you along myself.'

'Where would I have to go?'

'Well, there's Manchester of course, that would be the nearest, then there's London, but I would really like Stefano Marcello to hear you play. I don't suppose you've ever heard of him?'

I shook my head.

'When I studied at the London College of Music, Stefano was a pupil there, a violinist, the most wonderful violinist I've ever heard. Afterwards he played all over the world on the concert platform but unfortunately he developed arthritis in his hands. He became a teacher, first in Milan then in Rome.

'He married an Italian girl who was not a musician, and they came to England to open a music academy in London. It's very expensive, and he takes only pupils he considers extraordinarily gifted. I would like him to hear you play.'

My heart leapt with excitement, but in the next breath I said, 'Grandmother Marston would never let me go to London, and I'm not sure if my Father's parents would be willing to pay the fees.'

'You must approach them, Lisa, explain the circumstances. Couldn't you perhaps visit them?'

'Perhaps. I haven't seen them for a very long time.'

'You do that, then, and I'll write to Stefano.'

'Suppose he takes me on, where would I live in London?'

'The academy is residential, that would be no problem. Now you run along home and write to your grandparents.'

It was a difficult letter to write. I told them about my music and what I had been doing during the last few years, and I asked if I could visit them. I told them a little about the Academy and that it was expensive, but that I couldn't put everything in a letter.

That night I told my Marston grandparents and Aunt Edwina. Predictably, Grandmother objected.

'You can't go to London Lisa, I won't allow a girl of eighteen to live there. You won't know a soul. If you must go to a music college why not Manchester? Chetham's has an excellent reputation.'

'I know, but Madame Levison says Signor Marcello takes only the best.'

'And what makes you think *you* are the best? Music colleges are full of brilliant pupils. Suppose he turns you down, you'll feel more hurt and embarrassed than if you'd never made the attempt.'

'I've written to my other grandparents to see if I can visit them, they said they would pay for my education.'

'They didn't say they'd be responsible for financing you in a college in London. Minnie Jeffries should have spoken to me before she told you about this academy.'

'Why don't we all wait until the Ralstons write back?' Grandfather said reasonably. 'We're talking about something we know very little about.'

'This is all very ridiculous,' Grandmother snorted. 'Edwina and I are off to Harrogate on Saturday. I haven't been feeling very well, the holiday will do me good. We shall be away ten days, but on my return I shall make it my business to have a talk to Minnie Jeffries.'

The house felt incredibly peaceful when Grandmother and Aunt Edwina had gone.

A few days later I received an answer from the Ralstons. They were pleased that I had done well at school and that I was happy and doing well with my music. Aunt Constance and Mark were now living near them in Devon so they were seeing the child grow up, which was so wonderful for them.

There was no need for me to visit them. They agreed to pay for everything I might need in London, and they asked me to understand. It would be too painful for Constance to see me after all these years, just when she was beginning to put the past behind her.

I felt again the sharp pain of desertion. I too had managed to put the past behind me, but never completely. That morning in Kenya would never leave me entirely, I still dreamt about it, though not as frequently. How could I ever really forget those moments when death had stared me in the face and tragedy had taken from me all those I loved?

I wrote back thanking them for their help but said no more about visiting them, nor did I mention Aunt Constance or Mark. I was too hurt.

Another incident during the week was to join that other memory. I waved to Grandfather as I walked down the drive and he waved back before entering the summer house. It was deliciously warm. The garden was filled with bird song and the scent of flowers, and even the moist earth was fragrant.

I had no premonition of tragedy, and was in a happy and contented mood when I came home, looking forward to the evening with just Grandfather.

Meg was waiting for me at the gate and I knew immediately that she was anxious. 'It's yer grandfather,' she said at once. 'I took 'im 'is lunch and 'e wouldn't open his study door for mi so I took it back, then just 'alf an 'our since I took 'im 'is tea and 'e still wouldn't open the door.'

'Perhaps he isn't in his study, Meg. Or maybe he's fallen asleep and hasn't heard you.'

'I've pounded on the door, loud enough to waken the dead in the churchyard. I'm right worried, Miss Lisa. Will ye come and try yerself?'

I ran as fast as my legs would carry me, every step making me more anxious.

The door was locked, and I pounded on it with both fists, calling out for him. I was met with silence.

In the end we got the gardener's boy to break the study window and climb in. Seconds later his startled face appeared back at the window above us and in a frightened voice he said, 'E's sittin' in 'is chair, Miss. I'll open the door so that you can come in.'

Grandfather was sitting with a faint smile on his lips, a smile of surprise, and gingerly I touched his arm. At my touch his head fell forward on to his chest and his arms slid down at the sides of his chair. He was dead.

It was the second time in my life that I had been faced with sudden death, but this time it had come gently.

Grandmother and Aunt Edwina returned the following morning almost before it was light. The inquest told us he had died from a heart attack, and Grandmother was distraught. For the first time I saw her as a frightened, miserable old woman and I knew that in spite of his gentleness and her dominance, life for her would never be the same.

She blamed herself for being away, and stayed in her room for hours on end. Then when the family arrived there was the parade into the room where Grandfather lay in his coffin.

Jessica and I shared the same bedroom, and that night as we were preparing for bed she said, 'Wouldn't you just have thought Alex would have come? He's spent so many holidays in this house.'

'Maybe he doesn't know.'

'Oh, yes, he does, I sent him a telegram.'

'Well perhaps he can't get away, it isn't easy to drop everything and leave whatever you're doing. He's in Israel, isn't he? Maybe he hasn't even got your telegram.'

'One thing's for sure, you won't be playing that wretched piano for the next few days.'

'Is that all you care about?'

'Well of course not, but you are getting to be quite a show-off, Lisa.'

'Why do you say that? When have I ever showed off here?'

144

'You lapped up all the adulation at the school, and you'll be even worse on a concert platform.'

'Honestly, Jessica I've never meant to show off. I love music, I'm very grateful that I play well and that people want to hear me. Wouldn't you be proud of your accomplishments?'

'You're going to say next that I haven't any.'

'Well, have you?'

'I'm beautiful. I know how to dress and how to get any man I want. As it happens I want Alexander Hamilton. Why do you always change the subject whenever I mention his name?'

'I wasn't aware that I did.'

'Well, you do. I suspect you're in love with him yourself but the sooner you get that idea out of your head the happier you'll be. Alexander was sorry for you out in Kenya, and you were just a plain scrawny little kid who never left him alone.'

Her lovely face was vindictive and although deep hurting anger flooded my being I managed to control my voice as I stared straight into her eyes.

'Did Alexander tell you that, Jessica?'

'He told me how miserable you were at the lake and that he tried to comfort you.'

'He was very kind to me, and you're right, I was a plain scrawny little kid. Don't think I'm not aware of that. I've known for a long time that all the family hope one day you'll marry Alexander, and I've too much pride to ever think he'd prefer me to you. You've got Alexander; I've got my music, it's more important anyway.'

That was the last time we mentioned his name. He did not come to the funeral, but sent his regrets and a floral tribute which Jessica placed reverently on Grandfather's grave. The day after, they all went home.

Although the gravestone had been littered with wreaths and they had stretched along the paths and covered other graves nearby, Grandmother insisted on sending small bunches of flowers every day to be arranged in the black marble urn she had ordered from the stonemason's.

Mostly they were the flowers Grandfather had loved in

the garden and greenhouses, and if Aunt Edwina couldn't take them, then the task was mine. I was doing it one day when a shadow fell across the grave and I looked up to see Ted Hibbert staring at me fixedly. My heart started to race, for there was a mean vindictive look on his face.

'You're the ritch bitch mi sister-in-law was friendly with. Emmie told mi you'd taken that charm I gave er, yer'd no right to do that,' he said sharply.

'I had every right, it was mine.'

'I bought it from a feller I know, 'ow was I to know it was pinched?'

'I don't believe you, Ted Hibbert. I saw you at the house.'

'Oh ay, give a dog a bad name and it sticks. Yer grandmother's that stuck-up old biddy who sacked Emmie's father, and then most o' the village followed suit.'

'I didn't agree with her doing that, but you're not to be trusted, you have a reputation for taking what doesn't belong to you.'

'I think you and me 'ad better 'ave a little talk, Lisa.'

He grabbed my arm and dragged me across the gravestones, scuffing my shoes and laddering my tights. When I screamed he placed a huge grimy hand over my mouth, then pushed me along the path towards the back of the church. I kicked and struggled but my puny strength was no match for his.

By this time he was tearing at my dress and I heard it come away at the seams. I could feel his hot breath on my face as he pushed me to the ground, and then I was writhing desperately on wet soil from a newly dug grave. My hands were threshing wildly above my head when they felt something hard lying on the soil. Realising it was a spade I lifted it with both hands and brought it down on his head with all my strength. I heard him moan and in that sudden shock of surprise I tore myself free and stumbled down the path. He came after me with the blood pouring down his face and I faced him with the spade lifted high above my head and the promise in my eyes that I would bring it down on his head if he came an inch nearer.

146

Suddenly on the still air voices came. I didn't dare take my eyes off him until the vicar arrived at a run, his white robes flowing, followed by two young policemen and three women with shopping baskets over their arms.

'Are you all right, luv?' one of the women said while one policeman disarmed me and the other struggled with Ted Hibbert.

It took both policemen to control him, then they led him away to a police car and I sat gingerly on a headstone, nursing my bruised arm. My dress was torn from shoulder to hem and one of the women – Mrs Sommers – took off her cardigan and placed it round my shoulders.

'I've allus known 'e was a wrong 'un,' she said, 'but I've never known 'im do owt like this 'afore.'

My teeth were chattering, and she said anxiously, 'Would ye like to come over to the cottage, luv? It's just there near the church gates, I'll make ye a cup o' tea.'

I went with her gladly while the vicar fussed and fretted at the back. We all trooped into the cottage, including the vicar, and in no time at all a huge brown teapot appeared on the table, with thick wedges of home-made currant loaf and hot buttered scones.

'Ye must eat,' Mrs Sommers encouraged me. 'Ye'll soon feel better, and ye don't want to go 'ome and let yer grandmother see ye like that. The poor lady's had enough to worry about these last few days.'

I stared at her. 'You know me?' I asked quietly.

'Bless ye yes, luv, I knew yer mother afore she went and married young Mr Ralston.

'I allus said she was the nicest o' the Marston lasses, bonny she were with that blonde 'air of 'ers, and allus ready to pass the time o' day. Terrible it was what 'appened to 'er.'

A discreet cough from the vicar brought the warm blushes to her face, and with an embarrassed smile she said, 'I'll just go and fill up the teapot. Yer've not eaten anythin', luv.'

'Thank you, I'm not very hungry. Have you got any cotton so that I could just stitch up my dress?'

'Come into the kitchen, luv, I'll lend you mi mackintosh to put on while I stitch it up for ye.'

The other women were making short work of the repast on the table and after a while they left. The vicar was the last, and after making sure that we were alone he said gently, 'This has been a terrible experience for you, Miss Ralston. How much are you going to tell your Grandmother?'

'Nothing at all, Vicar, I just want to go home and forget about it. Do you think those women will say anything?'

'I shall ask them not to.'

I stared down ruefully at my bruised arms and hands, flexing my fingers with relief that they hadn't suffered in the struggle.

Mrs Sommers came back with the dress. She had done wonders with it although I would never feel able to wear it again. I thanked her warmly, then left for home.

As I walked along the road I couldn't believe that only a short time ago I was struggling desperately with Ted Hibbert. It was all so peaceful. The air was filled with the scent of clover and birds sang rapturously in the branches above my head. Around me was the sound of bees humming as they moved from one flower head to the next, and the homely sound of lawnmowers and country voices.

The house was quiet as I let myself in through the conservatory.

I was halfway across the hall when I heard the door to Grandfather's study open and I started nervously.

'Is that you Lisa?' Grandmother called.

I stood in the shadows, hoping she wouldn't notice my dress.

'I'm feeling rather better today,' she said. 'After dinner we must have a talk about your going up to London. I don't think it's a good idea at all.' I agreed hurriedly, and managed to escape to my room without her noticing the state I was in. But I was worried. How was I to convince Grandmother that on this point she *didn't* know best?

She started immediately we had finished our evening meal. London was an unsafe place for a girl, if I had to

148

go to a music college then it had to be Chethams. 'That way you can come home each evening,' she said firmly.

I felt like a rat in a trap. I squirmed with resentment as I stared into her resolute face and when I opened my mouth to protest she merely said calmly, 'We won't argue about it, Lisa, my mind is made up. If you don't wish to tell Minnie Jeffries then I will.'

She rose from the table to show that the conversation was over but I sat on while she and Aunt Edwina left the room. I wanted to rage and storm about the room, I had the ridiculous desire to throw something valuable across it. Instead I put my head down on the table and wept copious frustrated tears.

Some time later Edwina came in, her face anxious. 'Lisa, Mother wants you in the drawing room.'

She sat at the window writing letters, and took some time to lay down her pen before she looked at me haughtily through her glasses.

'I won't have you sulking, Lisa. Although your other grandparents are paying for everything you need, *I* am giving you a home, and you should be grateful.'

'I am grateful.'

'Then I don't want to hear any more about you going to London.'

'If London is such an unsafe place to be in, Grandmother, why am I so unsafe here in the country?'

'What do you mean by that?'

'Ted Hibbert attacked in the churchyard this morning, and would have raped me if help hadn't come.'

Their expressions were comical: stupefaction, disbelief and horror.

'My dress was torn from top to bottom. I hit him with a spade, because he would either have raped me or killed me. Grandmother, how can you say that London is unsafe when I'm attacked within sight of my own home?'

'I'm concerned for your future but I always said your involvement with the Stevens girls would do no good. This has been the result of it.'

'Oh Grandmother, this had nothing to do with it. He's angry and filled with resentment. You stopped Mr Stevens coming to the house because he gave Ted and his daughter a home. In some strange misguided way he's blaming the disasters in his life on us.'

'That's ridiculous.'

'I know it is, but he doesn't think so. He's lost his home, his wife and his daughter because the Stevens family has moved away, and even though it's all his own fault Ted Hibbert has to blame somebody else. He resents what we have, this was one way he had of getting back at us and when they send him to prison it will go on festering inside him. Pauline once told me he'd always been in trouble, it's bred in him and it's never going to go away.'

'I shall telephone the Chief Constable. Something has to be done about that boy. If they let him off again we shall all be murdered in our beds.'

'I doubt if they'll let him off, Grandmother, he's wanted for several burglaries in the area.'

'No doubt he's the one who stole your Aunt Edwina's watch. She never did get it back.'

Then, staring at me intently she said, 'You have bruises all down your arms. You'd better have a very hot bath and get into bed. You've had quite an ordeal, you won't get over it in a hurry.'

'And after this you'll allow me to go to London?'

'I don't know. I shall certainly need Minnie's assurance that you'll be in good company and that where you live is respectable.'

'The academy is residential, Grandmother.'

'Well, we'll see, I shall think about it. Now upstairs with you and into that bath.'

All night I had nightmares about the scene in the churchyard, and the last most frightening one of all was having Ted Hibbert wrench the spade out of my hand, and I cowered on the ground as he began to rain blows on my head.

I slept no more after that. If those people hadn't come in time, what was now a nightmare might have been fact.

CHAPTER 20

From the first morning when I played for Signor Marcello in a huge studio overlooking the Thames at Richmond everything went well. He spoke English with a musical Italian intonation that was fascinating, and he was a handsome man with iron-grey hair and a patrician Roman profile.

He greeted Madame Levison graciously and immediately set about putting me at my ease. I was told to sit at the piano for several minutes before starting to play and I realized immediately how wise that advice was. In those minutes my confidence came back and my hands felt more supple, then at a gracious smile and a gesture from his hands I started to play.

The instrument was so beautiful, the room so quiet, all my nervousness vanished and only the melody existed for me. Chopin's music, sad and haunting in its theme, and then the Adagio cantabile from Beethoven's *Pathétique.*

After, there was quiet and polite applause while I sat with my head bowed over the keyboard.

When I looked up Signor Marcello was standing near the piano and he was smiling. I looked round quickly at Madame and she was smiling also. In that moment I knew he would take me.

'You have considerable talent, Miss Ralston,' he said quietly, 'but Madame will already have told you that succeeding will not be easy. It will need work and work and more work, several years of it, and there will be no room for anything else beyond your music. Are you prepared to give yourself exclusively to such a project? Can you forget all the normal joys other young women experience, can you forego sports like riding and skiing, tennis and the like because you must care for your hands? They will be the most important things in your life. Do you have a boyfriend?'

'No.'

'So much the better, then. Boys will come later, much later. As for now, let music be your life, the be-all and end-all of your existence. One day when you take your place at the piano before a vast audience your reward will be their applause, their adulation, their homage to your talent.

'You will place your life and your entire future in my hands and for three years you will live like a nun. They live their faith, you will live your music, is that fully understood?'

'Yes, Signor.'

'Then you will come to the conservatoire next Monday. Today we will take tea with my wife and she will show you where you will live. I am the best teacher in London, my wife is the best cook. Come along and we will see what she has for us.

Signora was small, plump and motherly and she talked with her hands. He sat beside her smiling occasionally at her chatter, and we were plied with cakes and biscuits. There was an upright piano in their sitting room and I was intrigued by the collection of photographs so that hardly an inch was left on the top of the piano and tables.

Seeing my interest Signor Marcello said, 'They are from old students who have succeeded in the musical world. We also have a large family.'

'Are your children musical?' I asked him.

'All except Maria, she takes after her mother.'

Laughing a little Signora Marcello said, 'It is true, I am no musician but Maria is a good wife and mother. She has a degree in domestic science. We have five besides Maria. Nino sings and Angelina plays the cello, Fernando plays the oboe, Bella is playing the piano and Carlo plays the violin. It is my husband's dream to take an orchestra of young musicians abroad. If you work hard, Signorina, you could travel with them and perhaps play solo piano.'

'You can be sure I shall work hard. Oh, I do hope I shall be good enough.'

'That is good then, the gods and my husband will smile on you.'

On the train home Madame Levison went over and over the interview, stressing the hard work and the care I must take of my hands. By the time we reached Lancaster I was almost afraid to use them to open the carriage door.

I stood on the platform feeling suddenly sad. I would be losing a dear friend, and I owed her so much. As the train drew away my last sight was of her standing at the window waving and smiling.

Aunt Edwina was waiting for me. We had both learned to drive Grandfather's car but I couldn't honestly say I enjoyed driving with her, she was far too nervous and hesitant. When she stepped into the passenger seat and I realized I was to drive home, I felt nervous that my precious hands were on the wheel.

I had never talked so much. About the conservatoire and the view from the windows, my room at the side of the house with its chintz covers on the divan which would serve as both sofa and bed, and the tiny ornate period desk tucked away in a corner. There was an easy chair covered in the same chintz and a small coffee table, and if the room was small, it was lofty and charming. My home for the next few years.

Grandmother and Aunt Edwina listened politely but they didn't really understand what those years would mean to me. Grandmother would have preferred me to study something concrete like physics or even biology, and Aunt Edwina believed that the dedication I had spoken of was robbing me of other and more necessary joys.

We went shopping, and Grandmother saw to it that my new clothes were businesslike and unobtrusive. There would be no tempting Providence in the form of pretty feminine clothes, I must make do with serviceable skirts and blouses, a beige tweed coat, mackintosh, and low sensible shoes.

As I packed on Sunday afternoon I couldn't resist saying to Aunt Edwina, 'I hope I'll be able to choose the gown for my first concert. If Grandmother chooses it I shall look a positive frump.'

'That's very unkind, Lisa. Mother doesn't think you should go to the conservatory looking like a chorus girl.'

'It wouldn't hurt to let me wear high heels and use a little more make-up. Jessica wears lots of make-up, and fashionable clothes.

'Jessica's father spoils her, and she looks well in anything. But I do think a little less eye shadow and lipstick would be more ladylike.'

I made no further comment. My Ralston grandparents would be sending my allowance to me direct, and I intended to buy a new pair of shoes and some pretty clothes as soon as I could get to the shops. I didn't realize that I would have to save up for them, or that I would find London very expensive.

I arrived on Monday afternoon and as soon as I entered the conservatory I was aware of violin and piano music from the room on the right of the hall.

A young maid took my coat, then turned aside to close the room door.

Seeing my surprise she said, 'All the rooms are sound-proofed, and the master insists the doors are closed. I expect Miss Bella or Mr Carlo forgot.'

I smiled at her explanation and followed her up to my room.

'I'll bring you a cup of tea and some biscuits while you're unpacking, then dinner's at seven,' she chatted on. 'What is it you're studying?'

'The piano.'

'I likes that best. I'm not overfond of violins, they screech somethin' awful sometimes, but most of the students are very good, particularly Mr Carlo.'

'I'd like to hear him.'

'Oh, you will. The master likes to have concerts, mostly on Sunday. Everybody plays something, and then there's the singers but it's mostly something from one of the operas and I don't much like the opera. I likes music a bit more lively. Mi name's Peggy by the way, everybody calls me Peggy.'

'Have you been here long?'

'About four years. Mi aunt works here, helps in the

154

kitchen she does, and when I left school she asked if I could come here.'

'But you're not a Londoner, Peggy?'

She laughed. 'No, not me, and I've never lost mi Devonshire accent. Mi father's a farmer near Bideford. Devon's that beautiful, I missed it terrible when first I came 'ere.'

'My Grandparents live near Ashburton but I've never been there.'

'That's in the south I fancy, but ye should go there miss, the soil's that red and the lanes are that green, I gets 'omesick somethin' awful just thinkin' about them.'

'It's pretty here.'

'That it is with the river and all. Me and mi boyfriend gets a boat most Sunday afternoons, it gets pretty crowded on the river.'

I smiled. The river and boats wouldn't be for me, or the boyfriend.

It was like being back at school I thought that evening as we sat down to dinner. The Marcellos sat at a round table in the centre of the room while the rest of us were at long tables, just like Ashlea. I was placed between a stout boy who informed me he was learning the trombone, and a tall languid girl who was a mezzo soprano. The teachers sat at a table near the window and I looked at them curiously.

The men wore dinner jackets and the women long black dresses. None of them were very young and the stout boy, Eric, pointed them out one by one in between mouthfuls.

'Which one is the piano teacher?' I asked.

'There are two. Signor Vichenti and Madame Gasparde.'

The girl singer said quietly, 'You're a pianist, I believe?'

'Yes.'

'New?'

'Yes, it's my first day.'

End of conversation. After that she devoted her attention to the pale young man sitting next to her, and their

155

talk was all of music and the opera. I asked Eric what the young man was studying.

'You'll never believe it, the french horn. He doesn't look to have so much wind in him, does he?'

If I closed my eyes I could hear the hum of conversation from every part of the room and happily I thought: I'm a part of all this, I belong here.

I opened my eyes and they met a pair of dark laughing ones at the round table. I blushed. Later as we left the dining hall he asked, 'Did your neighbours send you to sleep?'

'I wasn't asleep,' I denied hotly, 'I just wanted to hear all the conversation, it was so intense.'

'It usually is. My name's Carlo Marcello, by the way. Who are you?'

'Lisa Ralston, it's my first day here.'

'Have you formed any impression?'

'Oh yes, it's wonderful. I can't believe I'm really here, if I pinched myself I'd wake up.'

'You'll know you're here when you get into your routine. You'll never have been so tired in your entire life.'

'I won't mind when I'm doing what I want to do.'

'They all come here dedicated, but I should tell you that some of them fall by the wayside.'

'How can they?'

'Too much work, not enough leisure and not enough outside interests. Then some of them fall in love and that's the end of them.'

'Why should falling in love end it all?'

'They think of each other instead of music.' He was smiling down into my eyes and in some vague way he was deliberately provoking me, particularly when he went on to say, 'They see cornflower-blue eyes and hair like sun-kissed corn, and if they are foolish they forget what they are here for. Your hair is so pretty, why do you have it tied back in that ridiculous bun?'

'It isn't ridiculous, it's businesslike,' I retorted.

'But music isn't business, Lisa, it's an enchantment. That bun would never do for the concert platform.'

'I've a long way to go before that.'

156

Just then I saw Signor Marcello watching us impatiently and hurriedly I gave Carlo a brief smile and walked away.

He grinned at me cheerfully and he was so Latin and attractive I could feel myself blushing furiously.

He was right about me feeling exhausted. I was glad to crawl into bed every night about ten and waken at half past seven with another gruelling day before me. My head spun with talk of music, from shoulders right down to fingertips I ached agonizingly in the first weeks, then miraculously they didn't ache at all and I knew I was winning.

Sunday evenings were a joy when we congregated in the huge hall at the back of the house. Here a grand piano took pride of place on the dais, and on the first evening I sat at the back while those who had been there longer went to their favourite places.

I was surprised when Carlo sat beside me. 'Have you settled in?' he asked quietly.

'Yes, thank you, and like you said I'm very tired.'

He grinned. 'You'll get over it. I don't suppose you're performing this evening?'

'Good gracious, no.'

He dived into the music case on his knee and produced a typed programme.

'It seems we are to hear my brother Nino singing from *Tosca*, followed by a duet between Nino and Gabriella from *Turandot*. After that there's to be a piano recital by your teacher Signor Vichenti, and then I am to perform the third movement from Brahms' Violin Concerto. Do you promise to sit perfectly still and not fidget during the performance?'

He was laughing at me, and suddenly I joined in.

'Lisa Ralston,' he said softly, 'too much dedication is as bad as none at all. Smile a little, be happy, and do take away that ridiculous ribbon that is tying up your bun.'

He reached out and pulled out the ribbon, and as my hair was cascading round my shoulders he removed my glasses.

'I knew it,' he said impudently, 'you have the promise of great beauty, and one day a great many men are going

157

to fall in love with you. It is almost unfair to have talent and great beauty – take care, Lisa, the Gods are often jealous of their gifts.'

In spite of his banter his eyes were remarkably serious, and it was a discreet cough from his sister which brought us back to reality.

That first night and so many nights that came after I sat enchanted while the music surged around me, and then one evening to my amazement Signor Marcello announced that Signor Vichenti's newest pupil would perform for them and a nod of encouragement from Carlo sent me on my way to the dais with a fluttering heart.

I chose Liszt's 'Liebestraum' because I loved it, though most might have preferred something less well known, then after the encouraging applause died away I launched into Chopin's Nocturne No. 2 in E Flat.

When I took my bow Signor Marcello was smiling, Carlo was on his feet applauding and there was all round appreciation of my performance. I had made my first bow before a discerning audience, and I did not think I had acquitted myself badly.

I had been at the conservatoire three months when Carlo invited me to spend Sunday afternoon with him on the river. I asked if it would have the approval of his father, but he merely said airily, 'He has no complaint about the way we work. Besides, all work and no play is not going to do either of us any good.'

'Your father made it very plain when I came that that was exactly what he expected. No room for anything outside my music, no sport, no boys.'

'No boys outside the conservatoire, he didn't mean me. You and I are different, Lisa, we understand about music, we understand it comes first, but what's so wrong with our getting to know each other? I've only asked you to come out on the river, I've not suggested we elope.'

So I went out on the river with Carlo and I loved every moment of that afternoon. To be like other young men and women, to laugh and tease a little, to feel the sun warm and gentle on bare arms, and to wriggle my toes happily in the grass while I told Carlo that my Grandmother would have apoplexy if she could see me attired like a shop girl, and with a man who wasn't English.

She would have been horrified if she could have seen the things I had bought in London: sandals in various colours, gay summer skirts and cotton tops, one or two colourful silk scarves and a large floppy white handbag. I had had my hair cut properly and wore it long, bobbing around my shoulders and almost hiding my long fashionable earrings.

Grandmother Marston would consider it degenerate and common, indeed I had often heard her remark that young girls were all of a pattern these days with their short skirts and flowing hair. I was to be different, just as Aunt Edwina had been different. We were to be the classy ones with our severe suits and twin sets, pulled-back hair and discreet make-up. Poor Grandmother, she really thought that by keeping me plain and ordinary I would be saved from the damaging influences that had beset my mother, but oh how I longed to be like her. To be beautiful and graceful, to have men love me honourably and decently. Love didn't need to end in tragedy. And Grandmother had never been able to see her own hand in my mother's unhappiness.

I was happy all summer long with Carlo and the crowd we thought of as our own. It included his sister Bella, a pianist like myself, and other boys and girls who had discovered an affinity with each other. On the nights we were not working we went to concerts, the opera and the ballet. We went to musicals and sat in the gods, and we discovered London's parks and thoroughfares.

On the day I went home for Christmas I tied up my hair and packed my serviceable skirts and blouses. Carlo thought it was hilarious.

'Why do you have to put on that charade, Lisa?' he said. 'Why can't you let your Grandmother see that you're beautiful and normal?'

'She doesn't want me normal, she wants me perfect.'

'I knew a boy once whose father wanted him perfect. He kicked over the traces when he was twenty, went on

159

drink and drugs, and died at twenty-two. He'd been pushed too far.'

'Grandmother's not like that Carlo, and I'm far too sensible.'

'We always thought he was sensible.'

'He couldn't have been. You see, Carlo, I understand Grandmother, I know how she thinks, and there's been plenty of provocation.'

'What sort of provocation?'

'One day I'll tell you, but I don't like to talk about it, I'd much rather forget it.'

'You're being secretive.'

'Yes, perhaps I am, about this. One day I might tell you, but it has to be in my own good time. Are you coming to the station to see me off?'

'Of course.' He put his hands on my shoulders and brought my face so close I could feel his breath against my cheek. Then he kissed me lightly on the mouth and let me go.

Right from the beginning we had kept our friendship light-hearted and without passion, now I felt strangely insecure. I knew that he liked me, admired me but I didn't think he was in love with me. As for me, I was in love with love. It was wonderful to have a nice attractive man in my life, between us, always, was our music. When he looked, strangely solemn, into my eyes and I could feel my heart fluttering painfully, always I told myself: Remember your music, this isn't real, only your music is real. And because he recognized my withdrawal his eyes would grow dark with something I hardly understood and the moment would pass.

This was the first time he had ever kissed me, and it had been light-hearted, hardly a lover's kiss, yet it had stirred in me emotions I was trying fiercely to hide. As I passed before him out of the room my throat felt tight with embarrassment and he picked up my case nonchalantly and walked humming softly to himself at my side.

160

CHAPTER 21

It seemed that my life had been measured in Christmases.

It was sleeting as I stepped down from the train and I looked round the forecourt hopefully but there was nobody waiting for me, and forlornly I turned away. Then a long low sports car came to a halt with a screech of brakes and everybody turned to stare as Jessica stepped out.

'Put your luggage in the boot, the parcels can go on the back seat,' she greeted me.

The boot was already almost filled with parcels, gaily wrapped Christmas presents and several large cardboard boxes.

She drove swiftly over the slushy streets, then we were crossing the bridge in a stream of traffic and heading north.

'I thought Aunt Edwina would be meeting me,' I said by way of conversation.

'She got out of it. You know what she's like in traffic, besides that little car of hers would have been all over the road. I'd have been there sooner but I had to pick up some things at Madame Hilda's. She's new, and awfully good. I should pay her a visit if I were you.'

I didn't take her up on that, I hadn't the money to shop at Madame Hilda's.

'How is Grandmother?' I next asked.

'Complaining. Her usual aches and pains.'

'And Aunt Edwina?'

'Uncomplaining.'

'Are all the family coming?'

'Well, Mother and Daddy are here. Aunt Claudia and Uncle Henry have arrived without Angela. She's got herself engaged to some worthy cleric and they're spending Christmas Day with his parents in Staffordshire. They'll be here on Boxing Day.'

'How about Uncle Raymond and Aunt Georgina?'

'They'll be here Christmas Day but they're not staying at Granny's.'

'Will the boys be here?'

'I expect so.'

'Don't you know?'

'I know that Alex won't be with them even if they come. I'm so furious with Alex. I told him I'd be here as far back as September and I was looking forward to seeing him. It'll be deadly dull without him.'

I could see her angry tight-lipped face in the lights from passing cars. She was staring ahead, unconcerned with me, obsessed with her own resentment.

'Why isn't he coming, then?'

'He's spending Christmas with his father in Dorset. It's rotten of him, and so ungrateful. All these years he's been jolly glad to come to Grandmother's whenever the cousins came, now just because his father is home he has to go off to Dorset. It would serve him right if I never spoke to him again.'

'You surely can't begrudge the time he spends with his father, they've met so seldom over the years.'

'That's just it, isn't it? We were good enough when there was nobody else, now his father's suddenly turned up so he has to drop us like a load of hot coals.'

I didn't argue with her. She was being totally unreasonable, but then that was Jessica: anything or anybody who interfered with her enjoyment was in the wrong.

'I'm surprised you've come up from London, there's bound to be a lot more going on there,' she said.

'Most people go home for Christmas.'

'I wonder why you say "home" for Christmas. Do you think of Granny's house as home?'

'Of course. It was the only home I had after my parents died.'

'And I suppose Grannie's always good for a hand-out.'

There was a silence until she said, 'I might as well tell you that on Christmas morning we are all to go and pay homage to Grandfather's grave, so lunch will be late. After that it'll be much as usual. I suppose you'll be showing everybody what the conservatoire has done for you, but I do hope you're not expecting to play every hour that God sends. It would send me up the wall.'

'I must remember to practise while you're out.'

'I'd appreciate it if you did.'

'I remember you playing the piano years ago, on my first visit to Grandmother.'

'Granny always liked to hear me play, that was before we realized we had a genius in the family.'

There was silence again until we arrived at Grandmother's where, with another screech of brakes Jessica reversed the car against the south wall.

I said curiously, 'Are you leaving it here?'

'It'll take no harm until I go over to the Templetons' later on.'

'Aren't they the people in the old Ralston house?'

'Yes. You should see what they've done with it, transformed it completely.'

'It was a lovely old house.'

'It was stuffy. They've knocked a lot of walls down and built a cocktail bar across one corner of the lounge. They've got a sports room at the back and a pool in the garden, and now they're having another pool made inside. It's like a private hotel.'

'How do you come to know them?'

'Daddy's their accountant. They're having a dance tonight and I'm invited with the parents. You'll have Granny and Aunt Edwina to yourself.'

In the hall Aunt Edwina fussed round as we took off our coats. 'It's such a bad night, I was hoping you'd be all right on the road.'

'I'm a good driver,' Jessica trilled, then turning to me she said, 'You didn't say how you liked Daddy's present to me?'

'It's lovely, Jessica. I hadn't realized it was yours.'

'Did you put your car away, Jessica?' Aunt Edwina asked.

'No, I thought I'd drive us all over to the Templetons'. I have to convince Daddy that I'm safe, he's such a fussbox.'

Aunt Edwina had done her best with the elderly artificial tree standing in the hall, but it badly needed some more baubles and the tinsel was wilting. Seeing my glance at it she said, 'Mother said it would do for another year. It's amazing how expensive they are, but the real ones shed their needles and she complains about that.'

Christmas passed uneventfully. I saw little of Jessica who, when she wasn't visiting the Templetons was out riding or playing golf. Aunt Cecily seemed to delight in telling me what a popular girl she was.

'It's a pity Alex couldn't come, if he doesn't watch his step he'll lose her.'

'I couldn't resist saying, 'Jessica tells me Alexander has gone to see his father. That must be wonderful for him, they've seen each other so little.'

'We've had no word that he's coming up for the New Year and there's a big do at the Templetons'. Jessica was so hoping he'd be here to take her. There'll be lots of young men there and they were like flies around the honeypot on Christmas Eve.'

She was singularly uninterested in my life in London, and perhaps I wasn't surprised when I caught sight of myself in the mirror on Christmas Day. I sat on Roger's right while Jessica sat on his left. She was beautiful in red velvet while I was nondescript in faded blue crepe, my only jewellery the monkey's tooth, my eyes hidden behind glasses and with my hair caught back in the bun which Grandmother considered distinguished.

I listened to Robin's talk about his prowess at rugger and cricket, to Roger talking about girls, and Rodney's obsession with Kenya and its wild life. Across the table Uncle Raymond winked at me and I found myself laughing cheerfully as he pushed away his wine glass and helped himself to whisky.

On Boxing Day Angela arrived with her fiancé Simon, a slender serious young man who stared at me earnestly through steel-rimmed spectacles and contributed little to the general conversation. He seemed to have plenty to say to Angela, however, and in his presence she dimpled prettily and appeared content.

164

Grandmother approved wholeheartedly. His father was a dean, his mother the daughter of a professor and Simon himself a physics lecturer at Oxford. I couldn't help smiling a little when I thought about Carlo with his flamboyant good looks, his gay Latin temperament and his enthusiasm for many of the things Grandmother thought not quite proper.

For the New Year's Eve Ball Rodney had been instructed to escort Jessica much to her disgust.

'Who wants to go with one's cousin?' she said to me peevishly. 'There are a lot of young men going, far more exciting than Rodney. They just want to be sure I'm not getting involved with anybody else, because they want me for Alex.'

'I thought *you* wanted Alex,' I said.

'I'm not so sure. If he'll neglect me now, what will he do in twenty years' time?'

I thought Rodney looked remarkably handsome in his evening dress and as always Jessica was too beautiful. New Year's Eve passed uneventfully for the rest of us. Jessica's parents went to the ball, Uncle Raymond and Aunt Georgina played bridge with Aunt Claudia and Uncle Henry, Grandmother snoozed in her chair and Aunt Edwina worked on her tapestry. Robin and I went for a long walk.

I felt exhilarated in the sharp wind that came off the fell while the frozen snow crunched under our feet.

At first Robin did most of the talking, then I found myself telling him something of my life in London, the shows and concerts we went to, the sort of people I went with.

Grinning a little, he asked, 'Have you got a boyfriend down there, Lisa?'

'I'm usually with Carlo Marcello, Signor Marcello's youngest son, he's a violinist.'

'I can't imagine you with an Italian boyfriend.'

'Please don't mention him to your parents, they'd tell Grandmother and she'd think I'd taken the first step towards perdition. That I have a friend in London would be bad enough, but an Italian would be worse.'

165

'What's he like?'

'Handsome, talented. We're not lovers if that's what you mean, Robin. We're good friends and our music comes first.'

Back at the house I showed him some photographs taken in the summer and he stared at them as though he couldn't believe his eyes.

'Is this really you, Lisa?' he said at last.

'Well of course it is. Who else could it be?'

'But you're beautiful. Why don't you always wear your hair like that instead of like a schoolmarm?'

I gathered up the pictures and put them in my handbag.

'As long as I'm dependent on Grandmother for a roof over my head I feel I've got to conform. One day when I can please myself it'll change, I promise you.'

'Why don't you show these snaps to Jessica? It would do her good.'

'I don't intend to show them to anybody else and I'd rather you didn't say anything to Jessica about them.'

'Why ever not?'

'Because she'd take great delight in telling Grandmother and the rest. Please, Robin, promise you won't say anything.'

He promised, but I knew before the holiday was over that he'd told his brothers. They treated me with a new respect and awareness, almost as though they were searching for another person behind my demure facade.

The conservatoire was closing for a month during the summer and the Marcellos were going to Italy. I wasn't sure what I would do, I told Carlo, but I couldn't face a whole month at Grandmother's.

Several days later he came to find me, beaming. 'Your holiday's solved, Lisa, you're coming to Italy with us,' he announced proudly.

I stared at him in amazement and he laughed. 'We're flying out to Rome on the fifth of August. You'll love Rome, Lisa, and our house, and you can practise as much as you wish. In the evenings I'll show you Rome before

we move on. Tell your grandmother it's a summer school,
that a lot of the students are coming.'

'But it will be expensive, Carlo, I don't have that sort
of money.'

'Why will it be expensive? You only have to pay your
air fare, the rest is taken care of. Lisa, Italy's our home,
my father has houses there, he's a rich man. Music has
made him rich, it'll make us rich one day.'

'What does your mother say about it?'

'She'll make you very welcome. Lisa, you'll love Rome
and Venice. Think of it, four whole weeks in places you've
only dreamed about.'

Fired with his enthusiasm I was under the spell of Italy
already, and to my amazement the battle I had expected
with Grandmother did not materialize – she was spending
August in Scotland and had been worried about what to
do with me.

So I went to Italy with the Marcellos, and fell in love with
it. I adored Rome and was enchanted by Venice, then we
went on to Naples and I fell in love again – with Carlo.
He had taken me to dinner at Positano, down the coast,
and it seemed all the charm of Italy – the beauty, the sun,
the song and the wine – was concentrated where we sat
in the garden of a small restaurant.

It was inevitable that we should fall in love, a love that
never looked beyond that first sweet elusive joy and the
heady conviction of the young that our happiness would
last for ever.

As we drove home in the white open car I listened
dreamily to Carlo's voice painting a picture of our future.

'We'll tell them at the end of our three years, Lisa. If
we tell them before they'll think it's going to interfere
with our music. It's only twelve months away, darling,
then we'll celebrate in Vienna.'

'In Vienna?' I asked sharply.

'Why yes, that is where Father is taking his young
orchestra, where you and I will play our first concerts.
Didn't I tell you?'

'Oh Carlo, of course you didn't. You'll be going, but I may not be there. Why do you think he'll choose me?'

'Because he thinks you're the most talented pupil he's had for years.'

It was too much to take in: love and Vienna, a future with Carlo in a world surrounded by music. Was it really possible that so much happiness would come to me?

It was in the middle of a rainy afternoon in London that I had reason to doubt it.

Signor Vichenti had taken one of his rare migraines and was unable to work, so I was at a loose end. I was passing the Marcellos' drawing room when I heard my name mentioned.

I paused doubtfully. The door was open by about four inches and although I knew I had no right to be listening the Signora was not troubling to lower her voice and there was an edge to it.

'Why are you so complacent, Stefano, why don't you mind about this girl?'

'I like Lisa, she's a nice girl, but not for my son. I don't want a daughter-in-law who isa not a Catholic.'

'Who is talking about a daughter-in-law?'

'I am. Are you blind that you do not see the signs? They are together all the time, they gaze at each other like lovesick puppies.'

'The young have to fall in love sometime, they'll get over it.'

'And suppose they donta? What sort of marriage could those two have?'

'Why couldn't they have a good one. They are both musicians.'

'And both of them playing anywhere and everywhere, concert platforms in different places, the jealousies and resentments. If she isa doing well and he isa not, if he's courted and fawned on and she is not. I won't have it Stefano, ita will be a disaster. I want you to talka to Carlo.'

'I'll talk to him when it becomes necessary. In the meantime, Maria, let them be young and in love. What harm will it do? In time they will decide for themselves whether it is right or not.'

168

I had heard enough. With my face crimson I made my escape silently to my room, reflecting bitterly that the young Italian girl who served at the dining table would be more acceptable than me in the eyes of Carlo's mother.

On Saturday morning Carlo met me for a walk in the park and I told him what I had overheard.

'I shouldn't have listened, Carlo, but it was hearing my name, I had to know what they were saying about me.'

'For a long time he was silent, his face pensive and morose. After what seemed like an eternity he said doubtfully, 'When my mother sets her heart on something she makes pretty sure she gets it. You might think my father's the boss of our establishment but it isn't really so. As long as he gets his own way with the musical side of his life he allows Mother free rein.'

'What can we do then?'

Suddenly his face cleared and with uplifting enthusiasm he said, 'We'll work hard and spend whatever free time we have together. We'll go to Vienna and do so marvellously everybody will be crying out for us, and when it's all over we'll get married and our families will just have to make the best of it.'

I threw my arms around him and hugged him. His young good-looking vital face smiled down at me tenderly and he looked so sure, so certain that our future lay together. Certainty was what I wanted, there had been so little of it in my life.

CHAPTER 22

We were to go to Vienna in March of our final year, and for months there was little time for relaxation. We all worked endlessly and happily and there were whole weeks when Carlo and I had to be content with smiles across a room, the swift touching of hands in some crowded passage.

As usual I would be going home for Christmas and on the last lesson I had with Signor Vichenti he said sternly, 'You are almost there, Miss Lisa – almost, but not quite. You will go home and you will practise every hour that God sends.'

I promised faithfully, at the same time impatient to get away. I had a free afternoon, and was meeting Carlo at the zoo.

The day was cold and frosty, but a pale sun shone out of a blue sky and as we laughed at the antics of the monkeys our breath froze on the air. I felt exhilarated and entirely happy as we strolled arm in arm.

I had not bargained for the past to catch up with me on that happy carefree afternoon but perhaps one can never truly escape from tragedy. We were walking by the lake when I saw them, standing dejectedly beside the water: tall slender birds, their beautiful plumage vying with the reflection of the red sky in the lake.

I paused, and there was something in my face that made Carlo say urgently, 'What is it, Lisa, what's the matter?'

I stood at the edge of the water, my eyes on the birds but my heart was on that other morning when they had descended like a river of flame on to the lake at Nakuru. Then I was remembering Alexander and the low gentleness of his voice, and the child who had loved him, desperately and jealously.

'It's the birds,' I told Carlo. Was that really my voice, pleading and filled with pain?

Gently he took my hand and drew me towards a seat hidden from the lake by a small rock garden. 'They're flamingoes, Lisa. You've seen them before, haven't you? In Kenya?'

'Yes.'

'Lisa, tell me about it. I know something happened in Kenya that you don't want to talk about. But it's better to talk about it, otherwise it could become an obsession, crippling your life.'

He put his arms around me and gradually the ice that was my heart began to melt. I felt his cheek warm against mine, his arms holding me fast, and the tears began to flow and he kissed my wet cheeks and breathed endearments against my hair.

I told him everything. About my mother and Uncle Philip, my father and Jubilee and the trauma of that terrible day when they died.

He listened without speaking, then he said, 'But what about the birds, Lisa? Why are you so afraid of the flamingoes?'

'I'm not afraid of them, Carlo, I love them. They came out of the morning mist like scarlet streamers on to the lake, and that was when I realized that there was still beauty in the world, that it didn't need to be all ugliness. That was when Alexander told me about his mother dying and I understood that unhappiness can be overcome.'

'Who is Alexander?'

'He was a friend of my cousins.'

'Were you in love with him?'

'I was seven years old, Carlo. How could I be in love?'

'But if you saw him tomorrow?'

'He's going to marry my cousin Jessica.'

'Do you mind?'

'Well of course not. Carlo, I haven't seen Alexander for years. How can I be in love with you and him too?'

His face cleared, and kissing me gently he said, 'I'm glad you've told me, Lisa. Even when we were happiest together I always knew that somewhere there was another you. When your eyes darkened and grew sombre with memories, I knew I couldn't share them. Today for the first time I've really found you, darling.'

'Don't you have any secrets you'd prefer to keep to yourself?'

'Absolutely none. I'm hopelessly transparent. Will you find that terribly dull?'

'Why should I? It wouldn't do for both of us to have deep dark secrets within our souls, and I love your normality.'

'And in Vienna we're going to set the city alight with our music, and when we've shown them how good we are we're going to waltz the night away and I'll buy you the biggest most vulgar ring I can lay my hands on.'

I laughed delightedly as he pulled me to my feet, and we were still laughing as we walked along the edge of the lake. It was only when we turned away that I looked back at the birds huddled together in pink splendour across the water.

CHAPTER 23

Signora Marcello smiled affably when I wished her a merry Christmas on my way out. I believe she thought Carlo and I had got over our infatuation, which was how she saw it, and that Carlo was simply being polite in carrying my luggage.

Signor Marcello came to the taxi with last-minute advice: 'You will come back to us as perfect as I know you can be, and there will be concerts and more concerts, exhibitions at which you will take all the prizes and I shall be contentedly at your feet.'

We laughed at his absurdity, but his presence prevented Carlo embracing me with the warmth I had anticipated.

Aunt Edwina was at the station to meet me, shivering in a cold north-east wind and impatiently I wondered why she didn't buy herself a new coat. She'd had that old Harris tweed since I'd first known her.

'We're a small party this year,' she told me as we walked to her car. Just the three of us and Jessica.'

'Isn't Alexander coming?'

'No, he was here in the summer. He and Jessica went sailing, riding or walking, they had a lovely time. But he couldn't come for Christmas, he's in the Sudan.'

'I see.'

'Jessica'll be at the Templetons' most of the time, there'll be plenty going on there. Would you like to drive, Lisa? I hate the traffic.'

So I drove Aunt Edwina's old Morris along the familiar roads leading north, exasperated by the poor gears and the scruffy windscreen wipers.

'Have you never thought of changing your car, Aunt Edwina?' I said finally.

'Oh, she's good enough for where I go.'

'She won't last for ever.'

'Who won't?' she snapped.

The car, Aunt Edwina, I wasn't referring to Grand-mother.'

'I really don't want to part with this car, I'm sentimental about her.'

'Oh well in that case you'd better keep her. I just hope she doesn't let you down.'

There was silence for some time, then she asked, 'How is your music coming along?'

'Very well, Aunt Edwina. Do you think Grandmother would allow me to have the piano moved somewhere else? I really do need to practise during the holiday otherwise I'll not be fit to go to Vienna in March.'

'What's this about Vienna?'

'Signor Marcello is taking an orchestra there, and if I'm good enough I shall be going with them as a soloist.'

'Well, we'll have to see what Mother thinks about it. She may not approve.'

'Then I shall have to go without her approval. This is my life, my career, it's what I've been working for. It would be ridiculous if she tried to stop me going. Besides, I'm twenty-one in January, old enough to please myself.'

'But are you financially able to please yourself, Lisa?'

'Aunt Edwina, I would beg, borrow or steal to go to Vienna. But when I'm twenty-one I shall have my own money to do what I like with, and Vienna is what I want.'

'Really, Lisa, that conservatoire is not doing you any good, you're becoming rebellious.'

'Not intentionally, Aunt Edwina. It's just that I've worked so hard, and now that I'm so close I can't allow anything or anybody to stop it happening.'

'Well I won't say anything to Mother, you'll have to ask her yourself about the piano, and tell her about Vienna. I'm warning you, that's all, she may not take to the idea.'

The three of us dined alone – Jessica was at the Temple-tons' – and I broached the subject of the piano.

'I can't think that it's going to look at all well in the hall, Lisa,' she objected.

'But I must practise, and you won't want to listen to my playing all over Christmas.'

'The piano stays where it is, and we'll use the morning room. It will mean keeping the fire going all day.'

'I'd be very grateful, Grandmother.'

'Have you thought what you are going to do when you leave the conservatoire?'

'We're going to Vienna in early March, we're all hoping something wonderful will evolve out of our visit.'

'Why Vienna? Why couldn't you perform in London or one of the other English cities? I still think you'd have been better going to Chethams.'

'Madame Levison thought I was doing the right thing.'

'Oh well, you've always been prepared to take more notice of strangers.'

I bit my lip resentfully. It was no use trying to convince her that Madame Levison had put me on the right track, and to call her a stranger was ridiculous. She had been my friend, my confidante, my inspiration since I first met her, and I resolved that I would pay her a visit, even if I had to drive the old Morris to do so.

My opportunity came on Christmas Eve when, armed with a large bunch of flowers and a beribboned box of chocolates, I arrived at her studio in Kendal.

We sat on the window seat looking down on the road crowded with Christmas shoppers and I told her everything about the conservatoire and Signor Vichenti and the friends I had made there, but I didn't tell her about Carlo.

When I paused for breath she said gently, 'And what else have you to tell me, Lisa? You've only told me about the things you think I wanted to hear.'

'How could I ever think I'd deceive you?' I said, smiling a little.

'Tell me about this young man who you think you're in love with.'

'But we *are* in love, we just don't think we are.'

'Who is he, one of the students?'

'He's Carlo Marcello, Signor Marcello's youngest son, a violinist.'

Her face was very thoughtful and for a long moment

175

she remained staring down at the street. When finally she raised her head I was surprised to see the gentle compassion in her eyes.

'Oh my dear,' she said wistfully, 'be very careful. I knew Stefano Marcello well in the old days, I knew his ambition, his striving, punishing ambition, and it did not include love, only a multitude of women he thought he loved.'

'Carlo isn't like that, he isn't interested in other women, he loves me.'

'And why shouldn't he?' she said stoutly. 'A young girl with a great talent, great enough to complement his own. But I know musicians, their jealousies and their vanities. All I am saying to you, my dear, is be very careful. What have his family had to say about this?'

'I think his mother would prefer him to marry a good Catholic Italian.'

'Of course, and the Italian mother is a powerful force within her family. Have you told your Grandmother about all this?'

'No, I'd prefer to wait until we return from Vienna.'

'Write to me when you get back, tell me about your success. Here am I teaching music to indifferent pupils and sometimes feeling very sorry for myself, but the mere thought that in Vienna I shall have a pupil who is taking the city by storm will be my reward.'

'You think I might take the city by storm?'

'I demand it, Lisa, you and that young man of yours. And you will find yourself listening to the applause – which is the greater, which has the most warmth? – and the next day the reviews – which one will be the most sought after, which one will command the most money?'

There was fear in my eyes when they met hers. 'Oh Madame, it won't be like that, he's a violinist, and I'm a pianist. Isn't there room in the world for us both?'

'Of course, it will be in your own hearts that the comparisons will be made. Not at first perhaps, but in time.'

All the way home I was wishing I had not seen her. I might have known that she would find difficulties. Perhaps she had once loved Stefano Marcello and couldn't believe

176

that his son would be different. Perhaps even in some obscure way she was a little jealous.

As I dressed for dinner that night, my door was unceremoniously thrown open and Jessica came in.

She stood with her back to the door eyeing me thoughtfully. 'What a bore having to dress up to eat dinner with Granny and Aunt Edwina. Is that dress new?'

'Yes, I bought it in London.'

'Mmm. Discreet enough to please Granny but expensive enough to grace a London restaurant. Who is he?'

'Who is who?'

'You didn't buy that dress to dine alone, Lisa, so come on, tell me who he is?'

'There's nobody special, I go out with a crowd.'

'I can see you're not going to tell me. Well, I've news for you. On Alexander's next leave we're getting engaged. But in the meantime I'm not going to live like a nun. I'm having a good time, going to dances and race meetings, and I've got a host of young men eager to escort me. I might flirt a little, I might even encourage them a little, but I am in love with Alex, and it's Alex I'm going to marry.'

'Allow me to congratulate you, Jessica.'

'Thanks, I thought you'd be pleased.'

There was sarcasm in her tone but, smiling, I ignored it, indicating that we should leave the room together.

She was as beautiful as ever, her eyes dancing provocatively behind their fringe of dark curling lashes and as we walked down the staircase I was aware of her dark shoulder-length curls bobbing beside me, her floating crimson skirt swirling round her long slender legs. At the same time I knew my dark blue silk jersey gown had class. Its simplicity shouted that it had cost a lot of money, indeed it had cost most of my clothes allowance for twelve months, but I knew how that gown could become me when my pale hair fell around my shoulders and my eyes without glasses reflected its colour.

I was a little taller than Jessica, even in my lower heels, and as we stood together in the hall she snapped with something akin to annoyance, 'Gracious, Lisa, you've grown so tall, you'll begin to look like a positive beanpole if you grow much more.'

'There was a time when I never thought I'd be as tall as you.'

'Well you are now.' Then, looking again at my dress, she said, I might ask you to lend me that gown one evening.'

'It could be too long for you.'

'It could be shortened.'

'I don't want to ruin it simply so that you can show off in it, Jessica.'

'Oh well, we'll talk about it again. I'm off to the Templetons' now.'

I had always envied Jessica's beauty and sophistication, now I began to see her in a different light. She was just three years my senior and yet her lifestyle was aimless, she had no job, no ambitions, her life was one merry-go-round of parties and boyfriends. But I knew Jessica of old. She could be all things to all people, and I knew the girl Alexander had fallen in love with would not be the Jessica who had just walked out into the night.

Alexander deserved somebody better than Jessica. I remembered his sensitivity, his handsome thoughtful face as he had looked across the water without seeing it, while he told me of the trauma surrounding his mother's death, then the way it suddenly became alive as he pointed ecstatically at the pink cloud of flamingoes lighting up the sky.

Suddenly I wanted to protect Alexander from Jessica, just as Madame Levison had wanted to protect me from Carlo, but I knew that nobody could protect anybody else from the things they wanted to do. Maturity was made up of mistakes and yearnings, only time would tell us if our decisions were the right ones.

On Boxing Day the snow started to fall and by lunch time it was thick and still coming down. We heard on the radio that several of the lakeland passes had been closed since dawn and accidents were reported all over the area. The

178

police were warning people to stay indoors and not make unnecessary journeys.

I wasn't troubled by the weather – I had made no plans to go out – but Jessica was like a caged tigress.

Her face was mutinous over lunch because Grandmother had forbidden her to take her car over to the Templetons'.

'It's ridiculous, they won't be expecting you on such a day. If they're so desperate for your company they'll come for you.'

'They will if I telephone them.'

'And endanger themselves. Really, Jessica, it won't kill you to spend a day here with us.'

With a set angry face Jessica flounced out of the room and that was the last I saw of her until dinner.

She seemed to have recovered from her ill humour and with Grandmother at any rate she was all sweetness and light.

She went with them into the morning room while I took my coffee to the piano. Grandmother was put out that a fire burned in both rooms, and I had been very careful to keep the fire in the drawing room low. Tonight however I added logs because if my hands were cold they were useless.

I was practising the Rachmaninov Third. I loved its glorious sweeping movements and was so involved I didn't know Jessica was there until she came to stand at the piano.

The discontented look was back on her face and she disconcerted me by prowling about the room picking up ornaments and noisily replacing them. Then she started to poke at the fire and I could feel my concentration slipping.

When I stopped playing she stared at me with a half smile. She was lying against the cusions on the couch, her dark hair gleaming against red velvet, hands playing with her heavy jade beads, and almost insolently she said, 'Am I bothering you, Lisa?'

'Not if you sit still and listen to the music you're not.'

179

'Can't you play something else, something a little more tuneful?'

'I can but it wouldn't help me get ready for the concert in Vienna.'

'You sound so smug when you talk about that stupid concert and Vienna, as though it's the only thing in the world that matters.'

'At the moment it does matter, terribly.'

'The world wouldn't stop if you didn't go.'

'I know. Somebody else would take my place and it would feel like death.'

'How terribly dramatic.'

'Yes, I'm sorry.'

It did sound dramatic. Other people might be ill and lonely and dying and all I was thinking about was my music, but I couldn't help it. For years I had been conditioned to think like that, though I couldn't expect anybody like Jessica to understand.

'Do you mind if I go on?' I asked.

'Suppose I said I do mind, I mind very much? This is my holiday as well as yours, and I don't really see why the rest of us have to be inconvenienced simply to accommodate you.'

'I'm sorry about that too.'

She was silent, staring into the fire, and after a bit I began to play again. I forgot Jessica and the spluttering logs in the grate. I forgot that outside the firelit room a blizzard swept across the fells, I was aware only of the beauty of Rachmaninov's concerto and the artistry in my fingers.

I had not heard her leave the couch, the room did not exist for me until in one blinding moment I was aware of danger. I looked up suddenly to see her standing over me, her face red with fury, then with one swift angry movement she brought the piano lid down with all her strength on to my hands.

Even in the midst of the excruciating pain I could hear the sickening crunch of delicate bones before I slid to the floor in a dead faint. I don't know how long I lay there, but I felt water dripping slowly on my face and a thousand

180

miles away I heard a voice saying urgently, 'Lisa, Lisa, please wake up, I didn't mean it, honestly I didn't mean it.'

She was standing over me with a vase from which she was taking water to splash on my face, and in that moment memory came back to me and with it pain such as I had never known.

I sat up dazedly against the stool. My heard hurt where I had bumped it against the piano and when I tried to flex my fingers they didn't respond. It was as if I had no hands to flex, and when I tried to get to my feet I could not use my hands to help me up.

It took all Jessica's strength to pull me to my feet, walking with her arm round my waist until I was able to sink into a chair.

For the first time I looked at my useless hands. Already they were red and painfully swollen, and the fingers of my right hand flopped uselessly and uncontrollably against my skirt. Anguish filled my heart and I lay back against the pillows while the tears flowed unchecked down my cheeks.

Jessica brought brandy but I was unable to hold the glass, and suddenly I was aware of her frightened face. The enormity of what she had done was terrifying her and at that moment I was hating her with a fierce and desperate hatred. If I had had the use of my hands I felt I would have put them round her throat and slowly choked the life out of her, but they were dead helpless things lying idle in my lap.

She was babbling now, pleading with me not to tell Grandmother. 'Please, Lisa, tell her the lid fell down, tell her your hands will be better in the morning. I didn't mean it, honestly I didn't mean it, it was just that the music got on my nerves, I couldn't stand it any longer.'

I couldn't answer her. I felt my life was over, everything I'd worked for, planned for and dreamed about was over. How would I face Signor Marcello, how could I tell Signor Vichenti, and how could I ever tell Carlo?

I tried to move my hands slowly across the fabric of my skirt but only the left hand seemed to have any life in it, the right was still useless. At that moment the door opened and Aunt Edwina came in.

Jessica jumped to her feet and faced her and I could smell her fear even in the midst of all the pain.

'Lisa's had an accident, Aunt Edwina, the lid fell down on her hands, I was sitting here near the fire when I heard it happen. Nothing's broken, I'm sure nothing's broken, they'll be better in the morning.'

She was babbling, implicating herself with every word, and without speaking Aunt Edwina came to look at my hands, her expression one of horrified dismay.

'How could it happen, how could the lid fall down?' Then realizing the impossibility of it she turned on Jessica sharply, saying, 'Did you do it Jessica, did you slam the lid down on Lisa's fingers?'

Jessica started to cry, great torturing sobs, and fled from the room. We heard her footsteps racing across the hall and up the stairs, then the slam of her bedroom door, and I pictured her sitting there like a cornered animal waiting for what would happen next.

Grandmother was angry, but with her anger was amazement that her favourite grandchild could have done this terrible thing. 'She must be ill, she would never have done it otherwise. Did you provoke her in any way, Lisa?' she said sternly.

I shook my head wearily. It didn't matter, all I wanted was a doctor to look at my damaged hands, and yet it took them some considerable time to reach this conclusion.

'We can't tell them what happened,' Grandmother said, 'we must make up some story so that the tongues don't start wagging. There's been too much talk about this family already.'

'Mother, nobody in the area will be interested.'

'Things have a way of getting out. I know that to my cost.'

'But not this, Mother, not something that has happened in our own home.'

'I'm not so sure.'

All this time I was sitting in agony, light-headed with pain, until at last Aunt Edwina said, 'We must get a doctor. Lisa looks as though she might faint at any moment.'

'We'll never get a doctor out on Boxing Day, particularly in the blizzard.'

'Then I'll ring for an ambulance, they'll have to come.'

She came back to say the ambulance was coming, but it would have to fight its way through the snow storm and on untreated roads from Lancaster.

She fussed around me, offering brandy, wrapping a rug over my knees because by this time I was shivering with shock and nausea.

I closed my eyes but the pain went on and on, and in the midst of it all I heard Grandmother saying, 'I must speak to Jessica, she'll be sitting up there torturing herself.'

It seemed a small eternity before the ambulance arrived. The two men quickly sized up the situation as they placed me on a stretcher and carried me out of the house.

The journey took some time on those dangerous roads, but at last I was carried into the casualty department where a cheerful Irish nurse said, 'My, but it's a rare mess you've been making of your hands. Broken that little finger is and there's a crack across your knuckles or mi name's not Hilary Murphy.'

'Are both my hands broken?' I asked feebly.

'Well the right one certainly us, you may have got away with a bruising on the left. What were ye doing to cause all this?'

'I had an accident.'

'Sure, I can see that, love, but it's the first accident I've seen that's had quite this effect.'

'Shall I have to stay in hospital?'

'You'll not be going home tonight, love. There's a nice little side ward at the end of the corridor, you'll be all right in there till the doctor's seen you.'

She saw me into bed and gave me an injection which sent me to sleep. When I awoke it was still dark and a young doctor was standing with the nurse by the bedside.

He smiled and took hold of my hands and I moaned a little with pain.

'Well what have we here?' he said cheerfully. 'Taken a hammer to them, have you?'

'Will they be all right, will I be able to use them again?'

'Of course you will, but you'll have to be patient. Lots of rest and a course of physiotherapy should see them as right as rain.'

'How long, Doctor?'

'A few months, I'm afraid. They'll be stiff when the bones have healed, but they'll soon improve with treatment. Plenty of massage and help from you.'

I turned my head away and the scalding tears coursed down my cheeks unchecked.

'What is all this?' he said kindly. 'Tears are not going to mend things. Give you an opportunity to have a good rest.'

'I don't want a rest,' I moaned, 'I want to go to Vienna.'

'Holiday is it? When are you going?'

'Early March.'

'Well, they'll be improving by that time but they'll still be pretty fragile. You'll have to go easy on them, hands are sensitive things.'

'I know.'

'You won't be able to do much skiing if that's what you're thinking of. I'm not even sure they ski in Vienna.'

He was being kind, treating my injury in a light-hearted fashion to reassure me, but my tortured expression made him say gently, 'What's so important about Vienna, something to do with your hands?'

'Yes. I was to play at a concert there.'

'Oh crikey, you're not a violinist are you?'

'No, a pianist.'

The concern deepened. 'I'm sorry. What on earth were you doing to cause this injury?'

'It was an accident.'

'Mmm. Funny sort of accident. Well, Lisa, your hands are not going to take you to Vienna just yet at any rate. It will be early summer before they're anything like. You'll get another opportunity, I'm sure, but I can understand your disappointment.'

'Can you?' I replied bitterly. 'Can you really know

184

anything about the years of dedication, the hours of practice, and now just when I was seeing the results for all my hard work this had to happen.'

He smiled sadly, and I regretted my anger. It wasn't his fault, how could he know anything about the gruelling years of self-discipline? And he was kind as he tried to reassure me over and over again that one day my hands would be well again.

In my heart I could only feel that it was too late.

CHAPTER 24

I spent my twenty-first birthday in that tiny ward, with my hands swathed in bandages coping unsuccessfully with the letters and parcels the nurse placed on my bed.

There was a thin gold chain with a single pearl drop from Carlo as well as a bowl filled with dark red roses over which the nurse drooled over every time she came in.

Grandmother sent a dark blue woollen dressing gown, entirely predictable as well as practical, and from Aunt Edwina there was a travelling clock which I had admired in a jeweller's shop in Lancaster. There was a substantial cheque from Aunt Cecily, Uncle Neville and Jessica, but I doubted if Jessica knew much about it and Mother had once said that Aunt Cecily believed money was the answer to everything. Uncle Raymond and Aunt Georgina also sent me money and from Aunt Claudia and Uncle Henry there was a very nice black leather handbag.

Flowers came throughout the day from my friends at the conservatoire, and from Madame Levison a jade necklace and earrings which I knew had been her own, a gift which touched me more than any of the others.

My grandparents in Devonshire sent a card and a very bulky registered envelope containing share certificates and the information that the sum of ten thousand ponds had been placed in an account in my name with the National Westminster in Kendal. They hoped my shares would perform well and they wished me every success with my chosen career.

There was no joy for me in this news, it was too late. Too late for Vienna.

It was the end of February when I sat in Signor Marcello's study at the conservatoire facing him across a desk littered with musical scores.

His face was bland but uncompromising. I had disappointed him, he had made that very clear. To Stefano Marcello his own disappointment was far more important than my damaged hands and in some vague perverse way he was angry with me.

He made me feel guilty, almost as if he accused me of deliberately sabotaging the concert in Vienna. Signor Vichenti had behaved in almost the same way. I felt they had wasted their time on me, that I was a failure, even when I insisted that the doctors had said my hands would heal.

The bandages and the splints were off, but my hands were stiff. As the doctors had predicted it would take months and weeks of massage and tender care before I could even think of doing justice to a piano.

'I stressed right from our first meeting, Miss Ralston, that you must care for your hands, but no, you had to have an accident. Your fees are paid until the summer. Do you intend to return to the conservatoire?' he asked coldly.

'Why yes, Signor, I intend to work hard when my hands are better, I want to be as good as I was before.'

He shrugged with a gesture entirely foreign and in that gesture I saw again the difference between us. The Latin temperament that was both volatile and selfish. I was not important to him as a person, only as a musician. Almost incongruously I thought: Now he will be in agreement with his wife, neither of them will consider me a fitting wife for their son.

'We will have to see, Miss Ralston. Maybe you will be as good as before, maybe not, but young people are coming to me all the time, young people who will go far and who will do as they are told. My daughter Bella will come to Vienna. She is doing well, she will do.'

He stood up to tell me I was dismissed, and as our eyes met he gave the briefest nod before I walked disconsolately out of the room.

I was to stay overnight before returning to Grandmother's, and for the rest of the day I remained in my room. My emotions were in such a turmoil of pain, frustration, fear and guilt that I didn't want to see anyone. Not even Carlo.

At dinner time I slipped out unseen and ate a light meal at a small cafe in the town, then I walked forlornly along the river. The cold seemed to eat into my bones and when my hands began to ache I turned back towards the conservatoire. It was dusk, with the lights strung out along the river banks dispersing the mist. I had almost reached the house when I saw Carlo standing at the gates. He came striding along the road to meet me.

'Why didn't you tell me you were coming?' he demanded.

'It's a very short visit, Carlo.'

'It doesn't matter, I should have known.'

He gathered me into his arms and his kiss was warm and gentle on my lips.

'Let me look at your hands,' he said, taking them lightly into his own.

'What rotten luck,' he said angrily, 'what absolutely damnable luck. There's no way you can come to Vienna with those, Lisa.'

'I know.'

'But you'll come back, you'll carry on with your music?'

'Yes of course, and I'll be just as good, Carlo. I'll be better, you'll see.'

'Yes of course you will. There'll be other concerts.'

He had to go then, but we agreed to meet for coffee in my room later.

For the first time that day I felt happy. Carlo still loved me, I would play again, and I would show them all that my poor hands had lost nothing of their skill.

It was after eleven when Carlo came to my room and there was exhaustion etched round his eyes and mouth. His talk was all of music and somewhat wistfully I asked, 'Will you still play the Bruch?'

'I would like to. My father wants me to play the Mozart.'

'Perhaps you should do what your father wishes.'

'I prefer the Bruch. I was playing it for you, remember? Now you won't even be there.'

'No.'

'Oh Lisa,' he groaned, 'tell me about it, how did you ever come to do this terrible thing.

I had no reason to protect Jessica, Carlo didn't even know her, and yet I couldn't bear to tell him that another woman, a member of my own family, had been sadistic enough to spoil things for me.

His voice was reminding me that Vienna was to have been our triumph, the city that would take us to its heart and where there would be nobody to say we shouldn't merge our talents and our lives. We would be the beautiful exciting Marcellos, the concert platforms of Europe would ring with our name, and tears rolled down my face with the knowledge that I had failed him.

I allowed myself to drift with the tempo of his lovemaking, tender and gentle one moment and the next filled with wild tempestuous passion. It had the rhythm of music but my hands which longed to hold him fiercely were helpless inadequate fragile things and my heart ached miserably with remembered pain.

CHAPTER 25

I returned to the conservatoire after Easter. I had received two rapturous letters from Carlo and one telephone call to tell me their concerts had been a triumph and they were not coming home. Instead they were going on to play in Budapest, Prague, Belgrade and even as far as Trieste and Istanbul. Signor Marcello's connections had ensured that they were received enthusiastically and the talent of the musicians had done the rest.

Carlo had played the Mozart at their first concert and the Bruch at their second. His name was in the newspapers hailing him as a wonderful discovery, the best violinist since Paganini and although I rejoiced in his success I became desperately afraid that we could never recapture the first glorious moment of our love.

My hands were better, but their sickness had left a strange fear in me. They ached more than they ever had before. After an hour at the keyboard I could feel my fingers stiffening up, feel my wrists become weak and tender. How could I ever think they would survive a gruelling concerto?

'What ees it, Miss Ralston?' Signor Vichenti said anxiously. 'Your hands, they are better, it is all in your imagination.'

I feared he could be right and I toyed with the idea of having psychiatric treatment, but he waved the idea aside as being ridiculous.

'You are a healthy strong young woman, Miss Ralston. You can play just as well as before, your hands are healed. Do you want to join the orchestra in Europe or do you want to go on feeling sorry for yourself?'

So I played until the ache in my hands and arms became a torment and at the end of a long gruelling day I wanted nothing more than to flop into bed exhausted.

At the end of May I had a week's holiday which

coincided with a letter from Aunt Edwina that I should go home to collect the car. Uncertain what it was all about, I went to find out.

Aunt Edwina had had an accident. She had driven her car into the banking after a slight argument with a corporation dustcart. The damage was negligible and she had had it repaired, but her confidence had gone completely.

'I want you to have the car, Lisa,' she said as we stood looking at it on its return after a good overhaul. 'It was Father's car and he always looked after it, and the mileage is very low. Mother never liked driving with me, she complained and found fault with every move I made so that I became very nervous. Actually I'm glad to be rid of it.'

It had long been my intention to buy a small car of my own, and now I hadn't the heart to deflate her. She was so proud of Grandfather's little car, so sure that she was handing me a gift to treasure. I thanked her warmly, and Grandmother forgot her prejudice long enough to allow me to take them to the railway station when they set out for Harrogate on Monday morning.

'But where will you go on your own?'

'There are a hundred and one different places to visit. I shall drive south, into Wales perhaps or through the Wye Valley.'

'Well do be careful, Lisa, it isn't a good thing for a girl to be driving about on her own. Suppose the car plays up?'

'I thought you'd just had the car gone over thoroughly. Nothing is going to go wrong with it, Aunt Edwina.'

'Well I do hope not.'

I finally saw them settled into their compartment and it was only when I eased the car into the traffic on my way back to the house that I suddenly felt wonderfully free.

A whole week lay in front of me when I could drive where I wished, and if I found a place I badly wanted to explore there was nothing to prevent me lingering on. Tuesday morning started warm and sunny, the birds sang

191

rapturously in the branches and I had armed myself with a good road map, a picnic lunch and very little luggage.

How I loved it. Gentle timeless stone villages and soft country voices, ancient churches and lonely valleys, gnarled English oaks and cottage gardens.

I drove unhurriedly, following the gentle Wye as it wound its way placidly towards the mighty Severn, and my confidence grew day by day. My precious hands were coping marvellously. They no longer ached and I told myself joyously that I was on my way back, love and acclaim were waiting for me.

One morning I found myself driving over a vast stretch of moorland with beyond it the silver line of the sea. Tall crags stood out in imposing splendour and as I dropped down towards the rambling villages beyond the moor I thought about Masefield's love for the West Country.

It's a warm wind the West wind full of birds' cries,
And I never hear the West wind but tears are in my eyes

and I was hearing my mother's voice reciting it on the banks of the Nakuru where we sat watching the birds.

Nostalgia filled my soul, and I stopped the car and for a few moments sat with my eyes closed and my heart plagued with memories. When I opened them again the leafy lane which lay before me seemed alien and incongruous until the memories receded, leaving me once more in the present.

I had no idea where I was, it seemed a long time since I had seen a signpost, so I drove on towards the village.

The name Ashburton seemed to leap out at me and I sat back bewildered. I had had no intention of coming to Ashburton and had not thought of my grandparents at any stage of the journey. It was almost as though my subconscious had led me to this place and now that I was here I had a sudden and desperate desire to see where they lived.

I stopped at the post office for directions and was told the house was a mile and a half outside Ashburton.

It stood on a low grassy hill just where the road wound

down, so that I came upon it suddenly. It was a long house with the sunlight tinting its mellow stone to shades of gold and there were a great many windows.

They stretched along the entire length of the terrace and many of them were open to the glorious spring weather. Rockery plants tumbled colourfully over the walls, and the lawns were as green and perfect as the baize on a billiard table. Tall wrought-iron gates stood at the end of the drive which curved up towards the house. Leaving the car I walked to the gates and stood doubtfully staring at the house.

I could hear voices and the gentle hum of a lawn mower, and even before I could decide what I should do a gardener appeared from the back of the house and the sound of the mower became louder.

Then along the terrace a boy came running with a white terrier, barking excitedly as he chased after his ball, then seeing me he headed for the gates and the boy came after him.

The boy had dark blue eyes and a keen sensitive face, and as we looked at each other the years rolled away and I was seeing Philip Ralston gazing at my mother.

'Hello,' the boy said with a puzzled smile. 'Are you coming up to the house?'

In another moment I would have opened the gate and gone inside, but just then a woman came out of the house, calling, 'Mark, where are you? It's time to leave.'

He smiled. 'Uncle Ronald is taking us to London for the weekend, but you can come in if you like. I don't want to go anyway.'

I looked across to where Constance stood impatiently waiting.

'Please don't bother,' I said hurriedly. 'I'll call later this afternoon.'

Constance came briskly towards us. 'Who is it, Mark? Don't leave them standing outside the gates.'

I started to turn away, but some strange elusive notion held me captive and I turned again with the urgent desire to see Constance, to face my past in the hope that it might stifle for ever the anguish of memory.

There was no recognition in her glance, and she had changed little. She was still the glacially perfect woman I remembered from my childhood. There was not a hair out of place. It was blonde shingled perfection, and her make-up was immaculate from the thin arched brows to the pale curve of her mouth. I thought that I was looking at a beautiful statue, without either warmth or life.

'Oh, are you from the church? Mark darling, do get the flowers for the altar from the greenhouse,' she said.

'I'm sorry no, I'm not from the church. I saw the house, I thought it was so beautiful I just had to take a closer look.'

'I see. Well yes, it is rather beautiful, I would have taken you into the garden but we are leaving quite soon.'

Her expression changed from aloof condescenscion to a bright smile and I turned to see a car approaching, then Mark was opening the gates and she was walking forward to greet the new arrival. Through the open window of the car she kissed him, then with a brief smile in my direction she walked back to the house while he drove slowly beside her.

Mark smiled at me. 'I'll have to go now,' he said softly. 'I don't really want to go to London, but we've all been invited.'

I looked towards the house, where my grandparents were welcoming the new arrival. They settled down on the terrace and drinks were handed round. Nobody looked in our direction, and I thought that by this time Constance would have forgotten my existence and the older people did not know I was there. I wanted to talk to Mark.

'The dog's called Hamish, he's Scottish so the name suits him, doesn't it?' he said.

'Yes. He's a very nice little dog.'

'Mother's not keen. He's really Grandfather's dog, and when Mother gets married at the end of July and we go to live in London, I'll not be able to see as much of Hamish. He'll never be able to visit, and Mother says dogs are for the country, not for towns.'

'But you'll be able to see him when you come here. Do you go to school in Devonshire.'

'No. I go to Marlborough, that's my father's old school.'

My father's school too I felt like saying, but I kept silent.

'Are you all going over to London?' I asked instead.

He nodded glumly. 'We're going to meet Uncle Ronald's family, the grandparents haven't met them yet.'

'I see. Well, you'd better go back to the house, Mark, or your mother'll have to come looking for you again.'

I held out my hand which he took firmly in his.

'Goodbye,' I said gently. 'It was very nice meeting you, Mark.'

As I reached my car I turned to see him returning to the house with the dog running beside him. As he neared the terrace he must have said something because they all looked down the drive in my direction. The boy raised his hand and waved, and after waving back I climbed in the car and drove away.

I would never see them again. If the afternoon had been different I might have bridged the gap left by the years, but perhaps it was better so. It was time I headed north, the holiday would soon be over and it was high time I got back to my piano.

I couldn't understand the vague feeling of rejection that swept over me. I couldn't possibly have expected any of them to recognize me and come rushing down the path to greet me, yet surely I should have been able to walk up their drive with a smile on my lips and every anticipation that I would be warmly received.

It was all in my mind, of course, and fortunately I was not to know as I drove eastward through Dorset and Hampshire the following day that Fate, with her usual humour and bad timing, had one more trick to play.

It was the inn itself which made me bring the car to a halt in its cobbled courtyard where clematis ran riot and where a stout oak door stood open to the sunlight, letting out the sound of a piano being played in a none too expert fashion.

I went in and stood hesitantly at the bar waiting for somebody to come to me, and trying very hard to recognize the tune being played on the piano.

195

After a rather long wait, when I began to think perhaps I should move on after all, a woman came down the stairs holding the hand of a small boy. Seeing me at the bar she became instantly businesslike.

'Did ye ring the bell, miss?' she inquired.

I looked around for the bell and somewhat irritably she said, 'It's that Polly, she's probably shifted it to dust.'

She rummaged underneath the bar and after a bit proudly produced a squat brass bell which she placed firmly on the bar counter.

'The number of times I tells that Polly not to touch the bell. What can I do for you, miss?'

'I'm looking for somewhere to stay just for tonight.'

'We've got two commercial travellers checkin' in this evening, but there's a nice little room at the side of the inn. It's quieter than the front and the room's newly decorated. Come on upstairs, love, and ye can see it for yourself.'

I followed her upstairs, saying 'You have a pianist in the family?'

'Mi youngest daughter Maudie. Comin' on nicerly she is but the lessons are expensive and she doesn't practise enough.'

'I suppose there are too many distractions.'

'That's about the size of it. Her friends playin' in the fields and the long summer evenings comin'. Do you play the piano, miss?'

'Yes I do.'

'The trouble with our Maudie is that she wants to play well, but she doesn't want to work at it. I wish you'd 'ave a talk to her, miss, tell 'er she'll get nowhere without the practice.'

'She wouldn't like that coming from a stranger.'

'Well the piano's in the sitting room just across there, miss, yer welcome to play if ye feels like it. There's music in the stool.'

The room she showed me into was charming. Soft colours in a chintzy wallpaper covered the walls, and the curtains and bedspread were in a soft rose pink. Off the room was a tiny bathroom also in pink and seeing my look of pleasure she said, 'It is nice although I sez it as shouldn't. We don't get the trade now, they all go off to the Royal, done us a lot of 'arm it has.'

'I'm sorry. What could be nicer than this?'

'We've no swimmin' pool and no ballroom, love. Ye'll get good 'onest food and ye'll know what yer eatin'. We can't say fairer than that. Now if yer'd like to have a tidy-up and unpack yer little case I'll have a nice cup of tea sent up to you in the sitting room.'

'But I wouldn't like to disturb your daughter, I can have it in here.'

'She'll be glad of a disturbance, and I'll be wantin' 'er 'elp soon with the evening meal.'

The piano was an upright grand standing across one corner of the sitting room. It was anything but new but it had been lovingly polished over the years and in front of it stood a velvet-covered stool. A sheet of music was opened on the piano and curiosity led me to it instantly.

It was a sheet filled with scales and arpeggios and I smiled ruefully. How many years of my youth had been spent agonizing over such things, and almost unthinkingly I began to play. No music came instantly into my mind, but after a few minutes my hands responded and I gave myself up to the joy of melody. The piano had been kept well tuned and I played on and on until I became suddenly aware that I was not alone. A yound girl stood immediately behind me watching my hands, her eyes round with wonder, and I stopped playing and smiled at her.

'How long have you been there?' I asked her gently.

'I don't know, miss. I 'eard ye playing from downstairs, ye plays beautiful.'

'Thank you. Is is you who is learning the piano?'

'Yes, but I'll never be able to play like that.'

'Would you like to play for me?'

'No miss, I couldn't play for you and 'ave ye thinkin' 'ow awful I am. It's mi mother that wants me to play the piano, just because 'er sister's musical. Singer she is with the Salisbury Operatic Society. She's taken leading parts and she does sing lovely. I can't sing at all so mi mother thought I should learn to play the piano. P'raps I should practise more.'

'If you want to play really well then you should practise a great deal.'

'I reckon I'll 'ave to. Now that mi mother's 'eard you she'll be more keen than ever.'

I laughed. There was something engaging about Maudie with her frankness and her dimpled smile.

I made room for her on the piano stool but she said hurriedly, 'Please, miss, don't stop to 'ear mi play. Yer'll only make mi nervous and yer'll 'ate it, I 'ates it miself.'

I made myself scarce and took a walk by the river, where I came across a charming old watermill, the wheel turning lazily with a gentle rumble. I stood entranced to watch a kingfisher darting with a sudden flash of blue across the water.

I hadn't gone much farther when I saw a boy staring moodily into the water and my heart jumped painfully as I recognized Mark.

I stood above him, saying, 'Hello, I didn't expect to be seeing you again.'

He looked up, then a sweet boyish smile spread across his face and he made room for me to sit beside him.

'What are you doing here?' I asked.

'We're staying at the Royal. There's a tea dance on and the others are at that. Are you staying at the Royal too?'

'No, I'm at the inn. I'm afraid there's nothing in my luggage grand enough for the Royal.'

He grinned. 'Are you going home to London?'

'No, my home's in the north of England, not far from the Lake District. I'm on my way back there.'

'How funny, Granny and Grandpa used to live near the lakes. I'll bet you know some of the people they knew. I've been to the lakes camping with the school, it was great fun.'

'Have you thought what you want to do when you leave school?'

His face clouded and for a few minutes he remained silent, then almost resentfully he said, 'I really want to be a vet, I've never wanted to be anything else. But we don't talk about it, it's not what Mother wants.'

'It's your life, Mark.'

'I know. I talked to Mr Jeffries my housemaster about it and he said it was a noble profession, but after Mother'd had a chat to him he advised me to think of something else. I wouldn't care but she won't tell me why she doesn't want me to be a vet.'

'Perhaps she'd prefer you to do what your father did.'

'My father was in the diplomatic service. Grandpa told me, Mother never talks about him.'

'Do your grandparents never speak of your father, or any of their family?'

'Grandpa told me Uncle Malcolm was a gamekeeper out in Kenya, he was Father's brother. I know there's some mystery about it but I'd much rather know. They'll have to tell me one day.'

'I'm sure they will when you're older.'

'The other chaps think I'm cagey about things. They talk about their folks all the time. Morris Major's mother's run off with his father's estate agent, and Tony Beauchamp's father's left his mother for his secretary, and we all talk about *that*.'

'I'm sure if there's anything you should know you'll hear about it one day, Mark. Is there nobody else you could ask?'

'I've got a cousin somewhere but I've never seen her. Mother says the grandparents are paying for her education, I think she's a dancer or a musician of some sort.'

'Is that all you know about her?'

'Mother said she was a very ordinary little girl with glasses and pigtails. I don't think that matters, do you?'

'She could have changed. Perhaps she isn't plain any more.'

'I think all girls should be pretty, don't you? I think all girls should be as pretty as you.'

'Well thank you, Mark, that is one of the nicest compliments I've ever had.'

I smiled as the rich red colour crept into his face, and he gave the river his full attention.

We sat in companionable silence for several minutes before he suddenly consulted his watch.

'Gosh, it's after five, and Mother said I had to be back by then.'

We said our goodbyes and walked in opposite directions. I had not gone far however when he called out, 'I don't even know your name.'

I laughed and waved, but did not enlighten him. I doubted very much if Mark and I would ever meet again, and I was sorry. I had liked him, and felt we could have been good friends.

CHAPTER 26

There was a long letter waiting for me from Carlo when I returned to the conservatoire. It had evidently been written over several weeks, whenever he had a few moments to spare. It was all of their triumph across Europe and I didn't begrudge him one single moment of their success, I only wished I might have been with them.

They were going to Rome for their last concert and flying home from there at the end of July.

He sent me his love and said he had not forgotten the largest most vulgar ring he could find. He also added that his mother was enjoying their acclaim from the sidelines, insisting that they ate regular meals and generally bringing them periodically down to earth.

I sat for a few moments feeling a little sorry for myself. Carlo had said little about his sister's achievements on the tour, though I had no doubt Bella had performed well, he was too full of his own performance. And wryly I wondered what his mother would have to say about the expense of the large vulgar ring.

Then, one day Carlo telephoned.

'Darling, I'll have to be brief,' he announced. 'It'll take weeks, months to tell you everything that's happened. For now I just want to tell you I've got the ring, I love you, and everybody is very happy for us.'

'Your mother too?' I couldn't resist asking.

'Well of course. Our plane arrives in at three thirty on Friday morning. Will you be there to meet me Lisa?'

'Yes, of course.'

'I want us to be together, just you and I, so that I can see your face when I put this enormous monstrosity on your finger.'

'Oh Carlo, is it very vulgar?'

'It's the biggest diamond they had in the shop. Don't worry, darling, it will look glorious on your slender finger

201

and it's designed to warn everybody else off. And are your fingers really as good as new, darling?'

'Absolutely.'

'Wonderful.'

Then he was gone, and I stood in the hall with a smile of pure joy on my face. Seeing it the little maid who was dusting the chairs said brightly, 'You look so happy, miss, have you won the pools?'

'Better than that, Janie, I'm in love. Everything in the world is going to be perfect from now on.'

I didn't go to bed, I was far too excited. I had spent the afternoon at a very expensive salon having my hair styled and my fingernails manicured in order to do justice to my diamond, and soon after midnight I set out for Heathrow.

As always the airport was busy, the night filled with the sound of aircraft. I went to the reception area and sat with a coffee and a book in my hands, but it was impossible to read. I checked that the plane had left Naples and was on its way and scheduled to arrive at three thirty, and I amused myself by watching passengers arriving and speculating on their relationship to others waiting to greet them.

I don't know when I first became aware of a strangeness in the atmosphere. Men in uniform talking in groups, doors opening and closing, telephone calls in hushed whispers, and covert glances from airport staff as they passed through the room.

I was imagining things, I thought angrily, but I found myself remembering that terrible morning in Kenya.

It was three o'clock and there was another half hour to wait. A man and a woman came to sit at the table and I remembered having seen them at the conservatoire with their son. I smiled, and she leaned forward with an answering smile, saying, 'I told my husband you were waiting for somebody from the conservatoire. We're meeting our son Noel.'

'Noel Martin, french horn?'

She beamed. 'Yes. Oh they've had such a triumph, why weren't you there?'

202

'Unfortunately I had an accident just before we were due to leave.'

'I am sorry. Of course they'll all be full of it when they return.'

Mr Martin was restless. He brought coffee to the table then wandered away to look at the notice boards. His wife said, 'Jim's nervous, he hates flying, he's always like this when we come to the airport. He said if we'd been meant to fly God would have given us wings.'

I smiled but my eyes followed him round the room. He stood for several minutes looking up at the list of arrivals, then he made his way over to the information desk.

'He never believes notices,' his wife said. 'He's probably checking up that the plane is on time.'

He appeared to be arguing with the two girls at the desk, then he hurried over.

'Jim, do sit down,' his wife ordered. 'The plane's not going to arrive any sooner with you badgering everybody in sight.'

'It's not on the notice board,' he said in some agitation. 'All the others are up there, and it should be in any minute now, it's almost three thirty.'

'Sit down, Jim, and please keep your voice down, people are looking at us. We don't want to alarm everybody.'

The girls at the desk were talking agitatedly, their faces pink and concerned, and I couldn't stand it any longer. Excusing myself I left them, trying to walk in an unconcerned fashion towards the ladies' room. On my way I passed the large screen announcing arrivals, and Mr Martin was right. The plane from Naples had been removed.

When I returned to the lounge things seemed much the same except that Mr Martin had buttonholed a young man in uniform and his wife was reasoning with him while people looked on uncertainly.

Taking my courage in both hands I went to the information desk.

'I am waiting for the plane from Naples, is something wrong?' I asked.

'Why no, madam, but it has been delayed,' said the girl. Please take your seat and as soon as it arrives you will be notified.'

'Why has it been removed from the schedule of arrivals?'

'No reason, madam, except to make room for others arriving shortly.'

'Isn't that very unusual?'

'Why no, madam, the airport is very busy this morning.'

'Please, I'm not a child, if something is wrong I want to know. Anything is better than this suspense.'

'When we have a revised arrival time we'll announce it, madam.'

I was on the verge of tears, tears of frustration because I felt I was battering my hands against a brick wall. Why were they treating me like a backward child, humouring me? Across the room Mr Martin was becoming more and more agitated and now others were joining in his tirade.

Eventually a message came across the loudspeaker for all those waiting for the Naples plane to congregate at the back of the lounge and one by one or in small groups they complied, their faces anxious and pale. The news was broken to us calmly by a senior officer whose pale bleak face registered the anxiety we shared.

The plane was missing. They had had no reports from the flight deck for almost two hours since it crossed the Italian-Swiss border. As soon as they had anything concrete to report we would be informed.

At just after eight o'clock we were told that the plane had hit a mountainside and the wreckage was strewn for miles. There were no survivors.

It was as though the pages of a book had suddenly slammed shut. I remember wandering out into the warm morning air and the blinding sunlight of a beautiful day. I felt like a zombie as I made my way to the car park. It was some other person who unlocked the door and climbed into the driver's seat, some other person who drove out into the traffic and headed for Richmond. I drove like an automaton but my heart was a dead thing in my breast. I had no thoughts for the future and the past was a remote cloistered thing belonging to somebody else.

It was only when I reached the conservatoire that memory came back to me in all its poignancy and I remembered Carlo waiting at the gate to meet me, his dark hair blowing in the wind, his face alive with laughter. Then his fingers were entwined in mine, fingers that had enchanted Europe with the virtuosity of his music which the world would hear no more.

I was unprepared for the scene inside the front door. There were flowers everywhere, great vases and urns filled with roses and carnations, and across the staircase stretched a white silk banner saying: Welcome Home.

Students and staff lined the hall, their faces alive with expectancy. As my eyes met Madame Gasparde's I felt the room begin to spin, and I remember nothing more until I awoke lying on my bed with Madame and the housekeeper leaning over me.

Memory rushed back with terrifying reality, and I was telling them what had happened, the words falling over each other as I tried to force them to make sense. Their shocked faces and cries of distress accompanied my story, and then they were gone to tell the others.

I lay on my back looking round the room I had thought of as home and I wept miserably for the ending of youth and love. This time there was no Alexander to comfort me with his words, no flamingoes streaming down the morning sky with their promise of beauty and solace. That little girl who had believed implicitly in a world filled with beauty and goodness had gone for ever.

CHAPTER 27

I packed all my clothes, all my music and the accumu-
lation of the last few years and then I rang for a porter to
take them downstairs. I could tell he had been weeping
from his swollen face but mine was composed, the traces
of tears covered by make-up and I told him tersely what
I wanted done with my luggage.

He could see I didn't want to speak, but my heart
lurched painfully when I recognized the pity in his eyes
as he closed the door.

My last act was to visit the studio where I had spent so
many happy hours. The Steinway stood open in front of
the window and I went over to it and laid my hands gently
on the keys, then I quietly closed the lid. From the garden
came birdsong and the scent of roses. The sun sparkled
on the river and the sound of laughter and voices came to
me unreal and incongruous, completely out of keeping
with the stone that was my heart.

There was nothing for me here. Without the Marcellos
the conservatoire itself was in doubt but even if it survived
I could never come back. I had no idea what I would do,
at that moment it seemed my life and Carlo's had ended
together, but I knew where I was going. Until I could
come to terms with life I would go home to my grandmother's. There was nowhere else to go.

It was a long journey but I was glad of something to
do and I made myself drive well. It was dusk when I
finally turned into the drive and I felt so unutterably weary
I could have stopped the car and gone to sleep curled up
in the front seat.

Halfway up the drive I braked. There must have been
at least a dozen cars round the house and I had to squeeze
mine in between a large Rolls-Royce and a rhododendron.
I could hear music and laughter through the window of
the drawing room.

Inside, groups of people stood around in conversation, and for the first time I thought about my appearance. I had not run a comb through my hair since I set out for the airport that morning, my make-up needed freshening and I was wearing a grey flannel skirt and white cotton jumper.

My eyes felt so weary they were not focusing properly and a party was the last thing I was in the mood for.

The front door opened to my touch. About a dozen people were standing in the hall, sitting on the stairs and generally staring at me in utter surprise. They were all wearing evening dress and there were glasses in their hands, and while I returned their stares silence descended among them and then Aunt Edwina was there.

She was wearing her only evening dress, light brown silk, and her amber beads, staring at me in amazement. 'Why Lisa, we weren't expecting you. Why didn't you telephone?'

She came over and kissed me, then taking my arm she introduced me to the room at large. 'This is my niece Lisa. She's driven up from London, and of course she wasn't aware we were entertaining.' Then softly to me she said, 'Mother's in the drawing room. Would you like to go upstairs and change before you go in there? Although I really think Neville is ready to make his announcement.'

'Please, Aunt Edwina,' I hissed, 'I'd rather not, I just want to go and get into bed.'

'You can't, Lisa, we've put a friend of Jessica's into your room. You'll have to have the twin bed in my room – only for tonight, dear.'

By this time we were in the drawing room where Grandmother sat in her favourite chair in front of a fireplace filled with flowers.

Uncle Neville was on his feet in front of the fireplace with a glass in his hands, and there was a sudden burst of applause.

Jessica, looking exquisite in pale pink chiffon, stood demurely between her mother and Alexander Hamilton and I was immediately aware of her haughty stare which took in my dishevelled state. Somebody thrust a glass in my hand and then Uncle Neville announced with rare pride that we were all there to toast the health of his daughter Jessica and her fiancé Mr Alexander Hamilton.

Surprise, exhaustion and weariness combined to mar the importance of his announcement when for the second time that day I sank to the floor in a dead faint.

The next few days passed in limbo. Jessica accused me of spoiling her big night. Aunt Edwina informed me that Alexander carried me upstairs and she sent for the doctor, who prescribed sedatives. News of the plane disaster had reached them, of course.

I was now in possession of my own bedroom. The Templetons had sent flowers and grapes even though I didn't know them. Alexander sent flowers and I had visits from the aunts and Grandmother.

True to form, the first thing Grandmother said was that she didn't like my new hairstyle. 'It doesn't suit you, Lisa, the sooner you revert to your old style the better I shall like it,' was her parting remark.

What did my hair matter any more, I thought after she'd gone. Carlo had loved it. He had run his fingers through its silky fairness and said it captured the sunlight like summer rain, but now there was nobody to care.

I wallowed in my grief but it was Jessica who brought me back most sharply to reality. She came one morning and stood in the doorway wearing tennis shorts and a white cardigan thrown idly round her shoulders.

'Aunt Edwina says you're better,' she said airily, 'does that mean we can expect to see you for lunch?'

When I didn't answer she said, 'What on earth are you going to do now? I expect the conservatoire will be closed. How dreadful that they're all dead. Alexander is going back to the Middle East tomorrow so we shall be out most of today, we'll probably see you later. Bye.'

Neither Jessica nor Alexander was in for lunch. Aunt Edwina said they were over at the Templetons playing tennis and so after lunch I set off on my own wearing a tweed skirt and blouse and carrying a light jacket over my arm. I had put my hair up to please Grandmother, reflecting that the Lisa loved by Carlo had gone. The old Lisa was back with a vengeance.

I walked briskly along the country lane and climbed the stile near the farm. A farmhand whistled at me cheekily and two children playing in the farmyard waved to me. It seemed almost like old times except that these were the new people. I hadn't heard anything of the Stevens for a long time.

It was warm and sunny on the fell with the distant lakeland hills shimmering under a haze of cloud. For about an hour I sat idly taking in the familiar scenery, then I walked on towards the brook that was little more than a trickle now between the stepping stones.

I hadn't gone far when I came across a man sitting near the stone wall with an artist's easel set up before him. A box of paints was open on the grass and he seemed unaware of me standing behind, watching him work.

I knew immediately that he was good. His painting caught the gentle colours of the distant hills and the coarse moorland grass. White clouds drifted in a pale blue sky and warm Pennine stone separated the fields, and it seemed that every brush stroke added interest and charm to the picture.

I was about to turn away when he said easily, 'You needn't go, I don't mind an audience.'

I paused uncertainly and he went on, 'What do you think of it?'

'It's very good.'

He turned round. I couldn't remember ever having seen him before, so I was surprised when he said, 'The last time I saw you you were lying in a heap on the floor at the engagement party.'

I could feel my face flaming with colour and with something like resentment I said, 'You were at my grandmother's that night, I don't remember.'

'Well of course not, I don't suppose you remember very much of that night. You're Jessica Mapleton's cousin.'

'Yes. Lisa Ralston.'

'I'm Desmond Colby. I'm a guest of the Templetons, that's how I happened to be at the party.'

'I see. Didn't you have an exhibition in London a little while back? I know I've heard of you.'

He laughed. 'You obviously didn't go to my exhibition.'

'I'm afraid not.'

'Oh well, we artists are wrapped up in ourselves, you in your piano and me in my painting. I don't suppose I'd have taken the trouble to go to one of your concerts.'

I stared at him in surprise, then he laughed and I laughed with him, the first time I had laughed for what seemed like an age.

'That's better,' he said brightly. 'You look much prettier when you laugh. What have you done to your hair? It looked much nicer the last time I saw you.'

'My grandmother prefers it like this.'

'So that she can turn you into an old maid like that daughter, Edwina.'

'Now you're being impertinent,' I snapped back.

'And now you're coming to life. And how long do you intend to stay here, Lisa?'

'I don't know, I have no plans at the moment.'

'And your music?'

I didn't think it was any of his business, but his eyes were kind, he was not trying to annoy me.

'You know what happened so I can only tell you I have no idea what I shall do now. As I feel at the moment I hate the piano, I don't think I shall ever play again.'

'Don't you think that's rather foolish? All that hard work and dedication should be a monument to the Marcello family, not a betrayal.'

His candour both antagonized and attracted me and when I didn't speak he turned away and went on with his painting. I couldn't guess his age, but he was attractive. He had intensely blue eyes under hair as fair as my own which gave him a Scandinavian air, and his hands were graceful and as delicate as his brush strokes.

I was content to watch him paint, and we were silent so long I looked up in surprise when he said, 'You're not in the least like your cousin but your mothers were sisters, I believe?'

'Yes. My mother had four sisters.'

210

'Didn't your grandparents live where the Templetons live now?'

'Yes.'

'I've heard all about it, and it was all a very long time ago. It's time you put it all behind you, Lisa.'

'I have, I hardly ever think about it now. How is it you're so knowledgeable about my family when you don't even live here?'

'Surely you must know that scandal never loses anything in the country. Besides it was bound to get mulled over when the Templetons bought the house. I must say you look too sweet and wholesome ever to be a femme fatale. Jessica looks more suited to the part.'

'Don't you like Jessica?'

'She's very beautiful, and an artist has a good eye for beauty, but then you too could be very beautiful. You have the right bone structure for beauty, you have poise and if you didn't adopt that ridiculous hairstyle and those silly glasses you'd be the beautiful cool English rose all artists want to paint.'

I wanted to be annoyed by his candour but I knew he would have been quite indifferent. Changing the subject I said, 'I was sorry to spoil Jessica's engagement party, it was dreadful of me.'

'I shouldn't worry about that, the Jessicas of this world can rise above anything.'

'You seem to know Jessica remarkably well.'

'I know her hardly at all, but I have great intuition.'

'I've known for years that one day she would marry Alexander.'

'And he never wished to escape?'

'Why should he if they were in love?'

'Why indeed?'

'You don't sound very certain about their engagement.'

'My dear girl, I'm only an onlooker. I see Jessica as a young woman who thinks she knows what she wants and a young man who has been acquired for her, just like everything else she's ever wanted.'

'Alexander is not the sort of man to be bought, he has far too much character.'

'I didn't say he'd been bought, my dear, I said acquired. They've been thrown together, he's been planned for. At the moment he sees her beauty, I doubt if he's ever discovered her soul. And it seems to me, young lady, that you were mighty quick to leap to his defence.'

'I like Alexander. He was sweet and kind to me when I needed somebody, I want him to be happy.'

'With Jessica'

'Of course, if he loves her.'

'Then I stand corrected, my dear Miss Ralston. Now what do you think of the finished picture?'

'It's beautiful. How do you know when it's finished?'

'I could go on, adding a bit here and a bit there, but I wouldn't improve it. Would you like to have it?'

'I'd love it, but I couldn't possibly take it.'

'Why ever not?'

'But you could sell it, probably for a great deal of money.'

'I know I could, but I'd like to give it to you. Frame it if you like it, if you don't, stick it at the back of a cupboard somewhere.'

'I shall do no such thing. I shall look for a frame tomorrow.'

He smiled and handed the picture over with the instruction that I hold it carefully until the paint had dried completely.

'It'll soon dry in this heat,' he said. 'The paint's acrylic so you needn't worry about it smudging after that.' He rose to his feet to collect his things and I saw that he was tall and broad shouldered.

We walked companionably back down the fell together and parted company at the stile.

I was so proud of my picture I went immediately to show Grandmother and Aunt Edwina, but Grandmother only said I should know better than talk to strangers on the fell and Aunt Edwina added that Mr Colby was reputed to be quite a man for the ladies and that he was divorced. His wife had been some sort of actress.

That put him quite out of the pale so far as Grand-

212

mother was concerned, and neither of them showed much interest in the picture.

CHAPTER 28

The following afternoon I drove into Kendal where I knew of an art shop who would frame my picture. When I handed it over the counter an earnest young man said in some awe, 'But this is lovely, an original! It's not often we get to frame an original, and never an original of Desmond Colby's.'

I chose the mount which I thought would do justice to the colours in the picture and a plain frame which did not detract from it, then I went to Madame Levison's studio.

She was just putting her key in the lock when I arrived and she turned to see who belonged to the hurrying footsteps, then her face was wreathed in smiles, before the tears came and she held me in her arms.

'Oh my dear, I'm so glad you've come, I haven't been able to get you out of my mind these last few days.'

I followed her up the stairs and into the familiar room.

'Now come and sit here near the window,' she said. 'I'll make tea and you can tell me all about everything.' She listened quietly and without interrupting until I had told her of that terrible morning when I had waited at the airport for the lover who was never coming back, and then said briskly, 'Is isn't the end of everything, Lisa, you still have your music.'

'At this moment I have no desire to play. It's as though my music only existed for Carlo and now that he's gone there's no point.'

'What nonsense, of course you'll play again. You've given your life to music, you don't know anything else, and presumably you need to earn a living. What else are you fit for?'

'Nothing, absolutely nothing.'

'Well then, you will have to go back to your piano.'

'But not yet Madame, I need to think about it. Too

much has happened, I need to be sure and there are so very many brilliant pupils.'

'Oh course there are brilliant people, the world is full of them, but that shouldn't stop you. You can't afford to forget music for months, years, and then think you can return to it . . . Wait a minute, I've got an idea – would you be willing to teach here while I'm away?'

'Why, where are you going?'

'I have to go into hospital. I've been ill on and off now for about three months and the specialist says I need an operation, a new heart valve or something. I've booked in at a private nursing home and when the job's been done there'll be a fairly long convalescence. I was going to ask a local piano teacher to take over but he'd poach my pupils, I'd probably never see them again. You could do it Lisa, I know you could.'

'How many pupils have you?'

'Nine. They come mornings and afternoons for four days. I never work Fridays, but you will please yourself of course.'

'Are they all very good?'

'Two of them are as good as you were, the other seven are mediocre. When I say mediocre they could make their living playing the piano, but not on the concert platform.'

'I'd like to try, Madame. It seems like the perfect answer to all my problems at the moment.'

'What about your grandmother, would she object?'

'I am over twenty-one, I should be able to do what I like.'

'Edwina is over forty-one and she's never been able to do what she liked.'

'I know, I don't want to get like Aunt Edwina.'

'I can take it you'll take over then, Lisa. I'm due to go into hospital in ten days. Come here on the Monday morning, I'll give you a key to the studio and tell you where to find everything.'

'Everything' consisted of tea, sugar and milk. There was music in the stool but the pupils would bring their own, and Mrs O'Flynn came in twice a week in the evenings to clean. Mary Prothero was indolent and I would have to be stern with her. Timothy Gray was the most talented but he always made an excuse to go early because he had to meet his younger sister after school. She didn't always believe that story.

As I drove home my head was spinning with instructions but there was a new interest in my life. Slowly but surely my heart was coming alive again, and after I had put the car away I snatched the pins out of my hair and allowed it to flow free. It was a strangely childish and rebellious gesture but it heralded in the new Lisa Ralston I was determined to be.

I was surprised to find Alexander walking across the lawn to meet me with a welcoming smile.

'I saw your car turn in at the gate,' he said, 'do you feel like a walk? I'm leaving in the morning, you know.'

'Yes, I know. Where in the Middle East are you heading for this time?'

'Iraq. Are you feeling better, Lisa?'

'Yes thank you, Alexander. I'm sorry I messed up your engagement party.'

'Well of course you didn't, and even if you had what does it matter? Are you ready to talk about it?'

'I think so. But perhaps you have to be a musician to understand.'

'No, Lisa, you just have to be a human being. You can talk to me, you know, you did before.'

So we strolled in the garden and then sat in the summer house while I talked about the Marcellos. I told him all about the triumph they had experienced on their tour of Europe, and the welcome the conservatoire had planned for them. I described Signor Marcello with his great presence and his vanities, and Signora Marcello watching over her family like a fussy hen. I told him about Bella with her shy doe eyes and her longing to be a great concert pianist, and a little about Carlo and his all-absorbing talent. I did not tell him that Carlo had loved me and that he was returning home with an engagement ring for me, and afterwards I couldn't think why I had been reluctant to give him this piece of information.

216

He listened without interrupting as I went on to describe those young men and women I had laughed with, played with and listened to, and I was reminded of that other time when he had listened to me just as sympathetically by the lake.

He too must have been thinking of that moment because he said gently, 'Do you remember the flamingoes at Nakuru, Lisa, what a beautiful sight they were?'

'Yes, I don't think I shall ever forget them. Have you and Jessica decided when you are getting married?'

'Not definitely. This job will last for about three years, after that who knows where I shall be sent. I'm hoping for leave in December, so we will probably make up our minds then.'

'Is your father pleased about your engagement?'

'They haven't met, but I'm sure he will be. He's always promising he'll put down roots in England but somehow or other he never does, he's in Nepal at the moment. We're good friends now. He really is a remarkable man, I regret all those years when we never really knew each other, the resentment was all on my side and he couldn't live with it.'

'Where do you intend to live when you're married?'

'Wherever my work is, but I do have a delightful manor house in Dorset which will be wonderful to return to whenever we come to England.'

'Your father's house.'

'Well, he's given it to me, he says I'll probably spend more time there. Actually it's been in our family for generations. It's beautiful, Lisa, the gardens go right down to the sea and it's built from that soft mellow stone one rarely sees in the north. In the autumn the virginia creeper that covers the front glows with red leaves and from the gardens there's a little rugged path that climbs right down to the beach.'

'It sounds lovely, Alexander.'

'Everybody calls me Alex, but you never have.'

'No.'

'What are you going to do with your life in the immediate future Lisa, or is it too soon to ask?'

So I told him about Madame Levison and he frowned a little. 'Can you really bear to teach others when you had such dreams for yourself?'

'I'm marking time, Alexander. Perhaps when you see me again I shall know what I want from life.'

'I would have liked to hear you play. One day you will play for me.'

'One day.'

I felt he would like to have said more. He was looking at me so seriously I felt suddenly awkward and strangely shy, then with a sudden bright smile he said, 'Well, this won't do my packing. If I get leave over Christmas I hope to see you here.'

'Are you leaving early in the morning?'

'Very early. I doubt if you'll be up.'

'Is Jessica driving you to the station?'

'No. I have my own car here. I'm driving home to Dorset and flying from Heathrow on Sunday.'

With mention of Heathrow my heart lurched painfully and the trauma of that morning when I waited for Carlo came flooding back to me and my eyes filled with unwelcome tears.

He leaned forward and placed both his hands over mine. 'I know, Lisa, it hurts like the very devil, but believe me each day the hurt will be less and less. I'm not saying you will ever forget, just as you never forgot that other tragedy in your life, but memories become dim with the years. Grief is the price of love, my dear.'

'Love!' I echoed stupidly.

'Yes, of course. It was more than the loss of friends that drove you here.'

'Oh Alexander, you always understood better than anyone. But I'm not sure any more. I don't seem to be able to remember his face, his voice, I only remember his music. I'm coming alive too soon, perhaps I didn't love him enough, perhaps I never really knew him, perhaps I fell in love with love.'

He didn't speak. Instead he drew me to my feet and for a brief moment held me in his arms. That was the

218

moment the door to the summer house opened suddenly and Jessica stood there, her face flushed with anger.

'How terribly touching,' she snapped sarcastically, then without another word she threw her tennis racket on to the floor and ran to the house.

'Don't worry, Lisa,' Alexander said with a wry smile, 'I'll talk to Jessica, make her see that this is nothing.'

Nothing! Why did the word hurt so much, why did his arms around me mean so much? All my old resentment of Jessica washed over me. I should be mourning for Carlo, not aching uncertainly for Alexander, who was probably by this time consoling Jessica and telling her that he had felt sorry for me, that it had been pity which had made him reach out for me and hold me close.

It was at that moment that I knew with frightening certainty that I wanted Alexander, and with all my heart I hated Jessica because he was hers.

I stood forlornly looking towards the fells but I saw nothing of the scene before me. Instead I was a little girl again, listening to Aunt Georgina telling me how wonderful it would be if Jessica and Alexander fell in love, and my hatred and anger now were as fierce and potent as on that morning.

That was when I began to ask myself what sort of a woman was I, that I could lose one man so tragically only days before I began to agonize over another. Alexander loved Jessica and I was a fool to think anything could change.

CHAPTER 29

Madame Levison went into the nursing home to have her operation and I started work in her studio teaching her string of pupils. I had not expected to enjoy the experience, but there I was wrong.

Margot Lewisham and Andrew Foulkes were brilliant and would no doubt go far. The others were good but not exceptional and three of them told me that they hoped to teach music rather than perform themselves.

When I went to see Madame on the Friday afternoon I found her propped up against her pillows looking pale but comfortable. The operation was to take place the following Monday and her doctor had assured her there was nothing to worry about. We talked about her pupils.

'Andrew's a charming boy,' she enthused so that I became instantly aware that he was probably her favourite.

'I have great hopes for him, but what makes him so nice is that quite apart from his music he's a normal boy with all sorts of interests. He collects stamps. His father started him off when he was three and he tells me he's now got quite a valuable collection. When he knows you better he'll badger you to pass on any foreign stamps you get.'

'I'll remember that. And Margot, she's brilliant too?'

'I know. Both her parents are dead and she lives with an unmarried aunt. The aunt's all right, but she has a heart condition and neither of them has much of a social life. I imagine the piano is all Margot has, and although I'm delighted she's coming on so well, sometimes children like that crack up. She's a girl who should be at Chethams or some other conservatoire like Marcello's where she would meet people.'

'Have you mentioned this to her aunt?'

'I have, but she didn't take to the idea. I'd be robbing myself, of course, but one has to think of the girl.'

'One or two of the others have told me they want to teach music in some school or other. I'm not quite sure what to make of Alison.'

She laughed. 'Encourage Alison, Lisa. She doesn't practise nearly enough and I can't remember how many excuses I've had to listen to, but she's John Barton's daughter and John Barton is a great patron of the arts, from Carlisle down to Preston. Concerts, amateur dramatics, choirs, he's generous with his money and he doesn't mind the time and trouble that go into it. Without people like him music in the north would suffer considerably.'

'I didn't know, but is he aware that his daughter isn't all that brilliant?'

'I'm sure he is, but she's good enough to entertain his guests, and the fact that she's one of my pupils is a bit of a feather in his cap. He's a dilettante, my dear, but he's a very likeable man and does more good than harm. His wife's one of these pretty fussy women who likes large houseparties and is always in the forefront of every good cause and charity in the area.'

'What are their ambitions for Alison?'

'I doubt if they have any serious ambitions for her. They're very wealthy so she doesn't have to think about a job, and believe me a job is the last thing Alison thinks about. They have a beautiful home, Maxton Hall, just south of Carlisle. In the summer it's opened up as a show place, they use the grounds for agricultural shows, and in the winter the local Hunt Ball is always held there. I get an invitation to it every year but I've never yet accepted. You on the other hand must certainly accept.'

'What makes you think she'll invite me?'

'Oh she will. I've told her a little of your history, she'll dine out on it, I feel sure. My advice to you, my dear girl, is to set your stall out, get your hair done and buy some pretty clothes. Hang your grandmother.'

Jessica came every weekend to Grandmother's but we saw very little of her. She was always at the Templetons' but I did manage to ask her to save me the stamps off Alexander's letters and I saved others I received from Aunt Georgina in Kenya.

Jessica was working during the week in her father's office, but she seemed to have so much time off even Grandmother said, 'What do you suppose she does in that office? She's hardly ever there.'

Aunt Edwina said, 'I don't suppose the other girls in the office are too pleased about it.'

When I asked Jessica what she did there she shrugged. 'I'm Daddy's personal assistant, I see to his mail and answer his telephone. After all I don't have to work, Mummy'd rather I didn't.'

'What would you do if you didn't work?'

'There's a lot I could do, at the moment it suits me just to go to the office. When Alex and I get married we'll be living abroad anyway.'

'Will you like living in Dorset when you're in England?'

She stared at me in some surprise. 'Dorset! I shan't be living in Dorset, besides it's Alex's father's house and we're not living with him.'

'I understood it was Alexander's house now.'

'Really. Oh well, even if it is I don't want to live in Dorset. I wouldn't know a soul. We'll probably sell it and buy something near London or even around here where I know everybody.'

'Has Alexander said if he will get leave at Christmas?'

'He must. Christmas will be awful if he doesn't.'

In mid November we got our first snow of the winter and instead of driving into Kendal I took the local bus. At the stop near the Templetons' house I was surprised to see a long low car pulling out of their drive driven by Desmond Colby. He had been with the Templetons several months and yet it was some time since I had encountered him sitting with his paint box up on the fell.

He was the first person I met when I stepped off the bus and he greeted me cheerfully, taking my elbow in a friendly grip as we walked along the icy pavement.

'Come and have a coffee,' he said, smiling. 'It'll warm you up.'

It was Friday morning and I had shopping to do before

222

going to see Madame Levison at her bungalow on the outskirts of the town. Her doctors had prescribed a long winter's cruise to somewhere warm but she said she preferred to wait until Easter at least. In the meantime I did her shopping and when I explained all this to Desmond Colby he merely said, 'There's oceans of time. You do your shopping and then I'll drive you where you want to go. My time's my own.'

'What are you doing in Kendal on a morning like this?'

'Shopping for holiday gear although I doubt if I'll find much in Kendal.'

'What sort of holiday gear?'

'For somewhere a little warmer than this, I hope. I have some friends with a yacht at San Tropez, I've been invited to join them on a cruise just before Christmas.'

'How wonderful. Where will you cruise to?'

'Alexandria perhaps, the Greek islands, the choice is endless. Would you like to come?'

Ignoring the question I said, 'I haven't seen you painting on the fell for some time.'

'No. I'm not one for winter scenery, I like the south. Bougainvillaea tumbling over terracotta stone, warm southern seas and white stucco houses set against a blue sky.'

'But that picture you did of the fells was very beautiful.'

'It wasn't bad, but it wasn't really my scenery. I'm known for my paintings of the Med and the tropics.'

'Your painting looks very well on my bedroom wall. I had it mounted and framed.'

'Good for you.'

'We'll try the pub for coffee,' he said easily, confident that I would agree to join him.

'So you're teaching music,' he said when we were settled at a table near the window. 'Have you given up all ideas of the concert platform?'

'Yes, for the time being,' I said shortly. 'How did you know I was teaching?'

'Your cousin Jessica informed me.'

'I see.'

'Why don't you come along with her to the Templetons'

223

some weekend? It's open house and there's always some-thing going on there.'

'I don't know the Templetons.'

'They're a decent hospitable lot, it can't be much fun for you living at your grandmother's.'

'I'm quite happy, thank you.'

'Now don't be prickly, I'm not trying to be condescend-ing. Jessica says you're a loner. Maybe she doesn't know much about you.'

'No, she doesn't.'

'Tell me something. Is this fiancé of hers coming home for Christmas?'

'I believe he's hoping to, I don't think she's heard anything definite. Why do you ask?'

'She's been invited to join us on this cruise. I doubt if she'll hesitate for much longer.'

'But of course she won't go if Alexander's coming home.'

He looked at me with a cynical smile on his attractive face and then nonchalantly helped me to another cup of coffee.

'You wouldn't go if Alexander was coming home, my dear, you wouldn't go if he wasn't, but you are not Jessica. That young lady sees life slipping past her and although she might think she loves that young man of hers, she loves life and its variety more.'

He lingered on while I did Madame Levison's shopping, much to my annoyance, and seemed to have little incentive to shop for himself. When I reminded him that he was supposed to be looking for summer clothing he merely smiled.

'There won't be any in Kendal, Lisa, it was silly to think there might be. I'll shop around in Manchester or London. I might even decide to wait until we get to San Tropez.'

'That seems the most sensible thing to me.'

'It does, doesn't it? Anything I buy there will be geared for their climate. What time do you go to this woman with her shopping?'

'Immediately after lunch. She's just out of hospital so I don't invite myself for lunch.'

'In that case we'll lunch at a nice little inn I know just out of town.'

'I really don't want to be late arriving at Madame Levison's.'

'You won't be. Why on earth does she call herself Madame?'

'She's a musician, a professional woman, it sounds better.'

'Do you call yourself Madame Ralston now that you've taken on her pupils?'

'Of course not.'

'What's the difference?'

'Age, I think. She's old enough to be my grandmother, in fact she went to school with my grandmother.'

'You're a glutton for punishment, Lisa.'

Out of town the roads were icy and I was surprised when he took a narrow side road towards the hills.

'Don't be afraid,' he grinned, 'I'm a very responsible driver.'

'It would have been more responsible to keep to the main road.'

'Well, it isn't far. Look, you can see it from here, that long low white building at the bend in the road.'

We were the only people dining at the inn but the food lived up to its reputation. After we had eaten we took our coffee into the lounge and sat in front of a roaring fire with the reflection from the leaping flames falling on brass and copper and old English prints.

He was a good conversationalist and we talked about all sorts of things from art and music to my travels in Italy and his in remote corners of the world.

I was staring into the fire when he said softly, 'You know, Lisa, you're a good person to be with. You have great poise, great self-control.'

I could feel my face blushing stupidly, and I was wishing with all my heart that I could find the gay rejoinder and when I couldn't I looked at my watch quickly, and he laughed.

225

'Time to go, is it? Come along, I'll drive you and sit in the car until you've finished your conversation.'

'I can't leave you sitting in the car. Really you've been very kind but I can quite easily go home on the bus, and she will expect me to stay a little while.'

'No problem, like I said my time is my own.'

Madame Levison insisted that I invite him into her bungalow and I was instantly aware that they were sizing each other up like two cats, and later when he went out to the car after saying goodbye and I was preparing to follow him she whispered, 'He's charming, Lisa, charming and dangerous.'

'Dangerous?'

'Easy with women, and I would imagine there have been a great many. I hope you're not falling in love with him.'

'Really, Madame, I hardly know him, and he's not at all the sort of man I would ever fall in love with. I must go, he'll be sure we're discussing him.'

'Oh I very much think that man is accustomed to being discussed.'

'He's been very kind, and very much a gentleman.'

'I'm sure he has. Worldliness and charm are his stock in trade. He has a reputation for being something of a charmer.'

'How do you know so much about him?'

'I only know what I've read in the papers. His wife was an actress, Pamela Roxburgh, there was all sorts of a scandal when their marriage ended.'

I took my leave of her and she was still frowning. Sleet was falling again as we made our way back and his driving needed all his attention. It was only when he stopped the car at the end of the drive that he said with a cynical smile, 'Well, did you believe her?'

'I beg your pardon?'

'Wasn't your friend and teacher warning you against me? If so there was no need. I have no ulterior designs on you, Lisa, I find you wholesome and charming and when you close the door I doubt if you'll spare me a second thought.'

'Thank you for the lunch and for bringing me home. I've spent a very enjoyable day.'

He threw back his head and laughed, then before I could gather my parcels together and get out of the car, he leaned forward and placing his hands on each side of my face he kissed me warmly on the mouth.

As I stepped out I was annoyed to see Margery Harris watching us from the gate, her face wreathed in smiles, her eyes bright with curiosity.

'Hello, Margery,' I said briefly, and hurried up the drive. When I let myself into the house she was standing where I had left her, still watching me.

CHAPTER 30

I always knew when Jessica received a letter from Alexander because she made a point of giving me the stamp for Andrew. When Aunt Edwina asked if he was coming home for Christmas she shrugged, saying she hadn't yet heard, and I waited for a mention of the cruise.

It came during a weekend when her parents were at the Maples. We were just finishing dinner when Aunt Cecily, who I feel had been well primed, said easily, 'Have you decided what to do about the cruise, darling? It doesn't look as if Alex will be home for Christmas.'

Jessica's expression was doubtful and a little sulky. 'It really is too bad of him, Mummy, he could at least write saying yes or no.'

'Perhaps he's still trying, darling. But the Templetons will be wanting an answer from you.'

'If Alex isn't coming I want to go with them. After all, what will there be here if they're all away?'

Aunt Edwina was looking from one to the other curiously but as yet Grandmother hadn't shown any interest, so Aunt Cecily tried another approach.

'Where exactly is the cruise taking you, Jessica?' she asked innocently.

'They haven't exactly decided, but probably Alexandria and the Greek islands.'

At last Grandmother woke up. 'Cruise! What cruise?' she demanded.

'It's something the Templetons are doing over Christmas, Mother, and Jessica has been invited.'

'But of course she can't go. Jessica's an engaged woman and Alexander will be coming home.'

'That's the trouble, Mother, we don't know that he *is* coming home, and if he isn't it's such a wonderful opportunity for Jessica to be with nice people visiting lovely places.'

'Well I think it's quite out of the question. Hobnobbing with young men, and your fiancé miles away.'

'Oh Granny, don't be silly. The Templeton boys are fourteen and fifteen. I'll be company for Sally, that's why they've invited me.'

'Well you certainly don't go with my approval. I'm surprised at you, Cecily, you should be encouraging her to think about her approaching marriage instead of going off cruising. Suppose Alexander gets leave at the last minute, what will you do then?'

'Then I won't go, Granny. The Templetons will understand.'

'Really, Mother,' Aunt Cecily said reasonably, 'all this is a storm in a teacup. Jessica isn't wanting to do anything foolish or wild but she does have a life to live quite apart from Alex. I don't think we should begrudge her this last little chance to see something of the world. After all she'll probably be miles from any sort of social life when she and Alex are married.'

'She'll have plenty of chances to see the world with her husband. She's wanted him long enough and if she doesn't want to lose him she should be patient and wait for him coming home. You're not saying very much, Neville, don't you agree with me?'

'John Templeton's mentioned this cruise to me several times and he's asked my permission to include Jessica. Personally I don't see anything wrong in it if Alex isn't coming home.'

Grandmother set her lips in a firm hard line, and next moment she had risen from the table and we all trooped after her straight uncompromising back.

As we crossed the hall Jessica whispered, 'I'm going to a party at the Templetons' tomorrow night, it's Sally's nineteenth birthday. Will you lend me your monkey's eye? It will go beautifully with my new dress.'

'Of course.'

'I'll show it to you if you'd like to come up to my room.'

I followed her up the stairs and into her room where the new gown was spread across her bed. It was a long chiffon creation in shades ranging from palest yellow to deep russet and when Jessica held it in front of her and started to move about the room the long draped skirt seemed to have a life of its own. It was a beautiful exotic gown and it needed something different to do it justice. My monkey's eye was a perfect choice, but as I handed it to Jessica and she laid it against the material she merely said, 'It's the only thing I could think of. Topazes would have been perfect but this will do. I'll let you have it back but you won't mind if I wear it whenever I wear the gown, will you?'

I was about to leave the room when I said innocently enough, 'I got a lift into Kendal the other day with Desmond Colby. He told me about the cruise.'

I saw the colour flood her face before she grabbed hold of my arm, pulling me back into the room and hurriedly closing the door.

'For heaven's sake don't mention it to Grandmother. How do you know Desmond anyway?'

'I saw him painting on the fell one day, he told me he was a guest at the Templetons.'

'He's very attractive but there's absolutely nothing going on between Desmond and me.'

'I didn't think there was.'

'Not that he wouldn't like there to be, he's quite a man for the ladies. I wouldn't have thought he was your type, Lisa.'

'No, he isn't.'

'You still haven't forgiven me for hurting those hands, have you? It's not because of that that you've changed your mind about your music?'

'No, Jessica, they healed a long time ago. It's something else entirely.'

'Would you like to be my bridesmaid when I marry Alex?'

My eyes opened wide and in some doubt I said, 'I'm surprised you've asked me, Jessica. We've never been great friends.'

'Well, you are my cousin. I can't ask Angela, I don't

want a matron of honour. I thought perhaps you and Sally Templeton.'

'Thank you, Jessica, I would like to be your bridesmaid.'

'I don't want you with your hair up and spectacles.'

'I'll try not to let you down.'

That was the last conversation I had with her before she departed with the Templetons ten days before Christmas. Grandmother was scandalized and Aunt Edwina noncommittal, while her parents saw her off in a flurry of good wishes and laughter. Her last words to me were, 'If you want your monkey's eye it's in the top drawer of my dressing table. Daddy bought me a topaz necklace for Christmas which looks absolutely divine, but thanks for the loan of it anyway.'

Grandmother's disapproval was so evident she hadn't even bothered to go to the front door, and Uncle Neville was decidedly put out. I heard him say to Aunt Cecily, 'After all John Templeton is one of my clients, it wouldn't have done the old girl any harm to be civil to him.'

'She'll get over it, darling,' Aunt Cecily replied soothingly. 'You know what Mother's like. It's my guess she's annoyed at not having Jessica around over Christmas, it's going to be pretty boring anyway.'

They weren't the only ones not looking forward to Christmas. Aunt Claudia and Uncle Henry arrived over the weekend and Angela and her husband came two days later, a very pregnant Angela and an over-caring husband.

The talk was all of babies and nursing homes until I felt I would scream if it went on much longer, and I was glad when Monday came and I set off for Kendal in cold driving rain.

I was surprised when Alison Barton arrived in the company of her mother and everything Madame Levison had said about her came immediately to mind. She was small and dainty, a blonde fussy woman wearing high-heeled suede boots and a pale cream mink coat. She came carrying an enormous bunch of chrysanthemums and holly which she said were to brighten up the studio, and embarrassed me next by handing me an expensively wrapped present which I was told I must not open until Christmas morning.

'Really, Mrs Barton,' I admonished her, 'this is very kind of you but there is no need. My piano lessons are very expensive.'

'I insist, my dear, and I want to ask a favour of you.'

I waited in silence for what came next.

'On the Wednesday before Christmas we are having friends in for supper. About twenty of them, actually all very old friends, and all of them devoted to music. My husband has asked if you will join us and perhaps play for us after supper. Alison says you play beautifully.'

When I still hesitated she hastened to say, 'You needn't worry about the journey, my dear, we have friends who can pick you up. Don't you live at that very nice house called the Maples? I always remember it because there isn't a maple in sight.'

I smiled, amused that one of Grandmother's foibles had been found wanting, and I warmed to Mrs Barton.

'Thank you, Mrs Barton, I shall be glad to come. What do I wear?'

'Oh, we dress up a bit, not ball gowns, but something quite dressy if you know what I mean.'

'Of course.'

When I told Madame Levison of the invitation she seemed well pleased.

'It's time you set your stall out, Lisa. Who knows, there might be one or two nice young men with money there.'

'I'm not looking for a nice young man with money.'

'I know, but your violinist has gone, my dear, and he is not coming back, and that other young man is engaged to Jessica – much good may she do him.'

I could never hope to deceive her, she was far too astute, but I began to look forward to Wednesday evening.

When I told them at home, Aunt Edwina said doubtfully, 'The roads could be bad just before Christmas, Lisa. I should take a taxi instead of driving yourself.'

'Friends of the Bartons are calling for me, Aunt Edwina.'

'I see. What will you wear?'

'My evening skirt and sweater. I bought them in London thinking I was going with the orchestra to Vienna, and haven't worn them.'

'I hope they're not too flamboyant,' Grandmother said caustically. 'I didn't approve of that gown Jessica was wearing, it was far too old for her.'

'Oh Mother,' Aunt Edwina protested, 'Jessica's not a little girl any more. Next year at this time she'll be a married woman.'

'Not the way she's behaving, she won't. Not if Alexander Hamilton finds out where she's spending Christmas.'

'Alex won't mind. If he can't be here then he shouldn't begrudge her spending Christmas with her friends.'

I left them arguing and went upstairs to sort out the things I would need for Wednesday evening. I fould gold kid shoes and evening bag, then I took the long skirt still wrapped in tissue out of the wardrobe. It was a beautiful skirt which fell in long sweeping folds to the floor. Made in heavy black and gold brocade, the pattern was exotic, almost Mexican in its design. With it I intended to wear a black soft wool sweater with a low neck and long sleeves, entirely plain so that it did not detract from the glamour of the skirt.

I tried them on, twisting this way and that before the mirror, and the heavy skirt moved gracefully with every turn of my body. The sweater needed jewellery and I thought immediately of my monkey's eye, the only thing I owned that would do justice to it.

Jessica had told me where I could find it and I went immediately to her bedroom. The drawer was untidy. I had to rummage underneath a pile of silk scarves and several rows of beads before I came across the box. When I took it out I noticed that it had been lying on an envelope addressed to Jessica at her father's house in Alexander's familiar handwriting. Curiously I took it into my hands and looked at the postmark, December first, but the envelope was empty and I wondered why she hadn't thought to give me the stamp for Andrew.

I smoothed the envelope out against my knee before

putting it back in the drawer but the drawer wouldn't close properly and I groped at the back to find out what was causing the obstruction.

It was a tight ball of crumpled paper and as I took it out to straighten it once again I was staring at Alexander's writing.

It began 'Darling Jessica', and every instinct told me I shouldn't read it but there were too many questions hammering in my head. Why had Jessica screwed Alexander's letter into a ball and thrust it at the back of a drawer, and why was I suddenly so angry that my hands were shaking?

In the first few lines I learned that Alexander was coming home for Christmas and that he was longing to see her. After spending a few days with his father he would be with her on Christmas Eve. Jessica had set out on her cruise knowing that Alexander was coming home and I was filled with such deep anger I flung the letter back into the drawer and slammed it shut.

Why hadn't she thrown the letter away instead of cramming it into a drawer here at Grandmother's? Then a picture began to form in my mind of Jessica receiving Alexander's letter just as she was leaving her home to come here for the weekend. She would put it in her handbag, forget about it for a time, then perhaps open it later when she returned from the Templetons'. I could feel her frustration, even her anger that her plans were in jeopardy and might have to be altered. It was her anger that had made her screw the letter into a ball and fling it to the back of the drawer.

Grandmother didn't approve of my evening attire or that I wore my hair long on to my shoulders. She said I looked like every other young woman where before I had looked classy and different. I took my glasses off when I went out to meet the people who had called for me, and even this simple act afforded me a pleasure quite out of proportion.

The Bartons made me very welcome, their friends were charming and I had not been long in their home before I realized that these were people intent on acquiring culture, who had never been brought up to it. On the walls were valuable paintings which Mr Barton showed to me proudly, and in the music room stood a Steinway every bit as grand as that at the conservatoire.

'Alison is a very lucky girl to have such a beautiful instrument to practise on,' I couldn't resist saying.

'Oh, she doesn't practise on this one,' he said quickly, 'this is my pride and joy, in fact it's only been played once when we entertained a pianist from America. Alison could never do it justice. I'm a dabbler, you know. I don't perform myself, I'm a hanger-on, a listener. I've made money quickly. I'm good at that but I'm a self-educated man. I've studied music, literature and art since I acquired money, and I'm willing to make such things available to as many people as possible by giving freely if that will help.'

'I find that very generous, Mr Barton.'

'It's my pleasure. They've recently made me a patron of the Musical Society for the area, and I'm the chairman or president of several societies. All that is very worthwhile to me, I only wish Alison had the right sort of dedication. What do you think of her, Miss Ralston?'

'She is competent, Mr Barton.'

'Only competent?'

'Good enough to entertain your guests, Mr Barton. But were you expecting her to make a career of playing the piano?'

'My daughter doesn't need a career, I just hoped she would want it.'

'Perhaps she is confused between the ballet lessons, the piano lessons, her riding and her tennis coaching. With me there was nothing outside my music.'

He stared at me, his face colouring slightly. 'You're right of course, Miss Ralston. When I was Alison's age I was just a kid from the wrong side of the town. My father was a quarryman. I won a scholarship for the local grammar school but my folks couldn't afford to let me go so I went to the local council school instead. I went into scrap metal with an old fellow and we prospered – God

235

how we prospered – then when old Jack died I got the business.

'I've got this house and a boat down at Glasson. I can afford to give my daughter all the advantages I never had, and you can't really blame me for wanting the best for her, can you?'

'Well of course not, Mr Barton, it's natural that you should, but where her music is concerned don't expect too much. It has to compete with too many other things.'

He grinned, and I realized that I liked him, there was something wholesome and honest about him and I found myself watching his delight in showing his guests a new painting or a new piece of porcelain. There were beautiful ornaments and pictures in Grandmother's house, bought because they had been expensive, but none of my family could have told any of our guests anything of the people who had painted or fashioned them. It was enough for Grandmother that they were there.

Mrs Barton fluttered round her guests in a pale pink chiffon gown that was really too young for her, but she was in her element encouraging us to partake of the mountain of food they had provided.

After dinner I was invited to play, and I decided there and then that it must not be too classical.

The piano was a beautiful instrument and I soon became completely engrossed as my hands performed Chopin's exquisite melodies. After the polite applause which followed I played modern tunes by Gershwin and Jerome Kern, and here I knew immediately I was playing at their level.

I stayed at the piano for two hours while over and over again they asked me to play favourite pieces of music, and when finally I lifted my fingers from the keys they were so appreciative it became embarrassing.

As we left the house around two o'clock Mrs Barton pressed two tickets into my hands. 'They're for the Hunt Ball on Boxing Day, dear, please do come and bring a friend. I'm sure you must know one or two young men in the area.'

When I seemed doubtful she said hurriedly, 'Come

236

alone if you don't want an escort, there's always enough men and more. John loves to have them here, and it's usually an evening to remember.'

I drove into Kendal to see Madame Levison. She was very interested in all I had to tell her about my evening at the Bartons' and I was relieved to see her looking so much better, and looking forward to her cruise holiday.

I told her about Alexander's letter and Jessica's perfidy, and when the tale was told she snapped angrily, 'I'm not surprised, Lisa, after all you've told me about her, but what has all this to do with you? I'll tell you what will happen, the family will close ranks to protect that girl, and Alexander will never know the truth. In the summer he'll marry her and they'll both be out of your life, thank goodness.'

When I didn't speak she said sternly, 'I hope you are not going to tell him the truth, Lisa. What good would that do?'

'I'm not going to do anything, but I don't know how I'm going to be able to stand it.'

'You love him, don't you?'

'I don't want to love him.'

'But my dear girl, last year at this time you were in love with Carlo.'

'I was in love with love, with his music, our music, I was in love with a world unlike any other I'd known. It was all so gay and carefree, I had my music and I had Carlo, it was a beautiful dream and now there are times when I can't even remember what it was like.'

'What makes Alexander so different, why is he suddenly so important?'

'Perhaps it was because he was the one who first made me see that in spite of tragedy life would go on and that love and beauty still existed when I thought they had gone for ever. He was the prince who kissed my sleeping heart awake. I wish I didn't love him, it hurts too much, but I can't help it.'

'My poor child. What can I say.'

'There's nothing to say. In the summer Alexander and

Jessica will be married and I shall be left to pick up the pieces of my life.'

CHAPTER 31

I decided I would attend the Hunt Ball at the Bartons' on Boxing Day. It was a desire to distance myself from the family, but more than that it was a rebellious need to emerge from the restrictions my grandmother had subjected me to and which I had seen fit to follow because she was giving me a home.

I spent money on a jade green chiffon ball gown that I knew she would disapprove of because it moulded my slender figure lovingly and enhanced the tender swell of my breasts. I spent an entire morning at the hairdresser's and I was determined I would not put my hair up again, consequently there were sulks and plain words spoken over the dinner table.

The family arrived on the morning of Christmas Eve and we were all drinking coffee in the morning room when Alexander arrived.

It was like watching a play where the actors betrayed their consternation too extravagantly, but this was for real. Neither Aunt Cecily's sophistication nor Uncle Neville's bonhomie could disguise their obvious dismay. Aunt Edwina looked on the verge of collapse and Grandmother sat stunned.

Aunt Georgina and Uncle Raymond knew very little about anything, and catching my eye across the room Uncle Raymond shrugged, wondering what all the fuss was about.

Only I greeted Alexander without surprise, then I sat back and waited for their defence of Jessica to start. She had not received his letter, the Christmas postal arrangements were blamed for that. She'd been so miserable they'd encouraged her to accept the Templetons' invitation, even when she hadn't really wanted to go.

Alexander was bemused. Too many people were trying to console him, promising him the best Christmas of his life, even if it was without Jessica's company, and Aunt Cecily surprised me by saying, 'Why not escort Lisa to the Hunt Ball? It will be a charming affair and Lisa doesn't have an escort.'

It was much later that evening when I heard Aunt Cecily and Uncle Neville arguing in the room next to mine. Uncle Neville didn't trouble to lower his voice, and Aunt Cecily had spent the entire evening extolling Jessica's worthiness to her daughter's obviously disappointed fiancé and its effect was catching up on her.

'Really, Neville,' she said caustically, 'you left everything to me. You spent all the evening talking horses with Raymond, both of you drinking Mother's best malt as though you hadn't a care in the world.'

'What was there to care about? If I'd fussed round him he'd have started to have doubts, as it is he'll know we've nothing to hide.'

'We haven't anything to hide. Jessica never got his letter, the poor girl would never have gone if she'd known Alex was coming.'

'I'm not sure it was a good idea getting him to escort Lisa to that affair on Boxing Day. In case you hadn't noticed, she's a very attractive girl.'

'Lisa!'

'Yes, Lisa. She looks entirely different with her hair down. Your mother's kept her under for years, now it looks as if the worm has turned. And Alexander is a man who could well notice.'

'The girl hasn't an idea how to dress. That thing she wore today was years old, and those glasses don't do anything for her. I know it's Mother's fault, she's done the same thing with Edwina.'

'Well, don't say I didn't warn you. I rather fancy that young woman might have a few surprises up her sleeve before too long.'

'What nonsense you talk, Neville, you're talking off drink. Anyway it's your turn to chat up Alex tomorrow, I've done my share.'

Only a few years before their words would have hurt and embarrassed me, now they merely annoyed me. I would show them, I would show all of them that I had the acumen to threaten their precious Jessica.

On Christmas Day Alexander was taken in hand by Uncle Neville and Aunt Cecily, immediately after breakfast. They walked to church together while the rest of us went by car, they took him out with them in the afternoon to visit an army of their friends, and arrived back just before dinner so that Grandmother grumbled and said it was inconsiderate.

Once, across the table, our eyes met and he smiled, the sweet slow smile that made my heart race madly, and later he asked me to play for them.

'Why not you, Alexander?' I said evenly, 'I remember you played with Jessica on my first visit here.'

'I get very little time for music these days, Lisa. In any case I'd rather listen to you.'

'Well, I'd rather play bridge,' Aunt Cecily said quickly. 'We have two fours and I badly need some practice.'

So we played bridge and I partnered Uncle Raymond and played very badly – largely his fault, I felt, since he made unrealistic bids which confused me utterly.

When I apologized for my bad play he grinned, saying, 'My fault, Lisa, I did it purposely to confuse Cecily.'

'Why is that?'

'She should have let you play for us, love. If Alexander can be stolen so easily he was never intended for Jessica anyway.'

I coloured and stared at him uneasily, but unperturbed he was shuffling the cards while our new partners joined us at the table.

I was helping to prepare our buffet lunch on the morning of Boxing Day when Aunt Edwina came to tell me there was a young man at the door with a large parcel for me.

I recognized him as the elder brother of one of Madame's pupils and he grinned at me cheerfully as he handed over his parcel.

'Madame Levison asked me if I'd drop this off,' he said with a smile, 'she's put a note inside.'

241

I caught sight of Aunt Edwina hovering at the back of the hall so I decided to take the parcel upstairs to open it in my room.

Inside were several thicknesses of pale blue tissue paper, and then I gave a little cry of pleasure. I was staring at a dark mink stole with pelts of luxurious thickness.

'Dear Lisa,' said the note, 'I want you to have this as a small token of my appreciation for looking after my pupils. I feel sure I would have lost one or two of them if it hadn't been for you.

'When I was your age I couldn't afford to buy mink, and now that I can afford it I am too old to do it justice. Beautiful furs are for beautiful young women and I know you will do it justice at the ball tonight. I shall be thinking about you. With love, Hermione Levison.'

I was so touched by her gift I sat on the edge of my bed, my eyes moist with tears, then I placed the stole in my wardrobe and returned to the kitchen.

Aunt Edwina eyed me curiously. 'Another present?' she asked brightly.

'Yes, Aunt Edwina, from Madame Levison.'

'How very kind. It was a very large parcel.'

'Yes, something to wear for the ball tonight.'

'Don't you want to tell me what it is?'

'You'll see it tonight, Aunt Edwina, I'd rather you saw me wearing it with my dress.'

The entire family were assembled in the drawing room when I entered it dressed for the ball that evening. I knew I had never looked more beautiful. The exquisite floating chiffon skirt shimmered delicately and the soft jade colour was so right with my blond fairness.

The richness of the stole around my shoulders hid the décolleté neckline and complemented my hair. I was not wearing glasses – I had no need for them at a ball – and I stood in the doorway enjoying their looks of stupefaction.

A few minutes later Alexander arrived wearing full evening dress and Uncle Raymond remarked lightly, 'Well, I'll say this for you, you'll be the handsomest couple at the ball tonight.'

Grandmother didn't say a word, but there was disapproval in every line on her face and Aunt Cecily gave her husband a look that spoke volumes.

Alexander smiled down at me. 'You're looking very lovely, Lisa. The car's at the front of the house if you're ready.'

It was heaven to be sitting in Alexander's fast car as it ate up the miles on the drive north. It was a bright moonlit night and the trees were etched in silver frost. I was very aware of the dark perfumed interior of the car, and beside me Alexander's dark, beautiful profile. Feeling my eyes on him he turned his head briefly and smiled, then he gave all his attention to the road.

As we arrived the car door was opened by a man in uniform who said he would park it for us so that we could go straight into the house. As we walked up the steps music poured out, and we could see people dancing.

I was conscious of his hand under my elbow and then the Bartons were coming to greet us and almost immediately I was dancing in Alexander's arms and I was utterly, ecstatically happy.

Extreme moments of happiness had been rare in my life. I had been happy with Carlo in Italy, but it had been a gay frothy happiness, and it had belonged to a girl who had died with Carlo on that mountainside in Switzerland. This was different. This happiness had a timeless permanence about it, even when in my innermost heart I knew there could be no permanence beyond this night.

Dancing with Alexander was a joy, and when our eyes met I knew that he was admiring me – but no more than any other man I danced with that evening.

It was after three when we left, and there were still revellers lingering in the ballroom or gathered in groups singing ageless hunting songs.

The parkland was a fairyland of frost, it silvered the trees and the shrubs and shimmered on the drive, then we were through the gates and out on to the road.

I sat with my eyes closed. My beautiful night was ending and I had no wish to see the countryside slipping away as fast as time. I had no light and airy conversation,

I simply wanted to sit quietly beside him in the darkness in moments I would hold close to my heart for ever.

Too soon however we were outside the front door and I opened my eyes to find Alexander looking at me. He smiled, saying, 'You've been asleep, Lisa,' and I did not contradict him.

'I'll come to the garage with you,' I said, 'I don't mind the walk back.'

I drove with him to the garage and waited while he locked the doors, then he took my arm and we walked back to the house. Inside the hall I thought desperately: This is the moment when he will thank me for a lovely evening and I will reciprocate politely and then it will be rest of our lives and he will belong to Jessica. Instead I was surprised when he said, 'Perhaps we should have a nightcap, Lisa, you look cold. What would you like?'

'Coffee, I think. I'll make it.'

'Then we'll drink it in the kitchen, I'll bring some brandy.'

It was warm in the kitchen and we sat across from each other at the table with mugs of rich coffee into which Alexander was pouring brandy. Like two old married people, I told myself wistfully, except that we would probably never sit like this again in companionable silence.

Alexander was the first to speak, and his question stunned me, setting my heart racing madly, and I could feel the warm blood rushing to my face and throat.

'Will you tell me something, Lisa: Why was everybody so amazed when I arrived here on Christmas Eve and you were not?'

I couldn't find the words to lie and I couldn't tell him the truth, and gently he asked the question again. 'You knew I was coming, Lisa, and I want you to tell me how you knew. Surely you can tell me the truth. I thought we were old friends, you and I.'

I remained silent, staring at the pattern on the table-cloth. He reached out and covered my hand with his, and his voice coaxed me gently. 'I want to know, Lisa, If you don't tell me I shall have to find out some other way.'

Hesitantly the words came in little above a whisper. 'I

found your letter to Jessica, probably the last you sent just before Christmas, and I read it.'

'You read it!'

'Yes. I was looking in a drawer in her bedroom for a pendant she'd borrowed and the drawer wouldn't close. I found this letter screwed into a ball and when I straightened it out I saw it was from you and the words simply leapt at me: "I'll be with you on Christmas Eve, darling, I'm longing to see you."'

'I see.'

'I hated myself for reading it, but then I just felt so terribly angry with her that I was glad I'd read it and I hated her even more than I'd hated her before.'

'You hate Jessica?'

'Perhaps hate is too strong a word, but we just don't get on, she's done things to me I could hate her for, and now I've done something to her, even if it was unintentional. What are you going to do?'

'I'm going to bed, Lisa, and tomorrow I'll think about what I'm going to do. I was glad you were here, you were the only honest person in that room. The others were too persuasive, too anxious to convince me that it was all a mistake.'

'People always forgive Jessica, Alexander, and you will too. She'll come back into your life beautiful and charming and you won't be able to stop yourself.'

He merely smiled, and holding out his hand he said, 'Come on, Lisa, it's very late.'

There was very little of the night left, and I was unable to sleep. For what seemed hours I tossed and turned, then unable to stand it any longer I got out of bed, bathed and dressed and set about laying the fire in the morning room. If I kept busy I didn't have as much time for thinking, and long before anybody else came down I had eaten mine and was walking the lane outside the house.

It was bitterly cold and I walked with my hands thrust deep inside my pockets, a soft woollen scarf covering my head. I felt that before the day was over it would be snowing, and I had learned to respect that wild north-easter blowing from the Pennines.

When I returned to the house they were all down for breakfast. Uncle Raymond said, 'Well, were you the belle of the ball then?'

I smiled and Alexander said gallantly, 'You should have asked me that question and I would have told you she was the most beautiful girl in the ballroom.'

'You're not wearing your glasses,' Grandmother said tartly.

'I'm not doing anything that needs them, Grandmother.'

'Nevertheless being without them won't do your eyes any good, and I don't like your hair like that, I prefer it up.'

'This is how I wore it in London and how I prefer it. Please, Grandmother, allow me to wear my hair how I like it.'

'Bravo,' said Uncle Raymond and received a sharp look from Aunt Georgina for his pains.

Grandmother sulked and the rest of them looked uncomfortable, then Uncle Neville said heartily, 'Well, Christmas is over for another year. When are you due back, Alex?'

'I've decided to return to Dorset today, I've seen very little of my father. I told him I hoped to have Jessica with me, naturally he wished to meet her.'

'Jessica will be devastated to have missed you, and the chance of meeting your father. Have you decided anything about your marriage? She's bound to be avid with questions when she gets back,' Aunt Cecily said easily.

They were all looking at him, but none of them more anxiously than I. What *would* Alexander do about his marriage? Could he still go through with it now?

He was staring down at his plate, idly moving a knife on the table, and when he looked up I knew he had made up his mind.

'Perhaps I could have a word with you in private,' he said evenly to Uncle Neville.

'Well of course, my boy, immediately after breakfast.'

A silence had descended on the table. My thoughts were racing. Was Alexander going to say he knew about the letter, and how he knew, in which case what would the rest of them think of me?

I watched them go into the morning room, and Aunt Cecily said irritably, 'What is there to talk about, for heaven's sake? We can't decide for Jessica.'

'She should never have gone on that cruise,' Grandmother said darkly.

'She would have been here if she'd known he was coming. It's not Jessica's fault. There was bound to be a problem with Alex in the Middle East, letters are a poor substitute.'

The Christmas tree looked somehow incongruous standing unlit in the hall and Grandmother must have thought so too.

'Surely we don't have to wait for Twelfth Night to take down that tree,' she remarked acidly. 'The floor's covered with needles.'

'Would you like me to take it down now?' I offered.

'Yes, I'd like the house to get back to normal.'

'I'll help you, Lisa,' Uncle Raymond said, 'I don't want you breaking your neck on the stepladder.'

From inside the morning room we could hear Uncle Neville's voice and he seemed to be blustering, so much so that Uncle Raymond said, 'All is not going well in there, Lisa. I thought Alexander seemed unusually thoughtful over breakfast.'

When I didn't answer he said impishly, 'Perhaps he's transferred his affections, Lisa. I wouldn't blame him.'

'Transferred his affections?'

'To you, my dear. After all Jessica's got nothing you haven't got in a far more subtle way. I know if I had to make the choice which I'd choose.'

My face was blushing scarlet but he merely laughed at my embarrassment. 'Come on, Lisa, you've had a soft spot for Alexander since you were a kid, now don't deny it.'

I was saved from answering because at that moment Alexander left the morning room and ran upstairs. Uncle Raymond remarked that all was not well, and Aunt Cecily hurried across the hall to join her husband. We heard their voices, then after a few minutes Aunt Cecily ran back across the hall, dabbing at her eyes.

'All is definitely not well,' Uncle Raymond remarked, while with a leaden heart I went on taking the baubles off the tree.

Just after eleven Alexander came downstairs wearing his overcoat and carrying his grip.

Uncle Raymond said, 'So you're off, Alexander. Well, you've a long drive in front of you, and the day's deteriorating. When can we expect to see you in Nairobi?'

'Perhaps on my next leave, I'll be in touch.'

'It's unlikely any of the boys will be home, they've all fled the nest, but we'll always be pleased to see you. Your father'll be glad to have you home.'

'Yes, we've missed a lot.'

'Pretty place, Dorset.' Then with a wink at me, he said, 'Your aunt and I did a lot of our courting in Bournemouth, it was considered one of the smart places in our young days. Now the kids go abroad. We never had the money.'

'Oh, Uncle Raymond, when have you never had the money? Besides, you've been abroad most of your life.'

He laughed. 'Well, that's the end of the tree, Lisa. I'll leave you two to say goodbye.'

He shook Alexander's hand warmly and with a wry grin said, 'I'll join Neville. I should think he's in need of a bit of company after Cecily said her piece.'

'What has happened, Alexander?' I asked quietly.

'I've told your uncle the engagement was a mistake, Lisa. I thought about it for most of the night and that was the conclusion I reached. I'm not blaming Jessica entirely, we're too far apart. I don't expect her to forego the parties she loves but I do expect her to put me before her friends when it's possible for us to be together. If Jessica loved me she would have stayed at home. None of us can have the best of both worlds.'

'I feel awful, I should have lied about the letter. I should never have told you.'

'Don't you think that it's better we've found out now rather than later? Jessica will bounce back, she'll find somebody else if she hasn't done so already, and perhaps in time so will I.'

'Shall I ever see you again, Alexander?'

'As I feel at this moment I don't want to see any of you again. But yes, Lisa, I think you and I will meet again, I think that's inevitable.'

He took my hand and held it, then with a brief smile he said, 'Say goodbye to the others for me, Lisa. I don't want to answer any questions, I just want to get away as quickly as possible.'

I watched him stride across the hall and, as I thought at that moment, out of my life.

CHAPTER 32

On the day after Alexander's departure Uncle Neville and
Aunt Cecily left. They had remained unduly subdued,
and Aunt Cecily was often tearful.

'How could Alexander have done this?' she moaned.
'It's totally unreasonable, it's not as though Jessica knew
he would be here. The poor child will be devastated.'

'I take it he'll have written, his letter will probably be
waiting at home for her,' Uncle Neville said quickly.
'I've no doubt Alexander will be gentle with her, he'll be
suffering as much as Jessica.'

'How can he give her up if he still loves her?'

'Maybe he thinks she doesn't love him enough,' Aunt
Edwina put in gently.

'Oh Edwina, what do you know about it? I don't think
you've ever been in love, and I'm telling you people in
love don't break off their engagement.'

The house was miserable. Meals were eaten in silence,
and even Uncle Raymond's sense of humour failed to lift
the gloom, in fact he was accused of adding to it. He and
Aunt Georgina left a day before they'd intended.

It was a lovely spring day, not long after Easter. We were
at lunch when Aunt Edwina said, 'Oh, there's a letter for
you on the hall table, Lisa, with a foreign stamp on it.'

'It's probably from Aunt Georgina,' I said casually.

'Oh no, it's not. I know her handwriting. Besides, it's
not a Kenya stamp.'

Puzzled, I left the table in search of my letter and stood
for some time staring at Alexander's familiar writing and
the Saudi Arabia stamp. We were only halfway through
our meal so I pushed it down into my pocket and returned
to the dining room. They both looked at me curiously.

'Who do you know abroad?' Grandmother asked
abruptly. 'Where is your letter?'

'In my pocket, I'll read it later.'

'Don't you know who it's from?'

'I think it's from Alexander.'

'Why should he be writing to you?' Grandmother snapped.

I didn't reply but went on eating my meal.

I had not seen Jessica since her arrival back in England, though Grandmother and Aunt Edwina had. They told me she was bitterly unhappy, she felt Alexander had treated her unkindly in suggesting that perhaps neither of them was quite ready for marriage, and it was unfair of him to expect Jessica to tie herself down to a man who was for the most part thousands of miles away.

I had known that Alexander would not implicate me but I was not proud of my hand in the affair.

As soon as lunch was over Grandmother said, 'Well, aren't you going to open your letter?'

There was nothing for it but to open it there and then. There was no reason to be secretive and I felt sure it was simply a letter from an old friend that I could show to anybody.

He was going to live in Israel where they were building reservoirs and a house had been provided there for him. He had a month's leave before taking up his new appointment and he hoped to spend it with his father in Dorset.

All this I told them as I read through the letter, then I remained silent while they waited expectantly for me to speak again.

'I remember you said you'd never visited Dorset,' I read, 'so I thought perhaps you might like to spend a little time here in the summer. I shall be home in July if that coincides with any holidays you have planned. My father and I will be delighted to see you.'

At last I told them, and Grandmother said sharply, 'Of course you can't go, it's out of the question. He's just broken off his engagement to your cousin. What are her parents – and everybody else, for that matter – going to think if you go tearing down to Dorset? It's your mother all over again, Lisa, and I won't have it.'

Such deep anger filled me that I could willingly have

251

shaken her, and bitterly I turned on her. 'How dare you bring my mother into this? There's absolutely nothing in this letter you or anybody else could take exception to, and I intend to go. Jessica is not engaged to Alexander now, and in any case she's probably found somebody else by this time.'

'I very much doubt it,' Grandmother snapped. 'You've always been jealous of Jessica, and there was never any need for it. I'm glad her parents have taken her to America. It would be terrible for her to know what you are about.'

'Oh, Grandmother,' I said wearily, 'I've had to pick up all the shattered pieces of my life on my own, Jessica's been shielded from life's disasters since the day she was born. I intend to write to Alexander and accept his invitation. You can read the letter if you like. It's warm and friendly, but that's all.'

I tossed the letter into her lap and stalked out of the room. I was angry and bitter, but I was elated too. In three months I would be in Dorset with Alexander.

How could I have ever thought that it would be so easy? Aunt Edwina knocked on my door while I was writing to Alexander. She looked pale and anxious, and for a moment I thought she might be ill, and she seemed to have difficulty in meeting my eyes.

'Mother wants to see you in the drawing room, Lisa. Can you come now?'

'Yes, of course. What is it?'

'I'd rather not say just now.'

Puzzled, I followed her down the stairs. If it was another attempt to dissuade me from visiting Alexander then they were wasting their time.

Grandmother sat in her favourite chair with a look of stern determination, and Aunt Edwina went immediately to sit where she could stare into the fire without looking at either of us.

'I've had all afternoon to think,' Grandmother snapped. 'Had you anything to do with Alexander breaking off his engagement to Jessica? Did you deliberately try to take him away from her when you went to that Hunt Ball together?'

'No, of course not.'

'But I feel it in my bones. You did have something to do with it, Lisa, and I want to know what. It's been on my mind for months, I've gone over that Christmas again and again, and all I'm left with is you. Somehow or other you knew Alexander would be here for Christmas. We were all amazed except you, and then there were the clothes and your new hairstyle. I want the truth, Lisa. There have been too many lies from Jessica and the rest of them, now I'm sure you too have been telling me lies.'

I could feel my face burning, my heart thumping painfully, and I was a little girl again standing silent before her after some childish misdemeanour. I had been unable to lie to her then, I was unable to lie now.

It all came out in painful syllables. My discovery of the letter, my anger and hurt at Jessica's deception, and my love that had started on that morning long ago beside the lake in Africa. I kept nothing back, nothing of my conversation with Alexander after the ball when I had told him how I found the letter and read it.

Aunt Edwina gasped, 'Lisa, how could you? Alexander wouldn't thank you for destroying his faith in Jessica.'

'She didn't deserve his trust, Aunt Edwina,' I snapped back sullenly.

'But he loved her, Lisa, don't you realize you were responsible for destroying it?'

'Be quiet, Edwina,' Grandmother ordered. 'Lisa knows what she's done. After this, Lisa, do you still intend to spend a holiday in Dorset with Alexander?'

'Yes, Grandmother, I do.'

'And you think he might fall in love with you now that he's had time to forget Jessica?'

'I don't know.'

'But that is what you are hoping for?'

'Yes, perhaps it is.'

'There is no happiness for you there, Lisa. He will always remember that it was you who told him about that letter, you who destroyed what he had for Jessica, however justified you felt yourself to be. If you can live with all that, Lisa, perhaps you deserve Alexander.'

There was nothing more to say. Her old lined face was strangely sad, and on the seat before the fire Aunt Edwina sat dabbing at her eyes with a tiny lace handkerchief. Outside the room the wind whispered through the branches of the beech trees and the distant lakeland hills stood out sharply against the sky. It was going to rain.

Madame Levison had recovered well from her operation, and had taken an enjoyable cruise. I had expected her to take over her teaching full time after that, but her doctor had a different idea, she told me. She was to spend a few months working no more than two days a week, and I was delighted to continue on helping her, even if it was only for two days a week.

By the end of June, however, she was fully recovered and ready to work full time again. I prepared notes on all the pupils I'd been taking, and went to see her one Sunday to make the final hand-over.

As we walked in the garden she said, 'What about your music, Lisa? Would you give it up for Alexander?'

'I don't think that's going to arise.'

'It could very well arise. He's free, you love him and you are going to spend time with him. It's not outside the bounds of possibility that he will come to care for you. If he does, what about your music?'

'If and when I marry surely it doesn't have to affect my music?'

'My dear child, think a little. Alexander is going to live in Israel, probably miles from anywhere, there probably isn't even a piano. Can you live without a piano, is he more important than everything that has gone before?'

I didn't answer immediately, thinking about my life without my music, how much it would weigh against a life with Alexander. And I knew it would count as nothing. I was unfit for the musical career Madame Levison had envisaged for me, I had to be unfit when I was ready and willing to give it all up for love.

I did not need to speak, she read the answer in my face.

254

Sadly she shook her head. 'There are men and women who would give everything up, Lisa, tell themselves that only their genius mattered, but you are not one of them. But suppose Alexander goes his own way and you never see him again, would you be willing to go back to your music as second best?'

'I suppose so.'

'But would you be the musician I want you to be? That's what I'm asking myself now.'

'Probably not.'

'Oh well, nothing is solved by talking about it. Go off on your holiday, enjoy your Alexander.'

I was packing for the journey when Aunt Edwina came into my bedroom. She stood silent for several minutes, then said, 'I hope you're not thinking of driving all the way, Lisa, the car's far too old for that kind of journey. I should get a taxi to the station and travel down by train.'

'I'd thought of that, Aunt Edwina. I'll telephone Alexander to meet me at the station.'

'You're looking forward to this visit, aren't you, Lisa?'

'Very much.'

'You know Mother isn't at all happy about it?'

'She's made that very plain.'

'Try to understand her a little, dear. There's been so much talk about this family in the past, she doesn't want any more. I thought she was wrong to bring your mother into the conversation but you must admit it has its similarities. Your mother fell in love with her husband's brother, now I think you might fall in love with your cousin's fiancé.'

'There are two very vital differences, Aunt Edwina. My mother loved Philip before she married my father, and Alexander is no longer Jessica's fiancé.'

'All the same, my dear, there'll be talk.'

'There's nothing to talk about. I'm going to Dorset for a holiday, to meet an old friend. Sufficient unto the day is the evil thereof.'

I took my case down to the hall and rang for a taxi. I was wearing a grey flannel suit, white silk blouse and high-

255

heeled black court shoes, and my hair fell in a shining page-boy cut. I was not wearing glasses.

I went into the drawing room to tell them goodbye and after looking me up and down Grandmother said, 'You look very nice, Lisa, but as you know I don't like your hair worn long and you seem intent on ruining your eyes without your glasses.'

It was the last time I ever heard her mention either my hair or my eyes.

Alexander met me at the station, and my first thought was that he looked fit and handsome, with sleeves rolled up over slim brown arms, his eyes startlingly blue in his suntanned face. He took my case and slung it into the back of the car, then we were driving along a wide road with the sea below us.

He pointed out the house as we climbed the hill and I gasped with delight. It was a stone manor house set above rolling green lawns and the tall wrought-iron gates stood open in anticipation of our arrival.

A man sat on the terrace reading a newspaper, but when he heard the car he came down the steps to meet us. I would have known he was Alexander's father, I felt sure, if I had met him in the street. He too was tall and slender, but although his hair was grey his eyes were the same steely blue and his smile had all Alexander's sweetness and warmth.

He took my hand in a firm grip. 'Welcome to Graylings, Lisa. We'll have tea first and then Alexander will show you round the garden and the house.'

'Hadn't she better see her room first, Dad?' Alexander said, smiling.

'Of course. We've put you on the sea side, the lawns slope down to the top of the cliff and it's a beautiful view.'

The room was charming, with white walls, delicate chintz and a thick oriental carpet. I enthused over the view from the window and when Alexander told me to come down when I was ready I said quickly, 'I'll change into a dress, if you don't mind. I feel too formal in this suit.'

'I thought you looked very elegant when you stepped off the train,' he said quietly.

I felt pleased by his words; and when he looked down into my eyes unsmiling, he said quietly, 'You know what I really thought in that first moment? Where is that little girl with the long pigtails and the glasses? It was almost as though I was welcoming a stranger. But I think I like this one best. See you in a few minutes, Lisa.'

I changed into a simple shirtwaister in a blue the colour of my eyes, then I ran down to the terrace. A middle-aged woman was pouring tea into delicate china cups, and there was an array of dainty sandwiches and small cakes on a tea trolley.

'This is Mrs Hollis, Lisa, she's been my housekeeper for a great many years.'

I shook hands with her and I felt her staring at me strangely.

'What is it, Mrs Hollis,' Alexander said, 'didn't I tell you she was pretty?'

'You did, Mr Alex, but you didn't tell me she looked so much like your mother.'

When I stared back at them, Sir Noel said softly, 'I noticed it when you arrived, my dear. You have Margaret's colouring, and there's a certain young colt look about you that I remember so well. I don't suppose you remember much about your mother, Alexander.'

'I would never have said Lisa reminded me of Mother until the night I saw her dressed for the ball,' Alexander said. 'I remembered my mother coming in to see me one evening just as you were setting out for a function. She too was in evening dress, and she was fair like you, Lisa. You reminded me very much of her that evening.'

'Then I'm very honoured. I know how much you loved her.'

Perhaps I shouldn't have said loved, I wanted to make no connection like that between us, indeed I wanted to keep our days together light and easy, and already it seemed there were deeper echoes stemming from a past I had not been aware of.

After tea Sir Noel said, 'Now show Lisa round the

gardens and the house Alexander. I won't come with you,
I have letters to write.'

The gardens were lovely, from the formal rose garden
to the enchanting wild flower garden and rockeries. The
house too was a treasure, and Alexander showed me por-
traits, including one of his mother. She looked so young,
a slip of a girl in a white delicate dress curled up into the
corner of a settee with a brown and white spaniel nestling
in her arms. Was I really as pretty as the woman in the
portrait? She was as fair as I, and her eyes were blue, and
as Sir Noel said, there was an enchanting young grace
about her that reminded you of a young colt.

'She *is* quite a lot like you, Lisa,' Alexander mused.
'Of course I would never have recognized it in that little
girl I found sitting oh so sorry for herself beside the lake.'

'I was desperately sorry for myself, I thought my world
had come to an end.'

'And then the flamingoes came, and you clapped your
hands with glee and your face lit up like the sun coming
out after rain. I don't suppose you've ever seen flamingoes
again.

'Yes, I saw them at the zoo, all dejected and somehow
colourless in our English weather.'

'Poor things. Away from their natural habitat they seem
to lose so much of their glamour.'

I loved Alexander and I loved Dorset. We drove out
into the countryside and we sailed around the coast in
Alexander's catamaran. The weather too was kind to us
and I became sunburned and rosy in the salt breezes that
swept across the downs.

In the evenings I played for them and once Alexander
joined me at the piano and we played together as I had
seen him play with Jessica years before, only this time our
music was more professional.

Sir Noel said, 'You play beautifully, Lisa. Alexander
has told me something of your story. It was a tragic
moment when that plane crashed into the mountainside,
it halted your career for a time.'

'Yes, I'm not even sure if it can ever be the same.'

One evening, when I was playing for Alexander alone, I found him staring at me across the top of the piano, his eyes so keenly intent they brought the rich colour into my face. 'Could you live without a piano, Lisa, or is it the most important thing in your life?'

'I'll never forget my music, and I'd come back to it again, but that punishing dedication may not be there any longer.'

'What could you put in its place, I wonder?'

'I'm not sure. Some other profession perhaps, but I don't know what.'

'Nothing besides a profession?' he insisted.

'I could put love before it.' I felt the answer drawn out of me against my will.

'Love, and marriage perhaps,' he still insisted.

I allowed my hands to finish the Chopin Nocturne, then raising my eyes to his I said simply, 'Yes, Alexander. Much as I need my music it could never take the place of love, and I would never marry where I didn't love, so I think I have answered your question.'

He knew that I loved him. It had been in my voice, my eyes, my music, and now I was in limbo waiting for the next twist in events.

It came several days later. I had helped him pull the boat up on to the beach and we were climbing the stiff path up to the house. I was breathless as we paused halfway up the slope, and he took my hand and pulled me after him. When we reached the top I was gasping, and with his eyes filled with laughter he pulled me into his arms and kissed the top of my head.

Startled I looked up at him and suddenly his face grew sombre and he said gently, 'Lisa, can you imagine living in a house near a reservoir which has still to be finished? It will be hot and desolate, and there will be few women for you to chat to. I doubt very much if there will be a piano, but perhaps in time we can get one. Think very carefully, I'm not the sort of man who goes in for collecting broken engagements.'

'Is it a very small house, Alexander?' I asked with a little smile.

He threw back his head and laughed. 'Actually no, Lisa, the house is quite large. Any more questions about the layout?'

'None, and I don't really need to think about it at all. I could live in a house beside an uncompleted reservoir, I could live without a piano if I loved the man I was living with. Are you asking me to marry you, Alexander?'

'I think I am, Lisa.'

'Then the answer is yes, Alexander. I'd have died if you hadn't asked me.'

I didn't ask Alexander if he loved me. He was sweet and tender, and he made me feel loved, but he never put it into words. I told myself that actions spoke louder than words, but I was never deluded. It was too soon for him.

He liked me immensely, he liked the way I looked and the way I loved him. Our engagement gave his father the utmost pleasure and that too counted in my favour. I did not think Sir Noel would have liked Jessica, he would have seen through her, but then Jessica would have hated Dorset and would have found him remote and a little anti-social, which was not surprising in a man who had spent most of his life in the world's most inaccessible places.

It was Alexander's father who said when we were all sitting out on the terrace on a warm balmy evening, 'Have you two decided when the wedding is to take place?'

My eyes met Alexander's and I left it to him to reply. We had agreed to marry, we hadn't spoken of when.

'Do you want a traditional wedding, Lisa, white lace and orange blossom, or would you prefer to be married quietly?'

'Entirely without fuss,' I answered quickly.

'That's what I thought. I'll drive you home on Saturday and talk to your Grandmother. I don't want you to have to face the family alone.'

'I'd *much much rather talk to Grandmother alone, Alexander. It won't make it any easier if you're there.

'I'm not afraid of meeting Jessica, if that's what you mean, Lisa. I didn't want you to face them alone.'

'I appreciate your concern, but that's what I want.'

I didn't want Alexander to see Jessica again, not so soon

in case the embers stirred and came alive, and to my
shame I think he saw through me.

'I doubt if any of the family will wish to come to our
wedding. You must admit it will be very difficult,' I told
him.

'Of course. Then as soon as they've been told perhaps
you'd like to come back here. I'll get a special licence and
we can be married at the church in the village.'

I agreed with everything he proposed. If he'd suggested
marrying me in Jerusalem I would have agreed.

I sent Aunt Edwina a postcard saying I would be home
on Saturday evening and would get a taxi at the station.
It was a slow stopping train, which gave me more time to
agonize over the evening ahead of me, and my heart sank
still further when I saw Uncle Neville's expensive Merc-
edes standing outside the door. I had hoped Grandmother
and Aunt Edwina would be alone.

I paid the taxi driver and he carried my case up to the
front door, then I was in the familiar hall with the sound
of voices coming from the drawing room where the door
stood ajar. Aunt Cecily's voice and Uncle Neville's, then
there was laughter followed by Jessica's voice relating
some adventure followed by more laughter.

My first thought was that I was glad Alexander wasn't
with me. Then fiercely I told my trembling heart to be
still, there was no way to evade the storm, they had to be
told.

Squaring my shoulders I entered the drawing room,
where five pairs of eyes stared at me haughtily and without
welcome, then Jessica jumped up, pushed past me and
fled from the room.

'We won't ask if you've had a good time,' Aunt Cecily
said coldly. 'We'll just assume that you made the most of
it.'

Grandmother had a frozen look on her face, Aunt
Edwina sat nervously twisting her beads, and Uncle
Neville puffed at his pipe, the typical example of a man
who did not wish to become involved.

Conversation resumed between them and I was ignored,

left to stand uncertainly at the door. Their attitude told me what I must expect from now on: they stood together and I was singularly alone. No one even looked up when I left the room.

I had barely reached my room when I heard goodbyes being said in the hall, then Uncle Neville's car drove off.

Telling myself there was no point in stalling, I returned to the drawing room to face Grandmother's wrath. Without giving her a chance to speak, I said simply, 'Tomorrow I am returning to Dorset to marry Alexander Hamilton. The wedding is next week. We're going out to Israel immediately after the wedding.'

If I had said I was emigrating to the moon I could not have dropped a bigger bombshell. Grandmother's face was scarlet and her hands were gripping the arms of her chair so tightly the knuckles showed white.

Aunt Edwina sat transfixed for a full minute, then she moaned miserably, 'What are we to tell Jessica? Poor Jessica. Lisa, how could you?'

I said quietly, 'I'm going upstairs to pack. Perhaps you will tell the others.'

When Jessica was late at a party she always slept in the next morning, but she was in my room soon after nine with her eyes blazing and deep anger etched on a face that looked anything but lovely.

'How I hate you, Lisa Ralston,' she stormed. 'I hope you have a rotten marriage. He doesn't love you. How can he, so soon after he finished with me?'

I couldn't answer her. I believed that every word she uttered was true, and yet I was remembering his sweetness and while I still looked into her stormy eyes and listened to the venomous words falling from her lips I felt suddenly calm.

The years that lay ahead belonged to me. I loved Alexander and I would show him by every word and deed that he had been right to marry me. I would be the wife Jessica could never have been. I would make Alexander Hamilton love me.

CHAPTER 33

Alexander and I were married quietly in a little stone church not far from the house, where the vicar seemed quite overwhelmed by the fact that he was marrying the son of the famous Sir Noel Hamilton.

There were spectators from the village but only Alexander's father and Mrs Hollis sat in the pews behind us. One thing had cheered me considerably the day before when my cousin Roger arrived to act as Alexander's best man, bringing with him his young wife Marcia to be my matron of honour.

I remember thinking that it was strange to be followed down the aisle by a girl I hadn't met before yesterday, but she was a kind friendly girl and she looked quite enchanting in the blue dress that had been her going-away dress.

For my part I wore cream wild silk, with a wide-brimmed hat of the same material trimmed with pale cream chiffon roses, all from the most exclusive shop in Bournemouth. It was a pretty, feminine outfit and Alexander said to me in the vestry, 'You look very beautiful, Lisa.'

We ate our wedding breakfast in the local hotel and Roger made a glowing speech after which we drank champagne. I remember looking down at my new wedding ring and my engagement ring, a large diamond that flashed colours of blue and flame over my slim fingers, and thinking about my piano with a vague feeling of loss. How long would it be before those same fingers ever played again?

I remember that Alexander looked at me doubtfully as we stood surrounded by our luggage in the living room of our new home. The view from the windows was simply miles and miles of dry and arid country. We lived on the edge of a building site, and while Alexander worked there was nothing for me to do besides reading the papers that arrived several days late from England.

Two young Arab girls acted as servants but their English was minimal, and when we entertained it was usually two of the engineers who were as yet unmarried.

I made the best of it, reflecting grimly that Jessica would have hated every moment – the heat, the noise and the flies. But there were times over the next three years when we escaped for a little while to the Israel I had read about but never expected to see.

Moments of relaxation for Alexander were rare, but we spent an enchanting weekend beside the sea of Galilee and another two weeks when we explored Jerusalem. We walked one evening in the garden of Gethsemane after most of the tourists had gone, and a rare and acute sadness washed over me. It had all happened so long ago and this land was still an unhappy divided land, yet there was about it still the love and passion of that lonely man who had met his death on the hill outside the city.

One other memory will always be with me, of the day when I stood with Alexander on the parapet of the dam looking down at the swirling waters rushing headlong into the valley, creating before our eyes a shimmering lake, and softly I heard Alexander quote some lines from Solomon's Song of Songs: 'For, lo, the winter is past, the rain is over and gone; the flowers appear on the earth; the time of the singing of birds is come, and the voice of the turtle is heard in our land.'

I was glad that we were going home. I was four months pregnant with our first child and I desperately wanted the baby to be born in England.

It was not a happy homecoming for us. We arrived on a cold dark January morning to be told by Mrs Hollis that Alexander's father had had a massive heart attack and had died during the night. I grieved with Alexander, who had deeply loved his father and bitterly regretted his early life when they had seen little of each other.

Mrs Hollis was very good to us. In spite of wishing to retire to live with her sister in Bournemouth she stayed on until our daughter Andrea was six months old, largely because it had been a difficult confinement, but also because she adored the child.

Andrea was a beautiful child, dark like Alexander, with a gay laughing face and a temper that defied description. She was totally like Jessica as I first remembered her, and this, I thought, was my penance for what I had done to her. She could have been Jessica's child, there seemed to be nothing of me in her.

Alexander adored her, and I resented it. I believed he adored her because he too saw Jessica in her. I think in those early days he never really saw Andrea as I did. He saw her cleverness, her brightness, her beauty, but I saw the tantrums and the precociousness that lurked behind every sunny smile, and when I was sharp with her Alexander looked on in dismay because he felt I had overstepped the mark.

When she was three I took her north for the first time to meet Grandmother and Aunt Edwina, and if they were distant with me they fell in love with Andrea. Indeed Aunt Edwina's first words were, 'But she's so like Jessica when she was a child, she's adorable.'

In front of Grandmother, Andrea behaved impeccably and with all Jessica's charm, and when Alexander came at the end of the week I was persuaded to leave Andrea with them so that I could go with him to Finland for several weeks.

I was reluctant, but Alexander said it could do her no harm, the child was quite happy at the Maples and Andrea showed no signs of wanting to leave with us. That was a pattern that repeated itself over the next four years, and by that time I had given birth to Jeremy.

Jeremy was beautiful and placid, and I loved him utterly. He cried when Andrea pinched him and she had absolutely no time for the new baby, although I tried very hard to show her that his arrival took nothing from her.

I had not seen Jessica since the morning when she had flung herself into my bedroom with hatred in her eyes and anger flooding out of her mouth, but shortly after we arrived in Israel her own marriage was front-page news.

265

She had married Desmond Colby and they were shown surrounded by wellwishers in front of the Ritz Hotel in Paris.

Alexander merely smiled, while I tried to remember the Desmond Colby I had known briefly. I had thought him a very astute man; I also thought he didn't choose his wives astutely enough. Grandmother thought him charming but unscrupulous, Aunt Edwina had doubts that the marriage would last, but Jessica's parents were delighted with the match. Desmond was a famous artist, he had money and he had style, he was a man worthy of their daughter.

Desmond's money had to be worked for. His first wife took a large slice of it, and in no time at all Jessica was saying he kept her short of money, that he was sarcastic and cheating on her. Two years later they were divorced and twelve months later she married for the second time, a second-rate actor five years her junior.

None of this was Jessica's fault, poor dear, she had been unfortunate in the men she had loved. If she'd married Alexander her entire life would have been different, but then Alexander had been stolen in the most devious way.

When I said all this to Alexander he merely smiled. 'We always knew what they would say, Lisa,' he replied evenly. 'You mustn't let it worry you.'

Two years later our daughter Linda was born and while Alexander travelled widely I stayed at home to care for my children. Andrea was at a very good prep school on the edge of the New Forest and we only saw her during the holidays or at speech days and sports galas. It didn't take me long to realize how she lorded it over the other children and tentatively I asked her headmistress if she was popular at the school.

She seemed evasive, but when I insisted she said, 'Among a certain section of the girls Andrea is very popular, Mrs Hamilton. She is clever and beautiful, and other children tend to make idols of girls like Andrea.'

When I seemed doubtful she said gently, 'Children's personalities alter a great deal as they reach maturity. I

266

will be very firm with Andrea, you needn't worry, Mrs Hamilton.'

When she was eight I took her to see Grandmother for the last time. I had my other children with me but it was Andrea they adored, Andrea they wanted leaving with them for the remainder of the summer holiday.

'You have your hands full with the other two,' Aunt Edwina said persuasively. 'She's so good with us, Lisa, and she loves being here.'

When I asked Andrea if she would like to remain behind she flashed me one of her bright smiles, saying, 'Of course, Mummy, I love it here, I get taken into Lancaster for tea and I can go up to the farm and play with the kittens.'

That decided me. I had loved going up to the farm, perhaps after all there *was* something of me in Andrea.

She stayed in the north for three weeks, and then I left the two younger children with the au pair while I drove north to collect her. I had no qualms about leaving them with Eva, she was a sensible girl from Sweden who would stand no nonsense and she treated them both with the utmost affection.

Andrea didn't want to return with me. She wept and stormed. She hated the school and she hated the pupils, why couldn't she go to Ashlea? I'd gone to Ashlea and so had Aunt Jessica.

'She's not your aunt,' I cried, 'she's my cousin.'

'She told me I could call her Aunt Jessica and so I shall,' stormed Andrea.

I gathered Andrea's clothes together and started to put them into her suitcase while she sat on the bed scowling at me.

'We'll go downstairs and say goodbye to Grandmother and Aunt Edwina, Andrea. You'll be able to come again on another holiday.'

'Why can't I stay here and come to you and Daddy for holidays?' she demanded.

'Because this isn't your home. Besides, we all miss you, darling.'

'I haven't missed you. Linda and Jeremy are too young

to play with and I told Aunt Jessica I hated Dorset. She said she did too, it was too rural and stodgy.'

I stared at her in some dismay. She was sitting cross-legged on the bed, her dark curls framing her enchanting face, and I felt I was looking at Jessica while instinctively I pressed my hands together. But the pain was in my heart, not in my hands.

I shut the case, picked it up in one hand and held the other out to Andrea. 'Come along, time to go,' I said brightly.

Ignoring me she jumped off the bed and ran out of the room. I heard her running along the corridor sobbing angrily, and I knew the sort of scene I would meet in the drawing room.

She knelt on the floor near Grandmother's chair with her head against her knee and she was saying between the sobs, 'I don't want to go back to that school, I want to stay here and go to Ashlea. Please, Granny, tell Mummy to leave me here, I'll be good, honest I will.'

Aunt Edwina looked at me entreatingly. 'She isn't happy at that school, Lisa. Perhaps you should talk to Alexander about it, he might agree with her to leave and come to Ashlea. We wouldn't mind having her, and she could spend all her holidays with you.'

'We'll talk about it later, Aunt Edwina. I can't just uproot Andrea, she's doing very well at her school.'

'I'm not, I'm not,' Andrea stormed, 'I'll never do well there, I hate it.'

By this time I too was angry, and I realized I had three determined people facing me, one of them my own daughter.

'We have a long journey in front of us, Andrea, and I want you to come with me now. Come along, I want no more nonsense.'

I had to drag her away from Grandmother's side, and she sat beside me in the car refusing to wave goodbye. All the way down the drive and for many miles I was remembering Grandmother's look of pure satisfaction.

It was remarkable how quickly Andrea recovered her high spirits once we were away from the house. The tears were drying on her cheeks and her head was looking this way and that so as not to miss a thing on the road.

'Feeling better?' I asked brightly.

'I still don't like Dorset,' she answered adamantly.

I decided to change the subject. 'I know a very nice inn where we can eat lunch. What do you say to fresh salmon and strawberry ice cream?'

'I'll think about it.'

It was Saturday and the inn was filled with other diners. I was therefore completely mortified when Andrea's childish treble asked, 'Mummy, what is a bastard?'

Totally embarrassed I glanced round at other diners who were pretending they hadn't heard, and I whispered, 'Darling, that's not a very nice word, you mustn't use it.'

'But what is it?'

'I'll tell you in the car, not here. Now eat your lunch.'

She picked up her knife and fork sulkily.

At last we had paid our bill and were out in the car, where Andrea once more asked the question I was wishing she had forgotten.

'Mumm, what is a bastard?'

'Where did you hear that word?' I asked sharply.

'Aunt Jessica was talking to Mrs Harris, they were talking about their husbands. Aunt Jessica said Desmond was a lying bastard who never gave her any money.'

I had no intention of explaining the word to her. 'I knew Desmond, not very well, but I liked him. He had a lovely sense of humour and I can't really believe he kept her short of money. She's been brought up to be extravagant, not all men can keep pace with a wife like that.'

Momentarily the word bastard was forgotten.

'She's got another husband now but they quarrel all the time.'

'How do you know?'

'I heard them at Granny's. She threw a book at him and he went off in the car and didn't come back for hours. He was talking all funny when he came back and Granny said he'd been drinking. Would that make him talk funny?'

269

That was when I decided Andrea was not going to stay with my grandmother again, and the decision was endorsed in the next moment when Andrea said, 'Aunt Jessica took me out to tea and a lady asked her if I was her little girl, we were so much alike.'

I never told Alexander why I stayed away. The children grew older and went to school. Alexander travelled widely in his work and I travelled with him whenever I could.

Andrea was clever with languages, Jeremy won a scholarship to Oxford and Linda wanted to paint, just as passionately as I had once wanted to play the piano.

Now I only played for pleasure and to entertain the family and our friends. Andrea was not musical, and perversely she hated me to play, but the other two would sit for hours playing quietly and happily together while I was at the piano.

One morning a letter arrived for Andrea which she hastily pushed unopened into her pocket. Amused, I wondered if it was from some boy or other, because she was almost thirteen and boys were beginning to notice her. Later I found the envelope in the waste basket and I recognized Jessica's writing instantly.

I felt a strange pang of jealousy when I realized she was writing to my daughter, and another when I thought that Andrea was keeping it from me.

She was far closer to her father than to me and there were times when I wondered if she talked to Alexander about Jessica. I never asked him, but as the years passed I realized unhappily that Andrea and I would never be close. We had nothing in common, we didn't even like the same people.

Jessica had divorced her second husband and was living in London, so I was not surprised when Andrea decided she wanted to go to London University. By this time I was so tired of crossing swords with her I made no effort to change her mind.

I knew she must be seeing Jessica in London, but I had no complaint to make about her prowess. She passed her exams with flying colours and quickly obtained a position

270

in London with a big firm of importers as an interpreter. We saw her seldom because she was constantly overseas in one country or another, and when she was home she shared a flat in London with two other girls.

It was Andrea who informed us that Jessica had married for the third time, and she seemed vastly amused that her husband was quite old, at least fifty she said gaily, and that he was quite bald but filthy rich. When he died two years later Jessica hoped to get all his money, but his three children contested the will and she got only half of what she was expecting, and much of this was swallowed up in legal fees.

I believed that contact with Jessica was making Andrea too old and sophisticated. She had nothing in common with Linda when the two girls were home together, and Jeremy largely ignored her existence.

Alexander was amused by their behaviour and when I chastised him about it he said with a wry smile, 'Children are individuals, Lisa, there's nothing either of us can do about them. They'll go their own way, all we can do is instil into them some of the values we were brought up with.'

I saw the logic of his argument but it didn't satisfy me. I had wanted so much more from all my children.

I had a good marriage. I loved Alexander with unchanging selfless devotion, and in my innermost heart I believed he loved me even if he was never in love with me.

The shadow of Jessica had become dim as the years passed, and my sense of guilt towards her became less severe now that I no longer visited the north to be reminded of the tragedy she had made of her life. I still believed they laid that tragedy at my door but I never allowed Alexander to see how much that bothered me. I loved being married to him, I loved our home and our life together, and our moments of passion were ecstatic and complete so that each time we made love I told myself that it was something neither of us could fake. Why then could I never entirely believe it?

Alexander had commitments in the Far East and

Andrea was off to Hong Kong on an assignment, so they were travelling together.

I saw them off in the morning and stood at the door until the car disappeared round the bend. Andrea had embraced me briefly, saying lightly, 'Don't expect letters, Mother. I'll send you the odd postcard but you know what a rotten correspondent I am.'

Alexander took me in his arms, discovering the tears in my eyes.

'I'll telephone you as soon as we arrive, Lisa, and I'll write whenever I can. In about three weeks I expect to be home.'

I nodded, unable to speak, and with light banter in his voice he said, 'Hey, what is this? You've seen me disappear from your life a great many times over the years, there's nothing different this time.'

He kissed me gently and was gone.

Saying goodbye to Alexander left me with a feeling of loss. Andrea was the problem, she always went away with a careless wave of her hand and an embrace that said nothing.

PART IV

CHAPTER 34

Footsteps passed my door before it was properly light, but I had lain awake for hours listening to the wind moaning in the chimney and the sleet pattering on the window. I knew the scene that would meet my gaze when I pulled back the curtains, a cold grey day with wet snow covering the garden and the distant hills shrouded in virginal white.

I put on the bedside light and consulted my watch. It was half past seven, so I decided to get up. There would be no more sleep for me and the family had to be faced, preferably with composure and sang froid.

I stood at last looking at my reflection in the long mirror and I liked what I saw, a tall slender woman in a deceptively simple black dress, a woman with pale blond hair framing her face and eyes like deep blue pools, an elegant woman with a calm assured air that came from deep inner contentment. Yet that contentment was betrayed by the trembling of my hand as it touched the pearls around my throat.

How long would I be able to maintain my air of calm, how long before the rest of them got to me, how long after seeing Jessica again?

Uncle Raymond was standing in the hall looking at the morning paper, and I thought he was there deliberately and out of kindness in order to walk with me into the breakfast room.

Grandmother's chair stood empty at the head of the table, and the others looked up expectantly as we entered the room. Aunt Edwina twittered nervously like a little bird, saying, 'Here you are, Lisa, are you feeling better?'

'Yes, thank you, Aunt Edwina. Where do you want me to sit?'

'Here I think, next to Angela.'

Angela favoured me with an absent-minded smile and

her husband leaned forward, saying with a toothy smile, 'Good morning, Lisa, pity we've had to meet again on such a sad occasion.'

I made inquiries about their children and Angela informed me that both were clever and in good positions, which prevented them attending the funeral. 'Absolutely couldn't be spared,' she said.

Across the table my eyes met Robin's and he smiled. It was so long since I had seen him but his face had lost none of its humour. I began to relax, and meeting Uncle Raymond's eyes across the table I felt a sudden surge of gratitude that he was there with his family to make me feel welcome.

'The funeral's at two,' Aunt Edwina informed me. 'There are still several people to come.'

'Who, for instance?' Uncle Raymond wanted to know.

'Neville and Cecily, Jessica too although she's driving up from London.'

Uncle Henry and Aunt Claudia came in next. They greeted me with some restraint and almost immediately Uncle Henry started to talk about the order in which we should occupy the cars and where we should expect to sit in church.

'I've invited Mr Scotson, mother's lawyer, to come back to the house for dinner,' Aunt Edwina said, 'he wasn't able to come tomorrow and suggested reading her will this evening.'

Just then Aunt Georgina entered the room and sat down next to her husband, dabbing her eyes. He looked at her somewhat irritably and she said in a trembling voice, 'I don't know why we had to eat in here. I hate seeing mother's chair standing empty there, it's uncanny.'

'I agree,' Uncle Raymond said, 'she's probably sitting there invisible and seething with annoyance because none of us can see her.'

'There's no call to be facetious, Raymond,' she said irritably, 'Even though you and Mother didn't get on, it is the day of her funeral. Why can't you show a little respect?'

276

Unabashed Uncle Raymond winked at me across the table and helped himself to toast and marmalade.

After breakfast some of us drifted into the morning room, others into the drawing room, and presently there was a constant ring on the front doorbell as wreaths began to arrive.

The sweet sickly smell of flowers seemed to fill the house and I helped to arrange them across the floor of the hall. It would seem that if Grandmother Marston hadn't been exactly liked she had been well respected.

I was standing at the drawing room window looking down the drive when a large grey car came slowly up the drive with Aunt Cecily and Uncle Neville.

She had changed. Always very svelte and elegant, over the years she had put on a lot of weight and her once slender figure had become well rounded. She was wearing a tight black skirt and a three-quarter-length silver fox cape which enhanced her extra weight, and on her dark hair she wore a silver fox hat which made her seem top-heavy.

She swept immediately into the drawing room, and as our eyes met hers became immediately hostile. Twenty-four years had not rubbed out the anger she felt towards me. She nodded coolly in my direction and I murmured a brief 'Good morning.' She left the room immediately and that was her last appearance in the drawing room that morning. Uncle Neville's greeting was a shade warmer when we met in the hall on our way to lunch in the dining room.

Seeing us in conversation Aunt Cecily interrupted, dragging him away to look at the wreaths and whispering to him furiously.

Aunt Edwina was consulting the clock nervously. In some agitation she said, 'Jessica's late. I suppose she is coming, Cecily?'

'Well of course she's coming, she's getting a lift. In fact they're probably here now, there's a car coming up the drive.'

Jessica and Margery Harris arrived together. For the

first time in twenty-four years my eyes met Jessica's, and she gave a half smile entirely without warmth.

She made it her business to sidle round the room until she stood beside me, then with that same maddening half smile she asked, 'Alex not with you then?'

I felt quite sure Margery Harris would already have told her that I was attending the funeral alone, but I made myself answer her casually. 'No, I'm here alone.'

'I must say you're looking very well, Lisa. Marriage seems to agree with you.'

'I've had a long time to get used to it.'

'You have, haven't you? I never got used to it. I probably never married the right man.'

I stared at her steadily but made no comment.

She was still a remarkably attractive woman but her enchanting beauty had gone. She was too thin, too highly strung, her make-up a little too heavy, her funeral attire too dramatic. She was wearing a black expensively cut suit topped with a black raincoat lined with dark mink, her black hair had been styled closed to her head and she wore long jet earrings and a lot of heavy gold bracelets. Her long scarlet nails emphasized the heavy rings on most of her fingers.

She was beautiful and repellent, sophisticated and yet in some way dissolute. Even her perfume was heavy and cloying, and standing next to her she made me feel chaste and clinical.

Later when we stood in the hall waiting to get into the funeral cars I saw her eyeing me over from head to toe, and I was glad of the mink coat Alexander had given me on my last birthday. When our eyes met she turned away quickly to hide the bitterness I surprised in hers.

I looked with compassion at Aunt Edwina's dark grey tweed coat thinking it could surely not be the same one she had worn on my last visit to the Maples, but then with Aunt Edwina how could one be sure?

The bell was tolling dismally as we made our way up the church path where a small crowd of villagers stood respectfully outside the door. A plump woman in navy blue smiled at me, and although I responded I couldn't remember having met her before.

It was bitterly cold when we finally stood in a small group round the open grave listening to the vicar's words of committal and the finality of those words coupled with the biting wind brought tears into my eyes.

I had never loved my grandmother, she had not invited love, and she had been afraid to give love to me because it might have encouraged me to be as free with mine as my mother had been. Now on this winter's morning, standing in that tiny churchyard under the ancient yews surrounded by a family who largely despised me, I found myself aching for those few bright hours of my childhood. I found my lips murmuring a prayer my mother had taught me in the ebony darkness of a Kenyan night and I thanked God for life and for time's golden memories that are good and sweet.

With my eyes misted with tears I was about to turn away when my arm was taken in a firm grip and looking up I found Alexander beside me, his eyes sombre and concerned as they gazed into mine.

I stared at him in wonder and then he smiled, and happiness flooded my being as I murmured, 'Oh Alexander, I'm so glad you've come.'

We mingled with the others to look at the wreaths laid out along the paths and Alexander paused to speak to Uncle Raymond while I wandered on alone.

The woman in navy came up and with a little smile said, 'You don't remember me, do you, Miss Lisa? It's been a long time.'

'I'm sorry, no. I don't remember you, but I feel I should. Who are you?'

'Mary Stevens that was, Miss Lisa. Many's the time I took you up to the farm to play with mi brothers and sisters.'

'Mary, of course! Oh, I'm so sorry I didn't remember you, but I can see who you are now. Are you living in the area?'

'Yes, we 'as a little cottage about twenty minutes from 'ere. Mi mother's livin' with us, but mi Dad died four years ago. He never really got used to bein' without the farm and 'e never settled away from 'ere. Our Joe's farmin' in Shropshire and our Danny's workin' for a shippin' firm in London, doin' very well 'e is too.'

'And Pauline, how is Pauline?'

'She was the clever one o' the family. She's a lawyer, livin' in Canada. She's bin over there fifteen years now.'

'When you write to her will you tell her you've seen me, Mary? That I've asked about her and wish her well. And what about Emmie?'

Her face clouded. 'We 'aven't clapped eyes on our Emmie for years, we don't know where she is and her bairns'll be growin' up now. Ted was allus in and out o' prison, 'e just couldn't go straight much as mi dad talked to 'im, it made no difference and ye couldn't talk to our Emmie either. She stood by 'im, but the last time 'e went away for five years and she vowed 'e wouldn't find 'er waitin' for 'im that time.'

'And was she?'

'We don't know. One day she just upped and left with not even a note and we've seen nothin' of her or 'im since that day.'

'Have you tried to find out where she went?'

'Oh yes we tried, but we didn't succeed. We can only 'ope somewhere she's fallen on 'er feet.'

Alexander joined us and I reintroduced them. He took her hand and smiled down at her. 'I remember you perfectly, Mary. Didn't your father have the farm on the fell?'

She dimpled prettily. 'Yes, that's 'im, Mr Alexander. I won't keep ye any longer, they're comin' this way.'

My heart skipped a beat when I saw Andrea walking with Jessica.

Andrea smiled brightly. 'Hello Mother, didn't you see me earlier?'

'No, where were you?'

'Standing with Jessica. I looked straight at you but you were too busy looking at Daddy.'

'I was surprised to see him and I didn't know you came with him.'

'We thought you'd want some support.'

Jessica smiled. 'I wonder how long everybody's staying. At least until after the will's read, I suppose. Are you expecting anything, Lisa.'

'No.'

She raised her eyebrows archly. 'Well I am, in fact I'm relying on it.'

'Nobody deserves it more than Aunt Edwina. She's devoted her entire life to her mother, now at last she should see some recognition for it.'

'Oh, come on, Lisa, it's suited Aunt Edwina to trot around after Granny, she's never had a home to buy or furnish, she's always lived at the Maples and I expect Granny fed her and clothed her. If you ask me she'll have amassed a small fortune simply living off Granny.'

'She never lived off Grandmother. She fetched and carried, shopped and chauffeured. And she looks so incredibly shabby, I don't suppose she's anything decent in her wardrobe.'

'I agree with you there, that coat looks like year one. I expect she's only worn it so that people will feel sorry for her.'

'Why would she do that?'

'Hasn't it always been poor Edwina? Everybody'll think it's a sin if she doesn't get most of Granny's money and it's my guess she won't. I doubt if Aunt Georgina's boys will get any either, Granny never liked the wives they've chosen. And Uncle Raymond'll be lucky if he sees a brass farthing. They never got on.'

By this time we had reached the waiting cars and I felt impatient that we should even be discussing money at such a moment. Alexander had distanced himself from our argument and Andrea was amused by it, so much so that she said, 'You'll not get anything, Mother, you left off visiting. You've probably stopped me getting anything too.'

'That's enough, Andrea,' Alexander said sharply. 'This is neither the moment nor the place to be talking about what any of you are getting.'

'Oh Daddy, don't be so stuffy. It was only just something to talk about, wasn't it, Jessica?'

'Well of course, dear. We've nothing else to talk about, have we, Lisa? Come to think about it we never had, unless we talk about you, Alex. You're looking very well, and every bit as handsome as I remember. I've always been attracted by dark men, how I ever came to marry Desmond I'll never know. I expect it was on the rebound. Andrea dear, never be tempted to marry a man because you've just been given the air by another.'

Alexander put his hand under my elbow and guided me to a car, and to my chagrin Jessica and Andrea followed after us. I was unprepared for Jessica's caustic humour, and even more unprepared for the fact that Andrea was enjoying it. Alexander's expression was unruffled, faintly cynical, but we were saved from any further examples of Jessica's wit when the lawyer joined us in the car.

Dinner was a silent civilized affair. Conversation was largely unconnected with the funeral.

Uncle Raymond and Alexander talked about the relative virtues of coarse fishing and fly fishing, and Robin and Rodney joined in with anecdotes of their own. Nobody had elected to sit in Grandmother's chair, and I could see that Aunt Edwina was only picking at her food while occasionally she wiped away a tear.

Aunt Cecily said sharply, 'Stop sniffling, Edwina, you're quite putting me off my meal.'

The lawyer said he hoped to be away before ten as the roads were decidedly treacherous, and we shortly adjourned to the drawing room. The scent of flowers still lingered in the hall and I held back there wishing with all my heart that I didn't have to go in.

'It won't take long,' Alexander assured me. 'If we don't go in there it will cause more talk than if we do.'

'The will has nothing to do with us, Alexander. Sitting through it is farcical.'

'I'm sure you're right, but we'll be very generous and congratulate all the beneficiaries,' he said with a smile.

The lawyer sat at a small mahogany desk which had

been Grandmother's pride and joy, while the chairs had been arranged so that we could face him. Aunt Cecily and her husband sat on the couch with Aunt Claudia and Uncle Henry. Aunt Edwina sat alone at the side of the room, and Alexander whispered, 'Shall we join her, Lisa? She looks very lonely over there.'

We drew our chairs close to hers and watched while the others took their places. Jessica sat on a low pouffe near the fireplace where the firelight burnished her dark hair, and she held out her long slender fingers to the blaze.

'Is everybody present?' the lawyer asked, shuffling his papers in front of him.

Just at that moment the door opened and Andrea stood on the threshold uncertainly until Jessica patted the pouffe, and without hesitation Andrea went to join her.

I couldn't take my eyes off them, they were so alike: two people cut from the same mould with their dark beauty, their exquisite profiles caught sharply in the glow from the dancing flames. I had to drag my eyes away when the lawyer began to speak.

'I am here to read the last will and testament of the late Annabel Marston. There is a sum of two hundred and eight thousand pounds to distribute – there would indeed have been more but she dabbled unwisely and against the advice of her accountants in dubious shares over the last four years.

'Apart from the sum of one thousand pounds to Miss Amelia Margaret Jarvis for long and faithful service, and four thousand pounds to certain charities and the Church of St Mary, all other monies are to be distributed among Mrs Marston's family as she has directed. Mrs Marston has also seen fit to explain her decisions so I will read her will exactly as written:

'To my daughter Miss Edwina Marston I leave the sum of forty thousand pounds which I trust will purchase the bungalow it has long been her aspiration to possess somewhere near the coast. She should be allowed to take any furniture she wishes although it will hardly appear at is best in a modern bungalow. She has however always been a most devoted daughter, and if she desires to live in bourgeois obscurity, so be it.

'I leave the sum of forty thousand pounds to my daughter Claudia. The clergy has never been a lucrative profession and my son-in-law will now be able to retire with a good conscience and the knowledge that a life of genteel proverty has been avoided.

'To my daughter Georgina I leave the house known as the Maples and twenty thousand pounds which will help towards its upkeep. I am aware that my son-in-law receives a good pension from his employment in Kenya but I was extremely saddened when they elected to live in Yorkshire on their return to this country, a decision no doubt occasioned by the fact that Yorkshire is well blessed with race courses. If they elect to disregard my instructions, then the twenty thousand pounds will be divided between my other three daughters and the Maples will be put up for sale. Any proceeds from the sale will also be divided between the same three daughters.

'To my daughter Cecily I leave the sum of ten thousand pounds, being assured that she is adequately provided for by her husband. She is however to have first choice of my jewellery, the rest to be divided between my three other daughters.

'To my grandchildren I leave the following: five thousand pounds each to Mrs Angela Ruddledge, Mr Rodney Chandler, Mr Roger Chandler and Mr Robin Chandler. I also leave five thousand pounds to my great granddaughter Miss Andrea Hamilton, even though I was deprived of the pleasure of watching her grow up.

'To my granddaughter Jessica I leave the sum of one hundred and fifty thousand pounds in token of the courage she has shown in the face of adversity. As a child she brought great joy into my life and has remained close to me. That she has been cheated of life's early promise was something that caused me great personal sorrow, and I now trust she will use this legacy wisely and for the ultimate improvement of her future.'

That was it. The lawyer rustled his papers with a bland face, graciously declined the drink Uncle Neville offered on the excuse that he had a fair distance to travel, and made good his escape.

That was the signal for the arguments to start.

Aunt Edwina sat staring in front of her, too stunned to take any part in the general discussion. With one stroke Grandmother had deprived her of her home, showing her no special consideration for the years of devotion, and as Uncle Raymond was already pointing out angrily, forty thousand pounds was hardly likely to buy the longed-for bungalow at the coast.

'Didn't the woman ever look at the price of houses?' he stormed, 'for forty thousand pounds she'll be lucky to find a small terraced house well away from the sea. And what does she want to do leaving the Maples to us? It's not an ancestral home, for heaven's sake, it's a big old house like a thousand others and I for one don't want to live in it.'

'If we don't live in it we don't get the money,' his wife argued. 'That means giving it to the others, who already have more than we do.'

'I certainly don't,' Aunt Cecily objected.

'Your daughter does, and you don't need it,' Aunt Georgina snapped.

'My God, the old girl has us sewn up properly, we don't want the damned place and we can't afford to say no,' Uncle Raymond stormed.

I could sense Alexander's distaste. Looking down at me he said softly, 'Shall we go for a walk, Lisa? Anything is better than this.'

'I'd like to see if Aunt Edwina's all right. Do you mind, Alexander?'

'I'll come with you, Alex,' Uncle Raymond said quickly. 'I'll be glad to get out of this house for an hour or so, even if I'm not going to be allowed to stay out of it for the rest of my life.'

They went out together, and leaning towards Aunt Edwina I said gently, 'Are you all right, Aunt Edwina, can I get you a brandy, or perhaps a cup of tea?'

She shook her head dismally. 'You didn't get anything, Lisa, not even a piece of her jewellery.'

'I didn't expect anything, I didn't want to be here.'

'I know, it was my fault you came. Still, she left Andrea something, that was kind.'

'No, Aunt Edwina, it wasn't kind at all. I have three children, she ignored Linda and Jeremy.'

'But she didn't know them, Lisa, you never brought them here. That wasn't kind.'

'Oh, Aunt Edwina, there are so many things I could tell you, but I think we should let sleeping dogs lie. You've been conditioned all your life to accept that Grandmother was right. I couldn't change all that, not even if I'd wanted to.'

'I did want a bungalow at the coast, Lisa. I thought it would be less work, and Meg was leaving us soon. I have a little saved, but I can't afford to spend it all on somewhere to live.'

'No, of course not.'

'I don't know what to do.'

'You'll think of something, and perhaps Uncle Raymond will help you. He doesn't want to live here.'

'You heard the will, if they don't the money will go elsewhere.'

I shivered miserably. Even though Grandmother was dead and buried she still watched over us, malevolently dictatorial about her money and her property.

Everybody studiously ignored my presence, but I sensed their discomfort. I was their sister's daughter, and I might have been a stranger. I wished I could make them see that it didn't matter, I didn't want anything that was theirs. I had my home and children and I had Alexander. I wished I had gone out with him, anything was better than the atmosphere in that room, even the icy wind.

Jessica was still sitting on her pouffe watching the others with a half smile, and Andrea's face was flushed with excitement. I went across to them.

'We're leaving in the morning, Andrea. I'm going upstairs to pack.'

'I'm not sure yet exactly what I'm doing. I'll tell you later, Mother.'

'I don't understand. You'll be returning to Dorset with your father and me, surely?'

'I'll tell you later, Mummy. Isn't it exciting? Five thousand pounds and I haven't seen Granny Marston for years.'

Jessica's eyes met mine with tantalizing candour. 'You didn't play your cards at all well, Lisa, though I didn't think she'd cut you off without a penny.'

'I'm in the very happy position of not needing anything, Jessica.'

'Well, of course. I know a little about the position you're in, don't I? What does Alex think about this afternoon's circus?'

'Not very much, he showed no desire to linger here.'

'So you're leaving in the morning?'

'Yes.'

'Well, there's nothing for you to argue about. I'd get on with your packing if I were you.'

It didn't take long to pack so I had a long leisurely bath and was sitting in my dressing gown brushing out my hair when Alexander came into the room.

Our eyes met in the mirror and I said, 'Are they still arguing downstairs?'

'I expect so. I didn't go into the drawing room, all I heard was their voices.'

'I'm packed, Alexander, I think we should go home tomorrow.'

'I agree. We shall never be coming back, Lisa.'

'No.'

Alexander, Uncle Raymond and I were the only people breakfasting the next morning and we had to listen once again to his tirade about not wishing to live at the Maples.

'I've never liked the house, and if we live here I'll be seeing the old girl round every corner, I'll feel her eyes on me from every wall. I've told Georgina to hell with the money, we'll manage without it, let her sisters have it and that niece of hers. I've always known Jessica would get the bulk, she was forever visiting the old lady with some sob story or other.'

When neither of us spoke, he said contritely, 'Don't mind me, I'm in a foul mood. But that will stank to high heaven. The old girl was sound of mind all right, but she'd been got at, there's no doubt about it.'

One by one the rest of them drifted in to breakfast but it seemed all most of them wanted was coffee and toast. Aunt Edwina's eyes were swollen with weeping and I guessed she hadn't slept much.

Jessica on the other hand came in with a bright smile and a cheerful good morning, followed by Andrea who looked at us sharply before helping herself to coffee.

Alexander said quietly, 'Your mother and I are leaving before lunch, Andrea. Have you packed?'

'Not yet, Daddy, I want to talk to you after breakfast.'

'What is there to talk about?'

'Not now, Daddy, later.'

Jessica's eyes met mine blandly, but there was something in her expression I recognized. I had seen it before whenever she had something planned that could injure me. Next moment however she was chatting to Alexander about the Far East and how much she had loved it.

Alexander surprised me by saying, 'Didn't you find the Far East very expensive, Jessica? Were you there alone?'

'No, I was there with Desmond. And you're right, it was expensive. There were so many glorious things to buy but he kept me short of money. My recollections of the Far East are very mixed.'

'We're going to go back, aren't we, Jessica?' Andrea said quickly. 'I can get a job there any time I want and Jessica's always wanted to return there. I've only ever seen Hong Kong, now I want to go to Malaysia and Penang. I have the money, I can find a job when that's gone.'

There was silence round the breakfast table and I could feel my heart racing sickeningly while Alexander went on calmly cutting his toast.

I felt the others were staring at us, waiting expectantly for our reaction, and when nothing was said Andrea seemed to relax. Beside her, Jessica stared defiantly at her mother.

Aunt Cecily said somewhat sharply, 'I hope you're going to be sensible with your money, Jessica. You've cost your father and me a lot over the last few years.'

'Well, I don't suppose I'll be costing you any more, Mother, but I don't intend to deny myself a thing. I want to travel. And who knows, I might conceivably meet the right type of man this time. My luck's due for a change.'

Uncle Raymond was looking down at his plate with a dour expression while Robin remarked brightly, 'Coming to see you and Mother here'll be like coming to see Grandmother.'

'Exactly, we'll all be under her thumb just like we've always been. If you ask me, Alexander and Lisa are the lucky ones. When they leave here they'll have cut the family strings for ever.'

'They did that years ago,' Jessica snapped, 'neither of them had the nerve to come back.'

Alexander raised his eyebrows maddeningly and in a quiet voice said, 'We're talking history, Jessica, nerve never entered into it. Lisa and I made a new life for ourselves away from all this, it's been a very happy and contented life.'

'Lucky for you,' she commented sarcastically.

'Come up to the bedroom when you've finished your breakfast, Andrea,' he said shortly. 'I want to talk to you.'

Andrea's face was rebellious, as her father and I rose from the table and left the room.

I asked no questions, I knew in his good time he would tell me what he had in mind.

Several minutes later Andrea came to our room and I knew immediately that we were in for a scene.

Alexander asked calmly, 'Now what is all this nonsense about leaving your job and going with Jessica to the Far East?'

'It isn't nonsense, it's what I want to do. When we've travelled around a bit I'll get work in Hong Kong. I'll have no difficulty and I'll love working over there.'

'And Jessica?'

'We'll get a house or a flat, I know a lot of business people out there who can advise me.'

'The time when an English girl could compete with the orientals and win is rapidly coming to a close, they've beaten us at our own game. I don't want my daughter living at a loose end in Hong Kong, nor do I think Jessica is the right companion for you.'

'You didn't think that when you were engaged to her. Why was it so right for you and so wrong for me?'

For a moment his faced paled, but he kept his anger in check. 'And are you supposing that Jessica will wish to remain in Hong Kong or anywhere else for that matter once she's exhausted every ounce of pleasure the area can provide?'

'Well I shan't mind if she moves on, after all she'll have the money, I'm just very pleased that she wants me for her companion. We really do have an awful lot in common, Daddy, and I am old enough to look after myself.'

'That's the tragedy, Andrea. I can't prevent you going if you've set your heart on it, you are old enough to make your own decisions. I doubt if you are wise enough, but you don't go with my blessing or with any of my money.'

'But I shall need some money to start with. I'll pay you back once Great Granny Marston's money is available. Oh, I just can't believe that you'll let me sponge off Jessica.'

'I doubt if you need have any worries on that score, nobody sponges off Jessica. She'll make very sure that you repay anything she's had occasion to lend you, with interest.'

'It's Mother who's poisoned your mind against Jessica. She had to do that to keep you.'

'Don't be such a little fool, Andrea. Do you think, if I was so easily stolen, I was worth having in the first place? You're talking of things you know nothing about, and you owe your mother an abject apology.'

I was sitting white-faced on the edge of the bed, and she turned to me with a hotly burning face and defiant eyes.

'I'm sorry, Mother. I only ever heard the story from Jessica, never from you.'

'I intend to speak to Jessica, Andrea,' Alexander said quietly. 'The sooner the better, I think.'

Alexander and Jessica, raking over the past, talking about our daughter's future together, I couldn't bear it. This was what I had been afraid of all our married life, and now it was here, in Grandmother's house where it had all begun.

I had to get out into the cold morning air, I needed desperately to walk it out of my system, and after they'd left the room I thrust my feet into my boots, and wearing my fur coat and a large silk scarf over my head I ran downstairs and out of the house.

The icy wind met me and for a few moments I stood uncertainly on the doorstep, then I set out resolutely towards the gates. I walked quickly as if to put distance between me and all those congregated in the house, and as I walked the frozen sleet crunched under my feet and my eyes pricked with unshed tears.

Through a blur I saw the solitary figure of a man walking towards me along the road, his head bent against the wind, his white trench coat flapping round his knees, and something about his tall broad-shouldered figure seemed familiar.

We were almost level when he raised his eyes and I paused in surprise, then his face suddenly broke into a smile.

'Lisa,' he said with evident pleasure, 'I hadn't expected to see you on such a morning. Come to that I hadn't expected to see you in these parts again.'

His smile was engaging, and he had hardly changed from our last meeting except that there was more grey in his fair hair and his face seemed a little more weather-beaten. In the face of my scrutiny he said, smiling, 'I know, a few more grey hairs, the years don't stand still. But they have for you. You're looking very beautiful, Lisa. It was always there, it was your grandmother who kept you looking so plain and chaste, she made you hide whatever beauty you had. I'm looking at you with the eyes of an artist, I'm not attempting to flirt with you.'

Desmond Colby had lost none of his charm, and curi-

291

ously I said, 'I'm surprised to see you in these parts, Desmond. You are still visiting, then?'

'Well of course, the Templetons were my friends before they ever met Jessica, and our divorce never altered their friendship for me.'

'I'm glad.'

'Your grandmother died. I believe the entire village went into mourning regardless of the fact that she wasn't exactly a popular woman.'

'She'd lived in these parts a long time, I think they respected her.'

'Are you here alone?'

'No. My husband and daughter are here. We're going home later this morning.'

'Just walking the atmosphere of the house out of your system, I suppose. Tell me, Lisa, have you been very happy in your marriage?'

'Yes, very happy. I have three children, two girls and a boy.'

'And did you agonize a long time about taking Alexander away from Jessica? I only heard the story from her.'

'Need we talk about it now, Desmond? Do you enjoy talking about your broken marriage?'

'I enjoy talking about it, it convinces me that I was entirely right and she was wrong. Look, it's too cold to stand out here arguing, let's go into the pub for a glass of sherry.'

'I must be getting back, Desmond, I shouldn't have come out.'

'Well you are out, and it would be terribly wrong of you to desert an old friend when he's feeling particularly low.'

He was the same old Desmond, cajoling and impudently charming. Besides, he was in the mood for talking and I was curious.

Our presence in the lounge bar of the local inn would cause some consternation: Jessica's unfeeling cousin and her ex husband drinking sherry together and indulging in amiable conversation.

There were several men at the bar and one or two

couples sitting at the tables. They eyed us curiously and Desmond bade them a cheerful good morning, saying in an undertone, 'The place'll empty in no time. They'll be rushing home to give an account of our presence to the rest of the village. Do you care, Lisa?'

'Not really, I doubt if I shall ever set foot in these parts again, and we're doing nothing to be ashamed of.'

He grinned so much like a naughty schoolboy that I warmed to him. I could understand why Jessica had married him, I could not understand why he had married her, and as if he could read my mind he said, 'You can't understand why I married Jessica, can you, and I'm damned if I can understand it myself. It's a question I've asked myself constantly since we separated.'

'Why did you when you never really liked her?'

'You helped to push me into it, you should be ashamed.'

'I did!'

'Well of course, she came home to England expecting to marry Alexander in the summer only to discover that he was no longer available. He was about to marry her cousin Lisa and spirit her off to Israel or some other godforsaken place. She made the most of that episode, I can tell you, and in the summer she went off with the Templetons to Venice.

'I was holding an exhibition of my paintings in Venice and I was doing remarkably well. Along came Jessica with her broken heart and her beauty. I'd never really liked her very much. When she came on that Christmas cruise I thought she was a spoilt brat and wanted a good spanking, now I couldn't see anything beyond her beauty. I looked at her with an artist's eye instead of a man's. Alexander used his intelligence, all I used was the moonlight on the Adriatic and the heady intoxicating Venetian nights.

'There was Jessica bewildered and crying out for love, and here was I suddenly besotted. I believed I was immune to love, I was a selfish contented loner completely in love with myself and my painting. God knows how she convinced me to change the way of life I'd been happy with.

'At first it worked remarkably well. I understood her, we were both greedy for life, rich, spoilt people with money to spend – and God, how that girl could spend money. We saved nothing and we had no settled home. Then I had a bad year and I had to insist we draw in the reins so that I could buy paint and canvases. That was when it started to go wrong.

'Then in the autumn my daughter Joanna came to stay with us in Malta.'

'Your daughter! I didn't know you had a daughter.'

'Not many people do. I never talked about her but that didn't mean I didn't idolize her. I couldn't get along with her mother. We married very young and I was too eaten up with my work, a struggling young artist with his way to make, and when Joanna was two her mother upped and left me and went to stay with her folks in Scotland. She remarried a few years later, some American chap her family approved of, but I kept in touch with Joanna and saw that she was never short of money, and I saw her whenever I could.

'To cut a long story short, she and Jessica didn't get on. It ended when Joanna said she was going home and never coming back, and Jessica said she would leave me if I ever had Joanna to stay again. That was when I realized our marriage was a disaster. I'd had doubts for a long time, but that morning the row between the two women finally put the crunch on it.

'The divorce was acrimonious. She threatened to take me for everything I'd got, and she damn near did. The rest was for Joanna, and for three years I was practically broke. I lost all interest in painting, I lived like a gypsy in southern Spain without putting a brush to canvas, and I drank like a fish until Templeton came down and told me I was a disgusting spectacle and a disgrace to humanity. I didn't care, somehow the will to survive had gone, and then one day when I was sitting by the roadside thinking about the next drink I saw a little girl bowling a hoop along the street.

'There was something about her that reminded me of Joanna, she was so pretty, so small and dainty, I suddenly wanted to paint her. It was a beginning, a return to sanity if you like. I went back to the hovel where I was living and took out my paints and brushes. Most of them were ruined, the paints dried up, but with the ones I salvaged I managed to paint that child, and her parents bought the picture for a few pesetas. The money wasn't important, I had started to live again.

'That's the real story, Lisa, not the one Jessica's told so many times and come to believe in. Did she get her hands on any of the old lady's money by any chance?'

'Yes, quite a large share of it.'

'She kept her grandmother pretty warm, as a matter of fact I often felt like warning that aunt of hers to stick out for what was rightly hers or Jessica'd take the lot.'

When I didn't enlighten him he said gently, 'It's not been very pleasant for you these last few days, has it, Lisa? I expect you're glad to be leaving.'

'Yes. I suppose I'll keep in touch with Aunt Edwina and Aunt Georgina even if it's only the odd Christmas card. It's strange, isn't it, my grandmother had five daughters and none of them are really friends. My mother's been dead a long time but when I remember her I think she was the nicest of the lot.'

'And the most talked about.'

'Yes.'

'And now you're going home to Dorset with your husband and daughter and the good life.'

Suddenly my eyes filled with tears and he looked at me in some consternation.

'I say, what is this?' he exclaimed.

'I'm not so sure about my daughter, I left her arguing with her father. I've been away too long, Desmond, I must go.'

He nodded briefly and I was glad that he didn't ask why they were arguing. We left the inn and he insisted on walking up to the gates with me. We stood for a few moments in the biting wind with him holding both my hands, his face robbed of its customary cynicism and strangely sombre.

'I doubt if we shall meet again, Lisa. Have you still got that painting I gave you?'

'Yes, of course. I had it framed, remember? I treasure it.'

'I'm glad. What a pity I didn't fall in love with you before Alexander saw his mistake and spirited you away. Things might have been very different.'

'No, Desmond, they wouldn't have been. I loved Alexander then, I think perhaps I always loved him even when I thought for a short time I loved somebody else.'

He bent his head and kissed me for the second time on my lips, gently and without passion, then he was striding away through the gloom of the winter's day and I stared after him until I could see him no more. Our lives had been strangely interwoven, and Desmond like me had been a part of all that anger and bitterness. But for him it was over, while for me there was much still to be resolved.

Aunt Edwina was the first person I met when I let myself into the house. She was looking as desolate as before and I couldn't help asking, 'What will you do now, Aunt Edwina?'

'Stay here for the time being. I'll have to look around for something soon, probably a cottage in the village.'

'But you don't want to live in the village, you want to live near the sea.'

'Mother was right, I'd hate a modern bungalow, they have very little character. All that silly talk of wanting something on one level to save work must have antagonized her terribly. She knew if she left me more money that is what I would do with it, and her lovely home would go to strangers.'

For a few moments I looked at her in pitying silence. Grandmother Marston was still here in this house, dictating her will to a daughter who was painfully receptive. I watched her watering the plants, resigned to whatever might come, then I mounted the stairs to face whatever awaited me.

Alexander was sitting at the bedroom desk with his briefcase open and his papers spread out. He looked up with a smile. 'I'm just working on some papers I hadn't time for at home. You've been gone a long time, surely you haven't been walking on the fells?'

'No, I walked towards the village and met an old friend.'

'Are you all packed and ready to leave?' he asked.

'Yes, what about Andrea?'

'She's going with Jessica.'

'Oh, Alexander.'

'I can't forbid her to go with Jessica, she's old enough to please herself. I've told her that she's on her own now, spending her own money. She knows where she can find us but she also knows not to expect us to bail her out whenever she decides she's fed up with anything. That, I'm afraid, has been Jessica's attitude all her life. I don't intend to encourage it in Andrea.'

There were tears in my eyes. Andrea was my daughter, my first born, and I loved her. I was remembering her as a child, beautiful and headstrong, and so often a torment instead of a blessing.

I turned away and busied myself with my hair so that Alexander wouldn't see my distress. I was unprepared for his gentleness as he came and took me in his arms. 'Darling, try to see that one day all our children will fly the nest, hopefully not this way, but it's a fact of life. One day there's just going to be the two of us. I can bear it, can you?'

I stared at him through a haze of tears. 'I mind because she's going with Jessica, it's just as though Jessica's paid me back for what I did to her, I stole you, she's stealing Andrea.'

'You never stole me, Lisa – or if you did I was willing to be stolen. Surely you haven't been torturing yourself all these years about something so unimportant? What I had with Jessica was a love affair, what I've had with you has been a marriage. I love you, Lisa, I love your serenity, your gentleness, the qualities that have made our marriage something to be prized in a world of changing values. I thought you felt the same.'

'But Alexander, you never told me you loved me, never once in all those years.'

'But I thought I showed you by everything I did, every action, every meaningful moment. I'm no good with words.'

'But Alexander, you're so very good with words. Your words were the ones that brought me back to life, made me see how wonderful things could be. Surely you haven't forgotten the flamingoes.'

He held me fiercely against him so that I could hear the swift beating of his heart, and my spirits soared to think that he loved me as I had always dreamed of being loved by him.

At that moment nothing else in the world mattered, not Andrea, not this house or the memory of the tragedies that had changed my life. For a moment he held me away from him, looking down into my eyes, his own strangely serious, then when I smiled tremulously he said, 'Time to go, I think. We'll say goodbye to the others.'

They came out into the hall – all except Andrea and Jessica – to see us leave the house, and Aunt Edwina wept a little. Robin kissed me and whispered, 'You'll not be coming back, Lisa, nor will I.'

Alexander had brought the car down earlier and I waited while he put our small pieces of luggage in the boot, then we got into the car and farewells were called. At that moment Andrea came running down the steps, her face flushed, and I could tell she'd been crying.

'Mother, were you really leaving without saying goodbye?' she cried.

'I thought you didn't want to say goodbye to us,' I answered her.

'I'll write, Mother, honestly I will, I'll tell you where I am.'

She made no effort to kiss me, or to speak to Alexander who sat impassively beside me, then when neither of us spoke she said angrily, 'Daddy wouldn't give me any money. But I'll show you both, I'll manage very well without it. Jessica says I'll probably meet a wealthy man and marry him, that way I'll never need you again.'

With a last stormy look she turned away and ran headlong into the house. I reached for the door handle to follow her, but Alexander held me back.

'No, Lisa,' he said sternly, 'she has to grow up, she has to want us on our terms, not on hers. Let her go with Jessica, one day if she's any sense she might see Jessica for what she is. Other people have, they can't all be wrong.'

I knew he was right, but as the car moved away I looked up at the windows of the house for the last time. Jessica was at the window overlooking the front door. She raised her hand in a gesture of farewell, but it was a mockery of farewell, a gesture of triumph. There was no sign of Andrea.

Alexander's hand left the wheel for a moment and covered mine tenderly. 'Don't worry, darling,' he said gently, 'you win some and you lose some. We'll find Jeremy and Linda waiting for us, they're both home for the weekend.'

At that my spirits lifted and I smiled up at him.

'I can't promise you flamingoes, Lisa,' he said softly, 'but life can still be pretty wonderful. I'm very contented with what we have, and I want you to be too. We can't let Jessica win.'

He was right. She had won so many times, even when I played the role of wife and mother somehow her shadow had always been between us. I knew now that it was my conscience and not reality at all that had been my enemy, but my conscience had troubled me with Jessica's beauty, Jessica's maddening scorn. Now she had taken Andrea but she could not take Alexander. Miraculously, Alexander loved me.

CHAPTER 35

Linda and Jeremy were surprisingly philosophical about Andrea. She was the older sister who had bossed their childhood. They had witnessed her alarming tantrums with dismay, her preposterous and absurd battles about nothing at all had left them bewildered and miserable. Now that they were grown up they hardly understood my pain at her rejection.

Sadly I chose not to think about the bad times, remembering only the gay smiles and sunny enchantment when she got her own way, and the beauty that strangely had been Jessica's beauty.

It was Jeremy on his last morning at home who put his feelings into words as we walked along the cliff top with the dogs on a frosty morning.

'I don't care if she never comes home, Mother, and you mustn't either. If she can simply walk out of our lives to go with that Jessica woman then she isn't worth bothering about.'

'She's my daughter, darling,' I remonstrated gently.

'Fat lot she cares about that.'

'I thought when you were older you'd all be good friends.'

'She wouldn't want to be friends with us, she was always so superior and bossy.'

'I know. I don't think she could help it, it was the Marston in her. If you'd known Grandmother Marston you'd understand what I mean. She ruled my childhood with a rod of iron, and it took every bit of willpower I had to finally rebel against her. There were so many things she never forgave me for.'

For several minutes we walked along in silence before he changed the subject. 'I'd like to bring Andrew Brooks home with me next time I come, Mother. Would that be all right with you and Dad?'

'Yes, of course. Are his parents abroad?'

'No, they live in Shropshire. I want him to hear you play. He's mad keen on music, plays his wretched piano every opportunity he gets, but he's a natural, he's never had a lesson in his life. I think he's marvellous, you will too. I've talked about you all the time, told him how you were going to be a famous concert pianist but settled for marriage to Dad instead. Do you mind?'

'It wasn't quite as simple as that, Jeremy. Fate had an awful lot to do with what happened to me.'

'I know, but you did fall in love with Dad and you could have chosen music instead.'

I didn't speak. I had no words to tell Jeremy of my feelings that terrible morning when I waited for the plane to arrive at Heathrow. How very different my life would have been if Carlo had come home to place his ostentatious ring on my finger.

As we tramped across the short grass with the grey sea pounding on the beach below us my thoughts were entirely on the past. Could I really have married into that volatile pulsating Italian family, each and every one of them larger than life, imbued with a towering talent yet surprisingly dominated by Mama from her favourite place in the kitchen.

I was seeing Carlo as I had seen him on that last morning, his dark hair shining raven black in the sunlight, his handsome laughing face and black eyes shining with enthusiasm for what lay ahead of him. How would it have been for us across the years, and had his mother been right when she prophesied that our talents would clash along with our ambitions? And yet on that night when he played the Bruch I had been transported into the realms of the blessed by the sheer poetry of his music and the longing to be a part of that life which had seemed wholly glamorous and close to my heart.

For a time I had forgotten Jeremy beside me, now I took up our previous conversation as though my memories hadn't interrupted it. 'Bring your friend whenever you like, Jeremy, but perhaps he may not care for my sort of music.'

301

'He just loves any sort of music, Mother. He'll enjoy playing on your Steinway, he's got an old crock that Noah took into the ark.'

'Is it his ambition to make music his career?'

'He's studying history, but I'd say music is his first love. Has he any chance, do you think?'

'Darling, I would have to hear him play, but it can never be the concert platform, not without formal tuition.'

'I don't suppose that would worry him, every pianist doesn't aspire to the concert platform.'

'No that's true. When are you thinking of bringing him?'

'The new year, perhaps, he'll be going home for Christmas. It makes it easier now Andrea won't be coming home. She always showed off in front of my friends and flirted with them all simply to amuse herself.'

I didn't reply. It was too hurtful to talk about Andrea in derogatory terms. Looking up at the thick black clouds hanging low over the stormy sea, I suggested hurrying back to the house.

The two dogs walked with their heads down and glum dejection in every line of their stocky bodies, and as soon as we reached the warmth of the kitchen old Gemma flopped into her basket while Jet, her son, stood hopefully at the refrigerator door.

The sound of the piano came faintly into the kitchen and Jeremy looked up from where he was filling the dogs' bowls.

'Doesn't it bother you that none of your children have been musical, Mother? I know that's Linda at the piano without seeing her.'

I smiled ruefully. Linda didn't play well and the other two didn't play at all. When they were children I had hoped that one of them might fill all the expectations I had so lamentably failed to fill, but it was not to be. They had other talents which made me very proud.

Linda stopped playing when Jeremy and I pushed the tea trolley into the lounge and Alexander looked up with a smile. It was a happy family gathering over afternoon tea, and yet my thoughts returned to Andrea and the future she had planned with Jessica.

The talk was all of Christmas which was only a few weeks away, and here again my thoughts were on all those other Christmases I had spent under the despotic eye of my grandmother and surrounded by a large and some-times quarrelsome family.

Once my eyes met Alexander's across the hearth and he smiled, that singularly sweet smile that still had the power to make my heart flutter. Alexander knew that I was thinking about Andrea, he was aware of the pain she had left in my heart.

The weeks up to Christmas passed all too quickly. There had been no word from Andrea and I fretted about this silently.

Jeremy and Linda arrived home at the beginning of Christmas week. They had both been invited to a party on Christmas Eve at the home of one of our friends. Christmas Eve coincided with the twenty-first birthday of their youngest daughter, but because Alexander was in London all day we had said we would go along later.

I wasn't too anxious to go, it would be a young people's party, but any kind of party would keep my mind off Andrea, if only for a little while.

In the afternoon it started to snow, fine fluttering flakes at first that quickly blew away in the strong wind coming from the sea, then by late afternoon the wind changed and the flakes became strong enough to cling to the trees, covering the lawns with a carpet of shimmering white. I hoped Alexander wouldn't be late, in weather like this the train could be delayed.

I saw Linda and Jeremy depart for the party at six o'clock and still Alexander hadn't arrived home. By this time I was a little anxious because he had promised to get away soon after lunch.

The two dogs lay stretched out in front of the fire and I turned on the television, which helped to deaden the sound of the wind howling round the house and the insist-ent ticking of the clock on the mantelpiece. The screen was filled with Christmas Eve jollity so incongruous to my mood that I switched it off impatiently, electing instead to play records, and soothed by the music I curled up on the settee and tried to find some enjoyment in listening to Chopin.

Gemma came over and thrust her soft muzzle into my hand and I leaned over and kissed the top of her head, whereupon she climbed on to the settee and curled up beside me. Gemma had always known when I was upset or worried, now her warm spaniel eyes looked anxiously into mine and she whimpered a little in sympathy.

It was almost eight o'clock when I heard a car and I ran to the window. Alexander's car was stopping at the front door and I ran back to build up the fire.

The room looked warm and welcoming with the Christmas lights on the tree and the leaping firelight on the walls and furniture. I was wearing the dress he loved best, a dark red velvet, expensive and deceptively simple, and one which lent itself to the three strands of pearls at my neck. I waited on the rug for him to come into the room, but when he opened the door he smiled across at me, then waited, holding the door open.

She came into the room diffidently, a little shamefaced and unsure, so unlike the Andrea who had always been so confident. Her eyes met mine, eyes that pleaded and begged for forgiveness at the same time, then without a word she ran across the room and my arms closed about her in spite of the melting snow on her coat.

I knew the moment was not one for questions, it was enough that Andrea had come home, and briskly Alexander said, 'Why not go upstairs and change out of those wet clothes? I expect you're starving. We'll all have something together when you're ready.'

We heard her running up the stairs followed by Jet, who had always been Andrea's dog, and Alexander came across and took me in his arms.

'Happy now, darling?' he asked gently.

'Where did you find her, why isn't she with Jessica?'

'I know as much as you do, darling. I found her sitting on her suitcase, waiting for the train. If I'd caught the earlier train I'd have missed her but I was delayed in the city.'

'But what did she say, what has happened? Surely she must have told you why she was coming home?'

'She said she wanted to come home for Christmas and she said nothing about Jessica. She'll tell us in her own good time. As for now, she's home – that's what you wanted, isn't it?'

So for a while I had to be content.

She ate ravenously, and across the table my eyes met Alexander's. It was a silent meal, not yet it seemed was she ready to talk. After we had eaten she helped me with the dishes then we went into the lounge to drink our coffee. Alexander had opened a bottle of champagne, and after handing the glasses round he raised his to Andrea, saying, 'Welcome home.'

I saw her lips trembling with emotion, and unsteadily she put her glass down before sinking into a chair where she put her head down on her knees and sobbed uncontrollably.

We made no effort to go to her. All we could do was look on in uncomfortable silence and I reflected how many times I had seen her cry in one of her tantrums, but this was real and genuine sorrow.

At last by a visible effort she squared her shoulders and the bleak smile on her tear-ravaged face twisted my heart.

'I'm sorry, Mother,' she said in a trembling voice, 'I wasn't going to cry, honestly I didn't mean to.'

'Are you ready to tell us about it, Andrea?' I asked gently.

She nodded, and encouraged I said, 'When did you decide to come home?'

'Last night.'

'You were staying in London?'

'Yes. Oh, Mother, it was horrible. I've been such a fool.

'It was great at first. I thought everything was going to be so wonderful. We went to stay with Jessica's parents and we went round all the travel agents and got lots and lots of brochures. We pored over them all day, planning what we would do, then after a week we went to Jessica's flat in London.

'It was still wonderful. We went to the theatres and we shopped for the sort of clothes we thought we'd need. Jessica knew a lot of people and we went to parties. I didn't enjoy them very much, the people were arty and some of them were queer, not at all the sort you'd expect her to know, then she met up with *him*.

'She'd known him a long time, from when she was married to her first husband. He seemed nice at first, you know, amusing and friendly, and he was good-looking. He seemed to have plenty of money, but then one day he came to the flat and said he was broke, he'd gambled and lost. And he moved in with us.'

She paused, biting her lip nervously, then she continued in a small anxious voice. 'I hated living in that flat with them. I used to lie in my bed hearing them giggling and laughing next door, and I knew they were making love. Some days they were in the bedroom until mid-day, sometimes all afternoon, and he never seemed to get dressed, he was always lounging about in that towelling dressing gown. And Jessica wasn't the same either.

'She dumped all the dirty dishes in the sink and left them for me to do, she never shopped for food, if I wanted anything I had to get it for myself and when they went out at night they never bothered about me. The daily woman left in a temper because she couldn't get into their bedroom to clean it and when I talked about us going to the Far East Jessica was sulky. She said I was becoming a bore about it, and not to let Gordino hear me.'

'Gordino!' Alexander exclaimed.

'Yes. He came from South America, Brazil I think. Then one afternoon when Jessica'd gone to the salon to get her hair done he made a pass at me and I hit him with a bookend. I said I'd tell Jessica when she got back, and he said he'd tell her I'd egged him on. After that he kept calling me the Kid, the Kid wants this and the Kid wants that, and Jessica giggled about it and thought it was funny.

'She hardly talked to me at all and finally I made myself ask her what she intended to do. She told me it was time

I left, that it had all been a silly mistake, I should get my job back and forget about her.

'She knew I didn't have a job any more, she knew I'd given that up to go with her. I left the following morning to come here, and Daddy found me on the station platform.'

We all sat silent for several minutes.

'What happened to your job, Andrea?' Alexander asked gently.

'I told them I was going to live abroad. Mr Calmus was very nice about it, he said they were sorry to lose me and he wished me well. They bought me a set of fabulous luggage, which I left at Peter Rawlingson's house. I'm glad I didn't take it to Jessica's, as things have turned out.'

'Who is Peter Rawlingson?' Alexander asked.

'He worked for Calmus. He's nice, we used to have dinner now and again and I've seen him once or twice since I left. They've advertised my job but they haven't filled it yet.'

'And how do you feel about it, would you like your job back?'

'I don't know, I was happy there and I was doing very well but if I went back I'd have to eat humble pie. They'd all be laughing at me and asking too many questions.'

'And you'd have to be just a little humble and truthful. The company might be disposed to take you back and your colleagues could be forgiven for gloating a little. I expect you left with your head in the clouds.'

Her beautiful face was set in the sulky lines I knew of old, then hopefully she looked up to ask, 'You could talk to Mr Calmus, Daddy, you know him very well. Couldn't you explain what's happened? Peter says they'd jump at me, I was good at what I did, after all.'

'I'm sorry, my dear, but this time you're going to have to do it alone. Calmus will have more respect for you if you face him without my assistance.'

'Then I won't face him at all, I'll look for work elsewhere.'

'That's your decision, of course. Your mother and I are

going to America in the new year, and would like to see you settled in a decent job before we leave. I suppose you also gave up your share in the flat in London?'

'No. I don't know why I kept that on, but I did. The rent's paid until the end of March.'

'That at least was sensible. We'll talk about this again after Christmas, you can do nothing about a job until then. But I'd advise you to think very carefully about it, Andrea, this is one time when you have to stand on your own two feet.'

For a moment her face was mutinous, then miraculously it cleared. Andrea had always been able to reassure herself that in the end things would go her way, and tonight was no exception in spite of recent experiences.

'You and Daddy are all dressed up, Mother, does that mean you were going out?'

'Yes. Linda and Jeremy have gone over to the Prestons', it's Mary's twenty-first birthday. Your father and I were going later.'

'Would I have been invited?'

'Well of course, if you'd been at home.'

'I'll wear my new dress, it's one I bought in London for the sort of life we said we'd be living in the Far East. You'll love it, Mother, nobody at Mary Preston's party will have anything like it.'

After she had run upstairs to dress, Alexander smiled at me ruefully. 'Andrea won't change, darling, we shall simply have to accept her the way she is. Don't you have the feeling that she's a throwback to one of your more disreputable Marston ancestors, just perhaps as Jessica was a throwback?'

'My mother was the one people talked about, but she was never like Jessica or Andrea. I remember that she was sweet and gentle, her fault was that she loved too much and too unwisely.'

Later that evening I knew that Alexander was right about our daughter. Andrea wouldn't change. She queened it at the party in her new too-sophisticated gown with its low décolleté and deep split on the tight skirt which left a great deal of thigh exposed, but she looked enchanting and so thought all the young men who crowded round her, much to the annoyance of many of the girls.

Jeremy came to my side, hissing under his breath, 'Just look at Andrea showing off as usual. When did she come home?'

'Just a little while ago, darling.'

'I thought you said she was going off to Japan or somewhere. I've a jolly good mind to put Andrew off, she'll be up to her old tricks with him.'

Mrs Preston remarked that Andrea and Linda didn't look like sisters and I had to agree with her. Linda with her fair English colouring danced by with a tall earnest young man, looking pretty and ethereal in white lace, while in the middle of the floor Andrea and a slender energetic young man gyrated and postured with a great deal of handclapping and stamping of feet that would have done credit to a flamenco dancer.

Alexander and I returned home alone in the early hours of Christmas morning after making sure that our children would be given a lift when the party was finally over.

It had stopped snowing, and as we drove to the front of the house we could hear the dogs barking their welcome. By the time Alexander had put the car away and returned to the house I had made coffee and poured out the sherry.

He came immediately to my side and took me in his arms. 'Merry Christmas, darling,' he said softly. 'Happy?'

'Happier. What are we going to do with our daughter, Alexander?'

'She's a grown woman, Lisa, we can only hope she's learned something from this sorry business.'

In the days that followed I had my doubts. Andrew Brooks came to spend New Year with us and much to Jeremy's annoyance Andrea immediately captivated him. For a few days he seemed to lose all interest in what he had come for, that was to hear me play and talk about music.

It was Andrea he walked with along the cliff top, Andrea who accompanied him to the parties they were invited to. Then one morning I looked out of the window and saw him walking with Linda and the two dogs along the cliff path.

Jeremy's spirits brightened considerably and Andrea sulked. That night all the family sat in the lounge listening to me play, and then Andrew took my place and played quite beautifully in spite of the fact that he had had no training. As Jeremy had said, he was a natural.

Scathingly Andrea snapped, 'You'll get nowhere without training, Mother trained for years. I'd stick to your history degree if I were you.'

Across the room Alexander frowned at her, and suddenly she jumped up and flounced out of the room.

Jeremy whispered, 'She's only peeved because Andrew's transferred his affections.'

'Why did he do that?' I asked curiously.

'He's probably found her out. She left him the other night to flirt with some other chap.'

In my innermost heart I pitied her. There was some devil in Andrea that couldn't be denied, the same devil that had driven Jessica, and even now when it was unlikely we would ever meet Jessica again, her restless flighty spirit was still here in Andrea.

It was several days into the new year and I was alone in the house. Alexander was in London and the boys and Linda had returned to their colleges. From the kitchen window I could see Andrea standing on the cliff top with the dogs. She was gazing out to sea with her dark hair blowing about her face, her white trench coat billowing, and I wished she would come indoors instead of brooding out there.

I was about to call her in when Aunt Edwina telephoned. Her voice was plaintive, little more than a whisper, and there was crackling on the line so that I had to ask her to speak up.

'I take it Andrea's with you, Lisa. I do hope so, I've been so worried since they left.'

'Andrea's here, Aunt Edwina, there's no need for you to be worried.'

The anxious mournful voice went on. 'Jessica was here,

Lisa, she's married, some man she says she's known a long time. I didn't like him, he doesn't seem to have any sort of real job, he's dabbled in a lot of things and that's all. He isn't even English and now she's talking about leaving the country and taking all that money with her.

'She's had a terrible quarrel with her father, who's washed his hands of her, and this time there'll be no grandmother to come running to. They're going out to South America, I think he comes from there, but what they're going to do there I can't imagine. Jessica says he drives racing cars and is going out there to join a new team. That can't be a proper sort of job, Lisa, I can only think they'll spend all that money and then the marriage will come to an end, just like the others did.'

'Aunt Edwina, you must know that Jessica's never listened to anybody. If she makes another mistake on top of all the others, she'll simply have to face it herself and make the best of it.'

'We always made excuses for her, it seemed so much easier to blame you, Lisa, and the men she married. I always liked Desmond but she blamed him for everything. He called to see me, Lisa. I thought that was very nice of him in view of what happened between him and Jessica.'

'Why did Jessica come to see you, Aunt Edwina?'

'She came to collect all her share certificates and everything else she was entitled to. I didn't have them, she'll have to get them from the solicitor, and she came to find out if Georgina and Raymond are coming to live here. I expect she was hoping for more money if they'd decided against it.'

'Have they reached a decision?'

'Oh yes, they're coming here, they really can't afford not to. The house is in a bit of a state, I'm sorting things out before I move. Is there anything you want, Lisa, furniture, pictures?'

'Nothing, Aunt Edwina. Grandmother didn't see fit to leave me anything, and Alexander and I have everything we need.'

'You're not just saying that because Mother didn't include you in her will, Lisa?'

'No, Aunt Edwina, I really don't want anything. Are you moving out quite soon then?'

'Yes. I've bought a little cottage in the village, there isn't enough money for a bungalow near the coast. Mother couldn't have known how expensive property had become.'

'No, perhaps not. You're very welcome to visit us any time you like, Aunt Edwina, you know that.'

'Thank you, Lisa, but I doubt if I shall be doing much travelling and Dorset is such a long way off. I got very tired of travelling about with Mother. She never really needed all those health farm holidays, she just liked all the pampering. Raymond always said she was as strong as an ox.

'Perhaps you and Alexander will call to see me one day, and I'd dearly like to meet your other two children.'

'The next time we drive up to the lakes we'll be sure to call, Aunt Edwina. I can't promise the children will be with us, they have their own friends now and choose their own holidays, but one of these days you will meet them, I promise. Try not to worry about Jessica. She's not your responsibility, she never was.'

'I know, dear, it's force of habit I suppose. Goodbye.'

I replaced the receiver and stood for a moment looking through the window. I hadn't heard Andrea come into the room, but suddenly she was beside me, asking, 'Was that Aunt Edwina?'

'Yes. She telephoned to see if you were with us.'

'Why would she do that?'

'Because Jessica has married the man she was with in London and they're expecting to go to South America as soon as possible.'

'Oh Mother, she's surely not married *him*. I thought he was a terrible man, he looked like some foreigner and he never had any money. She knew some awfully strange people, but he was the worst... I do wish it would stop raining, I'm so bored with the weather and having nothing to do.'

Suddenly exasperation took hold of me, and fixing her with a stern look, I said, 'Andrea, don't you think it's time you grew up? I'm so tired of seeing you wandering

312

about the house and gardens looking forlorn and bored. You should be doing something about a job. If you had any sense you'd eat humble pie and ask for your old one back.'

'Daddy could help me but he won't.'

'No, he's made that very clear and I agree with him. Andrea, I'm so desperately afraid you'll end up like Jessica, spoilt and aimless, the prey of any charming adventurer looking for a soft touch. I can see Jessica in you, I don't know if it was born in you or if it's her influence that has made you the way you are, but it frightens me.'

She stared at me, her eyes dark with hostility. 'Why don't you admit that it was your fault that Jessica became like that? You took Daddy away from her but she never stopped loving him.'

'If you want to believe that I can't stop you, Andrea, I can only tell you that Jessica has only ever loved Jessica. If you are disloyal enough to believe her instead of me then there's nothing more to be said.'

I left her staring after me. I felt an urgent need to get out into the open, the house oppressed me with its misted windows and the rain coursing steadily down the window panes. There was no colour in the sky and the sea rolled in glassily in long grey breakers. Snatching a trench coat off a peg and with a waterproof headscarf covering my hair I set off briskly towards the cliffs. The wind hit me like a knife and I quickly decided that work around the house was better therapy than trying to avoid the puddles on the cliff top.

Mrs Pearson was in bed with bronchitis and I had no idea when she would be well enough to return, consequently I had plenty to occupy my mind. There was no sign of Andrea in the downstairs rooms and after a while I heard her flinging things about in her bedroom.

Over dinner that evening I told Alexander about Jessica's marriage. When he made no comment Andrea said sharply, 'Don't you mind, Daddy?'

His eyes met hers levelly, then he said calmly, 'Why should you think I might mind, Andrea? Nothing Jessica does concerns me in the slightest.'

She looked down at her plate, and I could see that her face was flushed with colour while her eyes refused to meet mine.

After dinner she went up to her room, saying she had letters to write and Alexander asked, 'What did she have to say about Jessica's marriage?'

'Very little, except that she thought he was a terrible man.'

'She's very quiet.'

'Yes. I was cross with her, and said it was time she started looking for a job. Alexander, I'm so terribly afraid she's doing to be like Jessica, what can we do with her?'

'I think, my dear, that we are going to have to be very patient. Perhaps she'll come to her senses without any effort from us. One thing is sure, I'm not going to give her everything she asks for. It never helped Jessica, it won't help Andrea.'

We saw little of her during the next few days. She avoided me around the house and was constantly either out with the dogs or visiting friends. On Monday morning however when I went out into the hall with Alexander I was surprised to see her standing at the front door with a suitcase at her feet.

Our eyes met and with a shamefaced smile she said, 'Do you mind if I travel up to London with you, Daddy? I've decided to go back to the flat and see if my job's still vacant.'

'I'll be glad to have you aboard,' he said, smiling. 'When did you arrive at this momentous decision?'

'I've been thinking about it for days, I'll let you know how I make out.'

It was a beginning. I put my arms around her and hugged her, and if at first I found she pulled away a little, I knew it was her unwillingness to acknowledge that I had won, rather than lack of affection.

I watched her get into the front seat of her father's car and then Alexander turned and kissed me. 'It's going to be all right, darling,' he said gently. 'All we have to do is wait.'

I stood at the door until the car turned out into the

314

road and I prayed that she would look back, just once to show me that we were still friends. At the gate the car slowed and I stood with my eyes straining to catch my last glimpse of them, then I saw her bright red scarf waving frantically out of the window and I knew that Alexander had been right, all we had to do was wait.